Genevieve's
Such

G000162401

Odile's War

The Mad Game
Book Two

Chris Cherry

A Love and War Novel

I hope you enjoy the journey

A future worth protecting

Gifts left to us in Wills provide a wonderful opportunity to remember those to whom we all owe a huge debt of gratitude. Help us improve the lives of thousands of serving members of the Armed Forces, ex-Service men and women and their families with a gift in your Will. For a copy of our free Will guide or for more information, please call **020 3207 2259** or visit **www.britishlegion.org.uk/legacies** Registered Charity Number: 219279.

The Royal British Legion membership is made up of over 300,000 people who care about Armed Forces personnel, ex-Servicemen and women and their families.

You do not need to have a service background to become a Legion member. Becoming a member will allow you to support our campaigning work and give you a say in the future of the Legion.

Our 2,500 branches are uniquely placed to work with other community groups and organisations to remember the sacrifice of those that have fallen and promote the support that we give to the living.

You can find out more by visiting the Membership section of The Royal British Legion website http://www.britishlegion.org.uk/membership or via the Contact Centre 0808 802 8080

The author and publisher are proud to be working shoulder to shoulder with the Royal British Legion, supporting their valuable work with our Armed Forces, young and old

Copyright © 2014 Chris Cherry

The moral right of Chris Cherry has been asserted in accordance with the Copyright, Designs and Patents Act 1988

Published by Trench Publishing, Manchester, UK

ISBN: 0992935105
ISBN-13: 978-0-9929351-0-8

DEDICATION

This book is dedicated to the men and women, from all nations,
caught up in the tragedy that was
The Great War

Also by the Author
Love and War Novels

The Mad Game – William's Story
(*5 Star Bestselling novel released November 2013*)

The Third Light – The Mad Game Book Three
(*to be released 11 November 2014*)

CREDITS

Cover Graphic Design – Mark Bowers at The Devil's Crayon
Cover Photography – Bernadette at Bernadette Delaney Photography
Copy Editing – Helen Steadman at The Critique Boutique
French Language Consultant – Sandrina Parry-Bargiacci

CHRIS CHERRY

PROLOGUE – KOLN, OCTOBER 1918

The station clock struck eleven. Sunlight streamed in through the dirty glass panes above the platforms, a winter warmth welcoming the bereaved on their sad pilgrimage to the cemeteries. A little horse-drawn cab arrived at the front entrance to the wartime railway station.

'I am very sorry we are so late, Frau Wagner, but the horses have not been well this week. You will not be charged for this journey, of course.'

'That is all very well Hermann, but I will have most likely missed my train. Go and see will you?'

'Yes, Frau Wagner.' The man ran with a loping gait to the station entrance. He was a former soldier whose legs had been burned in an accident using an experimental weapon in Verdun, back in 1916.

Maria Wagner looked out of the carriage window towards the streets of Koln. Her hand rested on the little bump in her stomach, the little life inside kicking her. A reminder of her dead husband. And two more children at home, needing to be loved and fed, washed and educated.

At thirty-five years old, she felt her life already drawing closed. The black coat she was wearing concealed her pregnancy for it only drew pity. She did not want pity because it did nothing to feed her little family.

Maria thought of her wedding day in Koln. How handsome her husband had been, especially splendid in his uniform. How he had wanted to go and fight when the war finally came. Now he was under a little wooden cross in a remote field in northern Belgium, near some village that nobody remembered.

Hermann returned looking ashen. Maria snapped out of her thoughts and wiped away the tears from her eyes.

'Frau Wagner, I am so sorry, but your train has already departed. We are too late.'

'Did you enquire when the next one will be?'

'Not for two weeks Frau Wagner. On the eleventh of November, leaving at eleven as usual. I am sorry. Shall I go back to alter your reservation?'

Maria closed her eyes. 'Just take me home, Hermann. Take me home now, please.'

'Yes Frau Wagner. I will return tomorrow to rearrange your journey. Very sorry, the horses, you see.' Frau Wagner sat back in her seat.

'I will see you in two weeks my love. Heaven knows you won't be going anywhere.'

She looked out of the window. Her unborn child kicked inside her, demanding her attention.

'Be still, little one. There is no hurry to come into this world.'

CHRIS CHERRY

CHAPTER ONE – FRANCE, APRIL 1915

No girl should have to make this choice. A choice so base and degrading, the very thought makes me angry and still more resentful. That the number of buttons on a blouse, especially this rag of a thing, should determine whether we eat tonight. That bare, exposed flesh should account for the same as a loaf of stale black bread, or a slice of stinking sawdust sausage.

The tiny reflection in the window helps me to decide upon decency. I regard the girl in the reflection with a sad and cynical eye. But it is no use, it has to be done. It must look to them like I want to do it, not need to. So, one button open then, Odile.

I look down at the very moment Father passes, pushing a German transport vehicle that has boiling steam pouring from the front. He is being barked at by a young German administrative officer. Father nods politely and opens his arms in despair. The German kicks sand up towards him and turns away in disgust.

So, two buttons today it now must be.

'Darling girl, must you leave the house looking like that? You will catch a chill and we will all be the worse for it. Can't you put on a shawl? We have one here that is not too bad. Here, take this.' My Mother lifted a sad woollen shawl that was, even at its best, more hole than yarn.

'Maman, you know I must, it is the only way. Must we go through this pretence every day? Can't you see that our life is not improving and as each day passes Papa grows ever more bitter and resentful?'

Mother hesitated for a second, then recovered her stride.

'Odile, my love. We must keep hold of our souls. Without them we are lost and the devil has won. Your Grandmother taught me that. Whatever happens to us, we are true inside and always must be. Do you still believe that, little one?'

My Mother always did this, tried to carry on a life now so false and gone, it was unlikely to be imaginable again.

'I am not little any more,' I snapped at her. With that, I turned away and hurried out without another word and did not look back. I felt a tear chill on my cheek. Wiping it now would smear the little rouge I had managed to find in the empty camp that we had just left. So, I had to let it dry on my cheek, a reminder that perhaps the devil had not taken this soul just yet. It was time to hurry, for now I was late.

I turned the corner and saw to my disappointment a long line of shapes just like mine, huddled together at the back of the lorry. I was too late. Each girl wore just a skirt and blouse, even though it was cold enough to numb my fingers. Some wore little underneath their blouses, making the most of what little they had left on offer, just to get fed.

'Thomas, do you have one for me today? You promised that you would?' Twenty pairs of eyes flashed to Eugenie at the front, drawing blood with their stares. Then twenty pairs of eyes softened, knowing that if the truth were told, it was what they might do as well. Barter their charm for an extra ration. It was a necessary, if unseemly act, the outward appearance that none would degrade themselves at the feet of the wretched enemy who stole their land and their lives. But inwardly needing to betray and leave behind all that they held close. And to the very men who took away their husbands. Curse them for being here and having to beg to them for food. It was a painful existence filled with resentment, harshness and brutality, without justice. A life akin to the birds I suppose. Always cold, hungry and frightened, outwardly cheerful, never letting the world get inside to discover the secret brittleness within.

I stood at the back watching and waiting, wanting to see what the lorry brought to the camp today. Some black bread and sausage as usual, some milk that seemed not to have been watered down – but perhaps it had been tainted by soldiers believing it to be a game. At the front of the lorry, last to be reached, there was butter and sugar. Some flour perhaps? Yes, I would watch and wait my turn, steady and measured.

I looked down to make one final check, at the body that had not so long ago been a fresh young girl, eager for the world. Thinner now, drawn and clothed in little more than rags. I was breathing heavily, steadying myself. The flour and sugar were coming out now. The crowd bunched closer, also having noticed the more precious goods about to appear. They were all beginning to sharpen their elbows, anticipating what was about to happen. There was little time, little on offer and little chance to get anything more than the usual dry bread and sour milk.

For the sake of my Mother and Father I pushed forward to use my one advantage. Being seventeen, my skin was still clear and smooth. Thomas would find a loaf for me, I knew that.

'Get back, all of you, do not push in to me or I will take this all away for the dogs. Who wants this butter, huh? Which of you wants to cook for me tonight, eh?'

Thomas had a very heavy accent, but his French was sarcastic enough.

'You have one for me today?' Eugenie repeated her question, but with less conviction – she must have realized that the friendly façade was, as usual, turning into a miserable episode.

'Thomas? You promised me if I...Thomas?'

But Thomas wasn't looking at her. In fact, he seemed to make a point of turning his back on the poor woman. Eugenie was no more than twenty-five, but that made her at least five years older than Thomas, and it seemed five years more than his maturity could cope with. Instead, Thomas was looking at two new arrivals, fresh to the camp. To these he proffered a fresh loaf and a small parcel of butter wrapped in paper. By the time it reached their hands, it was squashed into a slimy lump of dirty grease. As it was offered, he spat on it, perhaps making sure they understood who was in charge.

'This you get today for no charge, eh? Tomorrow we see, we see. What you have for Thomas? Poor worn out boy, bringing you food to eat, better than this crap you eat here. What is this French shit you eat? I *know* what they put in it and it isn't good for you, ha ha.'

His laugh lacked mirth and we weren't really listening to the words. We just wanted to hear his voice. When he turned to us, would he be friendly or would he shun us today, having found a better prospect?

'You silly girl, now look what you have done.'

'Watch yourself, you, you fat cow.'

'A curse on your tongue, you rude child. Off with you.' A push and a shove and the two new girls went whirling to the floor, pulling hair and biting anything that wasn't covered. Both families would starve tonight, as the remaining women closed them off from the lorry and left them to their dispute, two less in this competition for survival at the back of the lorry.

Thomas watched the fight with a wide grin and laughed as first one and then the other tore off rotting blouses that gave way at the slightest touch, so poor was their condition. Quickly, an older woman, seemingly resigned to missing out on the bounty, threw her shawl over their shoulders before Thomas got sight of them.

'Right then, you sorry women. Who wins a prize today? I have, for very small cost, a little sugar and flour to give here. Who wants to see if Thomas is feeling generous?'

Now I was near the front, trembling and overcome with a wave of fear. This was my one chance, Thomas had always looked kindly on me although he had never asked my name. He knew other girls by name and perhaps that meant something special. Or horrible, if he was that familiar with them.

Still, I had to take my chance and I pulled my blouse a little so that it gaped at the front. Then, I swallowed hard and fought down a wave of disgust. I wanted to tear this man's throat from his stinking face but he was now the difference between survival and starvation. Quickly, I looked down. Yes, there was a little to see. Perhaps Thomas would turn my way and we would make the exchange.

'Well now hello again young miss!'

He turned to me, holding a small bag of sugar and flour. It was good British Army flour, captured from the Front. Probably milled in the south of France, far away from this stinking pit of Hell.

'Nice to see you looking so pretty. Little roses in your cheeks? Lovely.

Come and let Thomas have a look.'

Slowly, I moved a little closer, my face red and hot. Colour was good. I dared not look at his face and just lowered my arms to my waist and stood, being regarded as a marble statue in a gallery. Thomas stood for what felt like an eternity, just staring at me, his eyes upon my body. I fought the urge to tremble and run, thinking only of Father and his awful bruises, of Mother and her denial of the truth. So I stood still, hoping that my blouse would not, at this crucial time, blow closed in the breeze. Please Thomas, hurry and get all that you want. Let us get this over with.

'Would you like this, my little French fancy? I bet you do. Well, this isn't a bit of leftover bread, this is a nice bit of captured flour, top-of-the-shop stuff. No grit and sawdust and definitely no flour weevils. For this, I will need a little more.'

As if this degrading spectacle wasn't enough! I had no more to give. After all of this, I would go home with nothing to show for my shame. Voices started to whisper around me. They knew what I had done, had seen the outcome and must consider their own prospects worsening, knowing that this was a new price for a handful of stolen flour. A wave of shock passed from girl to girl, and from girl to woman. The women knew that if Thomas was the daily salvation, then they would be sacrificed.

Thomas turned back to get his answer. His face red and expectant, mouth opened just a little, allowing his tongue to slide over his teeth. I imagined him as a market boy in Germany. Probably beaten every day for being lazy, or late. But here, he was a deity. He was enjoying his moment in the sun and the pick of the French bounty in the Pas de Calais.

I wanted to kick him hard with my boots. But what of it? Shot most probably, and Father as well. Dear Father, please come now and help me. I have reached the limit of smiles and charm. From now on, everything would become dirty and shameful. The moment had come to cross the threshold from which there would be no going back. I was set. He could have me, would *need* to have me to seal this deal. I planned the words in my head, *Thomas, yes, I would like the flour and sugar if you don't mind*. I drew a deep breath and spoke. But those words would not come. Instead I simply bawled as a wave of panic and pent up hurt emerged, directed at this fool of a boy.

'William, come and get me please. I cannot bear this any longer!'

Startled, clearly not expecting to hear anything like that, Thomas took a step back.

'Who the fuck is William?'

Perhaps sensing an opportunity, the other women moved forwards, cutting me off from Thomas. From the front of the lorry, the officer emerged, no doubt having heard the outburst.

'You women, stand back. This is a fair distribution and you will all get your share.' He looked at me. 'And this girl can be first. This soldier will hand you this sugar and flour.'

I grabbed the parcels and fled, not daring to shed a tear. Weakness would be an undoing. They can prey on that, making it worse, both the Germans and the French. I looked at the small parcels. For these meagre packets I would have had to give up my body, in some meaningless act in the dark corners of the camp, to a disgusting brute soldier. But I had won today. Today, we eat. With a shudder, I realised that it would be the same tomorrow, perhaps with another German setting the price to a different French girl. None of us could hold out forever against this need for degradation simply to live. All of us trying to maintain a decency, which was really nothing but a lie.

As I looked up, two of the girls had linked arms, limping along in tears, holding on to each other for comfort. These were the two fighting cats, the new girls to the camp.

'Monique, we must never do that again. We will not live otherwise. We give those men a sight and something to laugh at, but no more. We are the losers and we have lost tonight. I am so sorry, so sorry.'

'Don't worry, dear sister. I have a little bread left from yesterday. You can have it. It was only a little kiss and he didn't hurt us so badly.'

The thinnest smile was shared between the pair as they moved away. A thin smile to cover a fight to survive.

I returned to our little doorway in the wooden accommodation. It smelled of burning embers so it was just a little warmer than the outside, which was a blessed comfort. In front of my Mother, I unwrapped the packets.

'Dear me, Odile. Is that all there is? Is that all you managed to get?' She paused, trembling slightly, 'and what did you need to give in return for this? I must ask, but I dare not.'

'Nothing Mother.' But my hands were on my blouse, pulling the still gaping fabric together.

'I see.' My Mother clearly did not believe me. But perhaps she had feared worse and this was at least an improvement on that.

'Well, at least we eat. The Collart family seemed to get nothing tonight, their girl is thin, you see. Those new girls came back in tears just now as well. Perhaps those women are not as beautiful to those brutes.' She was tapping the table loudly, as if holding back a scream.

'My lovely Odile, you will be our saviour, but what will be the cost?'

I moved to her and she held me close.

'Dear child, you are freezing. Go and put that vest back on, now that you have... Just go and get dressed again. Quickly!'

As I moved to my bed, my Mother opened the packets with the delicacy of a jeweller, daring not to waste anything. She would make every morsel count, thinking it had quite possibly taken her daughter's virtue to get them, in preference to the other families' girls. As I dressed, I pulled out my best blouse. I had been able to bring three. This one, I wore only at the weekends. The first time I wore it was September in 1912, when William had reappeared so unexpectedly. I held it close. If I tried really hard, I could smell him on it. Perhaps it was a fancy, my mind playing tricks to protect me.

I thought of the flour. British Army flour, given up after a battle, no doubt. To get it cost the lives of French and British, perhaps Australian and Canadian as well. We certainly didn't know. So little found its way to us. I imagined the sack being prised from the dead and bloodied hand of an English soldier; I just hoped it wasn't William. *Oh, William!* I thought often of you and our time together before you left.

'William, I meant it, my English boy. Come and get us. Take us back to our life in Bazentin.' I looked up, not knowing if he could hear me in his soul. Silly girl, of course he could not.

I looked at the date I had scratched each passing day on the floor of our hut. 22 April 1915. What was William doing today?

CHAPTER TWO – BAZENTIN, JULY 1898

'What is wrong with this stupid machine? All day cleaning it and still it won't damned well start. It is all I need, with everything else that is going on.'

'Pierre, I think you should take it easier, if you don't mind me saying. It is not helping Marie-Louise that you are in here all day every day, with this motor. She needs you by her side, surely? You know, what with…'

'I know Alain. But I'm no good with that sort of thing. Give me a gearbox to strip and I am in my space. Give me my wife and her poor pregnancy, well I do not know where to put myself. I only ever seem to make a wrong move.'

Pierre paused to wipe his brow with an oily arm.

'Besides, Alain, Mother Armandine is much better with that sort of thing anyway, and I am just an oily nuisance. Perhaps if I took in some oil, eh? We might see an end to this awful waiting.'

Pierre gestured towards the small leaking drum of engine oil and smiled at his farmhand.

Alain smiled back and shrugged, 'Perhaps it could make things worse.'

'Well, I ought to go in and see if there is any progress. I would like to see if the two little Lefebvre babies want to come into this world just yet.'

Alain gestured for Pierre to go. Pierre dropped the rag he was holding and nodded back to Alain.

'Thank you, my friend. Ha, I am worried though. If they are both daughters, I will never have my voice heard in my own house again!'

The men laughed and Pierre was gone.

'Ah, Pierre my love. There isn't much happening just now. Marie-Louise is asleep, but it is going to be soon I think, the babies are ready to be born. Why don't you get some rest? You will be needed later, I am sure. Don't worry, we Villiers women know our way around childbirth.'

'Yes, thank you Madame Villiers. I will get some rest since my skills will not be of much use here.'

'Not so many moving parts, eh? Nothing that you would understand?' Madame Villiers smiled at Pierre and poked him gently in the ribs.

A sudden scream made him recoil. It cut through his flesh to the bone, a percussion so strong that he stood petrified for a second in horror, unable to move or react.

'Dear God, Marie-Louise!'

Regaining his senses, Pierre quickly ran to the top of the stairs, swiftly followed by Madame Villiers, and pushed into the bedroom, terrified at what he might see. The sight offered little comfort. Marie-Louise was on her side, doubled up in pain. A wet patch of blood was forming on the sheets and it was getting bigger. Madame Villiers reacted first.

'Pierre, quickly. Turn her on to her back. Hurry up now, we don't have much time. Go and fetch Madame Bouchard, she can help me from now. Quickly Pierre, get her at once!'

Pierre dashed down the tiny stairs, out onto the road, and ran uphill to where Madame Bouchard lived on the corner. He had to be quick.

In a few moments, he was there. He pushed through the wooden gate, which snapped back with a large crash that brought Monsieur Bouchard to the door.

'My God, what is it Pierre? Is Marie-Louise quite well?'

'Your wife, Michel, call her quickly. Please, immediately.'

'My God yes. My God.'

He disappeared inside and within seconds Madame Bouchard came out, pushing past Pierre, and setting off towards the Lefebvre farm.

'Pierre dear, it will be fine,' was all she said as she disappeared, not even waiting for Pierre, who ran to catch up.

The evening wore on. The stairs were in darkness, and there were sobs from the bedroom. Marie-Louise was alive, but in pain and it was clear that she was giving birth. Giving birth in a hurry, in all probability.

Pierre stood at the door. It was not his place to see his wife giving birth, and she would not want him to see her in any case. Besides, it was a small room and he would take up space and become an obstacle. No, he would stay this side of the door. Perhaps he should go back downstairs. He felt useless, but such was the way with childbirth.

Half an hour passed, and sounds came and went, some were chilling and others reassuring. Marie-Louise was suffering, that much was clear, but the other voices were calming. Pierre hardly knew what to think.

Finally, the bedroom door opened, and a little ray of candle-light pierced the gloom. A shadow holding a bundle appeared on the stairs, coming down slowly, very slowly.

'Madame Villiers, so, are they—'

'Pierre, I am so terribly, terribly sorry. It is so very sad. I am anguished to my soul.'

Pierre could see the tear in her eye and knew this was to be devastating news.

'He was a little boy, Pierre, but not destined to live in this world. He is already in the next. God has taken this little soul already, so pure was he, that he could not be let into this sinful place. Pray for him and the other baby still to be born.'

Pierre dropped to the foot of the stairs as his legs gave way. The grief consumed him and he felt it press down hard on his head, which now suddenly felt as if it would burst apart. The expectation of joyous news turned to an almost unimaginably painful sorrow. At that same moment, a loud shout from upstairs startled him.

"Pierre! Are you there, Pierre? Pierre!"

"Yes I am here, what is happening? The other baby? Is it—?"

"Come up here at once! Hurry now, come up here!"

This did not sound like the birth of a second baby. There was no crying to be heard. Perhaps the second baby was not destined to live either.

'My God! Marie-Louise!'

He ran up the stairs and entered the candle-lit room.

'Oh my darling, oh my God. Oh my God!'

He looked at the bed. His beautiful wife lay peacefully on her back, tired, her pale face wet with tears. Her eyes were only just open, but a little smile crossed her wonderful face before she looked away from him. Pierre followed her gaze. Wrapped in a nursing blanket next to her on the bed was a tiny wriggling bundle. A little hand was just visible, the five fingers opening and closing in time with a little gurgling noise.

Madame Bouchard placed her hand on Pierre's face.

'Dearest friend, it is a time of sadness for one, but it must now also be a time for rejoicing for the other. You have a beautiful little daughter, healthy and very much alive. A daughter who very much wants to be in this world. Let her birthday always be a day for rejoicing the miracle.'

'Pierre, is that you?'

'It is, Marie-Louise. My love, let me see our, I can't now believe it, our daughter. Let me take some comfort from this day and look into her face.'

'I am so sorry Pierre. I am so sorry about our baby boy.'

'My love, there will be a time for him. But let us look upon his sister, our daughter here and now, with all joy and happiness. Shall we give her the name we agreed?'

'Yes, but I would like her to also take the name of my Mother since she saved my life.'

Pierre looked down at his new daughter. A tear fell from his eye onto her tiny face. He brushed it gently with his finger. He noticed how oily his hand appeared next to this pure new skin.

'Welcome to Bazentin-Le-Petit, beautiful, tiny, much-loved, Odile Armandine Lefebvre.'

CHRIS CHERRY

CHAPTER THREE – BAZENTIN, APRIL 1911

'Do you think the weather will hold this year, or are we in for another terrible summer?'

'You bloody farmers are obsessed I tell you, obsessed with nothing but soil, seed, and when to reap. Can't you sit here with me and enjoy the warm sunshine on your face just this once, you miserable old fool?'

Pierre pushed the half-empty bottle towards Michel across the makeshift tree-stump table, as both men laughed loud enough to bring Marie-Louise to the door.

'Are you two drunk again? Honestly, it is not yet evening and you are away already. It is not as if you don't see each other every single day.'

'Just sharing a glass of wine in the sun with my old friend.'

'Yes,' said Marie-Louise, 'just a glass of wine, and not a small cognac hidden about the scene somewhere, I can see that.' With a smile, she was gone.

'Pierre, how old is little Odile now, six or seven?'

'You old drunk, you see my girl almost as often as you see me! She is twelve and every bit the image of her Mother. Well, except for the mud and oil of course. I know she is trying to be her brother as well, when she can. How wonderful it would have been for her and Henri to have grown together.'

'Oh Pierre. Goodness, twelve years, who would have known? It was only yesterday that you told me Marie-Louise was expecting.'

Pierre looked down at his feet. For the briefest moment he remembered that awful day again. At the stairs he remembered Madame Villiers' face and the tiny bundle. Little Henri, who lived just the briefest moment in France before going to the next world. The pain was now at least more bearable, enough to live each day. They had tried again, hoping for a boy now that they had a lovely girl, but had not been blessed again. Perhaps the hurt to Marie-Louise was too great to have any more children. But that awful day was also the birthday of beautiful Odile. For her sake, they bore the pain of the date with happiness and joy, for in this world was the miracle child who had wanted to live. Goodness, was she making the most of it!

'Yes, she is twelve years old. Little Odile will be thirteen in three months, ah and indeed home right now!'

From the grass by the water pump, Pierre could see along the street. He saw the unmistakable outline of his daughter, almost skipping home from her lessons. She waved into the house of Great Aunt Madame Villiers, but did not stop to visit, hurrying towards home. Pierre had no doubt it was because today they would finish an invention together.

'Papa, Papa. I am home at last. Good afternoon Monsieur Bouchard!'

'Ha, good afternoon, little lady. I can see an air of excitement about you. Now why might that be?'

'It is today, isn't that right, Papa?'

'Yes, that is right. First go in and change, you never know you might get a bit oily today. Your Mother is expecting you to rush in and out just as usual. Hurry now, I want to be finished so we have time to try it today!'

Odile needed no second invitation. She bounded in and with much calling and fussing, she emerged moments later in her far-too-large overalls.

'Pierre, I will leave you two workmen together, ha ha. See you at the market in two days my friend. Good evening Odile, I hope you have fun! I will probably hear it anyway.'

'Ha Michel, everyone from Albert to Bapaume will hear Odile!'

Odile grinned at her Father and waved goodbye to his friend.

'No Papa! Hold it steady, no you are going to drop it down into the chamber! Left, before it... hang on. Get a grip, please. Papa!'

'I am trying Odile, but my hands are not as tiny as yours.'

'But you are wobbling all over the place and I am trying to slide the last bolt in here. Wait, I have the spanner in place. Here we go!'

'Steady Odile, not too much pressure, remember it will expand when it is hot!'

'There, it seems tight enough now, Papa. Enough for us to start it. Did you put in the fuel?'

'Yes Odile, enough for perhaps an hour of testing.'

'Did you oil all of the grease points?'

'Yes Odile, enough for us to test the motor properly.'

'Good, Papa, you have done well.'

They both laughed and Pierre kissed the top of Odile's head. Normally it would have been a tender touch, but the top of her head was the only part of her that wasn't covered in oil and grease.

'I think it is time we started the engine. What do you think? A ceremony, or just get on with it?'

Odile jumped into the passenger seat, and stood up, pretending to blow a bugle. Pierre cranked the engine slowly at first, ready for the motor to take the spark. It started first time, blowing puffs of black and blue smoke all over the garden and yard. Then it stopped. With a clunk.

CHAPTER FOUR – THE MOTOR CAR

I remember that moment very clearly. Almost a triumph followed by a dismal disaster. The odd little motor car, which Papa and I had restored from a pile of pipes and parts, was finally ready for the road. We had cleaned everything together, measured, cut, bent, hammered and spannered our way through this to our moment of joy. A moment which had then turned into a smoky bonfire of failure. We spent the next hour trying to work out what had happened until we discovered some loose connections in the electrical system. That had been one of Father's jobs!

'Right Odile, shall we try again?'

'Let us hope for success, the launch of the petrol car – Lefebvre.'

Mother had come out this time to watch our moment of joy. The engine rattled and clattered and sparked into life. This time, it didn't stop.

'Quick, Papa. Let's go before the engine stops again.'

'Yes, see you later Marie-Louise. We will not be long.'

'Bye Maman. This is going to be so much fun!'

'Oh you two, look at the state of you. Who is going to wash the oil out of your clothes? Hmm? It won't be me, just so that you know, ha! Wash in the pump the both of you before you come inside for the night.'

The motor car slowly moved forwards, with a clank and a rattle. I could sit and see over the top of the engine, just, but I had to stand for the first few minutes, because the fumes from the engine were sinking into the cabin.

Some of the village came out to see the launch of this new creation of Pierre Lefebvre. They were used to motors and tractors and other kinds of devices, but this one was different. A funny motor with a flat back. Ideal for taking goods to market, or moving furniture around. A very useful tool. But this one was to be sold.

The motor lurched along the road to Contalmaison. Going down the hill was easy, except for the brakes, which were not very good. At the bottom of the hill, Father turned right, towards the village. We passed a few bicycles and carts on the way and we received lots of surprised looks and cheery waves. The car was actually quite good. I kept looking across to Papa, who had a big smile stuck to his face as we drove.

'This is good fun, eh Odile? A bit smelly, but faster than a cart!'

'Yes, Papa. This is the future! Where shall we go?'

'Shall we drive the path to La Boisselle and see if Uncle's ducklings have hatched yet?'

'Maybe we might be able to bring some home for us to keep?'

'Yes, Odile. Why not!'

We drove on through the spring roads. Slippery for carts and bicycles, but the heavy motor car could keep going. At La Boisselle, the road narrowed to little more than a path, which would not take the weight and width of the motor car. We stopped to see if the ducklings were old enough to take away.

'Hello Olivier! How are you today?'

'Ah Pierre and... who is that oily child there? It can't be Odile! No, because she is a young lady? Hmm... what have you done with my niece, you dirty monster?'

I laughed out loud. Although I was nearly thirteen, Uncle Olivier always made me feel like a little girl, and I loved him for that.

'Uncle, it is me! Look, we have the motor car running at last!'

'So I see. A wonderful job, Pierre. So when will you have it ready to sell?'

'I have to make the seats, and the back axle needs to be rebuilt. With my other jobs, I think maybe in September. I'm due to go to Amiens then for the farming exhibition. Farming engineers from all over Europe will be there. Perhaps a buyer from over the sea? I don't know.'

'Well it will be worth every minute of effort. Selling this will feed your family for a year.'

'It's what I do, brother.'

I wanted to see the ducks and see if they could be transported in the motor car.

'Are the ducks big enough to come home with us?'

'Ah, oh yes, I almost forgot! We have nine that survived. They are all happy and healthy. Seven are female and their Mother was a good layer. What about taking six Odile? Five for eggs and one male to make new ducks with the two females that you already have?'

'Yes please!'

We loaded the quacking flapping ducklings onto the motor car in a wooden basket. We also brought back a few vegetables and a box of dried grain for spring planting. Our journey home was filled with joy as our work had been so successful. The ducklings looked confused by the wind in their little wings. Perhaps they did not know if they were supposed to fly, or maybe they did not understand how they were moving while their feet were still. It made me laugh. Father kept working on the motor car, whilst I busied myself on another invention, making a washing mangle into a food press, to wash and juice vegetables. This was the best time of year to try it, because I could work outside. If the food got too mangled, it could be used to feed the animals without upsetting my Mother.

Although life in the village could be harsh, in weather like this, it was blissful. I was happy to be here and I just wished I could have shared this with Henri. I looked down and rubbed the metal frame all the harder.

CHAPTER FIVE – BELGIUM, 22 APRIL 1915

Langemarck-Triangle Trench

We had just completed the installation of the light railway, to within forty yards of the rear communication trench 'Oscar.' LCpl Adams and I had just tested the water security of the light pumps for Triangle Trench and the two perpendicular reverses, lately occupied by the enemy. Wooden trench supports were weakened and we attempted to shore up the damage. However, two large holes remained, now available to the enemy as sniper bays. Hence, we were unable to complete repairs until nightfall. The French colonials have been instructed on preparing the defence line and I anticipate security by no later than 2100 (estimated to be 90 minutes after stand-to).

Added at 2200.
I have witnessed the most shocking effects of an enemy gas attack. At 1730, the enemy released a dense cloud of poison gas into the trenches of the French colonials from Martinique. Without the basic pad technique that we were testing, they succumbed to excruciating deaths. I witnessed dead men lying over the parapets and I realised that they had done so in spite of the snipers, in order to escape the low-lying gas. Their faces were gaunt, grey and yellow. I have not the words to describe the scene further. It appears death is not instantaneous, but a man may linger for minutes in this state, seemingly unaware of his surroundings and unable to think clearly. Evidence of finger scratching on the trench sides would indicate dying men trying to escape. Death appeared painful and disabling. From the enemy perspective, such attacks are successful without incurring losses of their own. The wounded are particularly damaged, their needs both immediate and visible. This is most likely the reason for the fear and panic evident in the troops, and their reluctance to defend further. There is no effective defence and no option to stand ground. Note: Engineers trialling a temporary effective measure of handkerchiefs soaked in fresh urine.
As requested, a note of enemy casualties. One enemy confirmed. Unit uncertain.
One German confirmed dead. A bald man. Death by skull fracture. The first enemy that I have killed.

Sgt William Collins
Royal Engineers. 22nd April 1915

I wonder what Odile is doing tonight? Whatever it is, I hope it gives her comfort and peace. There is no peace here. Odile, I hope you are safe and well my love. I would love to see you now, to receive your comfort and love. My knee is painful and the face of a bald, dead German is in my head. What might his family be doing this evening at home, awaiting news from the front?

CHRIS CHERRY

CHAPTER SIX – FRANCE, 26 APRIL 1915

'Odile, quickly, up and awake. We must move now, if we are to get anything again today.'

'Yes Maman. I am ready.'

'Your Father is already out with the soldiers. He is taking one of their lorries to fix something that went wrong. It was the one driven by that terrible stupid boy. I would give him something to make his ears ring.'

'I hope that Papa doesn't get any ideas – his poor face is still bruised from two weeks ago. I would not be surprised if his bones were not broken.'

'Hmm. Well come on. It is up to us now.'

My Mother had always been kind, with a softness to her voice and her manner, which everyone was drawn to. She was especially kind with me. But the last months have torn her spirit and hardened her nature, of course towards the enemy, but also towards the French citizens and the Belgians around us. To her, they seemed to be a different kind of enemy. Just others who would deny her family food and clothing.

'Odile, you must try to be at the front of the line. To do this, I will distract that older guard. Jurgen is it? I don't know, it is still quite dark.'

Mother had come to know all of the guards. She wanted to know their weaknesses and what they liked to talk about to distract them while the rest of us took advantage. The worst time was when the guards were rotated. Everyone was back to the beginning again and the cycle of suffering would start again.

'Good morning Jurgen. How are you today?'

'Lefebvre is it? I am well. What do you want?'

'I wondered if you had seen the Coffinet girls today? Also, little Amelie has a new dress that we all made for her.'

'Ah, no. Not yet. Why do you ask me about them? Why don't you look yourself instead of bothering me?'

'It's just that you are taller than me and may be able to see above our heads.'

'Ah well, I have not seen them.'

'Amelie would be sad that she has missed you today. She likes speaking with you.'

'She does what? Look, enough. Take what you want and go away.'

'Shall I ask her to come over to see you?'

'Look, just fuck off, will you?'

Jurgen pushed my Mother to the ground. She fell back with a grunt, stretching out a hand to stop me going to her aid, never once breaking her gaze from Jurgen.

'Jurgen, I thought we were friends?'

'Eh, friends with the... look I am sorry Madame Lefebvre. I just hate this bloody job.'

Mother had done it. She had found it again and opened up the wound.

'Help me up will you, Jurgen?'

'Yes, sorry.'

'You don't want this job, but it is your duty. Some day you can go back to your farm again?'

'Yes. I don't like this. It isn't proper soldiering, minding the bloody French. Where is the adventure in that?'

Mother was clearly in real pain, she placed her hand on her stomach and made sure her voice was calm.

'Well Jurgen, we all appreciate your kindness. You are a proper soldier to us. Someday soon, we can all live in peace together, but until then...'

'Look, just get what you want now, alright? I won't look for a ration. Take it and quickly.'

My Mother turned up her skirt, revealing pale matchstick legs. She was so thin next to the bear-like soldier she had just defeated. Maman loaded her skirt with anything she could lay her hands on from the lorry. When she had finished, Jurgen began giving others their small rations.

Mother was intelligent. She knew that keeping this to ourselves would cause problems, jealousy and accusations of favour. Although Father was beaten regularly for his defiance, it would make no difference to the women. Women, who each held their own secret relationship with the enemy. A relationship borne out of need, a strategy to survive.

Quickly, we returned to our camp quarters where we were housed in the wooden sheds that had begun as army camps in the first months of the war. Generally dry, but very cold, and the lack of privacy and the simplicity of the sanitary arrangements caused many unexpected problems. The Germans did not want to deal with outbreaks of disease that took extra time to deal with, so they tasked some men with keeping the drains clean. A foul job, reserved for the most defiant. My Father would long ago have been shipped to a labour camp to correct and punish his behaviour. But his genius with machines and his flat refusal to do anything if he was separated from his family meant that he was still with us, if not able to live in our hut.

Mother placed the proceeds of her transaction on the table. She carefully selected the choicest morsels for us — we did not know when we might get them again. The rest, she divided between the other families that we knew from our own village and also from Martinpuich and Longueval.

Quietly, she moved about the camp, distributing the parcels carefully. Not everyone could benefit from the day and she was careful not to create a scene, or to confront a jealous, envious or hungry family. Where she could, she gave food to families with children. Childless couples, she left to make their own arrangements.

To my ears, the German language was harsh. The younger girls here thought that familiarity with the soldiers was fun, and not in the least bit dangerous. What could possibly be the harm? I was not so sure. Any hint of danger, any hint of weakness and I felt the Germans would take advantage. In a different way to us, but exploiting the opportunity just the same.

Amelie had indeed thought that familiarity was fun. Whilst Mother had used Amelie with Jurgen, she knew that Jurgen was decent and his interest in her was no deeper than any glance at a pretty girl. His deep desire was home and his farm and it was the lever that she pulled frequently. Amelie, however, used the fact that young soldiers were here to occupy her time in a hobby of sport, teasing the young boys and then letting them go as the fun wore off. It was a dangerous strategy to relieve boredom and survive. Occasionally, it failed.

I was outside just for an hour that day, as it had been raining, using the light to repair my dress again. The threads were worn and weak and unpicking one area to mend another just meant that one day it would all fall apart in my hands. Amelie came past. We did not get along especially well; perhaps she was bored of my talk of engines, motors and *things*. She just wanted to talk about boys and silly books that were boring and far too young for us. But as a community we only had each other. Thrown together at random, our common bond was survival and for this reason, we had to set aside such differences. But she was fun and light, which helped, even though she quite understood the war we were in.

'Hello Odile, still just sewing again? How boring, boring, *boring*!'

'Amelie, I'm just mending this dress again. I won't be able to do it many more times, the material is so thin now.'

'Oh? Why not ask one of the boys to get you a new one?'

A shiver shot through my spine. *One of the boys?* I realised now we were never to get Amelie back. The silly girl from the *Tabac*, the girl who needed to be charming to put customers at ease, had most likely crossed the threshold, never to return to a life unhaunted by this war.

'Get me a new one? What do you mean?'

'Oh come on, Odile!' Amelie waved her arms theatrically. 'I mean, it's just a kiss, or a… well, just touching.'

'You would do that for a dress?'

'You've shown your breasts for a loaf! So what? It's nothing!'

To me it wasn't nothing. That degrading moment in front of everyone with the awful Thomas still sickens me every day. It was *something*. It was everything. William came into my mind. My lovely English boy, touching my face in the warm sunshine. I could not let him down. I would hold on for him, even through all of this torment. So? I did let some awful German see my breasts. My Father was bruised and beaten, with dirt and sand kicked into his face. We were hungry. They had not touched me yet, and would not ever get to me.

'I did, Amelie. But it was for food, and I did not have to touch him. A dress, well I can just do without.'

'You say that *now*, just imagine when it finally falls apart and rots. What will you do then? It won't just be a tit they see then, will it? Eh?'

This made me blush, I also knew it could well happen.

'Then, I will make one out of a blanket. It will never come down to *that* for me. It's disgusting.'

Amelie shrugged, clearly of a different mind to me. She was all for making it easier for herself and her family. They were only boys after all, just as we were only girls. So what?

'Look Odile. You know my thoughts are really the same as yours. It's just, well, I put those thoughts in a special place, where they can't ever get to me.'

I stood up and kissed Amelie gently, without knowing quite why, perhaps it was to show my understanding. She moved away, waving at one of the guards enthusiastically. For the first time, it felt like I actually knew her.

The evenings were the worst part. Once we had finished eating whatever had come our way, there was little to do. We would be allowed some time to speak with other families, but the Germans tried to keep us apart. We were an unwanted difficulty for the enemy soldiers, being evacuees from the towns and villages where the battles were actually taking place. There was talk that other towns in the north were being properly administered. The citizens were in their own homes, albeit only fed by the grace of the German Army. Meanwhile, for us evacuees, displaced by the invasion of 1914, it was a series of camps, privations and hunger. We were a forgotten population, a problem the Germans didn't want and didn't really know how to deal with.

The evenings were always a time for reflection, with conversations turning to our most basic needs. No more did Father and I speak of building motors, which made me sad. No more planning for school or for village gatherings with Mother. Now talk revolved around how to extract the last drop of juice from a mouldy cabbage or the last drop of fat from a tiny bone. We were simply existing, no more. Not for us the luxury of sleeping comfortably at night. And safety was as much of a luxury as being warm and fed. For my family, life was a nightly terror. We needed to be ever watchful for people among us, people who could take no more of the situation, finally losing the dignity of humanity and coming searching for satisfaction.

Mother's will grew stronger as the days of imprisonment went on. I never knew that my Mother had so much quiet strength to give. Perhaps it was the need to keep going for Father and me that sustained her through the misery.

'Odile, it is your turn to wash the clothes today. We have no soap, but the pump water is clean again as the pipe has been repaired. Go quickly, whilst it is still early, so you won't have to wait. But be careful on your own, those animals will be circling you as always.'

'Yes, Maman. I will go now. But these clothes will not last much longer. So few washes left in them and so many days of wear needed. When might we see new clothes?'

'Jurgen told me that there may be some next week. Some villages in the north have been raided. Perhaps a little might make it to us.'

'Someone else's dirty laundry – plundered laundry at that! I can't stand this!'

'Odile, enough. Go now. Go and get Papa's overalls clean. They smell and it makes him sad to be so dirty in front of the Germans.'

I remember that exact moment clearly. Stepping out into the early morning light, not cold, but cool as the day dawned. Everywhere was quiet and still. The Germans were guarding us, but they were not always on patrol. Most were brutes with us, I supposed it was a miserable duty for them, looking after dirty French civilians instead of shooting dirty French soldiers.

Into my head popped an image of my beloved William. The image was pleasing and I know it made me smile. A smile was a rare gift, to be treasured. I tried to imagine him in a uniform. I was sure he would have joined the war by now. I think he would have been old enough. I imagined him on a horse – perhaps not! On a motor-bicycle? Yes, he would do that, or perhaps some clever thing with machines. Perhaps he wasn't a soldier at all, but was at home, working for the war by making guns and bullets. Yes, I hoped for that. Vital to the war, but nowhere near the awful fighting.

At the pump, I felt the tug on my arm. A chill ran through me. Not again. This time, I may not be able to fight them off with words or tears. Perhaps this time, white French flesh through a blouse may not be enough to satisfy this brute.

"Excuse me, Fraulein, er Mademoiselle. It is Lefebvre isn't it? I think your family is in this block here, am I right?"

The uniform was unmistakably German, goodness knows what it meant, he was most definitely an enemy. But the language from his mouth was my beloved French and the voice with it was soft and the accent clean. He had clearly learned this language in a school. An officer then, perhaps?

"I am. Odile Armandine Lefebvre. I am from Bazentin-Le-Petit. A little village north of..."

"South of Bapaume, yes. I have been to that area. Miserable farmland, nothing to see for miles except fields and little houses, but charming villages in between the crops".

"You have been there?"

"Yes. My transport unit, with the third Guards, have been there at the front line".

"Where is the front now?"

"So many questions, but this one I cannot answer. May I ask why you are out so early this morning? Washing I see, am I right?"

"Yes, er sir. I am doing the washing for my Mother".

"Your clothes are shaming your beauty, Odile Armandine Lefebvre. Perhaps I could see if the stores..."

"No! I don't need any help from *you*".

The soldier was visibly shaken and took a startled step back. Perhaps he had not been here very long and did not know the unwritten rules of the little suffering community. I certainly had not seen him before.

"I, ah, am er sorry, if I seemed to offend you".

"You are *sorry*?"

"Yes, very. I meant nothing by it. I only said that I might be able to replace your worn-out dress".

"My dress is perfectly fine, sir. Now if I am allowed, I would like to wash these things before others push in front and the pipe runs dry of fresh water".

"Oh, I had that repaired yesterday. It was only a small hole, I don't know why it was not done before. I do not want cholera in this camp. It's quite safe and will remain so".

For the first time, I felt the shield in front of me soften and weaken. He was clearly not going to take me into a dark corner, at least it did not seem so, and perhaps I was safe for today. Now, Mother would be looking for weaknesses. What might be this soldier's pain?

"What is your name, sir? I have given you mine". I tilted my head to the right, I knew this seemed to be a favourite. William flashed into my mind. I heard myself tell him to go away, just for now.

"Sorry, who? My name is Kurt. Who is the person you were telling to leave? I do not understand?"

"Oh no-one. I was seeing if I knew any German to speak. Your French is good".

"I studied French at school. I want to be a writer when I am, well, when this war is over. But my family will not spend money on lessons to learn the language. So, I volunteered to be here, to speak and try out my French".

Mother would be proud of me. He has a family, perhaps it is a loving home, where they want him to study, but he cannot, there is a tiny conflict. He *wants* to be here, *wants* to learn French. I can do this. Odile, you must do this. This is a way *in* and it might not need your underfed body.

"Well, if it is allowed, perhaps I could help you with your French from time to time? Perhaps on days when food arrives, we could talk of the language and speak French to each other. Would that make you happy Kurt? Happy?"

I could see Kurt's eyes narrowing. Perhaps I had overplayed my hand in this transaction. This was all a façade anyway. Everyone knew the rules boiled down to favours, fair trade or sex. He was in thought, just for a second. Then he smiled back. I felt relieved inside and hoped my face did not betray me here. At least I was not half naked in front of him.

"I would like that very much, Mademoiselle Lefebvre". He tapped his cap and moved off. Perhaps he knew the rules and was playing along, bluffing this innocent French farm girl. Or perhaps I had something to work on, in time, that might mean something for us. Such little things could save our lives.

I made sure that afterwards, I remembered to tell Mother all that might be useful. Kurt, officer, wants to be here, learn French, isn't allowed. Thank you Kurt. We may survive here a little longer perhaps.

I turned back to the terrible rags in front of me. Giving Kurt something perhaps may not be so bad. A little time and a little smile may be enough to see these rags burned, replaced by something with dignity and more than a hope of a day's wear.

I worked the pump until the water ran clear. Kurt had been right, the water was sweet and clean. I washed the clothes quickly. Behind me a crowd had gathered around the fence where the motor lorries were kept. I thought for a moment it might be the French Army coming for us, but then quickly realised that could not happen here. The thought was replaced by a more terrible explanation. Oh my goodness, please no!

CHRIS CHERRY

CHAPTER SEVEN – FATHER! 26 APRIL 1915

'Papa! My God! Papa! No, please God, NO!'

There was a dirty and unmoving heap on the floor under the lorry furthest away from the fence. It looked like a pile of oily old rags, but why would soldiers point and shout at a pile of rags? It had to be my Father. He was the only non-soldier permitted in the compound. His genius with engines kept us together as a family, after a fashion.

'Papa! Please move, let me know you are alive.'

The crowd of French shouted and cursed the enemy. Here at least we could be united as one. For this, we were not in competition. But this was no victory for unity.

'Papa, darling Father! Let me know you are alive, it is your Odile!'

On hearing my name, the body began to move. He *was* alive!

With horror I watched as a nearby soldier him kicked him in the legs, then stamped on his knee. He must have known my Father's knees were weakened from the hours spent under their lorries. His cry was piercing, worse than a sick baby, worse than a Mother in birth.

He tried to lift himself onto his arms, clearly in agony. I tried to rush to him, but the gate was closed and two unfamiliar soldiers guarded it. To get through would be a lengthy process and Father needed me now. I was in no mood to negotiate. I rushed the gate and the two soldiers moved to stop me. A loud clear voice barked an order in German. The brutes let me go and the gate swung open. Kurt was at the fence, unsmiling, and a look of sorrow crossed his face before he turned away from my gaze.

'Oh Papa, Papa!'

'Eh, Odile, is it you my love? I cannot see you, for my eyes are kicked shut.'

My Father had two enormous red swellings around his eyes. His chest was covered in blood and his legs were streaked with dry blood and dirt from the compound.

'Yes my beloved Papa. What has happened to you?'

Although I tried very hard to keep the tears from my eyes, they would not hold back. I wept openly under that lorry, with my Father lying broken on the floor. This was worse than being touched by the enemy. This was heartbreak.

'I will be fine, Odile, I just need to get clean. Perhaps you would help me to the gate? You will not be allowed to stay with me here.'

I did not know how to lift my Father. Everywhere was painful for him. His clothing was ripped and covered in blood. His chest was a mass of bruises and his lips were cut. Blood pulsed from his leg. My blouse must now be a bandage, filthy though it may already be. I would have to let Kurt help me now, even if I had to degrade myself – whatever the price.

Another barked order. The soldier who had kicked my Father now helped him to his feet. Papa looked up and spat at him, hard into the face. A pink streak appeared on his attacker's face and the man stepped back in disgust. He slapped my Father's damaged face and pushed him to the floor.

'Papa, they will kill you! And that will kill Maman, and me as well. Is that what you want?'

'Curse these fucking pigs. Curse their boots and their Fathers. Disgusting pig bastards.'

He shouted loud enough for the crowd to hear. They seemed about to cheer, but perhaps seeing his broken body was enough to end any mutiny before it began.

Despite Papa's pain, I just had to lift him and get him to his feet. He shuffled like an old man across the compound. At the gate, the soldiers sneered but let us through as the watchful Kurt had instructed. As we passed, I heard a German speak to my Father in French.

'Tomorrow, I kill you, stupid fool.'

I looked across to Kurt. He did not meet my gaze, but instantly looked away, turning only to issue orders to his men.

Somehow, my Father made it to his bed. He had been a good engineer and the Germans had respected his work. But hunger and rags hurt the pride of a Frenchman unable to provide for his family. He was too strong and intelligent to tolerate the enemy fools. Today had been his last torment.

'Papa, what on earth happened? You silly fool of a Father. Let me wash your wounds.'

'No, Odile, you must go back to your Mother, you must not be here.'

'Tell me then, what did you do?'

'It is nothing. I poured water into the oil.'

On another day, I might have laughed. Nothing better than water to cause a blue smoke storm from the exhaust and ruin an engine.

'But why Papa?'

'It is not important, it is not important to know. Now, quickly, away home. Your Mother will be needing you this morning!'

'Papa, what could have been so terrible to make you do this?'

'Enough, child. Away now!'

I recoiled. This was my darling Papa, he never spoke to me that way. He had never raised his voice, unless in submission to my will.

'No, Papa, I must help you, I am broken inside to see you like this!'

A shadow appeared in the doorway, and spoke a few words in German. It was one of Father's attackers. Father turned at the sound of the soldier at the door. Then he turned to me again.

'Get out, you filthy child!'

To my shock, my Father slapped my face with enough force to spin me around. His fingernails caught my cheek, which burned with a fire I had not known before. In shock, and without a backward glance, I ran out, pushing past the startled brute at the door, who let me out with a sarcastic wave. I ran the short distance to our quarters and fell upon my Mother. No longer a grown-up woman, but a child once again, seeking the comfort of Maman's skirts.

'Dear child, what has happened to you?'

'Maman, Papa was beaten and I helped him and I helped him back to his bed and a soldier came in and then he hit me. He *hit* me Maman!'

'Odile, slow down, it is all coming out at once! Tell me again, I do not understand! Shh, come on now, it will all be well, you will see.'

'No it won't, Maman. Papa is gone. They beat him and he beat me.'

My Mother stopped stroking my lank and dirty hair and froze. She was silent for a moment and her hand tightened on my head. Then she started softly stroking me again, breathing heavily.

'He must have had a reason, Odile. Your Father would die for you.'

CHRIS CHERRY

CHAPTER EIGHT – MARCH 1912

Spring came early for us in 1912. I was especially pleased, as it meant that the motor car could be taken out and used. Twice, Father and I took it to Uncle Olivier in La Boisselle to pick up some vegetables on the back of the funny car. The second time I took one of his ducklings back, now a grown-up duck.

'Odile, my dear. Goodness, you have grown up quickly. You are so like your Mother, sorry, perhaps I should have not said that, ha ha. At least you are not like your stupid Father, how goes it baby brother?'

'Olivier, you fool, it is about time you showed me some respect. I am about to make our family a lot of money with this car and the second one that I am building now.'

'Yes, yes, I know. But these things will never catch on! They frighten the horses. Just look at poor Odile's face. It looks like you have shot her with a soot cannon!'

This made me laugh so much that I dropped the duck, which landed and quacked away, trying to escape the scene.

'Odile, shall we cycle over to Becourt to get some milk? They will have it all done by now. I won't get in this noisy thing, it might blow up, or worse.'

'Worse? What could be worse, brother?'

'Getting in this thing with *you* in charge of it!'

I smiled at them both, my lovely Father and adorable uncle, who always smelled of fruit! I turned to collect the bicycles, which I knew were inside the small shed in the front garden.

'They are already out, Odile. You must get out for some exercise. It will turn you lazy sat on your rear in this poisonous thing.'

We cycled to Becourt village through beautiful and peaceful scenery, pausing outside the village to take in the view. To the right we could see Albert down the hill in the distance. To the left, the ridge that sloped towards Contalmaison. It was such an idyllic spot, it seemed a shame that we had to leave.

On the way back, my Father explained to Uncle Olivier that the car was due to be sold to an Englishman who was coming to visit. He was also interested in farm equipment and Papa was hopeful of a successful transaction.

He would be coming over in early April. The price for the car would buy enough food for the next winter and leave enough to invest in some more farm equipment.

During late March, Father and I cleaned up the car. We oiled it, checked it and polished it. Every day we made sure that it would start, knowing how important this sale would be.

'Odile, it is time we went! Quickly now, my love. I will drive the car with you to Uncle Olivier. Put your own bicycle on the back. I will leave you there with him. If the car breaks down, then at least there are two of us to fix it. Then, at four, come and meet me in Albert, but don't be late, and we can drive home.'

'Yes Papa, this is the fifth time that you have told me.'

Ah, er, right. Good. Well, let's see if the car will start. Make a wish daughter!'

'Odile, are your chores done?'

'Yes Maman!'

'Look at the state of you!'

'No need to clean up, Maman. I might get dirty again today!'

My Mother threw a wet cloth at me to clean my face and disappeared back inside. She was shaking her head at me. I suppose I was a *bit* oily.

The car started straight away. It was not perfect, but it just had to last long enough to get us into Albert and back. The Englishman was well known for fixing these problems.

So it was that the funny motor car fired into life, and I hoped that this first good fortune would make for a day filled with joy.

At Uncle Olivier's house, I took down my bicycle and waved goodbye to Father. My job was to watch him onto the road and see that he made it into town. The road was clearly visible from the track to Becourt, so I quickly cycled there. The little car chattered and puffed its way into the distance, until it disappeared over the last ridge on its way into Albert. Now that my job was done, I was supposed to stay here until nearly four, before cycling into Albert. But it was boring just sitting here, so I decided to wait a little bit, and then cycle into Albert early to find the party with the Englishman, a Monsieur Collins.

When I got there, a little before three, still a bit oily, I spotted the motor car outside the café. Through the window, I could just make out my Father drinking coffee with the Englishman. There was a boy as well. I couldn't see him very well, but he looked tall and handsome, perhaps my age, perhaps a little older. What was I to do? *Oh, just be yourself and get on with it, Odile Lefebvre!* So I aimed right at the café, put my terrible wobbly bicycle against the lamp, put on a big smile and went in. The conversation seemed to be struggling a little as there were lots of hand gestures and the boy did not join in much – in fact, he looked quite bored until he saw me. The two Fathers were busy concentrating on their gesticulations and so he introduced himself in very slow and very loud English – perhaps taking me for someone deaf, or maybe for an imbecile.

'My name is William. That is, William Collins. I am from England. I like your country very much.

'Oui, yes, I know you are from England. William. Is a strong name, yes?

Like, William the Conqueror, who was from France, no?'

'No. Er, yes. Ha ha. I have travelled with my Father to see your Father. Do you go to school here?'

'Yes, they have schools in France. They teaching English to us better than French to you boys, oui? One, day, William-not-the-Conqueror, you come to France again and you learn French. You can show us how to build machines. Is a fair trade, you think?'

'Yes,' he laughed, 'is a fair trade.'

'Imbecile.' It was only fair to punch him on the arm since he had clearly taken me for the imbecile. He would soon learn.

'Thank you. Merci, mademoiselle.' He was still rubbing his arm, but he was grinning at me.

'Your French is very bad, William. I will have my work to help you learn French.'

The poor boy blushed. Since there was now a brief lull in the men's conversation, I turned to Papa now.

'Papa, that motor is nothing more than a thing for burning. Why do you still try to mend it? The dampening rods are bent away and the flywheel mount is so worn, it rattles the whole way home.'

'I know Odile, but we have discussed a solution to the problem with the bearings. Here let me show you the drawing that Monsieur Collins has come up with.'

'Yes, this is very good, if we can get the part to be made so accurately and to the size we need. Can we do this?'

'Ah, Monsieur Collins, William, this is my daughter, Odile.'

'A pleasure to meet you, Odile. You seem to know your engines. This is William, my son, accompanying me on this visit to France.'

Again I looked at this boy, now close up. Already, I feared that I might fall in love with him. He was strong and his face was so pure and full of life.

We took a walk that afternoon. I remember his strong hands on my arm, but he was always shaking and nervous. He was in such as state, it was very funny. But, he was kind and gentle, and if truth be known, a little like my wonderful Father, which went in his favour, of course.

As it began to get dark, we arrived back at Uncle Olivier's house in La Boisselle. My Father had driven there in the motor car with Monsieur Collins. We were to see them both the next day and I thought a picnic with William might be fun, knowing the weather would be warm and sunny. I knew at that time, that I wanted him to come back to France at some time in the future, for I knew that he was the boy I would fall in love with if he would only let me.

The next day, when we waved goodbye, it hurt my stomach when he left. As a farewell, I punched his arm and dug him in the ribs out of nervousness and not knowing what to say.

'Goodbye Monsieur Engineer.'

That was a very silly thing to have said! I did not want him to know that my longing for him was already strong. He was English, I might never see him again. I was being such a stupid little girl. My hand just brushed his, and the warmth rippled up my arm to my heart. As he turned away, I looked at his strong features, trying to remember them in case I never saw him again.

Over the following months, school became less interesting to me. I wanted to be out with Father working on the engines. The rest of the time was spent dreaming about William. Would I ever see him again? I thought about writing to him and knew that my Father corresponded with Monsieur Collins about the work to be done on the funny motor car. It would be completed soon and then it could be transported to England. Often, I would be found sitting under the trees in our garden, making drawings of two young people, hand in hand, walking the fields or riding bicycles. Underneath, I would write *Odile and William*, as if I did not know who they were.

By the time summer came, I noticed that my Father expected me less and less to stay outside at all hours. Although I wanted to fix engines, now I also quite liked other things. Perhaps it was William. Perhaps I was trying to grow up enough for him to notice me as a woman and not as the girl I still was. Perhaps I wanted to be a lady for an English gentleman. I suppose it was just growing up, when everything is confusing. Especially since there was no plan to see him.

When September came, the early evenings were my favourite times. The warmth of the sun was still strong and the light in the trees was magical. These were the days I most liked being outside with my Father. School finished early for harvest time and everyone was expected to help out, otherwise we would starve over the winter. The school rooms were very close to home, just a very short walk over the road.

Most of my days were the same. A walk home, hello to Mother, then get changed and go out with Father until it got dark. We would all then go inside, to eat and read before bed. The rhythm of country life was unchanged for us. It was the seasons that danced around us.

Early one September evening, I heard a terrible commotion in the bushes. From under the branch emerged a dirty, sweaty and unmistakable William Collins. My heart jumped and I smiled at him. But my Father advanced on him, a spanner at the ready.

'Papa! It is William. He has returned.'

'Ah, so it is. William! Idiot!'

'Hello Madame Lefebvre.'

'Er Monsieur Lefebvre, William. I am a man.'

'Ah, desolated, monsieur. Er.'

'Idiot, ha ha.'

Father slapped William on the back and welcomed him back to France. I walked him to the pump and made him wash. He was filthy, poor boy. He told us, in loud and slow English, that he had been travelling in farm carts to get to us.

He came with a wish to stay and work, which seemed odd for an English boy. Then I remembered the motor car, now owned by William's Father. Perhaps he had come to get it ready to go to England, but Father had said nothing about it.

Finally, it was agreed that he would stay above our little work shed, where it was warm enough and some furniture could be spared. He was not allowed to stay in the house. The village greeted him a little nervously at first, but his warm smile and generous heart won them all to his side. He was quite the popular boy. My Grandmother Armandine and my Great Aunt Villiers also took to him. He promised that he would learn to live in France, learn French and also undertake errands for a few coins. His earnest sincerity melted my heart and I began to desire only to be with William.

My Great Aunt Villiers was our chaperone when we went out. But she was mischievous and often did not feel the need to accompany us.

'Oh you two, off you go to Longueval. Mind the damp in Delville Wood, it's not safe in there, you know, ha ha. Be back by supper time, or you will be in trouble!'

On one of these trips we found a motor bicycle. It was not very old, but it had been neglected and did not work. William and I agreed to fix it, and then to ask if we could buy it or borrow it. If it worked, then it would be fun to use and practical for William's errands.

As it turned out, the motor bicycle was wonderful. We could go for longer distances, see more new things and explore our relationship together. William and I often talked of getting married. I had no idea whether it would be possible or legal in France, but it was fun to think so. Always the English gentleman, I often wondered if he actually did really love me. He said he did, but never tried to take any advantage of me – not that I would have let him. But it would be nice to know that he wanted to, if that makes any sense – but we were still very young, I suppose.

We had discovered a little toolshed on the road to Martinpuich, perfect for a hideout and a rest stop out of the wind. William and I loved to spend time in there. It was small, but it was always warmed by the sun and it had a view over the road. For fun I started to leave notes there so William could practise his French. He would be out and about and I would not know where he was. I would place a note, knowing that at some time, he would get it. The notes were things I could not say – desires and my growing love for this boy from over the sea.

Mother and Father adored William. I often used to think that Father looked at William as he might have looked at little Henri, someone to welcome into the family, not keep on the outside. In the evenings, he would often tell me that William was a good boy and that I should behave well towards him, with none of my silly girl nonsense.

William, my darling English boy, worked so very hard. He was doing it to show my Father he could provide, and my Mother loved him for that. I did too. We were not old enough to marry, and I did not know whether a boy from England – not even a Catholic boy – could marry a girl in France. Such things were for the future, not for now. For now, I loved the fun and the time together. We were innocent and our feelings so sincere and deep, which was enough for me and hopefully enough also for him.

We spent more and more time together at the toolshed, just talking or enjoying the sunshine. It was here that William finally told me that he loved me. Properly, slowly and in beautiful, perfect French. I did wonder whether Great Aunt Villiers had helped him – someone certainly had! I was always careful to call her Madame Villiers when William was around – because he once called my Mother 'Maman' by mistake. She did laugh, but I also know it cut through her soul to the place where she kept little Henri.

The year had been mild, but it turned quickly to winter. Christmas in 1913 was cold and dark, but it would be very different from the Christmas in 1912. William had just arrived and everything was different. He was still a shy boy, but everyone wanted to meet him at the traditional family night out in the village. My lovely village was full of kind country people, who would offer anything they had to friend or stranger alike. That was our way.

They took to William, even if they could not understand his terrible French – for terrible it certainly was. But his French got better very fast. Sometimes, it was fun to hear him struggle, earnest in his desire to improve. It was so very kind of him to try and it was kind of my village neighbours to embrace him so deeply. Even if it was only to enjoy some light amusement as the poor boy carried on regardless of what he said.

I read his notes in our toolshed, a little sanctuary of oil and dirt that was quiet and entirely ours. We could be alone together, not for any particular reason, but just for the calm and the chance to say what we could not say outside. Inside that shed was our world, our own time together, to determine our true feelings for one another.

In winter that year, the days felt short and the nights long. I would be home before William every day. At that time of year, he had to push the motor bicycle for much of the day. The roads and paths were slippery and the darkness took away the shapes, so riding was dangerous. He would arrive home breathless and cold and I was always the first to welcome my brave boy home.

'My brave William, poor cold English boy. Here, let me take that. Where have you been?'

'Today was a day for mending bicycles – two in La Boisselle and one in Becourt. Quite a ride home again, for the roads are terrible.'

'Well come inside. Mother and I have made vegetable soup and the bread is fresh. Are you ready to eat?'

'Yes my love, I am ready to eat.'

My Father was now at the door. William always shook hands with my Father in the evening. It was a very English thing and it always made Papa smile.

'William, there is no more work until the Christmas arrangements are over. You can rest now. You are a good, strong boy. Madame Lefebvre has changed your blankets and we have put some more furniture in your building. You should be more comfortable now. We are all at the village celebrations tonight.'

The day before Christmas in 1913 stretched on into a magical night. I looked forward a year to Christmas in 1914 and thought it would be the most magical year for us and could not wait for it to arrive. Soon, I would be old enough to marry, and Father might even consent, if it were legal and possible. Papa liked William for he was a strong, intelligent boy, who would learn a trade and make him proud. And Papa liked William's Father too, for they had done business together.

It really seemed that 1914 would be our year, and hopefully, we might spend more time alone. But also, it was necessary for William to visit his family for a time – returning to me, of course – for I would not be allowed to live in England.

'Perhaps in April, I will go back, exactly two years since we met. That would be good. I can come back to France in June and we can spend a lovely long summer together.'

So in April 1914, William returned to England for three months, just as he had planned. Under Papa's watchful eye, I kissed him chastely goodbye. When he turned to leave, I knew immediately that he was my true love. As I turned away, I took a step and then glanced back. Straight back into William's beautiful eyes. He held my gaze for a moment, then smiled, turned and went. My stomach fluttered a little, but then he was gone.

Dreaming ahead, I would be eighteen in the summer of 1916. I could be married here in the village church? Perhaps even on France's day on the fourteenth of July. It would be wonderful. The lovely street lined with the villagers, family and friends. And lots of English wishing William well. A village full of English – that would be so much fun to see! Nothing could stop it, and that day would be our special day. William, surrounded by his English friends and family, on the happiest day of our lives. Of course, it was silly to get so carried away in case William did not feel the same way, or in case being back in England changed everything. And yet it was set in my mind! The fourteenth of July, 1916, with a village full of English. Now, wouldn't that be a wonderful sight?

Over the weeks I wrote to William many times, but never had the courage to post my letters, although Mother occasionally sent one away for me. I received letters from him, in English mostly, which made me start to think his resolve was weakening. My letters became more desperate, so I would not even let Mother post any more. Once, I tried to send a telegram, making the telegraph officer in Albert cross with my insistence on sending an English translation. It was uncertain whether it was a successful attempt. It was possible that William heard nothing from me and it made me sad to think I had been so weak. Although the odd motor car was here, so there would be contact with William or his Father at least one more time, if there was no sign of William's return in June.

Then, we heard that a big war was coming, which would almost certainly involve France and Belgium, and we would be in the teeth of the coming storm. Newspapers printed maps with big red arrows and captions showing the possible paths of invading armies. When I looked closely at the maps of northern France, our little village was under the thickest red line. By this time, I did not know whether I would ever see William or a peaceful life again.

CHAPTER NINE – 26 APRIL 1915

Once Odile had run out, the soldier took a step closer to Pierre.

'I'd quite fancy slapping that little backside as well, eh? Felt good, yes? Well, my turn to teach *you* a lesson. You don't fucking well insult *me* in front of *my* men, you filthy French bastard!'

'Look at me, you pig. You think beating me again makes you more of a man? Well I don't care. I don't care for you, she is my daughter, speaking like that makes me sick. I don't care what you do to me. Hit me and fuck off.'

'So, the French troublemaker fights back! Well I enjoy this sport, after all, I have little love for the French.'

'And I have no love *at all* for the Germans!'

The soldier smiled without mirth. 'Perhaps I could give you a nice kicking so that you are in no doubt who is in charge. Or, maybe I will go and get your pretty daughter back and spank her arse in front of you...'

The blood rose in Pierre and he clenched his fists. 'No! That is a step too far!'

'Calm yourself, Papa French. I am not so base, I am a soldier after all.'

Pierre unclenched his fists slightly, but he was still ready to fight again. He knew that he was pushing his luck, that the Germans saw him as an inconvenience, like a pain, or a cut that won't heal. And he knew that he could get away with a little more since his skills were so valuable to them. But they had to deal with his insolence in case he inspired his fellow Frenchmen into starting bigger trouble. Pierre straightened up and glared at the soldier.

'Lefebvre, why must you try our patience, eh? Why must you insist on breaking our rules? We have won, you have lost. Accept it and we might all get along. You are good with my lorries. Today was disappointing. I would have every right to send you off for punishment for what you did today. But I will not. You have value, and for that reason I want you to follow the rules, you understand?'

'The way you speak my language makes me sick. Your horrible coarse tongue insults me, you fat pig.'

Pierre was still pained on behalf of his beloved Odile. He had wanted to send her home quickly, running to Marie-Louise without stopping. The only way to force her to go home immediately was to land that terrible and painful slap on her. He spat out a bloody mouthful, which landed on the floor, just as a black boot covered the spot, advancing on Pierre.

I was inconsolable that evening. My face stung, the pain amplified by salty tears. My face was red, with purple finger marks streaking across where

Father had slapped me. What had I said that was so terrible? What had we, Father and daughter, done for us both to be beaten?

'Darling Odile, let me put some cold water on your face. You must not bruise, or we might not eat for three days. Jurgen was not there this morning. It was that new young officer who you met at the water pump. He was with that awful Thomas.'

I shuddered at that name. The awful scene with him staring at me playing over in my mind again.

'Maman, why would Papa behave so? He has never ever been like that to me.'

'You say Papa was beaten and bruised? Injured, his face badly hurt?'

'Yes.'

'You picked him up, carried him to his bed, and still the Germans came for more?'

'Yes.'

'Do you think that you were safe then?'

'No.'

'Then, your Father protected you. He gave you the lesser of two beatings.'

I bit my lip. 'Do you think Papa was beaten again after I left?'

'Well, I doubt now we shall see him again for some time. The Germans will keep him locked up, I am certain.'

'My poor Papa. I am so very sorry. Maman please.'

I leaned over and hugged my Mother again. We stayed there for the next hour, gently sobbing to the beat of our hearts.

As it got dark, Amelie appeared at our door. She wasn't in the same building as us, but we all knew our way around.

'Odile, some milk has arrived. The officer won't give it out until all the girls are present. Here we go again. Time to get our br—'

'Amelie!'

I looked at Mother, and she looked at me, then looked down and dabbed her eyes with a dirty handkerchief.

'You girls had better go. Quick! Before the others get there.'

Once more the day had turned. Once more the ritual of the scavenger would be ours to perform. I did not bother to change or to clean up. If my best efforts, my clean blouse and my naked flesh had not been enough, then nothing I could manage today would secure any milk. Likely as not it would be sour.

But today was different. There was no sign of Thomas, and the lorry was stocked with fresh provisions. The first crates were removed and taken to the huts where the soldiers were quartered. Behind them were dusty and broken crates, but there were more of them than usual. Perhaps things were changing for the better.

'Form an orderly line. Name and family size. One each, no exceptions. No talking, and keep moving. We do not have all day.'

So today, there would be no contest of beauty or nerve. At the back of the lorry was Kurt. I guessed he was perhaps twenty-two years old and had some authority over the others. Two soldiers that were no older than me gave out small parcels. To some, those with young children, they gave a small bottle of milk. It was yellow, but at least it had not yet split. The scene was quiet. Perhaps we were civilised after all, and the breakdown of humanity was only temporary and driven by hunger.

'Odile Lefebvre, daughter of Pierre. I am also collecting for my Mother.'

'Sorry, nothing for you today. Officer's orders.' He nodded at Kurt, who looked away.

'I'm sorry? But my Mother and I—'

'Nothing for you, now move away.'

He shoved me and I took two steps away, but then I turned back, filled with anger and injustice.

'Why is there nothing for my Mother and me today? What have we done wrong?'

The young soldier shrugged. 'Just orders, girl.'

'Girl? Why you are my age, you brute!'

The second soldier looked up from his list.

'I saw your Father's attack today, and just look at the state of your face. He nearly broke the arm of one of my mates. The same fire burns in your eyes. I like it.' He looked me up and down for a moment, making me shiver. 'Now clear off.'

'I won't. I will stay here until you have finished. I will get my ration from you, or I will go to your officer.'

'Will you now? What do you think he will do? Special relationship is it? Besides, whose orders do you think we are following? The Kaiser isn't here is he? Ha ha.'

Both soldiers shared a dirty grin and then stared back at me. Once more I felt naked and exposed, just a piece of meat on a hook that they could devour anytime they pleased.

'You there, get out of the way. They aren't giving you anything. It's my turn and we're hungry. Get away.'

The French voices behind made me jump back. Just as I thought we had recovered from this nightmare, I was plunged to the bottom again. My face ached with blood pumping through my bruises. There were no more moves for me to make. All I could do was stand there, my red face throbbing and my dirty, torn blouse flapping in the breeze. So I made a wish, a wish that I wanted desperately to come true.

'William, come for me my love. Come for me and you can have

everything of me. I will be your true love. Please come for me now.'

'I wouldn't stay there if I was you dear!' The harsh voice made me jump out of my dream. I felt a pain in my stomach as the world came back into focus.

'That new officer is looking at you and not in a good way. You might end up with a problem. You aren't getting anything from this lot, so you might as well get out of sight. Quick, go on home. I will see if I can swindle a bit extra for you and your mother. Go now.'

I looked around. It was Madame Collart, owner of the Tabac in Longueval. A tough lady, every bit as angry as we were. Monsieur Collart had joined up early in the war, but been killed in the first action defending the French line near the Swiss mountains. Her son had also joined the army and she had not heard from him since. I knew that she hated the Germans and wished only agony on them, but she was wise to this game.

'Thank you Madame Collart. Thank you.'

She took my shoulder and turned me away, patting me just for a moment. My mother would be upset with my empty hands.

'Odile, did you manage to get some... oh, I see... was it like that again? Perhaps I should go tomorrow, until you get your spirits back. Is there much left? Shall I see if I can get us something?'

'Maman. We are getting nothing tonight. We have been struck off the list.'

'Daughter, please tell me that isn't true. Did you see it for yourself? Quickly now, did you see the name on the list? Was it struck out, or just underlined?'

'Maman! How should I know? They just told me to go away. Nothing for us at all.'

My Mother took a step back and slumped onto the stool. She wept into her hands.

'Pierre, my love. You have condemned us all. After everything we have come through.'

'Maman, surely not? This is just for a short time, surely? To punish Papa.'

'No, Odile. This is bad for us. The list is vital. Even when we are on the list, we get nothing without begging and... well, those other things. But to be crossed off the list! My God, it is almost certain starvation. Now, there is only one way to eat.'

'Steal Maman? Must we take from the Germans, or just from the other French?'

'No Odile, that isn't how we get to eat. We must play on them, to get what we want. We must encourage them to be kind to us.'

Of course, I already knew the answer. I had seen already what we had to do to survive. For the second time today, Mother and I sat and sobbed together. This was no life, this was not even existence. Our world was unendurable and it was now up to me to make it right again.

After dark, we both decided to try and sleep. We were hungry and thirsty, the only thing to do would be to drink the little water we were allowed and to sleep away the hunger. Hunger made me cold and I did not have the strength to keep warm. The blankets were so thin and worn they were no help. They smelled of sweat and were nearly always damp.

Then, there was a heavy thump outside the door and a shuffling of boots. Had Papa escaped his confines and found us here? Or were the Germans coming to exact more revenge for Father's insults? What more could they really do to us? Beat two weak women? Have our bodies? It was impossible to know. I was frozen in fear, but had to keep thinking. There was only one way out. Any injury or harm would mean death for us.

The shadow at the door moved to and fro, as if looking around. It remained for a few seconds and then moved away. Mother's grip on me lessened and she was still easing me behind her when the shadow returned. There were more thumps and the unmistakable sound of breathing. Whoever was outside the door was staying close to it. Looking for a way in perhaps? We froze again. The shadow remained for almost an hour, just standing there, outside the door. Why would those brutes torment us so?

'Odile, we must confront this situation. Stay out of sight. Papa is likely lost to us, if not for ever, then certainly for now. We must keep going. Perhaps I can reason with them. Maybe they might leave.'

'Maman, no! They will kill you. Then where will we all be?'

'Shh, daughter. Just keep down.'

I rolled away and hid under the wooden bed as Mother approached the door. She took a deep breath and whispered a quiet prayer. Maman opened the door although anyone could have opened it anyway, we could not lock anything away, not even ourselves.

'Oh my goodness! It is safe, Odile. Come quietly and see.'

I looked up immediately, still expecting to see an angry soldier wanting something I did not want to give. But the shadow at the bottom of the door was actually a small sack. Inside, Mother found a bottle of the yellow milk and some potatoes. Not mouldy, but firm and white.

'Oh Maman! Madame Collart was as good as her word. We can eat after all.'

'Odile, we have been blessed by the kindness of a friend. Quick, let us cook these potatoes. We do not know if we might get some more.'

We ate quickly. Mother kept four potatoes under the bed. If we saw Father soon, he could have some. The milk we had to drink immediately, as we had no way of keeping it fresh. The thick yellow liquid was only slightly sour, and every drop felt like it was nourishing us to our very bones.

In the morning Mother opened the door just after it was light. In the space between the door and the path was a parcel wrapped in cloth. It was a piece of cheese and a loaf of black bread – it was only a little stale, and some water would soon soften it.

'Bless you Madame. God bless the Collart family.'

Just as Mother moved the little parcel inside, we were all called to the water pump by loud shouts from the guards.

Kurt was there, with Jurgen by his side, along with the two guards that had struck me from the list. With horror I also saw the large serjeant who had seen my Father strike me. When he saw me, he turned, grinned and spat on the ground.

Kurt raised his hands for quiet, but we were all too frightened to say anything.

In French, he addressed the small crowd of women, a sermon for the beaten.

"French women, today you are all to be moved. I will not be telling you where, but it is to another camp, away from these village buildings. These are to be billets for the glorious advancing German Army. The soldiers cheered and waved their arms in the air.

"So, all, get on these three lorries and we will leave in five minutes. Quickly now!"

The soldiers spoke roughly to us in German. We had no time to take any belongings, we were not allowed back to the rooms we had been in. What we were standing in was what we had to travel in. But, the Germans had not counted on my Mother.

"Excuse me Jurgen. I must return to my room to collect some important items".

"Fuck off Lefebvre, just get on the lorry, we're late and I don't care about any of your filthy shit. Move!"

"But Jurgen, there are some items I simply must have!"

"What? Didn't I say?"

Mother gestured behind my back to go around and to our rooms. The potatoes were too precious to lose. But were they worth a beating?

"Jurgen, there are certain things a woman must have. Do you understand?"

Jurgen raised his hand to my Mother, but she did not flinch.

"Move now, or I will fucking break your face".

"I will Jurgen, but you need to know that women bleed each month. Do you want that all over the floor of your lorry? Hmm?"

Jurgen's hand lowered slowly. He neither knew whether that was true and might happen, or whether my Mother was playing him for a fool. But it was embarrassing for him and he wanted it out of the way, before anyone noticed.

"You have one minute, move".

But I had moved around, to the door of our room and had already retrieved the blanket, shawls the little piece of cheese and the potatoes. I also took the little loaf of black bread that came with the cheese. I quickly soaked it in water to soften it. We could eat it on the lorry later. The exercise had made my slapped face hurt, which throbbed so much I thought that everyone would be able to see it pulsating.

My Mother caught my gaze and I flashed her a quick nod and a smile. We had managed to recover some dignity for us all and the other women had noticed it. My Mother had saved a little humanity for them as well.

We were all loaded roughly onto the lorries, fifteen of us in each one. There were also Germans to act as guards. The one in our lorry was the awful man who beat my Father. He took the opportunity to humiliate us frequently on the journey.

The day was warm, as the year was turning towards summer. The lorry had canvas sides, but the Germans tied back the two rear corners so that a warm breeze flowed over us, along with showers of dust. None of us knew where we were, or where we were going.

I thought of the brave soldiers from the French Army who went off to battle in 1914. And I imagined darling William in uniform. These were better images of soldiers. Perhaps in Germany, girls of my age imagined their men fondly as heroes. And perhaps some of them were heroes, in their way. It was just a matter of fortune, which side of the war we were on. But it did not excuse the unnecessary violence towards defenceless women, with no weapons except our common sense and our bodies. A small ripple of muttering had broken out among some of the older women.

'No talking, you French cows! If I hear any noise, I will make it my pleasure to punish you, eh? You would like that, eh?'

Everyone fell silent and concentrated on the floor, anxious not to catch the man's eye.

'Well, would you? What about you, little peach? You want some – just like your Father, maybe, uh?'

I stiffened, about to look up, but Mother pulled my head to her shoulder, shielding my eyes.

'You have nothing to say to her, you brute!'

'Maman, no! I can handle him.'

'Odile, you cannot. You do not know what he might do.'

'Well, little girl? Do you want to know what I did you your stupid, pig-head of a Father, eh?'

'Leave her alone. Can't you see her face? She has had enough.' My Mother gripped me tighter. 'Whatever torment you want to give out, you give it to me.'

I was not sure that the German understood what Mother was saying as she was speaking so quickly, but he seemed determined to continue.

'I kicked him until he stopped breathing...' There was a pause with just the slightest sob from one of the women before he continued again. 'And then I kicked him some more, just to see if his bones would break. Guess what ha!. They did.'

Mother stiffened on hearing this, even though news of Father being beaten was now a recurring story, and she spoke again.

'You German pigs just use news like this as ammunition in a battle without bullets to defeat us troublesome women from France, who no one wants.'

'So, then keep quiet, or the same will happen to you too.'

After that, we were not in the mood to speak much anyway, perhaps too busy trying to overcome this new challenge. My one hope was that the officers would travel with us, I felt we had the measure of them, awful though they still were. Oddly, I worried about Kurt. Not for him personally. Because he had shown me some kindness, I had hoped he offered a way to survive. But Father's rebellion had ended that hope before it had really begun. Mother and I were at the bottom of the ladder again. Perhaps I might have rebuilt a friendship with Kurt to help us survive.

In the morning, the sun was shining. We were driving south. From the rear of the lorry, some of the women were able to see the countryside passing by.

We stopped abruptly with a jolt. The soldiers jumped out and talked in German. None of us knew what was being said and I heard only two familiar words, *Collart* and *Lefebvre*. My blood ran cold. We had been singled out. What had Father done to us? He had sealed our fate, along with his own. Clearly Madame Collart's kindness to us had been spotted and now she was condemned as well!

Then, the canvas was pulled back and the bright morning sunshine poured in. Four women were pulled out and moved into another lorry. Amelie was moved into our lorry. So our lorry now included both the Collarts, as well as Monique and Natalie Delaitre, Mother and I. There were six others, who were all given little blue books for some unknown reason. The writing was in German and none of us could understand that language.

The other two lorries drove away leaving us behind, which worried me. I had assumed that the blue books meant something good for those who had them. Because Mother and I were not given one, I reasoned that we were still being punished. Suddenly, our lorry started up and lumbered forward. We had a new guard, who was the young soldier who had struck me from his list. Judging by the mean flash in his eyes, he had not forgotten.

'Ah the Lefebvres, Mother and girl! Ha! No food for you again, eh? Not while I am in charge!'

'You are not in charge, you stupid ignorant boy. If you were my son, I would have taught you a lesson in manners. How dare you speak to an adult like that?' Mother had already started probing for his weakness.

'Look, woman. I am an adult and a soldier in the German Army. So shut the fuck up.'

'You should have your mouth washed out for that language. Look at you, not even able to dress yourself. You should be ashamed.'

'Look, shut up now, just shut up!'

But Mother was not about to let go. 'Your Mother would be ashamed to see you doing this to us. Do you think she would be proud of you, beating weak and innocent French women? What do you think?'

'What? What the fuck does my Mother have to do with this?'

'Oh dear, if she heard you speak to me. Well, at least your French is passable, but to *swear* in another language and to behave so badly to a woman. She would weep, boy.'

'Stop calling me boy. Shut up!'

Clearly uncomfortable, his face flushed, he would be no match for my Mother. The agitated soldier tightened his grip on his rifle.

'Oh, wave a gun at a defenceless woman. Your *Grandmother* would be so proud, dear.' Mother made a sweeping gesture when she said Grandmother.

She got no reply from him and smiled to herself. Once again, my Mother had got what she wanted, she had won again, but I worried for her safety all the same.

The journey was interminable. Eventually, after about half the day had passed, the lorry stopped and we were allowed to get down. We were allowed to go into the bushes one at a time. This took up some time and I was glad of the air and the chance to consider what was to happen next.

'Madame Collart. Thank you for what you did yesterday for us.'

'All I did Marie-Louise was to prevent your daughter being manhandled by these awful soldiers.'

'Thank you yes, but I meant the food you left late last night. The food this morning was very welcome as well. You were very kind indeed to share with us.'

Madame Collart looked blankly at Mother, raising her hands in bewilderment.

'I am sorry Madame Lefebvre. I wasn't able to get anything for you or for us. We were off the list as well.'

CHRIS CHERRY

CHAPTER TEN – THEY ARE COMING, 1914

I had never seen Father like this. He was pacing up and down our little kitchen, rubbing his hand on the back of his neck and then on his chin. He was humming a tune under his breath, but it was impossible to recognise it.

'Odile, my love, ask Alain and the boys to come here at once.'

'Yes Papa. Are you quite well?'

My Father did not answer, so I continued with all haste.

Outside, the late July sunshine was strong and the breeze was wonderful in my hair. I ran across the garden to the shed where Alain was whistling.

'Alain, Papa is asking for you.'

'Oh hello Odile. Tell him I will be there in minute.'

'Erm, I think he meant you should go now.'

'Oh, I see. Does he want all of us?'

'Yes, he asked for you all.'

'So, it's finally happening.' Alain put down his hammer. He tapped the table three times. Without looking up, he called out.

'Louis, Antoine. Come into the house for a minute. Pierre wants to speak with us all together.'

Alain turned to me and slowly began walking to the house.

'Odile, will you feed the ducks, little one?'

I smiled. Alain still called me little one, even though I was now sixteen. As he passed, he kissed me softly on the top of my head, as he often did. Somehow though, it felt different this time. He went into the house and the door closed softly. When I looked up, three other men from the village went into our home. They were stony faced and pale. I watched the door intently for a while, then went to the ducks.

The ducklings had all grown into excellent layers and we had fresh eggs throughout spring and summer. I fed them grain from the spring harvest. Just a few grains as it turned out, because the spring had been dry. They quacked contentedly and bustled about my feet, tickling them. Often, I wondered how many more of these days we could have.

When the members of Father's meeting finally emerged from the house, the parting was sombre, as if at a funeral. Papa beckoned me.

'Papa?'

'Odile, I have asked Alain and the boys to go home to their own families – and to stay with them.'

'Why Papa? Surely a war would not affect us? No one is going to come through our village, it is too small is it not?'

'I just don't know, Odile. But it cannot harm us to be prepared for anything.'

'Anything?'

'Just clean up a bit out here and come inside for the evening. I want us all to be together tonight.'

'Yes, Papa.'

So for four days we stayed inside, huddled together in the warmth of the summer sun. Father occasionally stepped outside and attended meetings with the other families from the village. Mother bustled around as usual, cooking and cleaning, just as she did every day. I think she hoped that if we carried on as usual, then this might all go away.

On the sixth of August 1914, news came to us that war had been declared a few days before. I did not know what making it official actually meant, but from this moment I knew our lives would be different. Men from the village were meeting and discussing what we should all do. In Albert, preparations were being made to move the local government further west, or even south towards Paris. For me though, in the little village, it did not seem that war might touch us at all. But word came on the fifteenth of August that changed everything. The official conscription officer had arrived in Albert and sent word to the surrounding villages that men were being officially called up to the French Army.

'For goodness sake, we will have to join. The Germans will come at us from the south and the north! Do you just want to stand here and be shot?'

'Of course not, but we are not soldiers. It will take months to train and by then, well it will be over, one way or another.'

'So that's it then is it? Stand and watch every other poor bastard fight, eh? You are such a fool coward Durmond and I curse the ground you stand on.'

'Fuck you Bouchard.'

'No my friend, I think it will be the Germans who do that.'

The two men stood face to face in the road stretching from Martinpuich to Contalmaison. A cart was trying to pass, but the driver was enjoying the stand-off.'

'We must join, it is conscription. We do not have a choice, do we?'

'So, we can choose where we might fight and die as amateurs? Pitchforks and shovels against the mighty enemy? Sounds charming.'

'So, do we do it?'

'Shit, what choice do we have? Let's get the others and see if we can get in to Albert before dark.'

Within just a few minutes, fourteen boys and men set off for Albert. That was it, they were called and just got up and went. This was really going to happen. The war had got into our village. We all hoped it would be as far as the war came for us.

'They will be back soon. The enemy will not cross into France from the north,' Madame Bouchard said as she waved the carts around the corner.

'Are you sure?'

'Yes, Marie-Louise. Our army will halt them at the frontier.'

For much of August, the village lived in fear and hope in equal measure. Sometimes the news was good; the British and Belgians had held up the advancing army. But on other days we became more fearful as we knew another town had fallen. It became increasingly clear that we would not be able to avoid the war. We were in the line of fire for Paris, that much had now become quite clear.

On the last day of August, the first French soldiers appeared in the village. The administration officer had visited all of the villages to the north of Albert. For now, we were allowed to stay in the village, but it seemed that we were ultimately to be moved north and west, away from the danger. The army officer feared the fall of towns to the south of us as the Germans crossed into France. He also feared the fall of towns to the north. We might be trapped. I did not like the sound of this at all.

'Please everyone, please! One at a time. We are not here because we fear the enemy will attack this village. We are looking for towns to base our soldiers as we go north. We will hold them at the border, please be assured, we are winning the fight to keep the enemy out of France.'

'So why are you here? We are many miles from the border? Why would you need to put soldiers here?'

'Madame, please. It is just a precaution. We are just trying to give our army some choices.'

'Will you protect us? What is to become of us?'

'For now, you will stay at home. We may ask for you all to be moved north or possibly south, to Paris or nearby. The Germans are trying to reach Paris, of course, but they will be stopped. Paris will never fall.'

'North, or possibly south? What does that mean?'

'Thank you, now I must continue my work.'

The village was officially put under the protection of the French Army at the end of August. Soldiers began appearing in the village and some of the outbuildings were used to provide shelter for them. Tents appeared all over the fields between our village and Longueval. The enemy was moving north from the borders and enemy soldiers coming from Belgium were coming south.

'Monsieur Lefebvre, I understand you are to be attached to the motor lorry units in Le Transloy, or even Bapaume. We are moving your family tomorrow morning. Can you be ready at seven?'

'Yes. It is for the love of France and to help our soldiers. Where will we live?'

'We have arranged a farm building for all of the working civilians to live in. It is not perfect, but it will be safe and dry. The food will be to your liking, I will make sure of that.'

'Who is being moved?'

'For now, just your family. Your daughter won't be needed to fix the engines, but she will travel with you. Although I see she is quite the mechanic!'

'You have no idea. We will be ready and pleased to help.'

'Good, it is just a temporary measure, until we are fully supplied, then you can all go off to Albert and then Paris.'

The officer stood upright, nodded politely at my Father and disappeared around the corner.

Father turned to Mother and me, mopping his neck with his hat.

'It seems that we are to move, to help the army with their lorries. At least it will not be the army for me. I had hoped to build machines for peace, but these will be machines for war.'

'Move Pierre? What will we be moving to? This is awful. What will become of our home?'

'Darling wife and darling daughter. We can do no more than we are told. Come, let us embrace one last time on our farm and enjoy the last rays of sunlight on this old world.'

'Oh, Papa, that sounds so dramatic. Will it come to that?'

'Yes Odile, with certainty.'

We were allowed to take few clothes and belongings as this was a temporary move, for a month, whilst the army was preparing to move north to Lille and Armentieres. I had not been to either town, but knew they were some miles away, so why stay here then? It all seemed to be moving so very quickly, in two directions.

The morning was cool and clear. We packed the few belongings we were allowed into Monsieur Bouchard's cart. The two horses would get us to the lorry in Pozieres and then return. A few villagers turned out to wave us goodbye. No one said anything, but everyone had the feeling that we would all be saying a last goodbye to each other soon anyway. It was just that we were first. The embrace was longer, the smiles thin and shallow. Father put his tool boxes on the cart and we were ready to leave.

'Marie-Louise, we will see you in a month. I am sure by then this will have ended. I will feed the ducks and Michel will keep the garden tidy. Odile my love, look after your papa. He will need your help with those engines.'

'Thank you Madame Bouchard, I intend to show Papa what to do!'

We all shared one more smile and the cart moved off, the hooves tapping out a rhythm that was hypnotic, ticking off the last seconds of our life in Bazentin-Le-Petit. As we turned to go down the hill, I looked at my home once more. I tried to imprint the picture on my mind in case I never saw my home again. If the French Army did not hold back the enemy at the border, we surely would be overrun in this little northern village. We turned right at the bottom of the hill, moving off towards Contalmaison. At that moment, the sun came out to warm our faces.

'We will be safe with the army, Marie-Louise. It is the best option in this uncertainty. I think the Germans have crossed the northern border and are moving south. This is really bad for everyone. If the army does not hold them, and our British friends too, we shall be under the rule of an enemy soon. We must help our army fight on. I have to.'

'Does that involve our daughter joining the army as well Pierre? Does it?'

'Of course not, but we can't stay here. It will be too dangerous.'

'I know, I am sorry. It is a worry for all of us.'

As we made our way through the villages of Contalmaison and La Boisselle, passing Uncle Olivier's home, I wondered what would become of all of this. What would be the fate of the French people?

'Odile my love. How are you?' Father called over his shoulder in an unconvincing calm and joyful voice. It told me all I needed to know about Father's deepest feelings.

'Just like you, Papa. Very frightened.'

Father just smiled and waved to the soldiers at the waiting lorry.

CHRIS CHERRY

CHAPTER ELEVEN – INTO THE UNKNOWN
APRIL 1915

Once everyone had visited the bushes, we were pushed onto the lorry again. The lucky six with the little blue books looked around nervously. They dared not take them out to examine for fear of seeing them snatched by one of us, or taken away by the soldiers. I still did not know what these books were. What was clear was that the six who had them, kept them away from us. Seemingly they had made up their minds and they were determined not to lose the little hope the books gave them.

We tried very hard to understand where we were. Mother was convinced she saw a sign for Lille in the roadside, torn from its wooden post. But which way it was and how far was impossible to tell. There were German signs everywhere, infecting our land. Curse these brutes to Hell itself.

The lorry stopped again. New soldiers with guns pulled open the canvas, the light blinding me. Two fat old soldiers jumped in and grabbed four of the six women in the corner, snapping their fingers at the women and making gestures about the books. When one was proffered, the soldiers opened them and spoke roughly between themselves. The oldest one held up three fingers on each hand.

'Is six. Six bitches, ha ha.'

The six were identified and taken off the lorry. I thought about saying something, but did not. A loaf of dry black bread was thrown into the lorry, and it had barely landed before it was pushed under Amelie's skirt.

'Don't worry, I will share it later. I don't want it taken away.'

'Thank you Amelie, we may even still have some cheese to go with it.'

We shared a weak smile, but neither of us was in the mood for laughter.

The six taken from the lorry were put in front of an unfamiliar officer, who spoke more gently to them, but still in German. None of the women responded to what must have been questions. Finally, one of the girls went forward to take his hand, begging not to be beaten. He took a step back, startled at the response, quickly removing his hand and speaking to her in French.

'Girl, I do not want that at all. Switzerland, I want you to understand, is where you will be.'

They looked at one another in astonishment. They would be safe, perhaps. But the canvas was pulled back down before we could understand more of what was happening. It was now clear to us that whatever was to be their fate, was not to be ours.

'You fucking French are with me, ha ha.'

'Do you miss school at all? I wonder if you miss the beatings from your teacher for being so stupid!' My Mother snapped at him.

'Shut up, just shut up you French bitch.'

I closed my eyes. Clearly, Mother was not going to let this fool of a boy get the better of her. What had become of my gentle, loving Mother?

We travelled more, and when evening came we reached a little village in a flat and open part of the country. The wind was cool and blew dust and dirt around us from all sides.

'You will stay in this house here. All together and shut up.'

The house actually had furniture and a hearth. There was plenty of wood around to make a fire and it seemed the Germans were not going to stop us using it, at least not tonight. The door was shut on us and locked. We were prisoners, but there were some comforts available.

'Are there beds here?'

'No'

'Blankets?'

'No'

'Any linen at all?'

'No'

'Is the wood dry?'

'Yes, and there is a lot of it. There is a water pump at the back, but the door is locked.'

We quickly made up a fire and Mother lit it using the dry kindling. There was a little bread and cheese left, which we shared between us. We sat all together in a big circle on the floor of the one big room around the fire. We were just beginning to get warm for the evening, when the door lock was shaken, which shocked us all. A tall officer stood in the doorway. Here was another unfamiliar face for Mother to deal with.

'Which one of you is Amelie Collart?'

Everyone looked at the floor. From the corner of my eye, I could see Amelie's hands trembling.

'I said, which one of you women is Amelie Collart? I will not ask again!'

His French was good, perhaps he came from the borderlands where many French and Germans understand both languages. From behind him, we saw the flash of a metal pail in the firelight. It was full of water and the soldier carrying it threw it over the fire, splashing most of us with cold water, and causing ash and steam to fly out and make us cough with the dust.

'That was your drinking water.'

'I am Amelie.'

'Stand up and come with me, quick now.'

Amelie stood up and was taken out. The soldiers said nothing more, but turned and left, locking the door behind them. I could hear boots outside, so one of the soldiers must be guarding the door.

We sat in silence, too terrified to speak and too worried to put in words what we were all thinking. Instead, everyone looked at the wet hearth, the wood too damp to start a fire again, shivering as the cool evening turned to a windy night. There were no sounds from outside apart from the sound of the occasional shuffle of boots as the guard was changed throughout the night.

In the morning, the first rays of light came in through the window, so I knew it faced east. This meant that the road came from the north, so we were still moving south. But none of us knew where we were, and the enemy had succeeded in getting us lost. We still sat in silence, with nothing to eat, no water, no prospect of cleaning our bodies, and no dignity of privacy. So, we simply sat, slumped against each other for comfort. My thoughts turned to Father.

'Odile, are you awake?'

'Yes Maman. I feel faint with thirst and hunger, but I am here.'

'Amelie is still missing.'

In my sleep I had forgotten that Amelie was not amongst us. I felt ashamed for forgetting, even temporarily, that one of us was not here.

'Odile, why do you think we did not get a little book to get us to Switzerland?'

'It must be Papa, Maman. When he upset the Germans.'

'Yes, but Madame Collart and the Delaitres. What did they do?'

'I do not know. Please keep your voice down, we might be heard.'

'Do you think that Madame Collart managed to—?'

The door clanked again and was thrown open roughly. What we saw in the doorway shocked us, even after everything we had been through up until now.

CHAPTER TWELVE – WITH THE ARMY, 1914

We drove to Bapaume in bright sunshine in a covered lorry. The French soldiers accompanying us kept offering Father cigarettes and tobacco for a pipe. Father took them all, perhaps hoping to trade them for food, or clothing or whatever might be needed. We just wanted to hold on to everything useful as the world slipped through our fingers. The officer in charge was friendly and kind. His face was grooved and had a worn look, as if he had been fighting wars since he was a boy.

'Monsieur Lefebvre. I am sorry that all of this has come so suddenly. We are moving quickly to defend our borders and we do not have enough engineers to keep the lorries running. They get hot and leak oil everywhere. When they break, we do not have the parts to repair them. We need your skills, sir, to fix them, just for the time being. There are other civilians, Madame Lefebvre, but not many. France appreciates your sacrifices.'

'France is welcome to every last drop of strength I have. I could never have imagined this and wish it to end quickly. Do you have the tools? An engineer can do nothing without tools.'

'Tools we have, talent we do not. Ha, what will you do Mademoiselle?'

'I can fix the lorries as well.'

'Did you hear that, Jacques? This little one can fix engines as well. Ha ha.'

My Father leaned over and put his hand on the officer's arm.

'Monsieur, do not underestimate my daughter. Do not underestimate her at all. Believe me when I say this. Take me, take her too.'

The officer shrugged.

We arrived just north of Bapaume, at the temporary junction built to link Cambrai and the local railway. Our rooms were small, but some furniture had been put there for us and it was comfortable. Mother was relieved to see two other families living in the same place.

'Good day Madame! You have just arrived? Welcome to our little workshop town, ha ha. Is this your daughter? She is the most lovely little lady.'

'Good day Madame. Yes, this is my daughter, Odile, and I am Madame Lefebvre, Marie-Louise Lefebvre.'

'Pleased to meet you. I am Madame Collart and this is my daughter Amelie. My son was here until a few days ago, but he went to Cambrai to see if he could help. Silly fool will join up, likely as not. I bet they won't take him, he is such a dreamy fool he will have forgotten his socks.'

'The family over here. The two women?'

'Ah, the Delaitre girls? Yes. Their Father is laying the railway here. He is simply the best railwayman in northern France. Their Mother is a bit unwell, she never seems to go out anywhere. There is an aunt or cousin as well. She is in shock at all this upheaval. She has seen a German in France as well. She lived in Armentieres or thereabouts. This may not be over so quickly, you know.'

My Mother's head dropped for an instant.

'Do we eat well? Is there bedding and clothing?'

'Ah. Food is plentiful, if a bit poor in quality. We make do with soups and such. If you can cook, it will be possible. Clothes are what you are in and bedding... well, you should ask. They are taking whatever they need to get the army on the move. Fuel for lorries, bedding for families. Same difference, eh?'

'I see what you mean. I am sure we will all be just fine.'

'Marie-Louise, come quickly!' Father was calling from over the street.

'What is it?'

'I must go north again to the artillery lines. They need someone to help maintain the wheels and bearings. I will be back in perhaps three days.'

'My God, Pierre. Will I ever see you again? Artillery. That's guns? That's where the battles are?'

'It will be fine.'

So Father was gone. Whilst we waited for his return, I was able to help out a little with the cars and lorries in our camp. There was always a need to grease the bearings and make sure the water was kept in the radiator. These were easy for me.

'Look at that delicate little flower, all greasy and smelly. Good for you, girl.'

The soldiers did tease me, but I know that they also respected me. Mother saw to it that none of them ever said or did anything else.

'Odile, when you are finished, come and help me prepare food. It is our turn to cook. Madame Collart has found some mutton and apples. I do not know how she does it, she knows everything about everyone.'

'Yes, Maman. Do we know when Papa is back?'

'I ask every day, but it is the same. They just say – maybe tomorrow, maybe the next day, we do not know.'

And so our lives went on, each day the same. We cooked and helped out but felt useless, marking time until Father and the troops returned. We thought this might go on forever, but we saw more soldiers pour through our camp, more lorries come and go, more oiling and watering for me. This was serious because the soldiers looked more and more alarmed.

'Who is this child under the lorry? Go away, you could be hurt!'

'Sir, this is the Lefebvre girl. Do not worry, she knows what she is doing. Really, she does.'

'What? A girl fixing engines? Whatever next!'

'She might have to drive them as well, if we suffer any more losses.'

'None of that now. We will be glorious!'

'Very good, sir.'

The camp was tense, the mood no longer light. Everyone went about their business determined, all too worried for their own families. Late on the fifteenth day, word came that the troops were returning with Father. They would all be tired and hungry and so the women helped the army cooks to make something special. Two pigs and any number of chickens were brought in and prepared. It would be a welcome feast.

The first car arrived just before sunset. The damp September evening was cool and uninviting. The officer got out, took off his cap and stroked his nose wearily. He walked back along the trail, saying nothing to anyone, just staring into the dusk, gently tapping his hips with clenched fists. Everyone drew towards him, seeking word of our men. Soldiers crept into the space, knowing that whatever the news, it would not be a joyous return. Victory was not written on his face. The officer stood in silent shadow for a moment longer and then turned to us all.

'Everyone, we are in full retreat. The enemy will be upon us in ten days or less. They are attacking in force. We must now be prepared to stand fast.'

He went off, issuing orders to soldiers who quickly marched off to their duties. Stunned and unsure what to do next, the women agreed that whatever was going on, we should still serve a warming meal. We just would not expect too much of them. The lorries began to arrive just before eleven in the evening. The thin lights were barely visible as each lorry bumped and bounced towards the camp, filled with dirty soldiers, many too tired to eat. Father was not to be seen. I began to worry that he was ill or had been injured. But then he emerged, already smaller and thinner. His head was down and he walked with a stoop, looking so much older.

'Ah, my darlings, I am so pleased to see you. Your clothes smell comforting, my family.'

'Papa, my lovely Papa. We have missed you.'

'The guns needed your help, Odile. You would have done well there. But it was no place for you. The enemy is advancing. I have never seen guns or bombs exploding before. We were close to the front lines.'

'My god, Pierre. You mean the front lines where there is fighting?'

'Yes Marie-Louise, the enemy is in France and advancing to Paris even as we stand here.'

'We cannot stop them?'

'Stop them? No. Delay them, yes. This enemy will be through our village and away to Paris in quick time. They think three weeks.'

We stood in a single embrace. Father was swaying slightly. He was hungry and thirsty and had been jolted in the lorry all day.

'Sorry, Papa. We have food. Are you hungry?'

'Yes, my darling daughter. Lead me to my supper.'

Father slept through the next day. He had given a strict instruction to be woken at seven. The army came to get him at noon, but decided to allow him to sleep.

'Your husband has earned his rest. He did not stop for six days. The guns were hot and often they jammed. He was able to get them firing again. He could have been a first class gunner!'

'Well, he is a first class engineer.'

'Madame?'

'Yes?'

'You know it is lost. Whatever we do will not stop this enemy. They have been preparing for too long. They aimed their guns at us only when they knew they could prevail. Please, take care to leave this area. Safe passage can be arranged.'

'My husband will not go.'

'Which is precisely why I am telling you.'

CHAPTER THIRTEEN – APRIL 1915

Mother was the first to react.

In the doorway stood little Amelie, her clothes loosely draped over her. She was cold, shivering, and holding out a hand to us. In her other hand was a canvas bag. She dropped it at the door and stepped in without speaking. Her face was streaked with tearstains and her hair smelled strongly of tobacco and rifle grease.

Mother opened the bag. Inside was a small loaf of white bread and a piece of cheese. A smaller bag inside contained a lump of dried meat, of what type, we could not tell.

'Well, we can make this last a while, keep us going through the next few days.' Mother was back to trying to make the best of it.

Madame Collart sank to her knees next to Amelie, put her hand on the girl's head and said a silent prayer. Amelie did not look at us or speak again that day, but leaned onto her Mother and fell into a fitful sleep. At noon, the soldiers came back for us. The same grinning brutes that brought us here.

'Everyone on to the lorry. You are to be moved again.'

As we stepped outside we could see that five others were to join us. I had not seen them before and they looked just as shocked as I was. Their clothes were less worn than ours, but they still clung on to every thread as if their very lives depended on it.

Again, we spent what felt like an age bumping along in a lorry, the canvas sides tied down so that we could not see. The guards had mercifully changed again, and the young soldiers looking after us were efficient and said nothing. Perhaps they did not speak French, perhaps they just treated us like a job, not a sport, like the others had done. In the corner, Madame Collart and Amelie sat huddled together, withdrawn from our group. Madame Collart was stony silent, a pale shadow of her normal self. When we stopped again, to be given water, Amelie spoke. She leaned forward, staring into the floor of the lorry, speaking to no one in particular, but into the empty space between us. Her voice was barely a whisper, harsh, parched and choked.

'The soldiers had heard I was available for comfort and entertainment. They heard from the guards in our camp that I was happy to beg for food with my body. That was what they had heard. They knew my Father and brother were soldiers, which meant I was a prisoner of war and not a civilian. They laughed at me. I asked them for food if I gave them what they wanted as they were going to take me anyway. When they had finished, they gave me the food from their packs. They told me that they would have given it to us anyway, so I was just there for fun.'

Amelie sat back against her Mother again, who was sobbing to herself. They both turned away.

'My God, what is happening to us? What are we to do now? We are helpless.' Natalie's voice was also weak and parched.

'Enough Natalie. Sister, we must keep going, for our families.'

My Mother put her hand on her shoulders and kissed her gently.

'We must stick together, or we will be lost to our families.'

Mother squeezed my hand and pulled me to her. I wanted to break down in tears but they were for Amelie, not me. The poor girl was silent and hard. If she could survive this, so could the rest of us.

The lorry moved off again. We were going south now, with the sun mostly in front of us, meaning we must be moving perhaps south and west.

Later in the afternoon, the lorry stopped again. This must be the final stop, because around us were many soldiers and some civilians.

'Get down. We stay here for time.'

We got down from the lorry. The Delaitre girls were ushered into a group with several others and they were given blue books. Perhaps they were to go to Switzerland after all, but why had they had to endure this journey with us?

Natalie came to me, her book in her hand.

'I have been given one of these travel books, Odile. I do not know why. It seems we were supposed to get one before, but we were forgotten. It was decided last night to give us books. I am so sorry.'

'You must not worry. Go and live, Natalie. Do not worry about Mother and me. We will survive.'

Monique could barely look in our direction. Perhaps she was embarrassed with a ticket to freedom, but she had no need to be. I wished her only a long life.

We sat at the side of the road, unable to do anything else. Mother went to Madame Collart and embraced her gently. Madame Collart just sat motionless, in shock and sadness. Amelie had no tears, and she just sat staring silently ahead, holding her stomach and rubbing her arms together. I feared for her survival, the yellow tinge in her skin told me that I had to help her, or she would not make it out of this.

The guards seemed not to notice us, just moving past us, grunting their annoyance at us being in their way. They took a look at Amelie, one even stopping to offer her water. She spat at him. He cursed at her and moved off, mercifully without exacting any immediate revenge.

So there we were, the four of us, sat at the side of the road. It was nearly dark when an officer came to us.

'Who are you?' He barked at Madame Collart. She did not reply.

'I said, who are you? Answer me, damn you! Why I—'

'We are the Lefebvres and the Collarts,' my Mother interrupted. I guessed she was already working out where this officer might falter.

'Lefebvres? Well here you are! Why are you at the roadside? A transport has been waiting for you for over three hours!'

'It has? To where?'

'Never mind. Come on, it is taking up time and soldiers that cannot be spared. Get up and get your things together. Move!'

'We are with the Collarts,' said my Mother, 'we all go together.'

'I care nothing for these women and know nothing about them. You, however... we must move now. You are already late.'

'Late for what?'

'Just move. Into that car there. Get on with it.'

'But what about the Collarts?'

'Not my problem. Let's go.'

My Mother was pulled back from getting to the Collart women. Madame Collart lifted her head and stared into Mother's eyes. We could see her pleading, but no words came. Amelie just looked ahead rocking gently forwards and backwards, rubbing her stomach.

'Maman, we must help them. What can we do?'

'Nothing Odile, we are powerless here.'

We were taken by motor car through the unknown streets. The buildings were partly in ruins where bombs had fallen throughout this war. Wherever it was, it would never be the same again.

Finally, the car turned into a camp of wooden huts, tents and buildings among recent ruins. We were outside of the town, but bombs could still fall. It was not clear why we were so close to the war, when others had been sent to Switzerland. The driver moved into the camp and stopped just after we passed through the gates.

'This is the camp where you will live. On the left is an office. You must go and make sure you are on the list. Out!'

'Maman, we are *on* the list! What list this is we know not, but to be on a list means we *do* exist and might get food and clothing.'

'Odile, it means nothing. Surely you have learned by now. We are the Lefebvres from Bazentin-Le-Petit, they know whose wife and daughter we are. Your Father has surely condemned us.'

Of course I realised this, but we needed to cling to every chance of hope.

'Your Father may not even be alive.'

'Maman, do not speak like that. He is a valued engineer. Even the Germans would not be so foolish.'

'We are the foolish ones!'

We reached the administration building, surprisingly without any escort. Mother spoke to the officer on the desk, who was gruff, but not unkind.

His French was very good – perhaps he was French.

'Yes? What is your name?'

'Lefebvre. Marie-Louise and Odile Armandine.'

'Oh, yes, ah. Pierre Lefebvre. You know a Pierre Lefebvre?'

My Mother fell forwards, almost grabbing the man by his arms.

'Yes, yes. Pierre Lefebvre is my husband! Do you know where he is?'

'Yes, he is here. Here in this camp, number seven.'

Mother screamed out his name, almost at the top of her voice. The sound penetrated to my heart. The officer jumped to his feet to stop her rushing out.

'Pierre! Pierre! Where are you Pierre?'

Mother was out in the open, grabbing her skirts and rushing from wall to wall.

'Madame! He is here, but he is out working on our guns.'

My Mother turned back, regaining some composure.'

'You are sure it is him. Pierre Lefebvre, from Bazentin-Le-Petit?'

'Yes.'

'My God, Odile. God has delivered your Father back to us.'

'He is a bloody nuisance though, causing us trouble every day.'

Mother smiled. 'That is him, my beloved. Come Odile, let us see if we can eat and wash before we see your Father again.'

We waited until nearly nightfall, as close to the gate as possible, looking for any sign of Father. As it got dark, the lorry returned. A figure emerged, grumbling in French, walking slowly, head down, almost stooping.

'Papa! Papa!'

My Father looked up, his face a picture of puzzlement. My beloved Father. A Father I had not seen since I ran from the hut in tears.

'Oh Pierre, my love.'

We fell into his arms and he breathed us in deeply.

'My beautiful family, I thought you were gone forever.'

We stood in an embrace until the driver got out.

'Uh, Lefebvre, we had better go, come on.'

We linked arms and went into the camp.

'Leave them, Lefebvre, you have to come with me.'

'Pity me a moment, soldier. This is my family.'

'I don't give a fuck if you are the Kaiser himself, I'm not interested. This way, you French bastard.'

'Oh Papa, they are still bad to you, why do you torment them so?'

My Father stood still for a moment, looking at me. He stroked my face softly, over where his hand had left a red mark.

'You are alive and unharmed. Good. My beautiful miracle girl.'

CHAPTER FOURTEEN – FRANCE MAY FALL SEPTEMBER 1914

'Odile, we must take what we can and try to move south. The French want us to move back with them. The German enemy is coming quickly over the hills. Your Father may not want to come with us, but he must. You must help to make him understand. Will you try?'

'I will try Maman, but we should stay and fight. Papa and I can make a difference. We really can.'

'I know darling, but what are two unarmed people against an enemy charging across the country. There is really no hope.' I looked down.

'Of course, you are right. I will speak with Papa.'

The afternoon was bright. In the distance we could hear the movements of our soldiers and horses becoming ever more intense and purposeful, but always back from the fighting. Guns and ammunition passed by constantly, with waves of dirty and tired French horses and carts thundering by at full speed. Father was occupied in the camp repairing the flimsy French lorries that had been hit by shots from the German guns. Some even had bullet holes in them. That really meant the enemy was close. The officers tried again to convince Father to come south.

'Monsieur Lefebvre, we are to move south at first light. The German enemy moves quickly towards us and is within twenty miles. They could be here in a day. We must move back. Will you stay with us? You could be released to Albert, of course, on my word. What do you say?'

Father looked at me, thought hard, looked around at his beloved France, listened to the guns firing in the distance. He then turned back to the worried French officer.

'Of course, I have to help our army. Will you take care of my family?'

'With all our power Monsieur, such as it is.'

With that, the conversation was over. There was nothing I could say to Papa to change his mind. We were to stand and fight shoulder to shoulder and serve France. Mother would not like it.

The afternoon was spent preparing the lorries to move out. Soldiers were marching north, taking with them supplies and horses. Others, including us, were moving south to prepare defensive positions. Father would be with those lorries that moved tools and machinery to build defences, walls and barricades – anything to hold the enemy back long enough for the army to defend.

That afternoon I saw my first British soldiers, which made me think of William and what he was doing. Was he lost to me as well? What was he doing today? William, I would give anything to be held by you, my love.

'Oh hello young miss, what is your name?'

'I am sorry, my English is not so good. But I have learned some. My name is Odile. I live in a village called Bazentin-Le-Petit.'

'Well I haven't heard of it and I probably won't ever see it. I am Major Davies from the Rifle Brigade. We are here, helping your countrymen send Fritz back over the border. What is a young lady like you doing up here?'

'Fritz? Who is he? I am repairing the lorries with my Father.'

'Ha ha. Very amusing. Anyway, nice to meet you dear.'

The soldier moved off. The British were here. Perhaps now we had enough soldiers to defend our country.

In the evening, Father, Mother and I ate together. Father had insisted that we have one more meal together in a normal France.

'From now, it will be anything but normal. Tomorrow, we move south. The enemy is upon us and we will be overrun. Their guns are close, and men are dying in the hundreds. Shells are landing amongst them, blowing them into pieces.'

'Father, what is a shell?'

'It is the bomb fired from a long gun. Most are explosives, but some contain small pieces of metal that kill everyone over a wide area. These are the worst I think.'

'Pierre, will we be safe? I mean, when we move, will we be shot at?'

'Darling Marie-Louise, nowhere in France can be truly safe. We may be shot at from any place at any time. They are here amongst us now in our homes and on our farms. They are coming over in the thousands and we might be finished.'

'Oh Papa, what can we do?'

'It is simple Odile, we must fight the bastards.'

'Pierre, please! Not at the dinner table.'

'Dinner table? This is a war! I am sorry, both of you, forgive me. The world has lost its innocence and this is no place for politeness and normality.'

Before first light, we were on lorries moving back towards Albert. We stopped in a large field where several big guns were pointing to the east and to the north, from where the enemy was certainly now coming. For three days we stayed here, living in a temporary camp, with the French struggling to hold back the advancing enemy. This was clearly no place for civilians. Father reluctantly went to the officer to ask permission to be moved south, out of the war completely. It was too dangerous for all of us, his job was done.

'I have been with you for nearly three weeks. I have fixed lorries, carts and guns that were no better than scrap. I have worked hard. Will you now move me and my family south to safety – it is now too dangerous to stay. Will that be possible?'

'Monsieur, with great reluctance I must agree with you. With your permission, will you stay until the twenty-fifth? I can arrange a transport for you and the other families back to Albert. The army is quartered there and it will be quite safe. Can you give me until then? Will you help my men to cope with the repairs?'

'I will sir, and thank you. But the twenty fifth, do I have your word?'

The officer stood and put an arm on Father's shoulder. 'You are a brave man, Monsieur,' he nodded his head towards me, 'with a remarkable family. You should be proud. A true servant of France. You have my word.'

This seemed to satisfy my Father, and he tried to spend as much time as possible with us.

'In two days, we move to Albert, in the town where it will be safe. The other villagers may be there as well. No one will be left at home alone. The Germans could be here at any time.'

The night was warm for late September. The breeze was light and there was the promise of a little rain. The harvest was late, as the farmers had left the fields in the early alarm. Now, it was too late to harvest at all. The Germans were upon us. It was just a matter of where and when.

CHRIS CHERRY

CHAPTER FIFTEEN – SEPTEMBER 1914

I was woken before first light by the most incredible explosion. It shook the hut and a window fell inwards and smashed, quickly followed by two more windows. Immediately, I could hear soldiers shouting and yelling in French and in English. It was terrifying and shocking.

Two older administrative officers told us to be outside immediately.

'Drop everything, pick up nothing and come in what you are wearing now. Bring no belongings – nothing military must be in your possession.'

Outside, it felt cold. Men were running to and fro, seemingly without direction, just a disorderly stampede. Lorries were starting up and moving off with soldiers and equipment. They were not waiting for long and none were full.

In the distance, horses were bringing in guns from the north. Guns that had fired at the enemy for days, according to Father. They were dirty and many had scorch marks on them, or damage from the enemy firing back.

Then we saw the ghostly figures of the soldiers coming back. Unwashed, faces expressionless, going through the motions of the living. None spoke and none smiled as they passed. There was an army photographer nearby, taking pictures in the early light. As a soldier passed, he punched the photographer and smashed the camera.

'This is no place for a fucking photograph you fool. The Germans are on the hill. Get a gun if you want to be of any use, you dog.'

More and more French soldiers rushed through the roadways. The temporary rails that had been laid were useless for such rapid movement. Soldiers marched, ran and stumbled back, some looking for their comrades and the temporary quarters. I did not understand the army names, but I knew this was not an organised retreat. This was a rout, an end to the life we loved here on the hills.

More and more guns were rattling through the camp on their way south. Sometimes they stopped and fired over the hill towards an unseen enemy. The enemy were close, very close.

Father was trying desperately to get an army transport south. The cars were gone and the lorries would only take soldiers. Civilians were unimportant, even talented engineers. Father's officer was nowhere to be seen and we considered walking. But walking kept us in the open and vulnerable to enemy guns.

All day we were left alone. Father could do nothing to help as the lorries did not stop long enough for him to grease the wheels and beg passage.

'For goodness sake, let us ride with you to Albert – you have room enough for three!'

'What? This is an army transport. Go away. Why are you even here, you are a civilian?'

'One who has been working for the glory of France?'

'France? Have you seen what's coming?'

'Yes. Please transport us to Albert. We have been working for the army.'

'Then my friend, you are lucky to still be alive.'

Father was getting nowhere. Mother sat quietly most of the time, jumping when there was a loud noise, which was often now the enemy were shooting at us. We were not yet in range for all of their guns, but it was only a matter of time.

Father grew desperate. Abandoned by the army, his papers were worthless – as if made of smoke. Whenever he showed them to an officer, asking for help, he was met with the same refusal.

'I am sorry Monsieur, I have no authority to transport civilians.'

The evening drew in. The camp was full of French soldiers, riflemen and cavalry. Soldiers busied themselves cleaning rifles and gathering weapons. It was frightening. This was going to be dangerous and we were trapped in a valley in the hills. We could not escape south and of course we could not go north.

There was little food in the camp, but the army shared rations with us. The soldiers were all new and unfamiliar, none of them knew Father and his presence drew interest and suspicion. Father explained the situation, but all he received was bread and a shrug.

'Marie-Louise, we must set off for Albert, we will probably walk. The Belgians have walked here from their borders. I will try for a horse or cart. We cannot stay here. The Germans will be here in the morning – the guns are louder and nearer.'

'Oh, Pierre! What have we done? If we had stayed in our village, we could be in Paris by now. We are trapped and the enemy is here.'

Father said nothing. He drew the tent flap closed, to keep out the wind, although it would provide no safety when the enemy came. But the tent flaps were pulled open in the early hours. This time, a friendly voice called out for Father.

'Monsieur Lefebvre, are you in here? It is Louis. You must come now, I have transport.'

'Louis? I thought you were gone and had forgotten us?'

'Forgotten, no. It is chaotic. My whole unit is to move out and you are still part of it. I can get you to Bapaume, you might get a cart from there. We are moving now. Bring your family. Good morning Madame Lefebvre. Please, the time is now and we cannot wait.'

'Quick my loves, we must go now. It will be the last chance I think.'

'Yes Papa.'

I stepped out into the night. It was well before dawn. I saw flashes over the hill, but the sound was muffled. Perhaps we were driving them back after all. But when a flash lit the sky, it revealed a most terrible sight. There were many more soldiers than there had been in the evening and now many of them were bandaged or on stretchers, hurt and damaged.

The lorry was being pushed, as it would not start. Father thought it had run out of fuel, but I thought that something was wrong in the electrical wiring. We had no tools or time to look.

'Get in you two women. We will push until it can start.'

'I don't think that it will start this way.'

'What do you know, girl?'

'Actually—'

'Odile!' Father cut me off.

Mother stepped up into the back of the lorry. As soon as she sat down, she was thrown out and onto the road by a huge explosion. A shell had landed at the front of the lorry. The three soldiers at the front, including Louis, were now gone. They had simply disappeared. Mother landed on the grass. She had hurt her arm, but she had survived.

The soldiers ducked and took cover wherever they could. Another explosion landed nearby. The Germans had found the camp and set their guns upon us. The next shell landed amongst the wounded. The anguished cries were terrifying and chilling. In the dark, soldiers ran about in disarray. The officers could not get control of the soldiers, the soldiers could not get control of the horses. In the darkness, the shock and death cries were unnerving.

At first light, the flow of soldiers from the north became a torrent. Wounded, dirty, worn and tired faces came through in a faceless wave of humanity. It was possible to make out the rattle of machine guns in the distance. We were now on the front line and we had no escape.

With Louis gone, there was no transport. The officers who knew of our existence had all been together and killed at once. We had no more friends here. The army were occupied with the advancing enemy, not with useless civilians getting in their way.

The French soldiers were setting up temporary barricades at the gates of the camp. The hill was little more than a rise, but we could remain unseen until the enemy were upon us. The army were setting up a surprise attack, to try and halt the advance.

With no other option, we began the walk to Bapaume. There was nothing else to be done – to stay would certainly mean death. We set out on the road in the half-dark. Shells fell regularly, not quite reaching the road. The battle was close and I could hear individual rifles shooting. It would not be long before the enemy appeared. We hurried on, Father leading the way, Mother holding her arm to her chest and limping.

'Mother, what of the Collarts and the Delaitres?'

'We cannot worry for them now. God protect them. Amelie was so pale and frail, as if the wind would blow her over. I cannot imagine that little one coping with adversity. Her Mother—'

'Maman, please!'

'Sorry. The Delaitre girls are strong and will fight, most likely with each other. I hope that does not get them killed.'

'Please be quiet, my loves. I want to listen for the guns to tell if a bomb is coming.'

We moved on. Our movements were slow and hampered by the need to stay out of sight. The sky in the distance grew paler and brighter as the day dawned. We had made some progress towards Bapaume, but were now being passed by line after line of horses, guns and men. Some threw us bread and water, which was welcome. Most who passed gave us a cheery wave, to keep up our spirits. But none stopped, not even for a moment, no doubt it was now army first, civilians last.

As the light came, so did the rising noise of guns and the new war. We stopped to eat bread and to rest. We had not properly slept and Mother was unable to walk normally. Father urged us into a ditch at the side of the road. Damp, with long grass, it seemed the safest thing to do.

From the far horizon, black shapes came over the hill, like ants coming from a nest. Father dropped the bread and fell to his knees.

'Oh dear God. No! It is finished for us. Finished.'

'Father, it is the enemy on horses isn't it?'

'Yes Odile, and there are no French soldiers there to stop them.'

The columns of soldiers passing us quickly formed a line, sheltering in the same ditch at the side of the road. Father asked for a gun, but he was refused. He asked for a rock to throw at them. The soldier pushed him into the ditch.

The German cavalry moved quickly over the hill, behind them came their horses carrying guns, like the ones we had been using. The French guns were now landing shots among the enemy, but did not hit their swiftly moving cavalry. The men in our ditch now started firing. The noise was terrifying and deafening, and we huddled down with Father covering us, telling us to lie still. Two French soldiers moved next to us to protect us, covering us with their large coats. But Father took them off.

'The enemy might think you are a soldier and shoot at the uniform.'

Mother dug herself into the ditch with her fingers, sobbing to herself.

'God please take us or protect us. Do not leave us at their mercy like this!'

'Marie-Louise, please. It does not help us. Stay calm and lie there, you are safe.'

'Safe? We are to be killed, I am sure.'

The enemy horses were coming closer. Over the hill came the walking soldiers. These men carried their rifles high and the ones at the front were firing towards us. They were too far away to get close, but also too far away for our soldiers to get them. It was almost in slow motion that the French began to move forwards, with a metallic clatter.

'Good luck, my brothers.' Father watched them move off.

As soon as they began to move, the explosions began amongst us. One after another, right near the ditch. The soldiers were forced back and they moved along the road. One was hit but he continued to run as blood began to stain his coat. He stumbled and fell, never to rise again. I could tell that Father wanted to go to him, but he was still shielding Mother and me, and he stayed with his family, with the living.

Soldiers from our little camp moved away to our right, further away from us. The horses that they were moving broke free and tumbled over us. I knew that they would not trample us if they saw us in time but I was afraid that one might be hit and fall on us. The horses were also frightened, running around leaderless and blinded. Anything could happen. The figures over the hill grew larger and more numerous. Our army were now well behind us.

'My darlings, we cannot stay. We will be overrun by the enemy. We must go back. I cannot stop a horse, they are too frightened. Come, let us move back. We have to take our chances.'

'Pierre, I cannot move. My legs are frozen, my arm numbed. You go and take our daughter back, go the two of you, now!'

'I will not leave without you. We stay or we go, but we do it together.'

Father stood up to take a look, ready to move away. His face went ashen and he raised his hands into the air and fell back into the ditch. Over the rim came the barrel of a rifle.

CHRIS CHERRY

CHAPTER SIXTEEN
CAMP NUMBER SEVEN, 1915

Father disappeared into a small hut. Outside, were lorry parts – bearings, bolts and pieces of gearbox, all clean and repaired. This was my Father's work and he was very good at it. This talent had got him into trouble, but it had also kept us alive.

When Mother and I were shown into our hut, we could see that we were the only occupants, not crammed in with other French prisoners fighting for every crumb of survival. It was uncertain whether this was a good thing or not. Mother and I sat together, whispering.

'Maman, why are we alone here? Where are the others? What happened to Amelie and her Mother?'

'There is no way to know, Odile. We have Father and we are together. That cannot be just chance. It is strange. So much to suffer and now we do not suffer. I do not understand.'

'Neither do I, Maman. The Germans have not been kind to us. Why would they start now?'

The waiting and worrying were almost unbearable. It was almost worse than the daily ritual for food and the awful Thomas. This felt like a torture and we did not understand why.

We saw Father from our hut, but we were too afraid to go outside. No one came to us. No food or water was offered. Perhaps we were to suffer a slow death of starvation to punish my Father for his disobedience, with Father helpless to prevent it.

The second night was worse. We were cold and hungry, and thirst had almost overtaken us. I remember the dizziness taking away my ability to think at all. Mother was already ill. There was nothing for it – I would have to escape and steal food from the Germans. Perhaps these soldiers were not like our former guards, enjoying sport against weak and defenceless French women. Perhaps these would be gentlemen, able to show kindness without wanting flesh in return.

Once it was dark I opened the door to our hut. It was not locked and there were no guards, everywhere looked deserted. The light in Father's hut was off and I did not know if he was there or not but I dared not risk looking inside for fear of punishment.

My chest heaved with terror and I feared that my every breath would give me away. I did not know my way around, and would have to chance a look into every window in my hunt for food. The doorways were all lit making it impossible to cross them unseen. To try would probably mean a beating, or worse.

The first window showed an empty room, probably an administrative office. On the table was a neat pile of brown papers and a pen. To one side was a bottle and two glasses. They were empty. This room had two people in it then, most likely. Two brutes that I would not be able to prevent taking me.

I crept around the back and saw a soldier in the light ahead. He was smoking a cigarette and gently humming. He did not appear to be guarding anything, but rather resting. Taking a break from guarding defenceless French citizens – I wanted to poke his eye with his cigarette. I had to pass by him, but had to wait until he finished smoking. As he went to turn, I froze, certain he could see me. He looked in my direction, standing very still for a moment. His head tilted towards me – had I been seen? No! He stamped out his cigarette, coughed and turned away. I took a step forward. At that moment a large hand landed on my shoulder, spinning me around.

'French? You is the Lefebvre girl?' Spoken in French, not German. The soldier knew me, which terrified me and made me tremble.

'Y… yes. Sorry, I was just looking for water and food.'

'You is speak too fast. For why are you here at night?'

'I am thirsty and hungry.'

'You are cold?'

'Yes, but thirsty and hungry.' I mimed drinking.

'Yes, yes. Already!'

'Already?'

'Yes, food ration was two hours before.'

'What ration?'

'Food given to civilians before two hours.'

'We had none.'

The soldier laughed. This was torture after all.

'Did you not know how to get food? You get food after the soldiers every day.'

'May I go?'

'Yes, you are not prisoners ha ha.'

I rushed back to Mother, not bothering to hide out of the light. Mother saw me and cried out.

'You will be seen, oh my darling hide from the light.'

'Maman, we are not being tortured, we were forgotten, that is all.'

'What do you mean?'

'The soldiers did not tell us how to get food, that was all. We go to eat after the soldiers.'

'We do? Well, we will see.'

I heard footsteps outside and froze in terror. Mother pushed me behind her. Although she was shivering, she took a deep breath and waited for the door to be smashed open.

Nothing happened, apart from a cough followed by a gentle tap on the door.

'Excusing me, I have things for you.'

'Maman, it is safe to open the door. I know this voice.'

Mother opened the door slowly, still holding me behind her. Suspicion learned from months in German hands was hard to let go. Clearly, she had no intention of trusting the voice, sincere though it seemed to be.

'Ah goods evening, Madame. I know you did not have eat today. I am sorry, the soldier is new and bad. Here, this are your ration for today. Thank you. Please takes them.'

Mother snatched the parcels and slammed the door shut. Clearly, she was caught off guard by simple kindness that in any other place would have been met with hospitality. The clank of a bottle or pail was heard outside, but no other sound was made. Mother waited for a minute and then opened the door again. No one was on the other side, but in front of the door was clean water, sparkling in the moonlight. We drank straight from the pail and saved some to wash our bodies. It was glorious nectar. I did not know if we would ever see water again. I thought about visiting Father, but decided that would be too big a risk.

The parcels were small but heavy. Inside was fresh-cooked pork, not the poor greasy meat we scavenged at the last camp. And there was a piece of cheese. It was dry on the outside as it must have had been left out unwrapped, but it was good. I could not believe our luck. Little things that kept us alive.

'Odile, we starve, we are beaten, moved, starved again and now we are fed. I do not know what is happening. Why this treatment now and not before? We are with your Father, but not with him at the same time. It is worrying – worrying and confusing – not knowing what is happening to us. The unexpected kindness of the enemy is as worrying as the beatings.'

'Mother, we must just live each day as it happens.'

We stared at the food.

'Odile, we shall keep some for your Father and try to get it to him.

'Of course, Maman. We will find a way.'

In the morning, the sun shone brightly making it possible to see a little of our surroundings. If Father was repairing battle-damaged equipment, we were probably near the battles, the war was still in France then. We had driven south and east for the last part of our journey. There were no hills or mountains and the ground was quite flat. Yes, we were really in the north of France, perhaps not so very far from home.

Mother and I emerged from our hut a little after daybreak. We must have looked odd, crouched down, eyes everywhere like little frightened animals. Our clothes were rotting on our bodies, and I did not feel that our fortunes were much improved, even with a meal inside us.

I was still expecting the usual daily struggle to eat and survive, with the hope that Father could survive his ordeals at the hands of his captors, for he was certainly a captive. His talents saved the lives of his enemy, whilst taking those of his countrymen, and this must be a heavy burden for one man to bear.

Mother spotted the hut where food was being given to the soldiers. I almost dared not approach for fear of a beating, or watching them eat whilst we were still hungry. To my amazement, when we came near, still hunched like scavenging rodents, a cook called us over. He spoke German but it sounded welcoming.

He gestured to some tin bowls. We each took one and he ladled stew into them. I could smell meat, onions and other vegetables. It was the same as the soldiers were eating, so it wasn't mouldy and rotten. Next to the pot were portions of heavy bread. We took the hot bowls and made to run to our hut, before the food was taken away from us. The soldiers watched us with amazed faces as we ran, a woman and her girl grabbing food and running away like damp rats, or thieves in the night.

The bowl was very hot and burned my fingers but I would not drop it, its contents were too precious. Back in the hut, we ate quickly, and the broth was good. I felt full for the first time in months and felt guilty for eating when Father was probably still starving. I knew this would end soon, it had to, but while it lasted I would enjoy the nourishment for body and soul.

Father came back to the camp late in the evening. He was guarded as always, but tonight seemed calmer. He was still stooped over, tired and drawn, looking thinner and his face was marked with red lines and black bruises. Tonight, he walked past his hut towards us. Father would be in trouble for this, I was sure.

'Marie-Louise, are you there?'

'Oh, I am here Pierre. Watching your every move, darling husband.'

'I have one hour. I am allowed to see you for one hour.'

Father came into our hut. He was hungry and thirsty, so we gave him the meat we had saved and the bread with some cheese. He was astonished at what we had gathered, especially when he saw the little covered pail of water, still clean and fit to drink.

'I will not ask what suffering you had to endure to get this. Just know that I am grateful for the love of my beautiful family.'

'Oh Papa, we love you always. You are most treasured.'

'Ah Odile. I must explain to you why—'

'No Papa, you do not. It is forgotten. You are here alive and we will make you well and strong.'

'Strong enough to fight these pigs. They beat me every day, Marie-

Louise. Every day they take more of me until the jar is empty. I work on their guns, cars and lorries. Just so they can shoot our soldiers.'

'Do you know where we are Papa?'

'We are perhaps near to Bapaume, on the road to Cambrai. The enemy are making me work on railway engines. The trains come in from Dusseldorf and bring more of the bastards every day.'

'Oh, Pierre, what is happening?'

'I think there is a battle here, but we are still some miles from the Front. There are not many civilians, but there are enough to get some information. The Germans have attacked in Belgium and here, perhaps Artois. I do not know. They seem jubilant and in a good mood, so things must be going badly for us. I have seen some prisoners as well. English and some even from India.'

'Papa, why are there prisoners from India?'

He shrugged. 'They are fighting alongside the British, it seems. They were quite badly off, so the battles must be hard.'

'And how are you Pierre? How are you in this?'

'My love, I cannot submit to them whilst they are on our soil, killing our sons and brothers. But I cannot see you suffer either. It is fortunate that you are here with me. The other men do not have their families.'

'Papa, we are blessed to be near each other.'

Father leaned back, raising his hands.

'You are right, my daughter. We have each other still. Come and embrace your poor Father.'

We held each other in silence for a time. Then Mother washed Father's face a little, just enough to see his pale skin.

'Lefebvre come out now. Enough. You did well today. If you do well tomorrow, we shall see, eh?'

Father stood up slowly, aches and pains visible on his face, his injured body stiffening in the cool evening. I worried for his survival.

These Germans seemed friendly. But it was surely only a matter of time before they were changed to the normal brutes we had to endure. For five more days, we saw a little of Father each evening, as he had suppressed his anger in exchange for a visit. For two evenings I walked around the camp whilst Mother bathed Father properly, tending his bruises. His clothes were often stuck to his skin and were now far too big for him, his body disappearing from underneath. Often as not, Mother would be weeping when I returned.

'I fear your Father is weakening from his treatment. I am ill most days, but can carry on. Your Father is ill and having to work like a dog for these men. Darling Odile, we must do anything and everything to protect your Father. It might not be possible, but we must not give up. He gets a portion of food each day. This is good, if not enough. We must still get anything we can to help build his strength. He is your Father. Will you help?'

'Of course, Maman. You do not need to ask.'

The soldiers were changed every few days, but they remained friendly. We were given food and water and occasionally hot water to wash our rotten clothes. Father went each morning to the railways and the lorries and came back each evening, tired and worn. He had fewer bruises, so perhaps he had reconciled his hatred and decided that his family would be spared if he worked hard, even on machines that could kill his brothers.

CHAPTER SEVENTEEN – SEPTEMBER 1914

A second and a third barrel appeared. There were shouts in German and a young soldier, who did not have a gun, put his head into the ditch. He looked down at us and spoke in French – a French from the borderlands.

'You are quite safe. No one will shoot a civilian in this regiment. Come quickly now, it is not good for you to stay, the war is here. You could be killed. Quickly, let us go to the rear.'

He beckoned Father up. It was clear there was no choice. Father clambered up and pulled me after him. We watched the French disappearing over the field, perhaps to fight another day.

'Good luck my friends. May God deliver you.'

'Help me up, Pierre. Perhaps this is not so bad?'

'I am sorry I have brought us to this. Into the very arms of the enemy I tried to resist. Forgive me Marie-Louise, for failing you. Odile, my love, forgive your Papa.'

'Pierre, don't. This war would take us anyway. We are alive at least. Let us hope our captors are kind to us poor French.'

'Poor? Hmm. You, soldier. Leave my wife alone. I will help her up.'

'If you say so, sir.'

'I do and you have no business looking at my daughter. She is barely sixteen.'

'Monsieur, please, I said, no harm will come to you. Come now, I must insist.'

We were guided quickly, but not unkindly, to a waiting lorry. Father refused to get in, telling us that the French would be shooting at the lorries. It would be safer to walk. Father shouted at them in French. But either the Germans did not understand or did not care, and simply pushed him away and pushed us after him. Clearly, they wanted nothing to do with stupid civilians who would not do as they were told.

As we began to walk back to our now captive camp, the ground erupted in bursts of gunfire. This time it was the French shooting at the Germans. Behind us was a terrible explosion. A shell had hit the lorry we were to be on. I stopped for a second to look. Father pulled my arm, and it hurt when he pulled me.

'But Papa, there were French people inside and they might need our help.'

'No Odile, they will be dead, we can do no more for those families.'

'But Papa, I see arms moving, look there!'

An arm pulled back the scorched canvas and a head appeared. It was a young girl.

'Please, please, help me. My leg is stuck. Help! Please!'

Father hesitated, turned and let go of my arm. Freed, I ran towards the lorry. Before I got there, second, third and fourth explosions quietened the sounds from within. They were all dead now. The burning hulk of the lorry was all that remained. I fell to the floor, covered in soot. My arm was cut a little, but I was alive.

A hand grabbed my shoulder, pulling me over. It was a German. I gasped, panicking. He looked over my body, I was terrified. My dress was torn and my uncovered legs were visible. I thought I was going to die.

'Girl. Injury?'

'No monsieur.'

'That is good.'

He pulled me up in one movement and pushed me towards my Father. He spoke in German and none of us understood. Then he pointed to another soldier who was waving. The young soldier had come back for us.

'Quickly, come this way, I said it was not good to stay. You were lucky, I think. That might have been you. This regiment means no harm to French civilians. We must go this way, now. You must go along this path. I must go and find more of you French hiding in the fields. Good luck to you now that the war is nearly over.'

Father moved towards him, looking as though he might hit him in the face with his fist. Father was much bigger than the young soldier. My Mother's calm hand on his shoulder held him back.

'Pigs of Germans. How dare they say such things? France will win and take back our land from these sons of devils.'

'Pierre, they are sons of Mothers, like the French. Are you saying that we are so different?'

Father said nothing, just scooped up the torn skirt of my dress and we moved away to where there were more waiting soldiers.

We were made to walk for the rest of the day. My feet hurt and I was hot and thirsty. We were moved into a camp of tents and wooden fences that had been hastily built. Inside, there were wounded Germans with beds being built to accommodate them.

Father looked at the wounded and said quietly.

'Serve you bastards right. Curse you all to Hell.'

'Pierre, please. You will get us all killed if they hear you.'

Father looked away.

'I wonder what the Bouchards are doing now, eh?'

'Yes I wonder. Perhaps they are in Albert? South? Not here, that is for sure.'

But we were not going to stay here. The soldiers quickly put us into a lorry, and this time there was no choice. We drove north, away from the battlefield. It was north because the soldier guarding us showed me with a compass. He spoke no French and smiled his gestures at us. He seemed kind and gave us water and a little bread. But we were not really hungry. We ate because there was nothing else we could do and none of us knew if more food would be given to us.

The lorry stopped after what seemed like all night. It was dark and I felt confused by what had happened. I could never have imagined in our village, with the sun shining and engine parts all over the floor, that life could ever become like this. But here we were. Unloved, unwanted and uncared for. We only had one another for company.

The canvas was pulled back and we were moved apart from each other. Father was put onto another lorry, without being able to turn towards us. He was pushed and poked with a rifle until he stepped onto the plate at the back, he tried to look for us, but his eyes never found us. We were amongst others like us but we did not know any of them. They were all terrified, separated from home and from safety. Here there was no safety, only fear. Perhaps France would be defeated and this would be our new life. From the lorry, the voices of Fathers and brothers shouted loudly, 'Vive La France' and some tried to whistle our anthem, but rough German voices shut their defiant voices. I am sure my Father was amongst them.

We were kept in tents for three days, given regular meals and water and we were able to mend our clothes. My dress was torn from the explosion on the lorry, but I was able to repair it with threads from the other women. Some of these kind women had managed to bring extra clothes and medicines. At this time we were all happy to share. The mood was softening. The enemy were perhaps not so bad.

Each day we were expected to clean the tents and we were put to work mending uniforms. It was boring and menial but if we did as we were told we were treated well. None of us knew where we were, perhaps Lille, or further east? Certainly it was France, as there were some signs, but for which villages I did not know. Some had already been changed into German names, which was deeply upsetting.

Sometimes, new families were brought in, terrified, just as we were. We tried to help them settle, sharing our food and clothing. Some had barely anything with them, caught in the fast-moving battle. Families were sometimes moved away to other places, which was terrifying. Why them? What had they done and where were they going? I worried that something terrible had happened to them. Our world was fear and confusion.

For almost three weeks, as the weather turned colder, we were kept in this camp. Every day we were given food, which was usually fresh and sometimes hot, which kept everyone calm. The enemy, if that is what they were, treated us well. If no one was going to rescue us, then at least life was bearable. But we did not know how long this would last. And we had too few clothes to survive a winter in tents. Bathing and cleaning were difficult.

We were not used to living outside for so long and soon changed our habits to cope. Dirty bodies and dirty clothes became a normal way of life and we just got on with it.

One morning, our routine was interrupted by new lorries arriving and we soon learned that we were to be moved. These new drivers and soldiers were older and fatter and they seemed disinterested in us as humans. We were just a job to them and they never spoke directly to any of us, only shouting in German, just above our heads.

Mother appeared very upset by the idea of moving, but it didn't stop her from using her wits.

'Odile, quick my love, get our shawls and the apron that I was given. We will need every bit of warmth we can get. I will get us a seat at the front of the lorry. Quick little one.'

'Yes Maman. Go now, they are already getting on the lorry.'

We had to become experts in pushing and shoving without causing offence. Getting what we needed, without causing another to suffer. Mother stepped up onto the plate at the back of the lorry. At that moment, one of the other women pulled her skirt, causing her to fall backwards from the lorry into a heap on the floor.

'Maman!' Foolishly, I dropped our shawls, and ran to Mother. Her knee was cut open.

'Stop you pushing in again eh? Stupid cow.'

'Don't you call my maman a cow!'

'Who do you think you are, eh? Miss high and mighty as well?'

I did not know what to say or do next. I had never seen anyone speak to me or Mother like that before. I was also now very upset.

'Odile, it is nothing. Come on, we had better get in.'

By the time we managed to get in, only the terrible seats over the wheels were left, where every bump in the road threw you off, often almost to standing again. There were many bumps in the road and the journey was miserable.

'Maman, why was that woman so mean and nasty?'

'I suppose fear makes you react angrily. Everyone here is afraid. Terrified that everything may be taken from them. We are powerless women at the mercy of the Germans. Without our wits, we will suffer.'

'Oh Maman. Will it always be like this?'

'I am sure it won't. It might just be one awful woman.'

'How is your knee?'

'It will be well, my darling. Thank you. Here, have some water.'

The journey was shorter than before and we found ourselves in a much better camp with small huts instead of tents. There was room for six of us in each one, but the Germans put ten of us in each little building. We were given a sheet of paper each, to write down our names, where we had lived and the names of any family not with us. There was also a space to write the names of any family in the army. We all left this blank.

There was some chatter that we were to be moved again, into Germany as slaves or housemaids. I was already certain that Father was not following behind us and that his journey had taken a different path. He might be dead, or he might be in a camp for men. More likely, he was being made to work for the enemy. If he ever got his hands on a lorry, they would soon know how good he was. They would look after him then, most certainly.

It was always cold now as 1914 turned to autumn. A lot of rain fell on our huts, which made an awful noise. There was some wood to make fires but we only used it for cooking. Water was used to drink and to wash sparingly. The little water we used to wash was then kept to clean our clothes, boiling it again and again. It became precious, as less and less fresh water reached us.

In November, we were given some clothes. Nothing fitted properly and it looked like they had been looted from dolls. But necessity meant we had to make them fit properly. I managed to get a nice blouse. It would keep me warm and make me feel like a young woman and not a little girl. I needed to feel more normal and not like a farmyard animal.

But little by little the food rations disappeared. Each day the lorry would bring less fresh food and more leftovers or mouldy vegetables. One of the Germans spoke some French and apologised for the rations.

'More of us in France, eh? Winning this wartime, I think. Need the food from your harvest for eating, this big army! Ha. I am sorry for this, but we must give eats to the soldier first. Sorry, I am sorry, true.'

So, we were no more than cattle after all. I noticed some of the women trying to be nice to the soldiers, perhaps to get first pick of the food. I could not blame them. Sometimes, Mother would also go and speak with them. Once, she came back with a jar of jam. Another time, she came back with a cut lip.

'It is no good, Odile. Asking isn't enough. They want something in return, I fear.'

'Maman, should I go and ask?'

'NO! It is for me to ask. For me to find enough to eat.'

November turned into December. Some of the women had been moved away. Their family forms had been read and lorries were brought for them. We did not know where they were going, but the soldiers seemed kind. Perhaps they were going to their families? I hoped for that to be true.

One morning, a lorry came for us. Six of us were called and we had to leave immediately. Quickly, Mother gathered up the jam, bread, cheese and drinking water she had saved.

'Quickly please. Fast into the engine. We must to go out.'

'Thank you, soldier.' Mother was trying to ensure we were treated well. The soldier smiled and offered his arm to me to get up. I felt less anxious, and Mother's face eased a little. The other four were older women, perhaps in their fifties. They looked afraid.

We were going south. The sun was at the front of the lorry, low on the horizon. After an hour, we stopped. The other four women were taken off and left at the side of the road with a soldier. We drove off and terror once again took over my thoughts. Why were they taken off and left at the side of the road? Mother must have been thinking the same thing.

'Soldier, why were the women taken off?'

'Ah, ha ha. Another camp for them. Not for you, no, not for you.'

'What do you mean?'

'You are going to Cambrai.'

'But we have come all this way from there. Why are you taking us back?'

The soldier said nothing. He just tapped his nose and sat back.

'Odile, this may be bad for us. Please let me speak with them, not you. Do not draw any attention to yourself. Keep quiet and do not look any of them in the eye. Will you promise me?'

'Yes, Maman, of course.'

Mother pulled me closer to her and kissed my head.

'Oh my darling. We do smell so terribly.'

The lorry stopped again. It was dark and I could hear a distant rolling and grumbling noise, like a line of lorries moving in the distance. There were flashes of orange and red, with silver and gold lights. This was the Front. Why had we been brought back?

'Lefebvre? Are you the Lefebvre women, eh?'

'Yes, sir. We are the Lefebvres. Marie-Louise and my daughter.'

'Odile, sixteen? Very pretty girl.'

Mother stiffened, pushed me behind her and squeezed my hand until it hurt.

'Why do you ask?'

'I have a daughter, same age, Madame. Looks like her a little, as well.'

Mother relaxed her grip slightly, but still kept me behind her.

'When was the last time you saw her soldier? When did you last see your family?'

He looked away for a second, in thought. 'What? Hmm. Go over there, go on, quickly.'

How raw a nerve can be in this war, for all sides, and how easily Maman was able to hit them.

As we went into the camp, a figure near the motors stopped, turned and stared at us. He waved and moved towards us, the figure looking familiar.

'Odile, let me speak. Keep quiet and stay behind me. Do not speak, even if he speaks to you.'

Mother gripped my arm and her fingers dug into it with fingers thinner than I remembered.

The figure broke into a stumbling run. I thought we were in trouble. But the figure outstretched his arms and the voice was unmistakable.

'My darlings, my beautiful family!'

'Papa? PAPA! It is you!'

'Yes, my love. They brought you to me!'

'Pierre! But how? Men are separated. All the other families—'

'Don't have me as their Papa, eh? Ha. Come, let me show you.'

Father held my hand. He was warm and smelled of oil and I felt like a little girl being taken for a walk. Papa took us to the lorries where there were three French men and four German soldiers together. Tools and parts for the lorries were everywhere.

'I have been made to fix lorries that have been hit by bombs and guns. I don't like it, but I can do it. They see how quickly I can fix them all. So I said I could fix them quicker with my family here. They refused, I stopped working and now you are here, ha! That will show these pigs.'

'Pierre! You must not. They will beat us all for sure.'

'No they will not. I can fix anything here. They need me. Now who is powerful, eh?'

We moved to our new room. The hut was simple with a small stove in the centre that seemed to be only for heating the room. There were some clothes in the corner, shawls and shoes.

'For you. I asked for these as well.'

'Oh Pierre. You are a good man. A survivor.'

'We must all be that.'

'Have you had any word of the war?'

'The Germans have passed through to Albert. I think the French have stopped them there. I am not sure. My darlings, our village has fallen to the enemy. Longueval, Bazentin, Pozieres, Martinpuich. All for the Germans. I do not know who survived from the village. Perhaps they had more time than us and went south? I hope so. None of them are here anyway.'

'Our home, Pierre. What of it?'

'I fear it lost. I fear all of our lives are lost, my love. All because of these awful pigs. I defy them.'

'Be careful Pierre. You have us to care for now. You have brought us here. Do not have us harmed for the sake of your pride.'

'Marie-Louise, I do what I must. Fixing lorries will not lose France the war. Perhaps I can make them break in such a way I cannot be blamed.'

There were only a few civilians in the camp with us. Most were engineers with specialist skills. Their families were also allowed to stay with them. It was a settled routine and if food was scarce, it was also scarce for the soldiers. Father was given a ration of bread each day, sometimes nice and fresh and sometimes hard and mouldy, fit only to soak in broth.

Soon the year turned to Christmas. Christmas in 1914 would be quite different to the nights in the village, when the families in the village gathered all together. The German soldiers made the best of it, singing and playing musical instruments. We were not allowed to be with them and were not invited to their feast of meat and vegetables. But we were given broth and bread with a little cheese, which had been discarded as hard and inedible. We ate it hungrily all the same.

Christmas Eve was a time for us to reflect on where we were. We had been in the hands of the Germans for three months and in that time we had moved camps many times. Although we had been given food and shelter, there was little else. Our clothing was in poor condition and our bodies were going the same way. Mother and I made the best of it for Father since he had clearly hoped that bringing us here would help us.

I sat on my tiny sloping bed, which was almost impossible to sleep in. It was hard, and the straw mattress was already jumping with lice and fleas. My last blouse was now grey, streaked with dirt that would never wash out. It was now so thin, it was almost see through. One careless wash and it would fall to pieces.

I looked at myself. Sixteen and in a place of hunger and misery. Not the beautiful village of Bazentin, but the holding camp of an invading army, with no prospect of rescue. My darling William, I could not often even spare you a thought. Perhaps you were in the army now you were old enough to join the British. If you were in the army, or perhaps even on the sea, I hoped you would be warm and safe, that you would not be hungry, alone or in pain. I wanted you here, to rescue us from this suffering, which was only going to get worse.

Over time, there would be less and less food. The Germans would care for us less and less. Already, they grew more and more irritated by us women, we were just some distracting task to endure. Mother still tried to find their weakness, to play on their minds. How were their Mothers? Had they written home? Were they happy to be minding little women, instead of a manly job, like invading France? Sometimes, it almost made me smile, but I worried constantly that they would react with violence.

Father, darling Papa. So angry with the enemy, but resigned to his fate fixing machines. It meant we would eat and we were safe. But it preyed on him that he had taken us closer to the guns and the war. His optimism of victory for France had collapsed into deep fear that France would never be the same again.

'Marie-Louise, Odile! A very happy Christmas to you. We are at least all together. We have survived these three months in the war. My hope is that we survive until the final victory for France and her friends over the sea. I am too old to fight, now little more than a captive. I wish this war over and a return to home, if there is anything left.'

Mother and I could barely feel happy for Christmas. This year, well it could come and go uncelebrated. But I was able to ask Father for a pen. I wanted to write to William. A letter he would never receive, but it made me feel better to write it.

France had been invaded, our little villages overrun by the enemy. In the south, where the Germans had not been, perhaps it was not so bad. I wondered if William thought me safe, perhaps able to have escaped. I did not want to think him in danger and I expected he thought the same for me. What a situation we have found ourselves in. Be strong and it may all soon be over.

Darling William

You will never read this, as I will burn it after I have written it. I ache for you, my love. It hurts in my stomach and I want only to be held by you, safe from this awful war that has come and consumed us. From nowhere the enemy came, over the hill to trap us like little animals hunted for sport. It hurts to think you might be facing them when they are angry, with guns and bullets. I miss our walks in the country of Picardie. I miss the motor bicycle, the awful petrol smell in my nose, ha! I miss pulling it to pieces and then building it again. I miss the smell in the Bois de Forcaux and in the Bois de Delville. So peaceful, I can imagine no more perfect place than in the wood, surrounded by the birds singing in spring. I want to be there with you on the road to Longueval, on our bicycles or on the motor bicycle, falling off into the ditch.

Darling, anything but this dreadful place. Full of dirt and hate. Come and rescue us, for Father and Mother look so pale and worried. The Germans are not unkind, but it is all difficult now. They have no food, no desire for us and I feel we may soon be unwelcome. Darling, just think of me as I think of you. I do hope that you feel for me as I feel for you. My missing you is real, it hurts and my body sparks at every thought of you.

Today is Christmas. A day of joy and peace. It is not to be so for us, or perhaps for you. Darling William, adieu.

Odile, your little flower.

CHRIS CHERRY

CHAPTER EIGHTEEN – CAMP SEVEN, 1915

It was on the tenth day of Father's railway routine that our world was once again turned upside down. Father was taken out early in a hurry. The Germans were all over the camp, cars coming and going more frequently than usual. When the wind blew towards us we could hear distant guns, just like the ones that we heard when we were taken by the enemy. The war was still very much in the balance. We had not moved, the camp was not moving, and the French had not reached us. But today felt different, and anxiety seemed to have fallen over the soldiers around us. Inside, I was happy that the enemy might be forced to leave France, but outside I was sad that it was costing the lives of French and the Allies to do it. It might even have taken my dear William. I tried to find strength to remember his face, my beautiful English boy. His memory was locked in my heart, but his face was hard to see through the pain of this war. The war that had taken hope and cast it to the four winds.

The car taking Father rushed through the camp gates, and turned in the opposite direction to the usual route. Away he went, his head down, with his little tool bag, and two soldiers accompanying him.

During the day we were unable to spend our time in the usual occupations of cleaning, mending or cooking. The Germans seemed not to notice us or care about the tasks we normally performed for extra food or water – sewing uniforms, cleaning dirty equipment and folding linen. Today was definitely different.

Three lorries arrived in the middle of the day, laden with wounded from the Front. As the canvas was pulled back, I saw the most awful spectacle. Each lorry contained rows of stretchers, perhaps fifteen poor wounded boys in each. Bandages soaked in black blood coated them completely, softening their outlines.

'They may be our enemy Odile, but no one could wish such suffering on another human.'

'But these soldiers may be fighting the boys from our village, or perhaps William...' My voice trailed off and I knew a tear was coming. These men pointed guns at our families and fired. We were torn between pity and relief. Of course, it was pity that triumphed.

'That is as may be, but they are some poor innocent woman's son or husband. They are no more to blame than we are.'

'One of those women is the Mother of the pig that beat Father.'

Mother waved her hand, dismissing the scene.

'Yes, you are right. But God bless them, bring them no more suffering. Let it be an end to their war and be done with it.' She went into the hut and shut the door.

I watched the scene unfold before my eyes. Stretcher after stretcher brought out. There were no hospital spaces here, as it was a camp for lorries and cars. The men were simply laid on the floor, the dust from the lorries' movements settling on their dirty bandages. The cries were piercing and painful, the orderlies no more able to help than I was.

'You, French girl. Come here and sit down.'

I looked up.

'You, come here now!'

I ran across, unsure what to do. I was told to sit with the soldiers and speak to them. It did not matter that it was French to their German ears, I was just a comforting face and a voice. I wanted to taunt them in French. Ask them if they had killed my friends or my wonderful William. Had they seen him? Did he join the army? But I could not bring myself to say these things. What could I say, a girl of nearly seventeen, to these men?

'I am sorry, I will sit with you until you are taken away. Is there anything I can do for you?'

'French girl? Nothing. No more help.'

'Hello, you are like my daughter in Heidelberg.'

'Is your Father in the war?'

'Is your Mother with you, ha ha?'

'Hello French girl. I too, am sorry.'

I offered them water, but could do little else. Some were silent. Their wounds were very bad. They needed hospitals and there were none.

The sounds of more lorries coming around the corner grew louder and soon five more were here. These contained men that could stand at least. Those who still had both of their legs.

Before long, there must have been over a hundred wounded in the camp. The lorries brought them here to be seen by someone – we knew not who – then perhaps they were to be moved further back to a hospital. I half expected to be put onto a lorry and made into a nurse. But I wasn't. The officer actually thanked me for my help and then left to load the men onto freshly fuelled lorries.

The lorry at the rear did not unload its contents. Men were inside and I saw movements behind the canvas. I walked over to see who was inside. It was men in French and English uniforms. They were prisoners. I went closer to speak with them and ask where we were, but the lorry started up and I was waved away by a bad-tempered soldier.

'Fuck off girl. No French!' They all seemed to know how to swear well enough in my language.

So we were near enough to meet soldiers from the Front. Either it was moving towards us, or the camp was changing its purpose. Irrespective of which, it could be an advantage to us. I was walking slowly back to Mother when a car came into the camp and slammed to a halt near Father's hut.

'Out, you shit.'

'Get off me, you filthy bastard. Your breath smells like a drain, you pig. I am speaking so fast you cannot understand me, can you? You shit-eating dog.'

'Be quiet and go in here.'

Father spat on the soldier's boots. The soldier raised his pistol to Father's head and pulled the trigger. It happened so quickly I could barely understand what was happening.

It clicked but nothing happened, and so the soldier hit my Father across the face with the gun and Father fell to the floor.

'Papa! Not again. Oh Papa, you will kill us all!'

'Away girl. Away.' The look from Father stopped me in my tracks. This time, I needed no further instruction and ran to Mother.

'Maman, Papa has done it again. He has enraged the Germans and they are beating him. He spat at the soldier and he hit Father with his pistol. Maman, he fired his gun at him – but it must have been empty, as nothing happened. They were just trying to frighten him, I think.'

'Odile! Slow down and take a breath. Oh no! Well, he must have been trying to frighten your Father, that's all. He is not easily scared by other men.'

'This will be bad, Maman.'

For once we had just begun to get a little control of our lives and now we were back to the beginning again. What had Father done again to enrage the enemy so? An enemy already fearful and tense at what was happening to them.

Just before the camp lights were put on, the door was pushed open and three German soldiers came inside. The first one pushed Mother and I into a corner, holding the butt of a rifle above our heads. He spoke no French and grunted at us in German. Mother could not get in front of me, so she tried to pull me back into the corner.

'You, Lefebvre woman. Do not move.' The voice was harsh, but it was French.

I had no intention of moving. The eyes were blazing and the rifle close. At least this time it was not the barrel pointing at us. The other two searched around, took our meagre rations, and left. But the rifle did not move. An officer then walked in; it was the one who had struck Father with the pistol, and I could not help myself.

'Why would you do that to my papa? Why shoot him with an empty gun, to frighten him?'

The German looked straight into my eyes. 'Empty?'

I fell back, stunned at his reply. My world turned to ice.

CHRIS CHERRY

CHAPTER NINETEEN – ON THE WESTERN FRONT, 1915

June was at least warm. Once again, I was underground, listening for the awful tapping of the enemy mining operations. It was when I was underground that oddly I felt calmest. Here I was, in probably the most danger, in hot, sticky, sweaty and dirty company, yet I felt most able to think. I could only think of the job, not of Odile, or France, my parents or of a life out of this war. But out of the ground, with the breeze, stinking of burning and decay, I could think only of the life that was lost to me.

I had been once again in the line. With the Scots, trapped in a German counter attack. Again, I had fired a gun and again I had killed to live. Was my life worth more than an enemy's? No, but someone or something was protecting me. I liked to think it was my soul shielding me, its love for Odile stronger than the enemy. But it was fanciful thinking, and could not possibly be true. I was wounded, and my body was stiff and ached all the time, but I was a soldier in the line, and I had a job to do.

'Chuff me Will, you look a bloody mess!'

'Thanks Fixer, you don't look so rosy yourself.'

Fixer Cowling, my friend the railwayman, had just set up a test rig to blow a shallow mine. If successful, it might show us a way to break through and end this war early. And if it meant that France was not to be shelled to dust, well all the better.

'Hot work in the tunnel today, eh? How far are we now? Sixty, eighty?'

'Bloody hell, Fixer, you never stop asking damned questions do you? I'd say over a hundred yards. It'd be sixty, if you were doing it. But you weren't.'

'Ha, what is that you are writing? Not another note in crap French for that girl, eh? If she ever read one of them she'd laugh so hard, her head would probably fall off.'

'Bugger off you fool. It is a note, yes, but my French isn't all that bad. Better than your command of English.'

'Well, it passes the time.'

Fixer drew a pipe and sat down next to me, patting my knee in sympathy.

'It was tough in the line, mate. I know that. You rest. I will get us some tea in a while, when I've finished my pipe.'

I looked back at my note. I could never post it to Odile, could never see it in her hands. But I imagined her reading it. Somehow, the words written down had more power, perhaps enough to float over the trenches to her in France.

Perhaps they would travel over the bleeding wound of the trenches that divide the ground, brought by this war. I knew not where Odile was, but hoped her safe. I hoped she had escaped south, with the others. I knew that Albert was held. It was not too far away from Bazentin. Perhaps today, she is in the South of France, in sunshine and safety. I liked to think that.

But deep down, I could not be calm. Something was driving me onwards, it was the destination that was mysterious to me.

June 1915

Darling Odile. It still seems odd writing to you. Why I feel the need to write down these words, I do not know. Perhaps it is in case I do not live through the war. My sincere hope is that you are safe, behind us, south perhaps in the country. Tending a crop, or more likely, building an engine for a tractor to work the land with your dear Father! In my heart, I feel sure you have moved to safety, and that you are alive and well. It is possible for me to bear this misery, the boredom and the horror if it eventually brings me to you, for you are worth the journey. It is not permitted to write what is going on, for fear of capture. But I am acting to get to you. My energy, my drive and my will, they are all for you. Not for glory, or for country – none of that matters to me. It is you, my love from over the sea, who pushes me to live. To protect my Odile. I will come back for you, and nothing will stop me. I hope that you are there for me on that day.

William

CHAPTER TWENTY – CAMP SEVEN, 1915

'My God, Maman! He wanted to shoot Father in the head! You heard, you heard it as well didn't you?'

'Yes, Odile. But did he really mean it or is trying to frighten us? I cannot think. We must try to think. We must find a way through this again. Have they taken everything?'

'The food is all gone and the little pieces of wood are missing. We have nothing.'

We spent the night huddled together, too terrified to move. There were no kindly women to leave us parcels tonight. Neither of us slept and neither of us were ready when morning came.

The door opened at dawn.

'Out, two of you, immediate to move.'

'Maman, say nothing to him.'

'You two clean floor of soldier shit house now.'

We were pushed to the floor and dragged by our collars. The thin and rotten material tearing as we were dragged across the ground. I tried to stumble to my feet, but could not steady myself and kept falling back. The pressure on my neck was almost too painful to bear and my face throbbed.

At the door to the soldiers' closet, was a bucket of hot water. There were no mops.

'Soldier, give me a mop. I will clean your floor.' Mother was trying one more time to find a way in to these men.

There was a silence, a few words in German and a roar of laughter from the waiting group.

'No mop. Use hands or tongue, eh?'

Another roar of laughter. One of the soldiers kicked my Mother's leg. She winced in pain.

'You spit at us, we spit at you two times.'

'Pierre, you have ended our lives, my darling and stupid husband.'

'Come on Maman, the quicker we do this, the quicker we can get away from them.'

We pushed through the door, still on our knees. The hot water burned, and the chemicals in the water made my hands sore. I poured some on the cold floor and swept it around with my hand. Tears appeared again and I fought them back.

'Papa, let them be and they may let us live. We are no prisoners, we are slaves and toys for their amusement. Please Papa. Please Papa.'

'Hush, my darling. It does us no good and he cannot hear you now.'

'But Maman!'

'I know my little one, I know.'

I began to cry, I tried to stop, but the hot water and chemicals hurt, stinging my arms and now my eyes.

'William, please come for me now. Please take me from this place, I can live no more like this. Maman, please find William, I want my strength back and I want to see him again. Maman, I am begging you, please, please.'

'Oh Odile, you break my heart. We must not stop. We cannot fight. Please my darling, he will find us, I know that he will. He will be here to find us soon. Stay strong, darling daughter. Stay with me.'

Her words made me feel better as her strength was still there for me. But my Mother's hands were red and sore, just like mine, which made me feel worse. My Mother was still a beautiful young woman, but looking old and worn long before her years. I looked away and scrubbed the dirty floor with my hands until it was as clean as it had ever been.

When we finished, we poured the water into the drain. Our hands were burnt and sore, crimson red to the elbows. As we stepped outside, our clothes again torn and ragged, our arms burning with pain, we were met by a different crowd of soldiers.

'So you are the Lefebvre women. Here they are!'

I saw the first stone coming. It missed my head by the thickness of a hair. The second hit my leg and the third, my foot. Mother had already leaned over, grabbed my shoulder, and pulled me towards her.

'You leave us alone, you brutes. We have done nothing to harm you. Leave us alone now.'

One of the soldiers pushed to the front, raising his hands for silence amongst the group. In broken French he spoke to us.

'You bitches. Your husband kicked and spat at a superior officer who gave him a reasonable order. He poured water into the fuel for the lorries and split the brakes. It could have killed any one of us. For that you will all be beaten. Good for it as well. Run if you want, it will do you no good, ha!'

At that point, they started kicking dirt from the floor at us. We were soon covered in dust and the dirt stung my eyes. I tried to move backwards, but the soldiers had come around us in circles. They were pushing us from man to man, the ones at the front grabbing at my Mother, touching her and pulling at her dress. I was just pushed from one to another, I was hardly able to keep my feet, almost falling into each one of them. It was so frightening. More than once, I bumped into Mother, but she was only able to make grunting noises through the pain of her arms and leg and the awful rough hands of the soldiers. It seemed they were just taunting us. Then I saw why.

Father had been brought out to see the spectacle of his wife and daughter, powerless and in pain. His rage was visible. Surely this day we would be taken to one of the punishment camps and would be unlikely to return. Almost as soon as it had started, it was over. The group stopped, we fell to the floor and they walked off laughing and smoking. One of them threw a cigarette end at us as he left.

Father was made to watch us crawl back into our room. Mother looked at him, in tears of pain and anguish. She tried to hold me to her, but her pain seemed too much for her to bear.

'Lefebvre, you do that again, we will take everything from you and make you watch, pretty wife and daughter, yes? It is last time. You work right, or it is all over for you, French pig.'

For a week, we were starved. We scavenged water from the pump at night, but without the handle, barely enough came out to fill a cup each. No food at all, and we were prevented from going out. Weak and fearful, I thought that we were to be starved to death here. After all we had come through. Father could not forgive, he simply could not. His grief and anger would consume him. It had doomed us as well.

Until now, we had suffered bouts of hunger interspersed with eating half decently, only to be plunged once more into trading for food and water, and then finding comfort again. But now it felt like there could be no going back. There was no one who cared and we were truly alone. We realised it with a terrible pain in our stomachs. The war had won.

.

CHAPTER TWENTY-ONE JANUARY 1915

January in 1915 was cold. The rain came down almost every day and the wind was biting. Our clothes were summer thin, with seams ready to rot away at any time. Father was working on the lorries and the guns every day. I knew he particularly disliked the guns because they were used to shoot at the French and the Allies.

Then came the day that changed everything for him when he returned at nightfall from the repair yards. He walked slowly into the camp, his head in his hands, kicking the ground as he walked to his hut. Then, he went into the hut and closed the door. We did not see him for an hour, but he came to us after dark.

'My loves, please sit. I have something to say.' Father was grey and serious. This was not to be good news.

'I was out with the artillery today. They have these awful big and wide guns. The shells can be fired for many miles, I did not know such things had been invented. They mount them on wheels and tracks. Anyway, I was oiling the springs, and oh, my darlings, the guns are aimed at our home in Bazentin, as well as at Albert and many neighbouring villages. I work to keep a gun firing that is aimed at our home, our neighbours and our friends. They take fun in telling me all of this. The French are holding a line, but the villages evacuated to Amiens and then Beauvais, which is good. The enemy have been stopped at Albert. They have got no further.'

'Papa, that is good then, is it not?'

'I suppose for France, yes. For us, no. Our home is probably blown into kindling by the guns I repair. The French Army defended our village, but were pushed back by these Germans. They have most likely been into our house, taken our possessions, and destroyed our lives. How can we forgive that? They are uncaring vermin. How dare they do this to us?'

We sat in silence. I imagined soldiers in our home, and hoped they were French. They were welcome to take anything – food, drink, clothes – whatever it took to keep them strong. William kept coming back into my head. Where is he now? Is he safe or in peril? Thinking of him made me happy. It brought a warmth over me, like an extra blanket, an invisible shield against this war. Papa interrupted my thoughts, speaking again.

'I also bent the spring I was cleaning, quite deliberately. They saw this and punished me. We will not get food tonight, or probably tomorrow. I am sorry.'

'Never mind, Pierre. We have had quite enough today. Let us get some rest now, you go and sleep. You will have to work again tomorrow. Perhaps if you work well, they will be kind to us, yes?'

'Yes, Marie-Louise, I am sure they will.'

CHRIS CHERRY

CHAPTER TWENTY-TWO – CAMP SEVEN, JUNE 1915

My hands were red raw and weeping sticky pus that clung to my clothes. Mother was the same. She sat in silence mostly, clearly upset at being so powerless to protect her daughter. Father was angry and bitter. He had been treated so badly. He mended guns that killed our families and friends. When he could, he tried not to help, but was beaten and tormented, as we had been as well. The enemy were not kind, and the French population paid for the enemy's invasion in blood and anguish. We were leaderless, starved, imprisoned and forgotten. France had forsaken us and we were cut off, as if we were in Germany itself. No one was coming for us, not even my beloved boy from over the sea.

Father was beaten and broken. Mother, brave and protective, but weaker than the enemy. She had nothing to trade, nothing to bargain away the pain and suffering. William, where were you when we needed you? I am sorry to blame you when you cannot know or help. Your memory feeds me life and makes me happy amongst this blackness. I will be here when you come my love, that is my promise.

The morning came and Father was taken out again at first light. He carried his little bag of tools, and I was sure that he wanted to use them to beat the grinning soldier who was with him. I knew that every bolt he tightened cut him to his soul knowing it would help grind our army into dust on the slopes of our villages. I knew a fire burned inside my beloved papa, but I also knew it would seal our fate. We were hungry, starved, and thirsty and we would become ill. The dampness and fog were descending upon us and if we were to survive, something had to change for us. Quickly, and for the better.

Again, no food was given to us. We were shunned at the camp. This was going on day after empty day. This was now the way. No mercy and no amount of begging would make a difference. The soldiers here all knew what Father had done and they were keen to remind me that a loaded gun had been pointed at my Father, but had failed to go off. All I ever heard was disappointment that it had not gone off. They wanted my Father dead and Mother and I were just to be their sport and comfort, when the time finally came.

My only hope was that these soldiers would be moved out and others brought in. New soldiers usually meant things would be worse because we had no relationship with them, and Mother did not know their weaknesses. They did not know us and had formed no bond with us, harsh or otherwise. But it was my only hope, however little.

Mother discovered a way to get food from the rubbish piles. Any leftovers were boiled into soup, or piled up outside for the horses. Luckily, this pile was in the shade and if we were quick, the food would be fresh. Sometimes, it was not fresh and we would be ill for a day or two, and Mother was ill quite often. She insisted I fetch spinach home, even if it was raw, and we would eat it. It made me sick every time, but still Mother made me eat it.

'You are a woman, Odile. If we live through this, you will thank me.'

'Maman?'

'Hang on to hope. Your Papa is doing his best to kill us all. Be strong and eat, even if the food makes you sick. You understand?'

'Yes, Maman.'

'We will not give in, burnt arms, poisoned bellies and torn clothing are as nothing to family and our love. Quick now, whilst it is quiet outside.'

So, as I had done many times before in this and other camps, I set out in the shadows, like a rat. Keeping out of sight, hardly daring to breathe, creeping up on the prize. A pile of refuse, fit only for horses and dogs. I wanted to cry every time, and to thrust a knife into the heart of the enemy. I had never felt like this before. In my life full of family and love, there had been no place for hate or despair. Now I was turning into a machine. Perhaps one that even Papa could not fix.

Tonight, the pile contained warm vegetables, mainly stalks and leaves, but it was fresh enough to eat. In amongst the warm pile was a little fat, a tiny lump of greasy flesh. Perhaps mutton, maybe even horse, but it would sustain us another day. We were meant to have nothing, and if caught, I would be killed, or perhaps something even worse than that.

I turned up my skirt to pack it with food. My hands diving straight into the warm pile. I tried not to dig too deep and pick up dirt or stones. We had no way to cook anything, so we would eat it as it was. Then, I looked about and waited for the right moment to make my way back. I half crawled, half ran across the yard to the corner of the next hut to ours, to catch my breath and to be sure it was clear. Behind me a door opened, and a streak of light poured across the yard. Trapped! I could not move back or forward now, as it was too risky.

Muffled voices approached, getting louder. My German was limited to the words needed for survival. The voices talked quickly, but seemed gentle, not the brutish tones of the soldiers guarding us. Then I heard it, an unmistakable word, in any language. *Kurt*. It was a common enough name, but *what if*? What if it was the Kurt who had been kind to me, at least at first? But it couldn't be possible, there must be hundreds of Kurts here.

Then it came again, *Kurt*, from the figures in the doorway that were no more than indistinct shapes. It was hard to recognise the voice, even with my eyes closed. But there it was, the sound that was so familiar!

'Ja Kurt, ha. Guten nacht!'

The figure moved towards me. Still some way away, but there was a risk of discovery here. I stepped back, slowly. The second figure, the one that may have been Kurt, stepped in again, closing the door. The footsteps moved closer, almost upon me, but then turned towards a lit tent. Although it was very risky, I needed to know if this was Kurt, who may yet feel some kindness towards the girl whose beauty was shamed by her clothes.

When all was dark and quiet again, I moved swiftly across the yard towards his door. The warm, damp food was still wrapped in my skirt. I had gone no more than twenty steps when the door opened again. I froze solid and stood up as there was no escape from the bright light piercing the darkness.

The food slipped from my skirts and fell to the floor in greasy clods. Blinded, I awaited my fate. There would be pain, and almost certainly shouting.

'Mein Gott! Fraulein Lefebvre! Er, how are you Miss Lefebvre?'

'Kurt? Is it you? How is it that you are here?'

'Odile Armandine Lefebvre. At last, I have found you again! Here, come in here, no one will see you here.'

A wave of relief came over me. His words felt like genuine kindness. This was not to be a punishment meeting.

'It has taken me many favours and much time to find you. Your Father is quite the trouble maker.'

'I do not understand. You have been *trying to find me*?'

'Yes. Your Father, sabotage of the lorries caused me much trouble.'

'But you turned away, shunned my gaze upon you.'

'Well of course, I could not be seen to favour you. Your Father makes it difficult to help you.'

'I know, but you understand why?'

'Understand? Yes, I perhaps do. I much enjoyed our first meeting at the water pump. It gave me hope and joy for the war. I wanted you happy to spend time with me.'

'You have helped us then?'

'I have tried often but your Father spoils it time after time. You remember the time you were taken from the ration list, but food would appear.'

'My God! That was *you* and not Madame Collart?'

'Of course it was me. The Collart woman is as bad as your father!'

'The milk was a kindness, Kurt. Thank you.'

'It was my own ration. I stood watch to make sure no one would steal the parcels. I watched for you to come out and take them. But you did not. So I left more in the morning. As for Madame Collart? She told our soldiers that since you were not to be fed, then she should get your rations. But they were wise to her plan and struck her family from the list as well.'

'Oh, Madame. God bless you.'

'You had to be moved, since you would have been the subject of attention. Your Father was too much trouble. I arranged for you all to be moved, ensuring that the Collart women stayed with you, because their kindness would have made them suffer as well. Some women got passes for Switzerland, but I could not get enough for all, so I arranged for you to be transported north. I wanted you and the Collarts nearby but away from the infantry. My superior brought you here, to be with your Father and I arranged for the men to behave respectfully towards you. My superior was only interested in your family since your Father is good at repairs. Sadly, the Collarts are not here.'

'I know where they were. Your soldier friends raped Amelie Collart! Did you know that?'

Kurt was shocked by the blunt words. He sat down slowly on a small stool.

'I am sorry for that, Odile. I am not the commander and all I could do was to move you to a better camp. To keep up a pretence of not caring, yet allowing you to live.'

'They tried to kill Papa! One of your men shot him, but the gun did not go off. Did you know *that*?'

Kurt sat in silence. He had clearly tried to keep us safe. At least I now knew the story of the little blue books and the separation of the Collarts.

'It is dangerous Odile, very dangerous. I only arrived here yesterday and the soldiers here are Guards. Better educated and older men with families. You will be safer now. I asked to come here, it cost me much to be here, to be near you. Your beauty has burned into my eyes and heart. I hope that we can be friends?'

'But we have been tortured, treated as dogs, we washed shit-house floors with our bare hands, tossed from man to man whilst my father was forced to watch. Did you know that?'

Despite my best efforts, my voice rasped with anger. Kurt sat back, visibly shocked.

'It is your Father. He is causing you all this trouble. I have tried to help you many times, but he takes away any hope of comfort and safety for you.'

'Can you help us now?'

'Is that all I mean to you?'

'My apologies, I did not mean it like that. Can we at least be spared the beatings and the floors?'

'Your Father is the problem, Odile. Let us see if he will work with us. He is well known, you know. His talent is famous. Do you know he repaired a gun to fire that had been declared as scrap?'

'Yes, so you can fire on my family!'

'Sorry I said that. But he is valuable, or else he would be dead and you also. For you to be here is unusual, but it is the understanding of my commanding officer that a better job is achieved if you are with him.'

'Will we stay here? Father as well?'

'Yes, you know we are only three miles from our guns? Perhaps six miles from the Front.'

'Really? So near to home.'

'Perhaps, yes. But to keep you all here will be difficult. Perhaps we can find a way. As long as your Father works well, it will be easier for you to be here. If he works with us, we can work with you, eh?'

Here at last was a chance for survival, a way to eat that did not include greasy waste, but food that might nourish us.

In the morning, Father emerged at first light. This time, before he went off in the car, he was brought to our door and allowed in for a few minutes. He embraced my Mother, who was sore and stiff.

'My beautiful wife. My love and strength. Mother to my most precious child. My heart was torn to see you so. My love, my daughter. You be strong as well. We may live through this. I must go to work. They will get the very least of me, but I cannot see that sight again. It would end my life. That gun was loaded you know, but jammed. I have a chance to make amends and I will my darlings.'

Mother wiped a tear from his eye and her own. She kissed him lightly and he turned to leave.

'Watchful always, Odile. You must have eyes everywhere. Trust no one here. No one. Perhaps not even me. I may yet let us all down.'

'Go to work, Pierre. Go to work that we may eat again.'

At that very instant, it became clear that my time with Kurt would be a necessary tool to help my family to survive this war. But it would need care not to make him feel he was to be used in our survival plan. He was not going to be let into my world, he was still the enemy, and I held only thoughts of William, my parents, and our home in Bazentin.

It was common enough for girls to use their friendship with the enemy to get privileges like clothes or soap. I needed none of these things and wanted nothing from Kurt, other than kindness to Father, a life free of beatings and enough food to sustain life. Kurt had shown us kindness, which had put himself in danger and that had to count for something.

The next evening, Father returned and was again allowed to come to us, for a few minutes. He was not bruised and walked taller, it seemed. The day had been better for him as he had worked on ambulances and lorries, not guns. At least the lorries and ambulances did not kill our soldiers.

Kurt came in the evening and knocked on the door. It made my Mother wary and nervous.

'Is this that boy? Why did he knock? The others do not. Be careful, Odile.'

'Yes, Maman.'

I slowly opened the door. Kurt bowed his head politely and asked to come in.

'Good evening, Odile. Good evening, Madame Lefebvre.'

My Mother was visibly shaking. After all we had gone through in the last week, an act of politeness must seem so sinister. After all, a wolf invited inside, was still a wolf. But now it was inside the circle, beyond the shielding wall. She watched everything, no doubt waiting for the inevitable trouble to follow.

'Perhaps Odile, you would like to take a walk with me?'

'Yes Kurt, I would like that. Let me get my shawl.'

Kurt took a look at my clothes. His uniform was clean and tidy, his boots shining. Here was I, a bundle of rotting clothing, damp and dirty. The body underneath, streaked in dirt and unwashed in days.

'I am sorry that it has been like this Odile, that my efforts have not helped you all. But your Father—'

'Is a patriot, Kurt. Please remember that your comrades are killing our brothers and Fathers. My own village has been invaded. What do you expect of us?'

'Expect? Perhaps nothing. This is a difficult time for all of us. My comrades are dying as well. I know yes, this is your country. Perhaps we can just make the best of it, whilst we can?'

'You wanted to practise your French. Well, I am listening. Tell me about yourself. That would be a start.'

'Well, I am from Dusseldorf, my Father moved around when I was young and so I have also been to Leipzig, Koln and Berlin. I am twenty-two years of age and I have trained to be an officer. My Father wanted me to join a regiment because it offered a life that he could not provide. I went to a good school and here I am. I no more wish to be an enemy than you perhaps want me to be one.'

'How many soldiers in this camp?'

'Er, why do you ask? You were asking about my life then?'

'Sorry, yes. Do you want to be here?'

'My country is important to me, so I am here. I do not want to grow crops on French soil. Do you understand?'

'I do not think I do. How long will you be here in this camp?'

'The British are attacking north of here, so we are here until more soldiers come. That is all that I will say. I may be here for some time. I am asking to work with the administrators for the region, not for the army you see. So I can live with the French people more.'

'So you will be here for some months then?'

'Unless we win the war, of course ha ha.'

I fought the urge to spit at him. My chest rose and anger swelled, but I had to keep calm.

'Do you think your superiors would approve of you being seen with a French girl? Perhaps one so covered in lice and filth, like a rat in a drain?'

'There have been clothes here for you, brought from some of the houses nearby. But your Father's behaviour means that—'

'We all get punished. Yes I know that. Punished, starved, tortured, beaten. Is there anything else you want to do?'

Kurt looked down, blushed and turned away, kicking the ground. He looked angry, but not with me.

'I am not that sort of man. No, I just want us to be friends. Can you do that?'

I wanted to say it all to him. I wanted to punch him and step aside whilst William came and put a boot onto his neck. I wanted my Father to come out and hit him with a bolt.

'Yes of course, Kurt. It will be nice to have someone nearer my own age to talk to.'

He visibly brightened. Perhaps we had both understood each other better.

'I will arrange your rations, and see if the clothes are still in the stores. It is dry in there.'

We talked a little more and then Kurt had to go. Around me were no stares, no calls, and no soldier tried to stop my movement. Here I was, in the open and not in danger. At least, not in any danger I could see.

Late in the evening, rations were brought to us. We were asked to remain indoors, except to fetch water. We had been asked, not told.

CHRIS CHERRY

CHAPTER TWENTY-THREE CAMP SEVEN, 1915

Summer came early, the weather turning warmer and drier. The rags had been burned and our lives improved, as if the clothes were a symbol of a past. With a future holding some prospects, not just hiding and pain.

The daily ritual of working for the army had not changed. But little changes made our lives bearable. Father was working on ambulance lorries. He was happier that it was not the big guns, firing on our defenceless villages.

Kurt and I had spent many afternoons together, when he was free. We had all been given newer clothing. The clothes had been brought from a chateau, when it became an army office. My dress was really meant to go out in, not every day, but it was better than the rotten rags that I had worn before. Mother said she was wary of being offered new clothes, suspicious of a motive. Father was convinced it was because he no longer poured water into the fuel and shoved rags into the engines. Mother and I had kept my time with Kurt a secret. He was not often in the camp and for now it was possible to keep them apart. Kurt was happier with that arrangement. Each time Father upset the Germans, it meant that he could not see me.

Some evenings, Kurt asked if Mother and I would accompany him out of the camp, for a pleasant walk, which we often did. One evening, he asked us to drink coffee in a village that was further from the war. I had to accept, to keep us all alive, feeling still that I was only one wrong word away from a world of misery for us all.

'Odile, Madame Lefebvre, it is pleasant to have time here with you both. To drink coffee in the evening sun.'

I wanted to remind him that at nearly seventeen, going for coffee in the sun was an entirely new experience. It would have been preferable to have Father here. Mother was bristling, but she managed to use a pleasant tone when she spoke.

'It is, Kurt, thank you. It is warm here and quieter than the camp.'

A French woman brought more coffee. She looked at me, looked at my dress and slammed the cup down, harder than necessary. She muttered to another serving girl as she walked away. Kurt did not understand her, because the French was too fast. But I did, and Mother certainly did, judging by the expression on her face.

'Look at that whore? Who the fuck does she think she is, eh? Fucking that officer and fucking us at the same time. Little Miss Prim with her chaperone, how do you do little cow? I bet the war hasn't even touched the surface on her fucking life. Sitting there like a fucking Countess.'

'I know. I bet she does not know the first fucking thing about this war, little tramp. And her Mother sitting there, selling her own daughter, whilst we and the whole of France suffers!'

Mother's jaw was clenched and she held her coffee cup so tightly, it was possible to see the whites of her still youthful knuckles, but I knew she would not risk losing this chance. I almost burst into tears. Here I was, barely seventeen, a month after cleaning shit-house floors with my hands, balancing survival with the prospect of a day without my Father being beaten. What did they know, these women? How dare they, how damned well dare they...

But Kurt seemed oblivious and continued talking to us. 'I liked Dusseldorf. It is a pleasant place to be on a day like this. You should see it.'

'Er, oh yes Kurt. That would be lovely.'

'Really? Oh, does that mean that you would...?'

'Perhaps, after the war, if it were possible to be friends and our countries settled our differences.'

'Oh, that is a cause for celebration. Let me get wine...'

Mother caught my eye and I read the warning there.

'No Kurt! I mean, save your money. We can celebrate another time. Besides, I do not really drink wine.'

'It will fine enough to have coffee, Kurt, thank you.'

Oh, Maman, how careful you are.

'Very well Madame Lefebvre. Hello! Can we have more coffee mademoiselle?'

We had to endure another round of slamming, with accompanying stares and whispers.

'Not from round here, is she? None of us would give up to the enemy like that little cow. Cow, yes! You can fucking hear me can't you? Yes, and your fucking Mother, she can hear me as well. That fucking German can't though eh? Yes look away, old cow, you should be ashamed – selling your daughter like this—'

'Perhaps we should go Kurt? Odile looks a little chilly.'

'Yes of course. Odile, let us find our way back.'

At the camp, dusk was falling. I hoped that we were back before Father and we quickly left Kurt and ran inside. When the door was shut, I burst into tears.

'Odile, my love. Don't cry, please.'

'I cannot help it Maman, it was that French serving girls.'

'Odile, they are only words and she does not know us and does not know our situation.'

'I know Maman, I cannot blame her really.'

'As long as Kurt is happy. It is very important that you keep him happy. It must always be so. Do you understand me?'

I sat down against the door and wept. The act was hard, my energy draining each time to keep this going. Living without giving any hint of fear or alarm for this silly boy. Can't he understand how terrible our life is? Of course not, for him, this is one long adventure. He wasn't fighting in a field, after all.

'Odile, quickly. You must wash your face in case he comes for you. You must be always ready. That is your duty. At least this is better than the alternative. You know what happened. You know how it was. Let us not be back there again. Let us work this to our advantage.'

'To be like Amelie Collart? Did it do her any good?'

Mother sank into her chair.

'My God, do not say that.'

'But Maman, do you not think it will end like that?'

'No, Odile. You are clever and quick. You can manage that boy to your advantage. You must be alert and clever. But more than that, you must act, be an actress, be a character, be someone else for the time with him, for the sake of your silly foolish papa.'

Each evening, I would sit on my little bed. Still made of straw and still alive with something, but at least it was not on the floor in the draught and cold. I would shut my eyes and imagine my lovely William there, standing in front of me, smiling and holding out his hand for me. Sometimes, I imagined him in uniform. It was a French uniform, because I could not remember an English one exactly, but he looked smart and alive. It helped me to keep him alive in my soul. In that place, he knew that I loved him and my time with this German boy was for the life that I had now and not the life that I might have had.

I would write him letters, try to imagine a normal life. But this camp was my lot and impossible to escape. I imagined sending them to him, with this address. Perhaps he would come with horses and gather us up to safety. Foolish thoughts, but it made me happy to hold on to him and nurture my love.

I imagined telling him of the days of fear. Having to leave at night as the enemy advanced, Father putting us almost in front of the Germans. Sights of them walking across the fields in their silly pointed hats. Almost making it into the lorry to go to Albert and safety. But here we were in this camp, prisoners but not captives, ha!

Sometimes I would be with Kurt for the whole afternoon. I was careful to be always polite, knowing at some point, this would have to go further. Perhaps he would sense my reluctance, or suspect this to be a fraud and punish me for my cunning.

Kurt did not really know my Father, although he helped him by controlling the soldiers, he showed little interest. Perhaps if he did, it would show his weakness and the army would be angry with him. He had many superior officers who would willingly send him to battle. We both lived a precarious lie.

'Odile, I cannot help your Father any more. There are no more favours and if he upsets our officers again... I tell you this, because it may be that we will move camp again soon. Without me, you may be cast to the mercy of a Prussian soldier and they will not show mercy to your Father. They clean their guns and theirs will not jam.'

'So you may be going soon?'

'Maybe, but perhaps I can stay and be an administrator in the villages here.'

I thought Kurt might see the disappointment in my face and realise it was not because I would miss his company. I had to change the subject.

'Are we captives in the camp, Kurt?'

'Oh. Well, the army have declared this region as occupied and disputed, not administered. Further north and east, the villages are administered. You may have seen them when you were moved on my request.'

'The villages we saw through cracks in the canvas with German names?'

'Well yes, but that is only so that the Germans can make themselves understood. French names are hard for a German tongue.'

I wanted to scream my rage and tell him how I felt. To scream that William would kick his stupid German backside back to stupid Dusseldorf.

'I suppose that is true, Kurt. It seems a sensible measure.'

He looked at me with a strange expression. I was not an actress and I was frightened. Perhaps he saw this. He held my gaze for a second longer than usual and my cheek twitched slightly. This was an important moment.

'So I think that you are not a captive, but perhaps not free to move as you please. It is dangerous. You have your identity card and papers?'

'No, Mother and I have never been given any.'

'Really? That is not at all proper. I can arrange passes for you and your Mother to come to the village, and give you a little war money. It is not enough to buy much, but it is the best I can do.'

'That would be very kind.'

'Odile, I have to go away for four days. I will arrange this all before then.'

'Four days? Why?'

'It is the war, I cannot tell you.'

Four days. I could get a pass and leave for four days. This would permit me to explore and perhaps find a way to escape. Perhaps we could get out, in the night, away to an area of France where we could be free. Here, we were slaves under the boot. At last, I saw a chance to escape the awful memories, including Kurt and his stupid ignorance of our suffering, his stupid misunderstanding of my attentions. Four days.

'Odile, before I go, I would like to…'

My heart nearly exploded. This was it. This was to be the moment I dreaded the most. To refuse now, might yet mean death to us. That idiot woman in the café, if only she truly knew my true peril.

'Yes, Kurt?'

'I want to ask you something.'

My neck was throbbing, my face perspiring, and my hand visibly shaking. In this comfortable place, I was in more danger than anywhere else. A cold and dirty shed had known dangers I could sense and see. A rhythm of peril that ebbed and flowed predictably. But here was a ticking clock of danger, a spring tide of emotion that could turn at any moment.

'Then, ask. I am keen to hear.'

'Is there a time when you think that we could have a life together?'

This was it. The moment had come sooner than expected, but I had rehearsed this moment with Mother. She had taught me the art of men, but I had never wanted to confront this moment. Thoughts of my Father being kicked, and the day he hit me were still vivid in my mind. Thomas and his greedy eyes, Madame Collart and the word of warning. Poor Amelie, battered and forever damaged at the side of the road. I took a deep breath and calmed my voice.

'Kurt. This war has changed much for us both. If you had passed me in the street, you would never have glanced twice at me. A shy, thin girl would not have interested you. The war has brought us together, and the absence of any other girl in this dangerous place has brought your attentions upon me. Should you assume that love can follow, when we are in unequal situations?'

Kurt deflated. I was trying very hard to remember the rest. I hoped it did not sound like I was reading from the page of a book. I wanted to hold it together just long enough.

'You have shown me kindness. For that, I have gratitude for the risk you take. Perhaps it will be love, perhaps it will be all you may wish. But I need time to adjust Kurt. Time to understand that the war has changed things. Can you give me time to understand my feelings? Can you do that Kurt?'

He raised himself in his seat. He rubbed his neck thoughtfully.

'I think so, Odile. I am no brute, and want you to love me.'

Inside, my heart calmed a little. My lip started to soften and the emotional relief rose in my body.

'Give me that time Kurt and I can be the girl you love and care for.'

Mother and I had liked that bit. *The girl you love and care for.* You can be the boy I use to survive.

Strangely, I did not feel satisfied and was unable to be decisive like Mother had planned. The lives of three French citizens turned on my impression of caring love. I had done it, but felt dirty, dirtier even than my body was. This boy that, despite my best efforts, I could not despise in the way I had expected and the way my Mother insisted, when we hatched our plan in the gloom of an old candle in the dirty hut.

I thought of William on this June evening and hoped him safe. A wash of thoughts for my English boy came over me. Not for the first time in this war, I felt a pain in my chest for William.

A pain that meant something, but I could not know what.

The breeze was gentle, the evening calm.

I looked at Kurt, the German boy so close to me. I saw the uniform, saw the man inside only as I would see a garden on a foggy morning through a misty window.

But I cleared my head, pulled Kurt to me and kissed William deeply on the lips.

CHAPTER TWENTY-FOUR
IN THE TRENCHES, JUNE 1915

The June night in the trench had been cool, but not cold. We all felt fear, but had been here long enough to look after each other and keep up our spirits. At least this wasn't bloody Flanders eh? Ha ha. In the morning, very early, the Germans came again. They were determined and brave soldiers. But so were we, damn them. My injured back had stiffened and it ached, throbbing to remind me that I had been lucky. It made me feel awful and sick, but I had to go to it again. Fight or die, simple as that. And I was not ready to die whilst Odile was in danger, somewhere over the lines in the north. I thought of her and hoped her safe in this place of horror.

The first figure appeared over the parapet a little before five, in the early morning light. He was young, breathless from the sprint over the short distance of No Man's Land. He had received a light wound from a bullet or shell fragment in his leg and it was bothering him, which proved to be a fatal distraction. I shot him in the throat and he was dead as he hit the trench. There was no longer any feeling of remorse in me. That emotion had been left on the Belgian plains. The enemy were intent on killing, there was no doubt at all. This was active brutality on a massive scale, across the whole of the line, from the coast to Switzerland. My brothers depended on my courage to be a soldier and I must not let them down. Around me was a writhing passion of noise and muscle, torn and dirty and I had to do my share of the fighting. It was up close and the breath of the enemy was no more foul than ours.

The next German appeared terrifyingly close. A Scot soldier on my right bayoneted him as he fell into the trench. The air was filled with groans in German from the wounded and dying. Despite waiting expectantly for more Germans to appear over the top, no more came. I was overwound, anyone could come for me now. Feeling like a wild animal inside, I would kick and spit and defend my life with all my strength. They would not take me. I waited, breathing heavily, but none came and my tension subsided slowly. That was the most frightening part, the constant and expectant waiting. Come for me Odile, come and take me from this place with your fair hand. Lift me above the clouds of death into your welcoming arms. My love, my true love. Be there for me when the time comes. I know it will come.

Along our trench, some Germans had made it across, but too few to take back the ground successfully. Around a hundred Germans had attacked this early morning along a section of trench held by Three-hundred. The soldiers that made it into our positions took many lives, but none this time were allowed to return. There were Germans with bayonets pushed through the skull. One had been fully decapitated. The head, minus the helmet, was thrown back towards the Germans as it was a ghastly medieval sight to look at in the trench. I would have to be an infantry soldier in this awful place and I had better get used to it.

Then, with relief, there was shouting in English from behind us and Scots voices were responding to our challenges. We were going to be relieved, if not rescued. A path back to the road was finally secured. I made my way back to my unit unhampered, apart from a sore and bleeding back. A day and a night in the trench. A lifetime of pain, fear and anguish vented on the field.

I wrote a short note to Odile. I wished her safe in the south of France, perhaps on our side of the line, but knew this was probably unlikely. She would probably be in a village, under a German administration, or in a labour camp if she had been caught in the invasion. It helped to imagine that she was here with me, that we were together in the sunshine, in the glorious summer of France. A warm June evening, like this one. I felt a sudden and inexplicable urge to pull her close to me, to kiss her deeply, something I had only done twice before. It was a good thought and it washed over me for a moment, her lovely open face close to me and her warm lips on mine. Hold on my love, be strong and brave.

CHAPTER TWENTY-FIVE
CAMP SEVEN, JULY 1915

'Why is he even here? This is quite irregular... He can do what with the lorries? Oh, well perhaps there may be some use for him after all... But sir, his family as well? Must we nurse all of the sick French in a time of...? Well I understand, of course, but would it not be better if... Very good, sir... Thank you, sir.'

The telephone line was working again after a week of broken messages and lost orders. Colonel Rahm glared at it and muttered to his aide.

'Moller, it seems the whole French Army have been sent here to annoy me and only me. The camp works well. The lorries go out each day as they should. Almost all in working order, irrespective of what happened to them the previous day.'

'Very good, sir.'

'This French man, the troublemaker with the foul mouth and cunning ways. He has a certain touch with machines.'

'The miraculous civilian engineer with the big mouth, sir? The one with the wife and the girl here? Can you not get rid of them, sir?'

The colonel nodded. 'If it were up to me, they would be long gone. But orders are orders. We must keep the French man happy, watch him, but give him everything he needs.'

Moller made some notes. 'And his woman and the girl, sir, what of them?'

'Accommodate them. That does not mean make them comfortable.'

'Very good, sir.'

Rahm looked through the window, at the quiet orderly camp outside, just the way he wanted it.

'If the lorries go out in good working order, well, we can make allowances for that, I suppose.'

'Yes, sir. I have made a note of your instructions.'

The colonel moved away from the window and watched his trusted aide completing his notes.

'Moller, where is Langer? Get him here at once.'

'Yes, sir. He is waiting to see you. I will send him in.'

Moller left the room and ushered Langer through the door.

'Langer? Are you settled in here?'

'Yes, Herr Colonel. You wished to see me?'

'This French family we have attached to our motor group. Do you know who I mean?'

'The Lefebvre family. Yes sir. I have met the woman and her daughter.'

'Good. Well this order may seem odd to you, but I need you to make sure that the family are... accommodated. It is important that Lefebvre works well on the lorries and ambulances. He must be kept happy.'

Langer frowned. 'Sir, you are ordering me to make the French engineer happy, and his wife and the girl as well?'

Rahm waved his question away with a swipe of his hand.

'That is an order, Langer, straight from the General's office. Right, when you get back from arranging the new ambulances, you get on with minding the Frenchies, eh? Off to it then.'

'Very good, sir.' Langer snapped straight and clicked his heels together.

Kurt left the meeting and smiled as he stepped back onto the square. He had been *ordered* to look after the French family. They would be grateful to him for their, what was the word? *Accommodation.* It was in his power to make it pleasant, or otherwise for the family. Of course he did not want to make it unpleasant, but it would be to him that their requests would come and it did not hurt to be the one who could make things happen. It was clear that the family had been through a lot and they would be most grateful. He had already done much for them and it seemed that Odile had shown him recognition of that kindness. She had kissed him, it had surprised him how passionate it had been. He smiled. A French girl on his arm, maybe in time, even in his bed. Today was already a good day.

"Good morning Odile, Madame Lefebvre".

"Hello Kurt. Are you not busy today? We are required to mend uniforms for the ambulance teams and to try and wash off the blood from the uniforms in the laundry. At least it is not cleaning floors with our bare hands".

"I was sorry to hear that, Madame. I hope it will not happen again. Of course, if your husband..."

"Kurt?" Odile wanted quickly to keep the mood positive and in their favour. "When do you finish for today? My back is hurting from all this and I was wondering if we could take a walk. Perhaps outside of the camp. What do you think? I will not see you for some time and I thought it would be nice".

"It would Odile, yes, that would be good". Kurt felt his spirits rise even further. Perhaps she could see past his uniform to the boy within. What he could give to her, give to her family, would certainly make her fall in love with him. It would just take time, that is what she said. Time here, he has plenty of that to give.

Odile had prepared well for the walk. Her Mother had talked through everything she needed to do, to look for, to watch for and what she should do in each circumstance. Every word she said to Kurt would be important for their survival.

"Your Papa could ruin this all in one moment Odile. You have to make sure the German boy wants to care for you. You must give him something to hope for, but not give yourself away. My darling, you are so young to be carrying such a burden, but it seems fate makes us turn to you for salvation. There, you look good enough to go out now. Stay calm little one and keep thinking. Keep yourself alert and look. You understand my love?"

"I do Maman. I will do all that I must".

"Off you go then. Remember, to let him lead you. Do not ask the difficult questions too quickly, or he may become suspicious. He must always think you an innocent girl".

"Quick, he is coming. Go now. Smile. Good".

Kurt was pleasantly surprised to see Odile come out to greet him. He took her by the arm and led her to the gate of the camp. Odile saw that there was only one guard at the gate again. That seemed to be the normal number now. He did not ask for any identity documents, perhaps that was because of Kurt. He did not look their way, only opened the gate and saluted towards Kurt. Yes, Kurt could be very valuable, very valuable indeed.

Odile squeezed his arm a little tighter. She felt the muscles in his bicep and felt herself blushing, just a little.

CHAPTER TWENTY-SIX
CAMP SEVEN, AUGUST 1915

'I am sorry for going away for a few days, Odile, and will miss spending this time with you. I will make sure that your work is light, it is not possible to prevent you from having to do work, you understand. But I will leave orders that rations should be brought to you at all times. Fresh water daily and perhaps some more clothing for you and your Mother.'

'That would be good Kurt. Is Papa receiving his rations?'

'Oh, your Father is quite well. He works hard on the ambulances and we are most pleased with his skills. You need not worry. He has understood the situation quite well and accepts that he must work to live. The alternative is quite bleak.'

'For us as well?' There was a silent pause. Odile regretted the words.

'Your Father will not be a problem to us, it is certain.'

'Will we ever be allowed out of the camp?'

Kurt stopped abruptly and turned slowly to me. The old fear crept upwards and into my face.

'Odile, it is good that you have asked. I can arrange for you to attend the village to collect supplies, because you will like that, yes? It was hard for me to arrange, but I have managed it for you.'

A wave of relief crossed over me. This was so hard to do and my face was surely giving me away at every word.

'In fact, you are able to leave tomorrow. There will be orders for you in the morning.'

'Orders for me? To go out of the camp?'

'Yes. There will be a list of supplies that you must collect. Now, let us return to our walk.'

As I began walking again, the wave of relief was palpable. Had he stopped to warn me? To let me know that he knew what I might be up to? I decided to pull back a little, just in case.

Kurt left early in the morning. He waved as he left, but did not come over to say goodbye. Perhaps he ought not to appear too friendly. It was clear that my Father's work was now valued and the soldiers in the camp were not the awful brutes from before. In fact, some of them were friendly and showed kindness. Perhaps they felt that these French were welcoming them into their country.

I was thinking fast. My head was spinning. Now that I was allowed out of the camp, I had been given some freedom. How would I use it? How could I turn it to the advantage of my family? Would I be able to bring things back into the camp? What were the rules?

There was an envelope on the floor of the hut. It was addressed to my Father, but my Mother opened it. Inside was a slip of paper, signed by Kurt. It was in German and appeared to show two times in the day when I was to leave the camp to pick up some items – but I could not understand what they were. The first time was at eleven o'clock, in one hour's time.

'Maman, do you know what these items on the list are?'

'Not at all. I do not want to go and ask, for fear of losing the opportunity. All I do know is that you have to go to this road named in German. Did Kurt not tell you?'

'No, he did not.'

'Right, well, you had better take care to get all of the items on the list and make sure you are back on time.'

'Maman, there is something I must do as well, when I have this pass.'

'You must do nothing that might make the Germans turn on us again. We have come through a terrible time, Odile. Your Father is better and our fortunes are improved. Do not send us back into the dark, my darling.'

'I will not Maman. It is for us that I must do this.'

CHAPTER TWENTY-SEVEN
CAMP SEVEN, AUGUST 1915

It was easy walking to the gate since I had papers that permitted me, well ordered me, to leave the camp. I did take an extra shawl and a woollen scarf, which might otherwise have been unusual on this warm morning, but the bored guard on the gate did not seem to see anything unexpected.

He looked at my note and my identity card and let me through without a word, just a shrug and a grunt. I knew where to go, but not what to collect. The orders showed the return time at the bottom of the letter, but I had folded it over, out of sight of a casual glance. The guard at the gate never unfolded the orders properly. As far as he was concerned, I could be out until anytime. He seemed not to care. The guard was always changed in the afternoon and if my luck held, no mention of me would be made and they would not expect me back through the gates this evening.

Before making any plans, I needed to know what to collect. It was probably some parts, or provisions, certainly nothing important. If it was anything important, it would not be given to a French prisoner, surely?

The errand was wasting daylight, which might be vital later, so I hurried on. At the main square, which had been hit by bombs in the invasion, I saw the street names properly for the first time. The Rue Charlemagne had been renamed Wilhelmstrasse and my destination was on the corner. It was a very small market stall, where two French ladies were talking. In front of them was a small bucket of flowers. A most unusual sight.

'Excuse me Madame. I have a note to collect a parcel from you?'

'Parcel? Ah, the little whore came then? I told you Sylvie, the tramp would come for her flowers. Of all the things to worry about in this war of the dead, eh? Some shitty flowers! Well, here you are Empress! Now fuck off.'

'What? This note is only to collect flowers? Is that all? Why do you speak to me like that?'

'You can fuck German pigs if you like, you tramp, but don't expect the Mother of a dead soldier to help you. I know it is probably all you have to give, but to give it to these bastards? Have you forgotten who you are? What they have done to us?'

I blanched, opening my mouth to speak, but the flower woman was unstoppable.

'I was ordered to be here, fucking ordered! To stand here with a bucket of fucking flowers, otherwise who knows what they might do to my children. The flowers, stolen from the church, if you please. The only thing that is growing now in this damned place of ruin. What a disgusting sight you are.'

'I am not with the Germans. How dare you! You have no idea what they have done to me and *my* family.'

'Well,' the woman spat at my feet, 'as I see it, you are the one holding a note in German, demanding that I give you a bunch of stolen flowers. You tell me how hard it has been for you, eh?'

The women turned away, clearly ending this conversation, without any chance for me to put my side. I was confused and deeply hurt and the fire died in my belly. Was that really me? Was I fooling myself? I was no collaborator, but perhaps this is what collaboration feels like? Be nice to a German, to avoid your Mother being starved and your Father beaten? If that is how it seems, then it must be how it is. It made me sad and upset. These flower women were my people, not Kurt and his invading army.

I turned away, looking for space to think. So, the errand was flowers, for me. Kurt had clearly thought that a pass out of the camp meant trust. Flowers perhaps meant something else. This was no order. It was an act of care, perhaps love. He could not have known what the women would do, could he? They could not be blamed. They are just scared and angry. No, this was just a simple kindness from Kurt. Good, if this was the errand, no one in the camp would be expecting a delivery from me, which set me free.

This place was in Bapaume, or at least near it. Mother and Father were sure that we were just a few miles from home. The confused journeys had spun us all around, but this place was unmistakable. The churches and roads were not all bombed and were still recognisable, even with their awful German names. My legitimate pass and my identity card, stamped with the highest authority in the region, allowed me to hide, to move quietly and unnoticed.

The road south from Bapaume towards Albert was crammed with soldiers and their machines of war. I was able to move about in the open around Bapaume. But any attempt to move south down the road home, might mean arrest, or worse. The buildings were not too badly hit by bombs and there were plenty of places to hide. I was used to hiding and good at it. If captured, I could pretend to be insensible and buy myself some time.

I turned off the road towards the villages east of the town. This was an area familiar to me, from driving around with Father. But the roads were not easy to see and the Germans had laid new tracks across the fields. It would be easy to get lost.

The afternoon was warm at least. The soldiers did not seem busy with anything, and all appeared quiet and ordered. Around the roadsides were piles of wooden planks, and what looked like hundreds of twig bundles lined up in neat rows, as well as heaps of small stones, tiny rocks and sand. It was unclear what these were for, but it all looked like a lot of new building. Irrespective of their intent, there were plenty of places to hide unseen in the shadows in the late afternoon.

Being so close to home, made me want to go there so much. It was so close that I could almost see it and seeing my home or even my village would make me feel normal again, even just for the briefest time. William was in my head always. Here were the roads of yesterday. I imagined us floating up and down on the motor bicycle, with me in his arms as we giggled our way around France. There had been scant laughter in this last nine months. I wanted so much for William to come around the corner and carry me away from here.

But then there was Kurt. Here he was as well. I hardly knew him, hardly cared for him. But this boy was suddenly so important and precious to my whole family. A man that could save us, or condemn us. A man in whose power we were caught. Would it be so terrible? Would it be so deceitful and treacherous? Would I betray my love for my English boy for a German one? Without this choice we would be dead. With this choice, we may yet survive. One love for another. Was it as simple as that?

My chest tightened at the thought of betraying my darling William and these decisions tore me to pieces. Kurt, kind and trusting, extending a hand of love, from within the machine of war. None of the Germans had shown us the slightest care and concern, we were cargo, baggage, an unwanted nuisance. We were a job that signified a lower rank, and minding us was beneath their stupid pride. But Kurt had only shown compassion, in the face of reprisal.

Darling William. If you were here now, I would love you from the bottom of my heart. You are my first and true love. It may be a wasted heart if I love you still. But I will try my darling, try to hold on to my love. But life has changed so much. William, I need you to know that I want you, only you. But in order to survive, there is a different path for me to take.

In the shadow of a wall, I sat, knowing tears were no use, a weakness that was too expensive here, at this time. In my head there was another war. On one side was William. He was shouting at me, but I could not hear. Smoke and fire separating us. On the other, across a stream of blue water were Mother and Father, calling to me. As I moved to them, Kurt's strong arm held me steady. When I looked back, there was William, a streak of clear skin down his cheek as he called to me. He was moving away, taken by the flames until he almost disappeared. Father held out his hands, which were streaked in blood and oil. Mother, looked to me, her dress shabby and torn, with tears in her eyes. Kurt looked at me, and he smiled when his eyes met mine.

I knew what I had to do.

CHRIS CHERRY

CHAPTER TWENTY-EIGHT
ALBERT-BAPAUME ROAD, AUGUST 1915

The lorry bobbed and rattled along the track. It was a temporary road, built by the Germans in 1914 during the invasion. It was an invasion, and Pierre could not forgive them. His ribs hurt, his back hurt, his knee hurt and his head hurt. These pigs had beaten and battered his body, but they did not have him yet.

'Lefebvre, there are four ambulances for you today. One has a crack on the wheel bearing and is leaking oil. The other three simply will not start. It is quiet today, so you have until nightfall to repair them. Understand?'

Pierre nodded. At least ambulances carried the enemy his brothers had wounded. The more ambulances there were, the better. I will make sure the springs are hard and bounce the life out of this awful enemy.

'We are here. Come on, get on with it.'

Pierre jumped down. The day had come out fine and dry, after the cloud in the morning. Cloud that had silenced the guns nearby. But now they occasionally fired in the distance. He thought that they were firing near to Albert, but was not so sure as the land seemed unfamiliar after the road-building. All he did know was that there were unburied French soldiers' bodies and clothing visible in remote corners of fields. This was the price of defiance. Well, if that was to be his fate, so be it.

He leaned under the ambulance and saw the cracked bearing case. A small puncture wound let oil leak out and away, seizing the wheel. He knew it could take a couple of hours to repair, perhaps a morning if the plates sent as spares did not fit exactly. This would need a proper workshop space. He could do it here, but just did not want to.

'Soldier, this will take a day to repair. I need the workshop tools and they are not here or on the lorry.'

Their conversations, always complicated by the differences in language, were blunt and brief. Today was no different, but the number of lorries to repair was great and patience was little.

'You have all you need. Get on with it, now.'

Pierre had won a little battle. A little flea bite to scratch, over and over. He smiled to himself.

'I will do what I can, but I cannot promise.'

He turned to the wheel. It was already removed and the hole easily visible. Through it he could see open countryside, France, home. He looked out towards what must have been Martinpuich, or Pozieres. He saw the church standing upright. Not yet damaged too greatly by the war. That was good. The summer breeze was warming. On another day, it could have been his shed in Bazentin, working on the funny motor car with the flat seats that his darling daughter loved. He could smell her on the breeze. Flowers and oil. His little miracle girl. The girl that wanted to live. He looked at the church spire one last time before going back to the ambulance wheel.

'Darling daughter. I don't think I can protect you from these men. For that, I am sorry.'

'What was that Lefebvre? Get on with your work.'

'Sit on a bomb, you filthy pig.'

'What did you say?'

'I said, this might take a couple of hours still.'

'Good.'

The wheel was stuck. A little grease and brute force dislodged it. What little was left of the oil leaked away onto the floor in a black, silky puddle.

Pierre drew the little puddle into his can, making sure lots of dirt came with it. When the time came to refill the wheel oil, this would go in first.

He hammered and worked the metal for the rest of the afternoon. The job was finished, could have been finished sooner, but Pierre did not care to do so. He refilled the wheel, sealed all of the moving joints and left it. For a day or two, it would seem perfect. Then the dirt would jam it and seize the joint. By then the blame would fall on the conditions and the tracks. It all seemed too easy.

The ambulances were brought by horses. Not fine animals, but small, sickly ones that had been worked for weeks already. He knew how they felt.

'They treat you just like us, eh? Never mind little fellow. You rest now.'

The electrical system was the problem on these machines. The wiring got torn apart by the rough roads, and the thick wires were also prone to water damage. Pierre made sure that enough little holes were cut in the wire to allow water in to rust and cause the batteries to fail. But not until he was long gone.

The German engineers working alongside Pierre respected his talents and left him alone. They often asked for help on their own repairs and Pierre took care to work perfectly alongside them. That way they might leave him alone to his private battle of will.

That evening, with the ambulances repaired and working again, Pierre was driven back to the camp, in the usual silence. The soldiers behaved more courteously here, not like the brutes who had punished him at every turn, for sport and amusement. At the camp, the guard at the gate looked at his identity card. He looked up at Pierre and back to the card, then waved him through, just like every other night. Except tonight, he held his arm for a fraction of a second.

'I have not seen your daughter today, is she unwell?'

'I, I do not know. I have not seen my wife and daughter for a little time.

Perhaps she has a summer chill.'

The guards spoke quickly in German and both roared with laughter. The gate guard looked back to Pierre.

'Ha, perhaps she is missing our Herr Langer.'

Pierre looked away from the guard. He quickly stepped away into his hut.

'Odile, my daughter. Be careful with these terrible people. Be careful my darling.'

For the whole evening, until it became late and too dark to see, Pierre sat at the window staring at the door of his wife and daughter's little hut. The light stayed out, apart from a flickering candle for a fleeting moment. Perhaps they were both unwell. He might be allowed to see them tomorrow, if he could mind himself long enough.

Marie-Louise sat in darkness. Odile had not returned, but she had not expected her to. The girl had her Father's wilful spirit and there was nothing to do. Because she had taken up with the German boy, if only a little, this must be a reward for her. It was worrying, but she would not yet make a fuss. Odile would be home tomorrow, for sure. It would not hurt to sit and look out of the window, just in case. Marie-Louise sat by the window looking into the square.

In the morning, there was still no sign of Odile and no one in the camp was looking for her. Nobody came to the hut to enquire, politely or at the point of a bayonet. It was calm and orderly, and Pierre had left as usual, with no sign of fuss or commotion. It was too quiet. Odile was nowhere to be seen. The guards at the gate seemed to be acting quite normally. The colonel moved to and fro, without the slightest glance at her.

'Odile, where are you? What did you say you were going to do?'

Marie-Louise thought for a moment. What was it she said? *It is for us that I must do this.* The note with her orders was clear, she had to come back. But no one was looking for her. What has she done, or worse, what had she arranged with the Germans? *There is something I must do...*

Marie-Louise could not think clearly. There were items for Odile to pick up, but she did not know what they were. There was a time for her to leave, and she had gone at that time. But there was also a time for her to return. And Odile had not returned. What was it? What was her daughter going to do? She could feel the panic starting to rise. Perhaps it was a ruse. She had met the German boy and gone with him, perhaps taken against her will on a false promise? Perhaps she had come to harm after all, in all innocence. Pierre was calm when he left, he might know something. What could have happened?

Her whirling thoughts were interrupted by a knock at the door. Quite politely, but it echoed through Marie-Louise as if an enormous chain had fallen down an iron staircase.

Get a hold Marie-Louise, they knocked didn't they? She opened the door breezily, just as if it was her own door in Bazentin-Le-Petit.

'Hallo Madame. I bring you things, yes?'

'Er, what do you have soldier?'

'I have been told to bring bread and cheese and water and milk and these vegetable.'

'Thank you. Who sent you?'

'You ask who made me?'

'Yes, er ja.'

'Herr Colonel Rahm.' He visibly stiffened when he said the name.

'Thank you, soldier. Did you write to your Mother this week?'

'Write? Mother. Oh. Yes, yes, yes.' He turned red and stepped backwards. Marie-Louise stored his surprised expression, squirreling it away in case it might help her another time.

So, no one is looking for Odile and the most senior officer has sent food. Looks like enough for the two of us as well…

Marie-Louise sat down next to the little pile of groceries. She reflected on the change in fortunes from the shared room and the daily parade of the flesh to this. A comfortable hut and the soldiers actually bringing them food. Instinctively, she hid the items away, not daring to eat them yet. She saved portions in different places. Inevitably, she reasoned, this would all turn against them. This was just a punishment of a different kind. Tomorrow, she thought, the door would again burst open and she would be dragged out and tossed between the wretched soldiers until she was burnt and bleeding again, for the amusement of these awful brutes.

CHAPTER TWENTY-NINE
ON THE ALBERT-BAPAUME ROAD, AUGUST 1915

The night was cool, but not cold. The extra shawl was enough to keep me warm. If I pulled it over my head and breathed into the gap, the warm air was quite enough to keep me going. Under the shawl, my head was filled with William. He danced around me, holding me, guiding me around our little garden. His smile, his face, his clever hands pulling apart the motor bicycle and touching my arm.

Oh William, my darling boy. Why did this have to happen to us?

It was better to move at night. I was not so sure of the direction, but I was now not going to Bazentin. Instead, I would cross the fields to Martinpuich because there was something I needed to do. There was an urge driving me on, although it seemed a strange idea to risk everything for this one thing, this one impossible thing.

The little path over the field to Martinpuich was littered with wooden stakes, piles of rocks and stones. Some had been placed deliberately and some lay where they fell. The paths were deeply marked by hooves and carts. Carts heavily laden with something that always moved south. There were small camps of tents in the distance, but the ground was so flat and the ridges so gentle, that I could see them from far away and nothing happening there would trouble me.

In the early morning I reached the village and walked through the disturbed rubble and buildings towards my destination. The village was deserted, although it was clear the war had been here. Buildings were filled with equipment and the materials of war. The Germans were building here, but it was not busy, and there were very few soldiers around. There were some signs marking the distances to the locations around. It had been a battlefield, but it wasn't today.

Finally, I reached our little tool shed. It had not been disturbed, possibly since the last time that William and I were there last. It had not been used by the owner for some time. There were cobwebs and the little stools were where we had left them over a year ago. That made me sad.

Breathing in the scent of last summer, I could hear William in here, his wonderful voice that reminded me of his love. This place was possibly the last time that I would feel close to him. My feelings of love for him were was real, that much was true. But this war had pulled him from me, as if we were falling. I needed to tell him that I wanted him, in every sense. To hold me close, to touch me, to make my skin feel alive, to love me. But none of those things would be possible, perhaps ever again. I had to draw a line so that he would know that if this war had not come and pulled us apart, I was his, for always. But now, I must live the life I had been given, however much of it was left. Whatever happened from this day onwards, he needed to know that his Odile truly loved him. I had an idea.

We had always left notes for each other in the little tool shed. Silly things really, now that they sprang to mind.

If you read this before Wednesday, you can have one kiss.
If you wait until Thursday, you won't get one!

When you see Madame Bouchard, go around the back to the well.
I have a surprise there for you.
Be there before dark my love.

So I decided to leave him a letter here. If he ever made it back to France, if the army ever broke through, he would know to come here, if anything was left. It would be impossible and stupid to think a letter could survive. But somehow, it made me feel better, to be honest with my feelings and for William Collins, my boy from over the sea. I needed him to know the truth about my feelings for him. I would write it and leave it hidden. If the war came here, he might follow. I had to do it. So I tried to think only of William. Thoughts of Mother and Father and the camp drifted away. My confused and shameful thoughts for Kurt came and went. I needed him to survive and to help my parents, but even so…

There was paper here, and pencils, too. At least there had been. To my relief, they were still there. The paper looked old and stained, and the pencils nearly blunt, but they were usable. The page was blank. I hoped that my words would find their way to my love and that he would truly understand, what I felt and what I wanted to say. When I began to write, the words just poured out of my heart.

Mon William adoré,

Je ne sais pas si tu liras jamais cette lettre ou même si tu penseras à la chercher ici. Je t'ai écrit bien des fois mais je n'ai jamais trouvé le courage de t'adresser mes missives. Je crains que les lettres ne soient lues par des gens qui ne doivent pas savoir ce que je ressens, quels sont mes rêves et comment nous menions nos vies…

I read the words aloud as I wrote them.

My darling William,

I do not know if you will ever read this letter, or indeed if you will even know to look here for it. I have written to you many times and never had the courage to send them. I fear that letters are read by people that I would not wish to have knowledge of my private feelings and my daydreams of how we used to live our lives…

I looked out of the little window and imagined him coming along the road to here, most likely pushing the motor bicycle, and continued reading the rest of the letter aloud.

My dear William I do not know how to say the things that I must, that have happened to my family, and me in the last year. The terrible war so close to us and the awful sight of the Germans in our villages, with guns and swords and bombs…

I tried hard not to cry, but writing the words, the words of my family, hurt deeply, and an ache rose in my chest.

Dear William, you must know how terrible it was to be here. Everywhere there was the sound of marching and boots, horses and carts and the terrible menace of the German voices. The soldiers did not seem to wish us harm, but we did not want them in our villages. They took our food and took everything from the fields and we ate so very little in the early days.

Oh William, how could I possibly tell you of the terrible times with Thomas and the lorry? It breaks my heart and it would break yours. You need to know these things, but not here. I looked down at the page, steadied myself and continued.

Father was made to work repairing things that had been damaged in the battles. He works on the large guns and repairing carts and motor lorries. He detests utterly this work and wishes only harm on the soldiers. Because of this, they beat him and we do not receive any food. I too wish we could be rid of them, but we must make the very best of what we can.

Make the very best, William. The very best of almost nothing.

Oh William, my love, my love from over the sea. I could not live my life with so little food and my Mother and Father suffering so in the hands of the soldiers. I wish nothing but peace and to be rid of the Germans, but I do not see the war ending soon. We were moved to an awful place, little more than a camp in a field, near Cambrai. We were with other families, but it felt like a prison. We could come and go but we were always watched, our every move was recorded, or so it seemed to me.

This memory made me think of poor Amelie, but I wiped away these fresh tears and carried on.

Some of the girls seemed not to care of the war at all and frolicked openly with the Germans. They seemed to be able to get more food for their families and were given new clothing, they almost looked like German farm girls. We were always hungry, Father came home often beaten and bleeding and I could stand this no more. So I decided that I too must behave this way to get more food for our family…

I looked up again, thinking of the Collarts and the Delaitre girls. Please understand William, please will you understand? My heart was on the page just as if I had lifted it out and placed it there on the sheet.

William, do believe me when I say that I wish you were here with me now as I write this. Before I was able to become friends with the Germans in the camp, I met in the camp a young German boy, who was the same age as me. He was in the army but had softness in his voice that set him apart from the awful brutes that marched through our villages in 1914. He spoke to me in French and he told me how nice it was to meet a beautiful girl in the middle of this awful war. He gave me food for my family, he did not know my Father, but it did not matter because he was kind and we could eat. I did not have to go and dig mouldy vegetables that other families threw away anymore. He gave me a new dress and we were able to leave the camp if he was there with us, which we would often do in the evenings. William, I just wanted to feel normal again. I do hope you could understand…

Seeing the words on the page brought back thoughts of Kurt. The kindness and his care for my Father. It was for my Father.

Life is so much easier now for us. We are able to live a life and we are not hungry and beaten. My Father thinks the food is because he has promised not to shout and curse the Germans anymore. Now his family is happy, he does not need to anymore…

My hands ached with the pain of writing these words, and my heart ached with the pain of reading them. But I kept going, trying to say how I truly felt.

I have to live the life I have and not the life I may have had before the war. It has changed so much…

It was time to end the letter, to get back to my family. Carefully, I read the final sentences, where my love flowed through the pencil.

My Dear William, my heart has hurt for you so much in the last years, but it is time to let you go as it is taking away my spirit knowing you are so very far away…

Do you understand? Will you understand? Do you know how I feel? Will you know, if you read this? Suddenly, I felt foolish. William would never read this letter. Why on earth would he come here again? This was all about my own selfishness, all about making me feel better. But did I feel better? Finally, I finished reading my letter. My handwriting was terrible and tears had smudged many of the words.

I write this letter more in comfort to me I suppose as I do not think you will ever be here to read it. I can see no reason why you would.

Good luck dear friend and love Odile, August 1915

I looked at the sheet of paper, and kissed the top corner, just in case. Then I folded it and placed it on the floor, under where we always placed the stools. It was out of sight, safe as usual. In truth, it would never be read by anyone. But somehow, putting my feelings and my heart on paper made me feel so much better. A release, perhaps. Did I want a release from William? My love was as strong as ever, but I feared a doomed love, a wasted heart, as William would say. I had to let go a little, a folly of love to hope that we could be united again. I wanted to be convinced. I looked at my skirts and shawls. Time to go back, before I was missed.

CHRIS CHERRY

CHAPTER THIRTY
CAMP SEVEN, AUGUST 1915

It was not long before I was back at the camp. The roads back were clear but still avoided using them, for fear of discovery. Very little attention was paid to civilians inside the town, and it was only risky out in the open. But I had been lucky, gambling on the guards at the gate not asking too many questions. It was late afternoon, so there was sure to have been a change during the day.

'Lefebvre girl isn't it? Yes, I know you. Where have you been?'

'I was in the town on an errand. I am sorry, I tore the papers by accident, picking up some baskets.'

'Show me.'

I handed the guard the old order, which I had torn up to remove the date. It just left the time out and the signature.'

'Hmm, good. I see that you are late back. These passes are normally for four hours. Where have you been today?'

I thought of the women in the square and the state of my clothes. I was trying to think of what to say. I looked down. This was going to go badly.

'Never mind, go. I am too busy.'

An officer's car drew up at the gates. The guard saluted and opened them without another word to me. It seemed he had put me out of his mind and he would hopefully think no more of my story. The arriving officer was much more important.

Inside, I went straight to Mother. She was sitting in the corner, weeping quietly.

'Maman, it is me, Odile. I should have told you my plans, but if you knew them, then the soldiers could have punished you.'

She looked up, saying nothing, it seemed she had no energy to give.

'Maman, I am here. Is it me or is it Papa?'

'No Odile, your papa is fine. I have been worried beyond measure. Where on earth have you been?'

She stood and beckoned me to her, then held me gently.

'I went to see home. But it was not possible to reach our village. It was easier to see Martinpuich. Soldiers are there, but it is not so dangerous.'

'You put yourself in much danger. After all we have come through, you risk your life. Silly girl, Odile. Stupid. You have your father in you.'

Anger rose in me at her words, but it quickly subsided.

'I had to go, Maman. I had to let William go.'

Mother's grip on me stiffened then relaxed. She began to rub my back.

'There will be many things we need to let go before this war is over.'

'Kurt will return soon. I have not been missed.' No one seemed to care for us, except for him. It was to Kurt that I must turn for salvation from this war.

The remainder of August continued to be warm, and at times it was hot. Soldiers came and went, but for us, all we cared was that Kurt remained. He cared. He wanted us to be happy. All I needed to offer in return was a smile and company. At least for the time being, that was true.

As the days grew slowly shorter, we continued to walk out of the camp in the evenings – sometimes with Mother, sometimes without –to watch the sunset. Sometimes, he appeared preoccupied with whatever was happening in the war. But at other times, he would look at the sunset and talk of Germany, of home. Each little detail of home I reported back to Mother, in case we ever needed to use it to our advantage. I could never let my guard down with Kurt. Never allow feelings to develop. This was, as Father put it, a war of transactions, which were never in the favour of the French.

Often, Kurt would look to kiss me and I tried to make sure that I was ready. Ready to separate the transaction from the feeling. As time went on, it would become much harder to manage it. The more that Kurt cared for my family, the harder it became to see him as an enemy. Father was treated well, he worked hard too, now that he was repairing ambulances and carts for transporting the wounded instead of the big guns. Even Mother seemed to soften towards Kurt, referring to him as *that boy* and not the *German boy*, or as an officer of the invading army to be teased or fought at every opportunity.

The summer faded fast, with rains in early September. With them came renewed alarm in the camp. The British were attacking to the north and west of where we were. Father noticed the increased number of ambulances coming in, although the new ones were mostly drawn by horses. Father had been less angry with the Germans. He had no love for them, but he was a kind man and took pity on the ambulance trains. Of course, it was their fault, all of it, but not the ordinary soldier whose life might be spared with his work and care. Just so long as they didn't heal, just to go back and kill more French men.

Our life had improved, there was no doubt. Father remained convinced it was because he was working hard to repair ambulances, even though he still poured water into the fuel tanks of the other lorries. We received food as a ration and it wasn't always leftovers or mouldy, and smelling of wet soil. We did not need to queue, beg, or engage in terrible fights at the tit lorry for every crumb. It seemed that our awful life as scavengers was now far behind us. We had been under German rule for a year now. My clothes were too big and I was much thinner. Mother was drawn and tired, but we were all still alive, in this, our private war.

It was in this autumn period that Father was allowed to spend more and more time with us. We all knew that this was most unusual, a Father remaining with his family. We knew how much the Germans admired Father, despite the beatings. Their life was also made easier by him, than if they had to solve all of their own problems. Kurt saw to it directly that we were never separated. We lived apart, but every day we could see Father and he could wave to us. This was a kindness agreed with Colonel Rahm and it took courage. Perhaps it took his love as well.

The winter would mean an extra worry about keeping warm. Even with the attentions of a German soldier, we would struggle to keep warm enough. The hut leaked, it allowed the wind through the walls and the fire was small and did not let out much heat. Mother asked more directly now for supplies. She asked for wood, or coals, sometimes for extra fat, vegetables and meat. Now, she was bolder and calmer with the Germans, and often said that they were softer towards her. Occasionally, she let down her guard and even smiled. Perhaps she was less wary, the edge eroded by better treatment, or perhaps she was still playing their game, letting them feel that they were in control. I still had the sense that all of this could tumble to pieces in an instant. One incident with Father, one unguarded word and we could yet be punished. Life was still very hard, but the edge of the hill over which we might fall, now seemed a little further away each day, even if it never actually went out of sight.

At the end of November came the news that we dreaded more than almost anything. After months of settled calm and gaining a little control over our lives, we were to be moved again. Something was happening again for the Germans, we could find out nothing from them.

I tried asking Kurt one last time, the day before we were due to be moved. So that I might plan ahead, or take an advantage from this. Kurt came for me at three, just as it was getting dark. He wanted to speak to me, I could see. He was nervous and agitated. Good.

'Why are we moving again Kurt?'

'I am moving again. If you stay, you may well be transported north to a holding camp. You may be granted free passage, or you may be confined to a local village. Your treatment will not be good, given your Father's record eh?'

'Why then, are you moving?'

'It is not possible for me to say, but the army is moving south and east. I am to go to Cambrai tonight to supervise train transports for the vehicles. That is where your Father is to go. I have taken a big risk, Odile. A very big risk indeed. I have arranged for a small house to be made available to you and your Mother. It is empty, there is nothing in it at all. But it is safe. Your Father will live with us in the station.'

'A house?' My heart leapt. This was again a step further towards normality. But I also remembered the last time we were in a house. When the door had opened, and Amelie tumbled in, broken and bleeding. I had still to be on my guard.

'Go and tell your Mother. A transport will be provided in the morning. I will make sure that you are cared for. You know that I truly care for you, Odile?'

'Yes Kurt, I know.' It could not sound convincing, even to a German speaker.

'Shall we walk, Odile?'

We walked until it was fully dark and then made our way back into the camp. As each day passed, I could feel more deeply his feelings for me in his kisses. He held me tightly, and caressed my dirty and unwashed hair. Of course it made me wonder how much I gave back to him, I felt always that I was in control of my feelings. But when he kissed me, sometimes, just occasionally, it felt good and I know my embrace softened just a little.

The morning was dark and it was raining. I had not slept well, my feelings now more confused than ever before. Until now, I had felt nothing for any German, apart from feelings of hatred about Thomas and the lorry, Amelie and her broken body, the taunting of my Mother, the beating of my Father. But after leaving the letter for William, even though it would never be read by anyone, somehow something had changed. A little of me had been left in the tool shed in Martinpuich.

Kurt was very kind to the three of us. His superior, Colonel Rahm tolerated my Father and allowed Kurt his "French family", as I knew that we were now called. The soldiers did not bother us. They were new and none were left that had witnessed the shit-house cleaning or the taunting in the square. There was respect for my Father, although he still fought back occasionally.

It had been impossible to sleep because William occupied my thoughts, especially when I was afraid, or cold, or hungry. But I did not want William to only occupy my thoughts when I was upset. He calmed me, but he also inspired me. His care and love was a comfort through the difficult times. But it was becoming harder to hold on to his memory. The image of him was less bright, almost a shadow behind a curtain. He would have joined the army by now, more than likely, so perhaps he would already be trained and fighting over here.

The letter was solely for my benefit, I knew that. To capture my soul on paper. It was a dream to hold on to William. A dream that he might read my letter and hold on to his love for me. Why should he? What prospect was there now for a life in France? An unlikely one. I had to live the life I have, not the one that might have been, did I not write something like that? Yes, but I still wanted that life, wanted William. I was gambling with his love and my love for him. That was what made it impossible for me to sleep.

'Odile, my love. Quickly, we must go. At least we are not to be bundled like goods into the back of a lorry.'

Outside, a young soldier stood by the back of the cart that was to transport us to Cambrai.

'Is horse cart, bitches. You not get a lorry, fuck that.'

I froze. It was to begin again. Kurt had arranged this, but somewhere, something must have gone wrong. Kurt was kind, he was, wasn't he?

'Come on, now!'

Mother and I gripped each other by the arm. We got up and on to the cart, which moved off with a jolt. The door to Father's hut was open and it looked empty. Soldiers were rushing to and fro, and the alarm of the last few weeks had returned. It seemed that the winter of 1915 would come with one last push by our Allies to free us all from the Germans. It renewed my energy. My thoughts for William and Kurt ebbed and flowed, as if the war were being fought by these two in my own head. It felt disloyal, a betrayal of William playing out. A betrayal, even in my mind, was a betrayal all the same.

Now, I felt myself a collaborator, this was what it meant. To be French, siding with a German. They had won. The cart jolted again, bumping on the broken roads towards an uncertain future. I wanted comfort. I wanted William but it felt selfish calling to him, only wanting love when it suited me, as if my calling William took him away from his uniformed duty. In my head, he forgave me.

'Odile, what is it dear? You are whispering to yourself.'

'Sorry, Maman. I am thinking.'

'Tell me daughter, what is causing your face so much pain?'

'I have said goodbye to William.'

'Yes, I know Odile. I heard your words in your sleep.'

'You did?'

'You went away for three days without a word. You went with almost all of your clothes on your back. What on earth could you do? You came back and asked only forgiveness from him. From our English boy.'

I looked down, my world splitting at my feet.

'You must keep in with this German boy, for as long as you can. Use every chance you have, Odile. You cannot love him, he is the enemy. But he is good for us. Your Father, Odile. Remember that.'

The house in Cambrai was empty, just as Kurt had told us. We were able to find very little nearby, and were not allowed into other houses, which held soldiers and other French citizens who were being forced to work. They looked at us, almost with disgust. Some spat at us as we passed. One threw a lump of mud at Mother. She managed to move away from it as it came towards her. As it landed behind us, another came. As she turned back, it hit her fully in the face. It was then I realised that it was not mud at all, but a lump of horse dung from the street.

'You fucking whores are no better than the fucking Boche. How could you, how could you take up with these bastards?'

Mother and I hurried away, careful to avoid going straight to our house.

'Mother, oh Mother! Are you hurt, Maman?'

'Ah, it is nothing Odile, ah. This is disgusting. Oh, this is terrible. I am fine Odile, quite fine.'

Mother quickly flushed her face with water and took off her dirty dress. We had a little water and she used it to wash her clothes.

'Maman, are they right? Are we collaborators? Is this what we have become?'

'No, Odile, no! We are not collaborators. They have got us quite wrong. We were forced from our homes by these people. We were caught in a ditch by a German with a gun, daughter remember that. We have been stared at, humiliated, starved, beaten and made witness to rape. You think that makes us collaborators, that we try to manage events to our favour? A favour that simply means that we are not ourselves raped and beaten?'

'No Maman, I understand.'

'Your Father is the limit. If he had not started a row with them, we might well have been given a little blue book and be across in Switzerland by now. Remember the talk of Evian? No, we are not collaborators, child, we are survivors. And if, and if, well if those peasants want to come at me with horse... shit again, I will tell them straight and they will not call at us again.'

I had never heard Mother use that word before. I had never known her to be so upset. Perhaps that might keep us alive in this new war.

I did not see Kurt for some time. He seemed either less able, or less willing to spend time with me. Something was happening, but where and when, it was impossible to discover.

The few French citizens in Cambrai were mostly working on the transports. We knew that Father was here, but there had been no possibility of seeing him at all. That was now strictly forbidden. When we were in Bapaume, order had seemed a little chaotic and there was a space to move between the lines. Here was a military machine. There were orders, operations and the amount of transportation was enormous. The lines of lorries, carts, cars, motor bicycles, bicycles and horses were endless. In the distance we heard the constant movement of railway engines. The German Army was on the move, to where was unknown. But they were not retreating because more and more soldiers came in from the north and east. They were building up to something, of that there was no doubt at all.

One evening in early December, Kurt came to see me.

'Odile, I am sorry that I have not been to see you. I have new work with the army and I do not work with Colonel Rahm anymore. The new Kommandant here is very strict and will not tolerate us spending time with the French. But I see your Father most days. He is working on ambulances, repairing the engines and making them go. He also works on the motors, keeping them on the road. He is a mechanic, not an engineer now, ha!'

'What of us Kurt – of Mother and me?'

Kurt looked at me slightly suspiciously. Perhaps I had asked the question too quickly.

'I mean, can we stay near to you?'

'Ah, oh yes. This house is designated for prisoners of war. All French civilians here have been declared prisoners of war. From Lille and Armentieres, to north of Maubeuge. You are prisoners of war. But it is only a title, you are allowed some freedom to move.'

'So we can stay here?'

'Yes, my work is now in Cambrai and I will not be moving again, at least until we are at peace, eh?'

With a sudden realisation, it hit me that I was a collaborator. This conversation revealed to me that we might be prisoners, but we had a patron in the German Army. We were not trying to cause trouble, or fight them. We were embracing them. Even with a heart of cunning, plotting our moves. We were both playing each other. Kurt looking for comfort and home, just as we were. We were using each other. We were both collaborators.

We did not see Father at all until Christmas in 1915. The French citizens barely celebrated Christmas, merely marking the days with a nod and a whispered word.

Father brought our new papers, for Kurt had seen to it that we were to be assigned as workers. Mother and I were to work in a factory making and repairing uniform items, whilst Father was an engineering supervisor. His fire had died and he no longer taunted and tormented the Germans. He would shout and curse, but these soldiers were tough and professional. They laughed it off, and as long as he performed his daily miracles with the machines, they cared not. He was no more than a unit of labour.

Kurt was, I reasoned, a junior officer of transport. Cambrai was a central transport point, linking the German operations north and south. Most likely, he would spend his war here now, however long it was to last. It seemed now that the French and British were not coming to rescue us, so we had better just get on with it.

In the January of 1916, a new group moved into the house next door to us. They had lived nearer to Lille, a town now administered like this one. There were several families of women, sisters and cousins. There were no children with them. We were all to work in the same factory. It was the same factory as the group who had thrown horse shit at us. When they saw us, they sneered and kept away. They never threw anything else, spending their time turning away and avoiding us. Perhaps they thought that it might bring down German anger on these collaborators. It suited us just fine, all the same. The oldest of our new neighbours was a wily woman, perhaps fifty. She took no time seeking our story to see if we could be trusted.

'Didn't you get away then? From here?'

'We live further south, nearer to Albert,' Mother replied. She too, was going to work out the situation here.

'Why on earth are you caught up here then? You should be in Paris by now, enjoying the lights, ha!'

'Unfortunately, my husband was working with the French Army. We were caught by surprise near to Bapaume. They were upon us. We nearly made it away, but my husband wanted us to be with him. He did not realise that meant preventing our escape.'

'I'm sorry, truly. We were overrun as well. Well, when I say that, we refused to go. The army were slow with us.'

'How has it been?'

'Mostly we have been hostages. We had to camp in the government buildings. Used us, if truth be told. If anything went missing, or got blown up, they would punish us with starvation or beatings. One of our girls went missing. We have not seen her since.'

For a month, we all worked together. I only saw Kurt when he inspected our little house, when he was often quite formal. It worried me that he might get bored with me and cast us away to a prison camp. He often brought news of Father. The occasional water-in-the-fuel rebellion was no longer considered important and he seemed now to be just one of many mechanics. Quiet and inconspicuous. We hoped that this would be good enough to help us all survive.

January cold quickly turned into February snows. We received pay, which was a novelty, but in reality we worked only to live. By rights, Mother and I should not be there, but this was better than bartering with our bodies, clawing for survival. The food was bad and basic, but we did not have to be humiliated simply to eat. So what if I had to step out with Kurt to keep things normal? I could manage this. I was sure that William would understand, wherever he was.

152

CHAPTER THIRTY-ONE
SOMEWHERE IN BELGIUM, FEBRUARY 1916

'Stretcher-bearers! STRETCHER-BEARERS! For fuck's sake, where are you?'

We were trapped. Three of us in a little shell hole with shells landing on three sides, including behind us, the direction we needed to move towards. The only clear way out would be towards the enemy, which was no good. If we stayed here, we would be dead, so we had to move. The percussions of the shells made my whole chest rattle with involuntary grunts at every burst. Hearing the sound meant I was still alive. Lives were reckoned in minutes here, under shellfire.

The new barbed wire was designed to snag a uniform, canvas webbing, flesh, anything really. The reels we had been testing were supposed to allow the wire to pay out silently and evenly. Tonight, we had been seen and heard and the enemy had found his range on us.

I had found myself in a wiring party, tasked with assessing these new silent reels. If we made it back alive, I would make my feelings known in no uncertain terms. The wire worked well enough, we were snagged to shit. The fourth member of our party had just lost his arm up as far as his elbow, trying to unhook another snag in this new snagging wire. His hand was above the shell hole just a couple of seconds too long. A sniper had shot it off, for sport, probably.

It was bloody cold in February, and it was even colder here, because everything was wet in Belgium and froze each night onto my body. I could feel the trickle of icy water down my back, knowing it was tinged with old blood, gore, shit, mud and my own terrified salty sweat. The sounds of pain bounced around the shell hole. Stuck here, it would erode our courage, dooming us all. We had one ampoule of morphine, which was clearly not going to be enough.

'Sarge, with your permission?'

'Yes, of course, be quick man.'

I knew what was about to happen, and it could not come a moment too soon. The corporal raised his fist and sent it crashing into the side of the poor bugger's head. Not only had he just suffered the agony of an amputation, he had just received a massive blow from his best mate. Unconscious, his agonies subsided. If he was to stay alive and make it out of this war, then it would be because we thought and acted fast and because we were lucky with the shelling.

Another heavy shell landed close by, then another. They had our range, sure enough. We had to take our chances now.

'Corp, stay here with Beech for a moment. We will go ahead and try and find another spot nearer the line to call for help. We need a bearer, but no one will come this far over. When I call, come, don't fucking wait.'

'Bollocks to waiting Sarge, we will be right there. Go on now.'

I clambered up the three feet of cover the shell hole gave us. In the open, the breeze was cold and the air thick with smoke. At least it was just smoke, for gas could quickly follow and the wind was with the enemy.

I could sense bullets in the air, slicing it with a ping and a snap. Right behind us was a bigger shell hole. At the bottom was the little flag I had dropped on the way out, to guide us. We were going in the right direction.

'Corp, go!'

Immediately, their shapes appeared. Beech was semi-conscious and flapping. Perhaps knocking him out was a bad idea after all.

The two men reached us and we all fell into the new shell hole. We would have to repeat this perhaps five more times before finally reaching our lines. I looked up again, it was a risk, but we had to get back. Another shell had hit our position. It had probably landed in the hole that we had just left. This time, feeling guilty about Beech, I sent the others ahead. They found the next hole, gradually moving back, then called into our hole. The stretcher bearers assigned to us could now hear and they came straight out towards us. No stretcher at night, it was too dangerous. But they had dressings, morphine and just a little hope.

There were now six of us, in a shell hole that was just about big enough to hold us. I sent the two unwounded men back and stayed with Beech and the two bearers.

'It's his arm, he was shot.'

'He is dead, Sarge.'

'How? He was just hit in the hand. Has he bled to death already?'

'Not from his hand.'

'Oh fuck it to blazing Hell, he must have been hit again? Where?'

'Back of the head Sarge. Looks like he took a clean one for you lot.'

So that was it, a life ended, just as quickly as you could say it. We decided to drag the dead body of Rifleman George Beech of the Rifle Brigade back into our lines. We were close and it felt right to bring in our comrade. He had given his life on this little research trip. It certainly was not worth it. The Royal Engineers would learn nothing useful from tonight, except that German snipers were still excellent marksmen and the reels we used were too small, but we knew that anyway.

Back in the trench, I had to make notes from the wiring party. Apart from reporting the loss of our escort from the Rifle Brigade, I wrote down the problems with the wiring reels; we could fix them though, the wire was good, strong and certainly snagging.

It was not possible to get out of the trenches until the morning, so I made the best of the wet night with a little coldish tea and rum from a dubious source, and thoughts of my love. Odile, tonight I imagine you safe and out of this war, somewhere in the south of France. I knew that many of the citizens from around that area had been evacuated and were safe. It gave me comfort to think that she was safe. I had no news and no way of proving that, but I thought her well and it gave me solace and a barrier from this freezing air on my wet uniform.

I closed my eyes and thoughts of the dead overcame me. The faces drifting here and there. Behind them, in light from a single candle, was Odile. Pure and bathed in a yellow glow. Her Father behind her, calling her indoors, into the safety of her family.

CHRIS CHERRY

CHAPTER THIRTY-TWO
CAMBRAI, FEBRUARY 1916

The number of lorries passing through the town increased in February. There were many more soldiers arriving and leaving in trains. It was clear that the Germans were going to do something soon, but I did not know what. Kurt would not say anything and I did not ask.

Mother had calmed over the last few weeks and she no longer looked upon the Germans as tormentors. She had not forgiven them for her treatment, not a bit of it. But there was a realisation that this was to be our life and we were simply not able to fight it, not with thousands of soldiers pouring in daily.

One day, I noticed some machines in the air. I had never seen aeroplanes before and was instantly fascinated by them. The large ones, with sloping wings, flew low and around the troops. The smaller ones with straight wings kept their distance and did not fly for very long. I had no idea how they could stay in the air, and made drawings of them to show Father when we could be together.

Kurt was very attentive to me in February. With so many soldiers around, I think he felt that he needed to spend time with me. I did not mind so much, but the factory workers remained suspicious. Some thought that we were collaborating, but Mother and I knew different. Still, I felt in control, at least I had convinced myself anyway.

In the middle of February, Kurt invited me to an army concert in Cambrai. The Germans had spent a lot of effort on this entertainment, although I did not know why. Kurt and I did not go into the main seating area, but around the side, where we sat through music and some dancing. I did not like it at all and for the whole evening, felt little more than a traitor to my country. During the German singing, a new wave of anger arose in me, which must have always been there. It was a wave of disgust that this spectacle was happening in my country. Feelings that had been pushed and kicked into the shadows reappeared and must have played on my face.

'Are you quite well, Odile?'

'Yes thank you, Kurt. But please, when can we leave? It is very cold.'

'We can leave immediately, of course. Let us go when this song is over.'

A soldier seated on the other side to Kurt leaned over and touched me. He was a young officer, like Kurt, with an earnest expression, and certainly did not look like a brute. In perfect French, he said, 'It is a good concert yes?'

'Er, yes. But I am cold.'

'Cold hands, but a warm heart, eh?'

I did not reply, but looked down at my hands. They were shivering and trembling, but not just because of the cold. I looked across the expanse of soldiers, laughing and smoking. The soldier to my left, also smiling and singing. Sitting on chairs in my town, my country. How dare they? No, this was enough. I remembered then who I was and what had to be done.

'Thank you Kurt. Please take me home.'

Kurt looked shocked and clearly saddened. He had been looking forward to this moment with me, it was clear. He had taken up favours to allow us to be there in nice seats. His hand was warm and the evening was not really that cold. I hoped that he was not suspicious. If he thought that any flame between us was out, he might cast us out.

If the Germans won this war, it would be helpful to have a German on your side. But at that moment, it was not possible for me to think of the Germans winning the war. I had to fight for my country, and no matter how little I could do, I would and surely must.

At that moment, I decided that Kurt must remain on my side and I would be everything he wanted from me. If only Father could be everything that Mother and I needed him to be. It no longer mattered what the French around us thought, or said. We had been spat at by Germans, had horse shit thrown at us by French women, and would surely be despised by the women we lived amongst. William was far from me, his memory still made my bones ache, perhaps now never again to be in my life. But I had Kurt and France, Mother and Father. So, I decided there and then on that night to do what I had to for France.

On the walk home I decided to turn left at the square. Every other night, I had turned right. A step into an unknown and uncertain destination.

CHAPTER THIRTY-THREE
HEIGHTS AT VERDUN, 21 FEBRUARY 1916

The evening was very cold. Kemper and his small platoon were shivering, but exhilarated. Tonight was the last night of the old world. The morning would bring fresh hope of an end to this bloody war in France.

The train journey here had been tough. Kemper had changed trains in the town of Cambrai so that he could supervise the loading of the three guns comprising his little command. He fussed over them, some of his platoon had given them names. He thought that idea was a little absurd, but whatever kept the men happy was fine in his book.

The evening in Cambrai had been pleasant. Not too cold, coinciding with a little show for the troops. He remembered sitting with a young officer, much like him. He was sat with a little French girl. Well, perhaps not little, but unassuming. He remembered her being very attractive indeed, if a little quiet and detached from the event. Well, she was French, amongst the Germans. He was a lucky bastard, luckier than Kemper was now.

The guns were set up and had been oiled and prepared under cover of darkness. It needed to be in darkness, there still needed to be secrecy about what was to happen next morning, especially the scale and timing. Kemper sat in the dark, studying the little books accompanying the guns. As an artillery officer, he was aware of range and trajectory, the effects of wind and temperature and the little idiosyncrasies of his guns. Helga favoured a lateral pull to the left when cold. Perhaps a little defect in manufacture caused it. The correction was easy enough. He would remember. The other two guns were true, but both sometimes jammed when fired repeatedly. Dust and oil could seize the mechanism. He had good soldier gunners, who knew their jobs.

Kemper was to receive his orders at 0600 in the morning. He had to collect them from the range officer, so he made sure orders were left to wake him at 0530. From now until the morning, all he could do was keep the men busy and focused on their jobs. At 0100, he allowed himself some sleep. The weather had been terrible for days, but the wait might at last be over. He thought back to the night, just over a week ago now, at the concert. All of the faces in the crowd that night were most likely out there in front of him, huddled in the trenches, waiting for the same moment to end the war in a stroke. He thought again of the French girl who sat next to him. The one he just had to speak to, in his polished French, learned from schooldays, reading French poetry in the afternoons. What must she have made of the spectacle? Well, he had no love for the French, but no hatred either. They were all just trying to survive. She was interesting. Attractive yes, intelligent, probably. Sitting with a German, definitely, but she did not look like the easy girls in some of the towns. Despite the state of her dress, there was something about her. A little unnerving. The officer with her seemed happy enough, so that was all in order. Time to think about the bombardment.

The morning was dark and gloomy, not ideal for starting an attack. Kemper was awake by 0400, the excitement was building and the noise growing, so sleep could wait. He picked up his orders early, the target for his guns would be a bridge in the city of Verdun, as the Meuse flowed around the fortified town. He knew the range, the distance to the target and his elevation. He would allow himself nine shots to get the range and then pound the bridge until it fell. Instinctively he went again to his numbers and informed the gunners. His deputy checked his arithmetic, it was impeccable. They were ready. He recited the code words over and over.

"*Unternehmen Gericht*". This was operation judgement. Perhaps the last battle in this awful war.

He looked over the ridge, towards the quiet town of Verdun. Birds were singing a little, despite the February cold and gloom. All seemed quiet in these first rays of light of a new day. It was still dark, but the first lines of the buildings were now becoming visible, at the limit of visibility with his field-glasses. He thought again of the vast numbers of soldiers out in the trenches in front of him, between his guns and the town. He thought of the concert, the faces, the lives and the families. This was no time for reflection. This was a time to fight. Enough of the French girl and the countryside. He looked at his watch. It was 0710.

"Are we ready Lieutenant?"

"Yes, Herr Captain. We are ready".

"On my order then".

"Yes".

Kemper looked again at the walls of sleeping Verdun and back to his watch. He was instructed to lead the artillery bombardment. Upon his order, his three guns would fire, setting off the next sixty guns around him. He knew that the massive railway guns about ten miles behind him would fire first, it was to be his signal. He was interested in seeing how well they worked. He looked at his watch again, 0713. It was nearly time.

"On my mark Lieutenant".

"Yes, Herr Captain".

The boom of the railway gun behind signalled the first shot of the battle of Verdun. It took some time for the shell to reach them and pass almost overhead. He saw the splash of the shell right in the town, amongst the still quiet buildings. He looked at his watch. It was time.

"Fire".

In an instant the ground erupted and vibrated as the guns set off their charges and launched their shells into the morning. A second later, the others opened up on Verdun below. As well as his own battery's sixty, there were nearly eight hundred others, all along the battle front. After a few seconds, Kemper looked at the result of his shots. All he could see now was a cloud of dust and smoke in the town and what looked like specs of dust coming off the walls in puffs. He knew that in fact, it was large lumps of masonry blown from the outer walls, falling on the unsuspecting population, soldiers and civilians alike.

He tried hard to find the bridge through the smoke. A tiny break in the smoke revealed that the bridge was gone.

He turned back towards his gun, ready to give the next co-ordinates. He would be here with his guns, firing into the walks of the town and the French fortifications until the infantry left their trenches in around ten hours time. By then his guns would be hot, his gunners tired, their jobs done as the infantry poured forward with bayonet, bullet and a new weapon of war, a gun that poured out flames, incinerating the terrified enemy. Kemper had seen this demonstrated and it made him shudder to even think of it. Especially when he saw one malfunction and incinerate the poor bugger demonstrating it.

He looked again at the bridge, the walls, all smashed to a pile of rubble and dust. He knew that death lay beneath. Under his breath, he said simply, "I'm sorry".

CHRIS CHERRY

CHAPTER THIRTY-FOUR
CAMBRAI, FEBRUARY 1916

My step quickened. I had left Kurt a little bemused and did not want to find out if he was angry. By the morning, he would be calmer and possibly even understanding. I reached the house that was now my home, still cold, but at least dry and sheltered. By six, I would need to be in the factory, but that gave me enough time to plan my next move. Although something of an outcast at the factory, I had kept my ears open to the whisperings, and so knew exactly what to do and where to go.

At five, I left the house. It was bitterly cold and foggy, which meant no one else was on the street. I was not supposed to be out alone, but this was not the camps. Providing I did not appear suspicious, it should be undisturbed. At the pale green door, I knocked once and entered, according to the agreed instruction. I was off the street quickly, hopefully unseen and unnoticed.

Inside, the room smelled of burning wood after the fire has gone out. The ash was still smouldering, and a tiny curl of smoke rose to the chimney. A meagre fire, but it kept the one room just warm enough. It was an enviable privilege.

'Madame? Are you there, Madame?'

'Shh, keep your voice down girl! Yes I am here. Come into the back room.'

The back room was dark, cold and damp. The roof had not been touched in years and the occasional rattling from shelling had loosened some of the bricks and timbers. It provided cover for our conversation.

'So you decided to come?'

'Yes, I have made up my mind. Please help me.'

There was the sound of the drawing in of breath. A little plume of smoke emerged from the shadow.

'All in good time, little one. I need to ask you some questions first. Why?'

'Why what?'

'Why are you here now? It is a simple question, girl. I suggest you answer it.'

I sensed the presence of a second person in the room. The room was small, and it was almost possible to feel the warmth of the extra person.

'Last night, it hit me that I could not slip further from France.'

A face appeared in the dim light from the other room, but it was impossible to see who it was. The woman concealed her voice, intentionally transforming her accent.

'What happened last night?'

'I was at the concert, with the German boy, Kurt. A transport officer. The concert for the troops going south, presumably to fight the British or the French. Large numbers of them in our country, happy and smiling, going off to fight our Fathers and brothers in our own country. Initially, I thought I could cope, so that Mother, Father and I survived. Cope with a little attention for bread and to escape the beatings and humiliations. But I was wrong. This war is too big, going on for so long, it makes me afraid that I may never come back to France. I do not want to be German. If Kurt stops liking me, we may be cast back into the camps, or punished, separated or killed. It almost happened. One of them pulled a gun on Father and shot him. It was loaded, but it jammed.'

A hand stretched out. First it patted the top of my head. Then it slipped under my chin, lifting it sharply upwards.

'How do we know you can be trusted? We don't know you, you are not from this town. You could be under the spell of this German boy.'

I wanted to shout out that Kurt was kind, but he was German. It made me feel confusion and shame both at once, as well as excitement. I wanted to feel French again.

'To get us what we need, I can tolerate being with him. He is educated and he speaks in French. He likes France, respects us, our way and culture. He is an innocent in this as well, possibly.'

The hand snapped back.

'There are no innocents in this war, girl. Only them and us. Which one are you, eh?'

'I am French, and not one of them. You know what happened to us in the camps, you spoke with Mother.'

The voice softened a little.

'We need to be sure, Odile. We need to know that you can be trusted.'

'You can trust me. I am in love, not with Kurt, but with an English boy, who is lost to me. That life is gone to me now, but I want to be normal, my heart and soul cannot take much more of this suffering.'

'Very well, yes very well. Have you been with this boy?'

'Yes, we have been together for some weeks.'

'No, girl. I mean, have you *been* with this boy?'

'Oh, I see. No. Why do you ask?'

'If he wants you, it will make *him* weak. If he has had you, it makes *you* weak.'

'I understand. We kiss, occasionally. But I don't really kiss *him*.'

'You imagine that English one, yes?'

'Yes.'

'Well don't. You have to kiss this German boy as if he were the last man on earth. If you want to live, to survive, to help us, this is what you must do. Be careful, don't ever let him… Well make sure you know what you are really doing, yes?'

'Yes, Madame.'

'Your Father is very well respected. Ordinarily, you would be in a labour camp somewhere, or if you were lucky, you would be in Switzerland or in the south. He is needed by them, which makes *you* currency. Your Mother is more difficult. She gives them nothing, but her presence keeps your Father working and so they tolerate her.'

'How do you know all this?'

'There are many Kurts and many Odiles, my girl.'

'I see. What am I to do?'

'For the moment, nothing. We will have to think how best to use your special relationship with this junior transport officer, this son of a retired General no less, Helmut Langer.'

'A General?'

'Yes, you did not know?'

'No.'

'My girl, you need to grow up, and fast.'

I needed to leave for the factory as it was nearly six, and lateness was not tolerated, even for the girl of a General's son.

'Madame, I promise to do all that is asked of me for France.'

'You will, or we will all be dead, or worse. We know it is a lot for such young shoulders. Go now, do not be late. Before you go, there is someone you must see.'

As I turned to leave, the second figure moved into the light so her face was clearly visible.

'Hello Odile.'

My legs weakened and I nearly fell back in shock.

'Madame Collart! My God! And Amelie? Is she—?'

'She is safe now, with her Father. Her pain and suffering are at an end.'

Madame Collart drew me to her and embraced me gently.

'Quickly, you must go.'

I desperately wanted to see Mother and tell her of Madame Collart. But the meeting had been a secret, something planned based on whispers and rumours overheard at the factory, and it did not involve my Mother. At first, I had worried that I was meant to overhear the whispers and that perhaps it was a trap, so they could beat me for being with a German. But here, here was recognition. It must have been Madame Collart. Perhaps she had told them that I could be trusted.

Today, we were all sewing uniforms. Some had holes, tears and buttons missing. The scale was vast. These Germans were planning something big. The workers had until evening to finish the enormous pile. If we failed, we would all be punished.

The German supervisor walked amongst us checking our work. Each woman was issued with two needles, which were inspected regularly, in case work was sabotaged. Sometimes a woman would be pulled out, a seam left unsewn, or something hidden inside as a gift for the Boche. Sometimes it was a beating, sometimes it was worse. There were stories of women being deported to Germany for punishment. The work was hard, but it was indoors and mostly dry. It was infinitely better than the camps storing the homeless citizens of France.

At the end of the working day I wanted to return home quickly as my body ached with exhaustion. The movement of soldiers was reducing daily, with more and more of them gone away, to whatever front they were going to fight on. But Kurt was still here, and he came to see me as I left the factory. We took a short walk, mostly in the direction of home, in streets quieter than they had been for some time.

'Odile, it is so good to see you. Did you receive the food I sent you?'

'Yes, Kurt and thank you.'

'I have a small gift for you. It is not much, but it is all I am able to find.' He pressed a small folded piece of paper into my hands with great solemnity. It wasn't a dress, or anything practical, it was most likely a gift that helped my family not a bit.

'I don't understand the German, Kurt. What does it say?'

'It is a requisition note for furniture and coal. I will give it to you and your family. It will be enough to light a fire every day until April. Enough to have a table and chairs in both rooms. Enough to sit and to talk.'

'Thank you Kurt, thank you.' I leaned up and kissed him gently. It felt like a moment of true tenderness and it made me confused.

'Thank you Kurt. It will mean so much to Father.'

'Ah yes, your Father. I have also arranged for him to be permanently attached to the motor pool here in Cambrai. That way, you will not be moved around again. Unless we lose the war, ha! Or he punches the Colonel in the face, which would seem more likely.'

'Let us walk Kurt, I have much to thank you for.'

I was very tired, but could not sleep that night. The coal was welcome, if truth be told, but it was French labour under a German occupier that dug the coal for their fire. But I would be hated and taunted for befriending a German boy. If only they knew. If only they understood why. Just like Papa, I was a patriot but thoughts of Kurt confused me. The uniform could do me equal amounts of harm and good. The little food parcels and coal, at the cost of words and spite. But I could keep my clothes on, I could keep my clothes on for now.

But what might be the result? It was almost too much to consider, too painful. But I could not look at Kurt and hate him. It was necessary to be dutiful even though it was difficult. William was there in mind as well, silent but beautiful. If only this awful war had not seared new lines on my heart. William, dearest English boy from over the sea. Perhaps you are with a French girl, giving her coal and bread. You are not here and that is that.

I lay back on my comfortable bed, one not crawling with lice or chewed by rats or mice. My blouse was buttoned to the top, if you please, no longer a tool of the camp. But I would have to be careful, being balanced between Kurt and life, or rejection and misery. I had seen enough misery and did not like it one little bit. But I was also a patriot, and could not let soft sentiment win. Kurt was a means to an end for my Mother and Father. Yes, he was just a means to an end.

My Mother slept soundly, breathing softly, with hands bruised and sore. But this time it was from working, not from the beating of a fat pig German soldier. That was better, and I had to hold on to that. Kurt was useful; he was only convenience. I tried to sleep but visions of Amelie Collart, her face streaked with blood and tears, came into my head. Then William came and took Amelie away, bathing her face in warm water. He placed his hand on my cold arm and I brushed the back of his hand as I used to do.

CHRIS CHERRY

CHAPTER THIRTY-FIVE
CAMBRAI, FEBRUARY 1916

Father was allowed a visit today. The Germans were pleased with his work. He still occasionally shouted at them for being incompetent fools, but his belly was full as were ours. He imagined his work earned these rewards. Ambulances were easily repaired and back on the road, no Frenchmen hurt doing that, well no more than through any other forced labour. At least he wasn't making shells. He never worked on guns, and thanks to Kurt, would not be expected to. This war was not ending soon, that was certain. The first waves of protest and rebellion had to give way to some acceptance, if not agreement. In the occupied areas, the citizens had to give way to the army, if only for self-preservation.

When Father came, I spent some time just sitting with him. We talked of machines and of home. It was difficult for him, visiting so infrequently. He tried to cover it up, but it was clearly upsetting for him. But at least he could still see his family. I wanted to tell him of Madame Collart, but dared not. Her presence here seemed to be unknown. Several times, I had almost told Mother, but managed to change the subject quickly. It felt wrong keeping secrets from Mother, but this one was essential, for if she knew nothing, then nothing could happen to her.

I stood up and kissed Father and left him with Mother.

'Such a good girl, Odile. Such a good girl, my little miracle.'

'Oh Papa.'

Once the door was closed, my stomach turned over. Father was such a mess, he was so dear to me and it made me happy that he was alive and with us. But I could still see that gun aimed at his head. My parents must never know, for the sake of their safety.

As was usual now, I hurried to the green door, knocked and entered. Madame Collart was waiting for me in the back room. On the fire was a little of our coal, and I handed her a small loaf that Kurt had given me, as if it were nothing. It was everything to Madame Collart.

'Bless you, Odile. Did you find out what we needed? Were you able to get him alone?'

'Not yet, Madame. But tonight we are going to the square to celebrate some unknown thing that went on today. I will ask then.'

'Good. Be careful, this is important. Will you come back here tonight?'

'If I can, yes.'

'Whatever you can find out will help. You know it is very bad in Verdun?'

These words cut me deeply. The French town was under siege and it was a horrible place to be a French soldier. Madame Collart knew it more than anyone.

'Yes, it is very bad there, Madame Collart. I will try my best.'

When I left to find Kurt, I took a deep breath, summoning enough courage to behave as if I had not a care in the world. I turned the corner towards the square, straight into a fist.

'You tramp, you whore. Fuck the Germans will you? Well I am going to teach you a lesson, you little slut. Don't you know what it is like for our boys in Verdun? Course you fucking don't. Too busy with a fucking German pig.'

The spit with the word pig hit me in the eye, blinding me with its sticky foulness. There was a sound of running water near me and I knew they were about to throw urine on me. I turned away from the sound, but still felt the warm wetness on my back. Terrifyingly, the figures instantly melted away, as if they had never been there. The unmistakable sound of German voices, laughing loudly were coming towards me. Two figures appeared, one outstretched an arm.

'Ah, miss. You fall, I help. Good?'

'Thank you, sir.' I spoke in German, trying to sound calm.

'No break yes?'

'Yes, no break. Thank you.'

The two soldiers resumed their conversation without another word and did not look back. I got up quickly, the stinking wet patch now cold and clinging to my back. It would be fine. My face ached, but was hopefully not bruised. At least, not yet. It took all my nerve to walk calmly, my head up, looking for Kurt in the crowd of uniforms.

'Odile, over here!'

'Kurt, it is so good to see you.'

Kurt squeezed my arms and smiled earnestly into my face. Hopefully, he would not put his hand on my back. I backed away slightly.

'Is there anything wrong?'

'No, no. Just a little tired from work.'

'Ah, your ticket for being here, unfortunately.'

'All the same, it is tiring, that's all.'

Across the street were three women watching suspiciously. I knew how it looked. A tramp fucking a German, eh? What did they know! It was understood though, that from now the enemy was my friend and my friend now an enemy. I would need to look both ways, all the time.

'Kurt, help me with something, please? The German uniforms are so very smart, I work on them all day, but I do not understand why they are all so different.'

'Ha! Yes, that is easy. Look. See. These here are infantry. You can tell by the jackets. Then, the knots on the bayonet are companies, can you see the colours? That means these men are the fifty-fifth infantry. They are about to go out to Verdun. There are three divisions here, going out tomorrow.'

Odile smiled and nodded, careful not to appear interested in anything more than colours and petty details in connection with her daily labour.

'And what about those men over there, why do they have such ornamental helmets?'

'Prussians. These ones are professionals from before the war started. Most of the others joined after the war began. They are with Guards, there is a division of those going tomorrow as well.'

'Oh, such a lot of men! How many men is that?'

Kurt looked at me and narrowed his eyes, just for a second. I had to be careful.

'All together, perhaps fifteen thousand men.'

I was shocked at the numbers, but tried not to let it show as Kurt was scrutinising my face.

'My goodness, that is such a lot of young men to be away from their Mothers, and perhaps also away from their sweethearts.' I gazed up at him, with as much concern on my face as it was possible to muster.

His expression softened. Perhaps he thought it was idle chatter after all.

'It is unfortunate about Verdun, it is such a big battle with the French. I wish it could be different, and not like this.'

Oh, me too Kurt. I wish you would all go home to Germany and let me live my life.

'It is not your fault Kurt. Here, let us walk to keep warm.'

'Ah, but it is time for me to go, Odile. It is this troop movement.'

He looked at me, kissed me, and went away. Our meeting had been so brief tonight. After ten paces, he turned and smiled. His wave seemed happy enough, and hopefully he suspected nothing. He often had to leave after a short time, it was just this was so quick, worryingly brief. Absurdly, I hoped it was not to go and see another girl.

Immediately, I hurried to Madame Collart. The other woman was there too, but her name was never given to me.

'This is good information Odile, well done. Fifteen thousand. It is more than usual. Either they are increasing the attack, or they are losing a lot of men. Hopefully, it is the second reason.'

Back outside, the evening was gloomy. The year was turning, but it was still cold. As I reached the street with our little house, my door opened. Two soldiers came out. I stopped, instantly paralysed and terrified. Kurt. He had been suspicious and it was now all over. We were dead, or worse. Instead, they both smiled and left with a tap on their helmets. Inside, my Mother was unwrapping a canvas bag.

'Your Father has earned a little treat, Odile. We have some books and a little fresh milk. The soldiers came to collect your Father, but he had already gone back.'

I breathed out. The sound of relief was overheard by Mother.

'Whatever it is, Odile, do not tell me. Just be careful with that boy.'

That boy, these Germans, this war. There was no joy in this life. I thought of Amelie. Be strong, be strong for all the Amelies.

For the next week, Kurt was hardly about, but now I was known in the town, it was possible to move about more freely without causing suspicion in the Germans. Some of the French ignored me, some even turning their backs. Others who did not know me smiled or passed the time of day, as if nothing had happened to any of us. Were we accepting this new administration? Had they forgotten the soldiers at the Front? No, they were all surviving like us, making the best of it.

Today, I was going to use the requisition slip to get a little extra coal. Some for Mother and home, some for Madame Collart in the little house with the green door. The stores officer was old and fat, another of the administrative soldiers. He was no fool, but he was kind. Kindness in a German uniform seemed scarce in northern France.

'Ah, Mademoiselle Lefebvre. How is you today?'

'I am well, sir. A little cold still, the year has not yet become spring.'

'It is coming, ha ha! Here, your requisition. There is also a note here to give you some wood. Can you carry it?'

'Yes, thank you. This is most kind.'

'It is my orders, mademoiselle. You are lucky.'

I smiled, gathered up the bag of coal and wood, ready to hurry straight home. Coal and wood were scarce and valuable goods. People would kill for coal, the rules were torn up under administration and everyone was cold, hungry and frightened.

Madame Collart had perhaps arranged for some protection for me. Although I never saw anyone on the empty streets, it felt like an unseen protector followed me home. Either that, or someone was spying on me for a reason not known to me.

The numbers of soldiers we saw in the town continued to fall. Whatever movements had been made east had long since been completed. Lorries and ambulances were fewer and Father became more involved in repairing staff cars and farm carts, which he detested.

In mid-April, the weather improved. The air was warmer and we had less need for coal and wood. This meant fewer trips for coal, which meant less chance of being attacked, robbed or beaten for being a tramp for the Germans.

More often than not, I found myself knocking on the pale green door, giving Madame Collart as much information as I could about the Germans, their movements and what Father was working on. Where the information went, I did not know. Madame Collart was a tough woman, and she seemed to know everything and everyone, although it was unclear how she had got here without arousing suspicion. This made me curious, but it had never felt the right time to ask.

'Odile, I need to ask you a strange question. One that you may not wish to answer.'

This took me aback slightly, but it also intrigued me.

'Yes of course, Madame.'

'Do you trust your Mother? Truly trust her not to be weak with the Germans?'

Mother had stood up to being provoked, survived the lorry with Madame Collart and she had taken her turn at the lorry with the dreadful Thomas. Why would she ask this now?

'Yes of course I trust her.'

'Think hard, Odile. Would you trust her to know about me and the things we do here?'

One word of this would be death to all of us, but Mother would be included anyway, even if she did not know any of this.

'Yes, Madame. With my own life.'

'Very well. You had better bring her here. Tonight after work and after dark. We will be watching for you.'

From the time the factory closed until dark, Mother always rested in the small chair that Kurt had requisitioned – no doubt from some poor farmer in the fields. The subject had to be brought up carefully, so as not to terrify her with news of my secret life for almost two months.

'Maman, there is something we need to talk about. Will you allow me to speak of my life in the past weeks, since the concert in the town?'

Mother seemed a little stunned at first, then she sat forward, rubbing her tired eyes.

'What is it Odile. Please tell me, my love.'

'First, there is someone here in Cambrai who needs to meet you. Will you come and see them tonight?'

Mother looked very suspicious. Did she fear that her own daughter was to lead her into some kind of trap? It was written on her face.

'Who, where? What is this, you are making no sense?'

'Will you trust me Mother?'

'Yes of course. Is it to meet a German? What have you done, Odile? Are you in some kind of trouble?' Her eyes fell to my stomach.

'Oh my goodness, no Maman. But will you come?'

'When?'

'After dark.'

'Oh, Odile, what has happened? You should have told me. Something is very wrong isn't it?'

We waited until it was completely dark. Mother was strong, but she was worried that she could not protect us. Her worry for Father had lessened in the last months, but we were vulnerable and exposed here. Being friends with a German, whatever the reasons, made us a target for both the French and the Germans. But we had other friends now. Secret friends in the shadows.

'Come on Maman, we must go now.'

'Odile, I am worried out of my skin to know what has happened.'

'It is all fine, you will see.'

We moved out of the house. Across the road was the figure of an older man, smoking in the street. He was the civilian supervisor of the factory where we worked. When he saw us, he dropped the cigarette and stamped on it twice, then turned away. He must have known that we had seen him, but he made no attempt to come to us or to move away. His gaze was fixed on us all the way to the corner of the street.

We moved quickly across the mud-covered road into the shadow of the houses. On the corner we turned into the street with the pale green door. Mother was behind me, holding my arm, with me leading her as if I were the Mother. My turn, Maman, to take the lead. You have protected me enough in this war. Now it is my turn.

'We go in here, Maman.'

I halted at the green door, knocked twice and went in. Twice meant that there were two of us. It made me wonder suddenly why the factory supervisor needed to stamp on his cigarette twice.

'Madame? Madame? Are you there?'

'In here Odile, let your Mother come first.'

Mother's head lifted to the sound. Her face brightened in an instant.

'That voice! Madame, it cannot be, Madame Collart?'

'Madame Lefebvre, dearest Marie-Louise, it is me.'

'Oh my goodness. Is Amelie with... is she?'

'Amelie is at peace, Madame Lefebvre.'

Mother put her hand to her face, tears forming in the lamplight made her eyes shine.

'Oh no, the poor child. The poor child taken like that. May I ask how you are here?'

'You should both sit. The day you left us at the roadside is still as vivid to me as any other. The Germans had no idea who we were, or why we had been brought back from the borders. They had orders to protect you both, but not us. The soldier that moved us on told us so. He told us to get away from the camp, as he had no orders to protect two stray tramps.'

'Oh, Madame Collart, that is so terrible.' Mother had closed her eyes, perhaps trying to cover the shame she no doubt felt for her friend.

'No matter. The freedom meant we could follow the road to Cambrai. Bapaume was unknown to me, but Cambrai was a little familiar. We walked in our bare feet, and Amelie was in a bad way.'

Mother leaned over and laid her hands over Madame Collart's hands. Although her words sounded strong, her eyes told another story. She blinked and continued her story.

'As we walked, Amelie would talk of God and Heaven, asking whether the angels would come for her. It made me want to cry, but I could not. My Amelie was slipping from me. The Germans had taken my husband and my daughter, and there was no news of my son. We reached Cambrai and slept in the street, taking food from the army stores at night. The Germans are very predictable and sometimes they do not notice a woman.'

Madame Collart's hands moved to her face, dabbing her cheeks, it made my stomach churn thinking of what these Germans had done to this poor brave woman and her family.

'Amelie was very ill. I was not sure if it was a physical thing or in her head. She would take a little water, but she refused food. I managed to break into an unused house, hoping to find a doctor. But as she lay back in my arms to rest, it was clear to me that she would not live through the night.'

Madame Collart drew a long shuddering breath.

'I was right.' Her face dropped and tears splashed from her face onto her hands. 'You know, I have never really cried like this. I am sorry.'

'Oh Madame, do not apologise.' Mother drew her close. 'You must tell the story, it will help.'

Maman took her hand, their fingers entwining, as if encouraging Madame Collart to go on.

'There was nothing to cover my poor daughter, and I had to leave her there on the floor. Outside, I found an old French man and asked for help. It was a risk, but he returned with another man. They took Amelie away and told me she would be buried, not properly, but well enough.'

'Oh, poor Amelie. Poor Madame. I am so sorry for you.'

Madame Collart looked up briefly. 'There was nothing else to be done. Because I had no papers there was a risk of me being treated as a spy, so the two men arranged for me to come here. I have been here ever since, living in the shadows.'

'My poor woman. What do you need from me – you have only to say the word?'

'I need to be you, for a short time. There are some things that need to be done now. I need papers and we are of similar age. To someone who does not know us, it will not raise suspicion.'

'What are you to do?'

'Will you let me have your papers?'

'Yes, of course. Anything to help. But tell me why?'

'After, maybe. After.'

'Very well. But you must not cause the Germans to come for us, Madame. After all we have been through, all of us.'

'It will be fine. I just need to be able to move outside in safety. There are many looking for us in the shadows.'

My Mother nodded. 'Very well. When?'

'Bring the papers to me tomorrow, after the factory. The manager there knows to see you out early. You saw him tonight?'

'We did.' My mind went back to the man putting out his cigarette with two stamps.

'He is one of us.'

'Us?'

'Patriots, Madame Lefebvre. I, for one look forward to a day without the Germans in our towns.'

'But what can we do, so few of us?'

'Something, enough. All we can. We must try. Our brothers and husbands are fighting and so should we.'

Mother appeared to resign herself to the cause.

'Yes, we should do something, but will the result be worth the price? Probably not.'

'Have faith, Marie-Louise. Until tomorrow then.'

CHAPTER THIRTY-SIX
NORTHERN FRANCE, APRIL 1916

It was a fanciful idea. The notion of attacking an enemy, from behind, with fewer men than it took to clean the latrines. Somehow, it could work, we were just worried that our equipment would not be up to the job. Anyway, I was out of the trenches and that was fine by me.

All this time, Odile had occupied my mind constantly. The unfairness of separation played heavily on me and fuelled a growing resentment at the enemy occupying France. Compounded by the ineffectiveness of our actions, it drove me to keep working, if only to get my life back. I thought often of the hills and valleys of France. The careless days riding precariously about the villages near Albert were given equal priority in my mind. So it was essential to do these things. My injured back ached so I rubbed it, threw my pen down, and went to the window.

'I don't know if this is possible, Odile. Can my heart survive the pounding of the war hooves on my chest? The devil may come for me and he could take me, if you were not there to find me.'

Perhaps there was an undiscovered ether that would transmit my words, but it was a ridiculous notion. Reality had to win this game in my head.

'Odile, I still imagine you safe in the south. Somehow, the south sounds like a sunnier place. It is good to think of you there. You cannot hear me, but if my words can float and have existence in the real world, may they carry to you. Those months in France were my happiest and I fight for no cause other than your love, your care and your touch. I am coming for you my angel, and hopefully you will be there. I will do all in my power to reach you, my love.'

'Major Collins, sir? Is everything alright?'

'Ah Serjeant Watkins. Yes, yes, thank you. I have been reading your army service record.'

'You have sir? Is there a problem?'

'Problem? Goodness no! It says here that you are the most contemptible of the Old Contemptibles.'

'I am a regular sir, the army has been my life, there's nothing else known to me outside of it. All that's lined up for me is to die as a soldier, dunno where or when, but it will be in uniform. Likely straight at the enemy, sir, with my arse on fire.'

'Ha, I can believe it. May I ask you something that may at first appear to be strange?'

Watkins looked puzzled, took a second to answer, but stiffened up as if the order had registered at last.'

'Anything, sir.'

'What do you want in life?'

'That is not at all strange! To do my duty, to set about the enemy and give him what for. I will do as ordered, and take my men with me, right into the heart of it, if needs be.'

'Would you be willing to try something a little different?'

'Always up for new ideas sir'

'Watkins, there is something we should discuss. Will you walk with me?'

We stepped outside into the sunshine. The days were getting longer and the attack, whatever it was to be, was surely getting closer.

We walked and talked. I introduced my ideas and Watkins did not laugh. In fact, he seemed to like the ideas and found them clever.

'But sir, can we actually do it? With so few men?'

'There are sixty like us, Watkins, I have every confidence.'

I looked towards the grass. Pushing up near the trees was a small bush, covered in leaves and buds, and bearing a solitary red rose. I crossed over to take in its scent.

'Beautiful, this time of year, sir. Makes me think of the forest and the wild roses that grow by the roadside.'

'Must be an early spring-flowering variety.'

I picked it and carried it back into my little room. In an army mug with a drop of water, it looked out of place. I spoke to the rose as if it were Odile herself.

'A rose, Odile. A spring rose for my love. Will I ever be able to give you a rose like this?'

A warm glow came over me, as if someone had laid a blanket over me and drawn it tight. It made me feel better to think it was Odile, somehow embracing me across the distance, and holding me tight.

The little rose dropped a petal, which gently spiralled down to the floor.

CHAPTER THIRTY-SEVEN, APRIL 1916

Mother sat in the darkness in silence. Madame Collart's story had been so desperate. Perhaps she wanted the shock of it to encourage Mother to help. It was impossible for me to stop thinking of poor Amelie and of her last hours of pain and suffering, and there was nothing any of us could have done to help. We had nothing, could get nothing, could do nothing. But enough was enough. Amelie was the last of us to be taken without our exacting revenge on these brutes. It made me determined to take extra care when spending time with Kurt.

Only minutes after arriving at the factory the next day, Mother was unexpectedly summoned into the office by the supervisor. He did this very publicly, in front of the German administrator.

'What do you call this, hmm? This is the worst work I have EVER seen. Don't look at the floor, you useless woman, look at ME! See here? These seams? They would not hold five coins. What are you trying to do? Get me in trouble, is that your plan? Look at ME!'

'I am most terribly sorry, I, er—'

'What? What? Did you say you were SORRY? You think sorry is going to work? Get out the back and make up the boxes, you will no longer have the honour of making the uniforms. Out with you! NOW!'

My Mother fled out the back. It was hard to tell whether this was real, or part of the plan. The man's anger had seemed real enough – perhaps we had been victim to a cruel deception.

Mother was gone for the rest of the day, with no word and no sound. The box room was always hot. No other workers were allowed in, and everyone seemed to think this was a punishment for Mother. Mostly though, they appeared too terrified to go in anyway, perhaps in case some of the blame reflected on them.

She reappeared just before we were allowed home for the day, later than usual, and it was almost dark. We were all tired, hungry and upset for Mother. The other women came around her. It made me happy to see that. We had got used to so much abuse from the French for my friendship with Kurt. At home, Mother told me what had happened. The supervisor had taken Mother's papers and gone to Madame Collart. Whatever Madame had done, she had taken all day and some of the evening to do it. She was late, and so we were held back.

'The supervisor kissed my hand and apologised for shouting at me. He said it had to be unexpected for the shock to work. It certainly did that!'

'What do you think Madame Collart did all day?'

'I do not know, we may never know, but my papers came back with a blood-red finger mark on them.

CHAPTER THIRTY-EIGHT
CAMBRAI, APRIL 1916

There was a knock on the pale green door and it opened.

'It is Bourdin, Madame, with the papers.'

'Ah, thank you Emile. How was Madame Lefebvre?'

'Perhaps I overdid it slightly. She was in tears, very hurt and upset by the look of her.'

'Good, well good for the plan, of course. She is out of sight, like you said?'

'Yes, she is in the box room as planned. No Germans go in there, it is too dirty, hot and uncomfortable. She is making boxes slowly, as instructed. You have four hours before there is a break. If you are longer, it may be difficult if there is an inspection. I should be able to cover you if you go now. Here are the papers. Remember, it is her life right there. Take care of them.'

'Of course. That family is almost all I have left.'

They both stood, ready to leave.

'For Amelie?'

'For Amelie. And Francois.'

'Of course.'

Madame Collart stepped out. It was the first time that she had been out in weeks. Her first time in daylight since she arrived in Cambrai.

She hoped that she would not be noticed. It was getting warm and she was wearing two coats and two pairs of gloves, gambling on soldiers not being expert in female fashions, or even noticing what she was wearing.

At the corner, she turned towards the canal and walked as fast as possible. Moving about the town was not a problem, but outside was more restricted. She could get stopped at any point and her reasons for hurrying out of town were unconvincing, she had to admit.

There were two hours to complete her task. It was always going to be tight, even though she had planned every detail. But sometimes chance plays a card that cannot be counted. At the canal, the road forked. To the right was the road to Arras, to the left was the road to the Somme Valley. She turned right, not stopping to look. On both sides, soldiers passed, but all appeared preoccupied with their own military business, resting, or smoking in the street. Not one looked up, or called out. Madame Collart was relieved that she no longer turned heads. Unnoticed was good for a French woman amongst German soldiers.

Along the canal, two figures came into view, exactly where she expected them. Both limped towards her, slowly dragging themselves to the agreed meeting point. Under the shade of the overgrown bushes, they would be out of sight of any casual passer-by. On the other side of the road, another figure lit a cigarette and leaned against a damaged tree. Curls of smoke rose into the air.

'Madame, do you have it?'

'Yes.'

Madame Collart slowly took off her right glove. Wrapped around her middle finger was a tiny sheet of yellow paper. The trio looked around once more before she took the paper and handed it over. The taller of the two men took the sheet from her and placed it on his own finger. Then, he placed his wedding ring over it, so it was almost unnoticeable.

'It took three lives to get this to you. It had better be worth it.'

'Madame, if it contains what we hope, it might change the course of this war.'

'Then, very good Monsieur. The next one, will be the last one, I think. When shall I expect to receive it?'

'We have not had contact with George in the last three weeks. It may mean nothing, it may mean everything. But this paper, Madame, this one is the key to all of this. Look to the skies, but stay away from the movements, you understand? Tell no one directly, but keep the citizens away.'

Madame Collart nodded slowly and turned to leave. Whatever the fragment of paper contained seemed to mean everything to these two men. Before starting back along the canal, she took out Madame Lefebvre's papers and studied them hard. The face in the picture was thinner than hers, but their hair was almost the same, she had planned for that. Her own bosom was bigger, she knew that, had needed it often. Perhaps she would need it again.

At the top of the bank, she rejoined the pathway. She never looked back, must not look back, but felt the presence of eyes upon her. Hopefully, it was not German soldiers, curious as to her intentions.

The town had occasionally been shelled by the Allies. The railway station and German camps were bombed frequently. Their little town, the city of the French, was not bombed. It might well be because the Allies knew where the French were, because of the little messages given to the French and British armies. Madame Collart did not know how these messages made it, but knew that some did, had to. Her duty was to France and to the memory of her beautiful dead family. As she hurried through the streets, she wondered which ones Hugo had walked down, so eager to join the army. Hugo was the first of her family to become caught up in the war.

'Hugo, my little boy. Be strong for your Maman.'

But for now, she must not worry, must not give away her sorrow and her fear for her son, not now. She pushed on, not yet late, but the quicker this was over the better. At the corner of the square, the most dangerous part of the walk back, her heart almost stopped as her arm was tugged back.

'Where is you go, woman?'

The soldier looked to be the same age as Amelie had been. She wanted to force her fist into his chest and pull out his heart. But all she could see was Hugo. He was no more a brute than her own dear son. She softened slightly, her voice betraying just a slight irritation at being detained.

'I am going back to the factory. I needed to take a walk to help my poor back, you see, my back?'

'Back? What is?'

'Here.' Madame pointed to her back, near her bottom. She was hoping the embarrassment would be sufficient to end the conversation quickly.

'Ah, walking. Papers?'

Under the German rules of the administration, any German soldier had the right to detain a French citizen and ask for papers. But they had to have a reason, not just ask for spite, revenge or as a game.

'Here, what have I done, soldier?' Madame Collart put on her Motherly voice, trying to gain some control in this conversation.

'Nothing, I think.'

He looked at her papers and handed them back. He turned away and did not look again at Madame Collart. She did not stop for a second longer than it took to put her papers back in her tiny pocket before moving off. It nagged at her that her expression had given something away, but the soldier was perhaps just curious and a pain in her back was enough reason for a pained expression. So she hoped.

At the last alleyway, she decided on a short cut back to the factory. It was not on the agreed route, but her alarm made her want to get back quickly. The alley was quite full of rubble and broken timbers from earlier bombing. It had not been cleared, as the buildings were only lightly damaged and the labour could not be spared. Madame Collart was still distracted by the scene in the square, and took little care where she stepped.

Her foot gave way from underneath her. The boots she wore were as rotten as any others and the sole split from the heel. She tumbled forward and was hit on the head by a falling wooden beam. Despite her best efforts at silence, she let out a pained scream. As she fell, the papers of Madame Lefebvre fell from her pocket. As the world spun around her, Madame Collart thought that today was the day she would die. Unable to move, her body was hot and the pain flowed in waves.

At almost the same time, a hand reached out and hauled her free. She could make out the figure only as an outline against the sun. She did not hear any words, but her whole body rose almost in one movement. Quickly, she was moved forwards, stumbling on her painful, naked foot. The hand was insistent, not letting her stop for a moment. At the end of the alley, she was pushed into a doorway and then to the floor, expecting nothing but a painful, tortured death.

'Madame, stay quiet, we might be lucky. There is a bombing raid starting on the railway. Keep still. Your head is cut, but it is not too bad. Your foot is, probably sprained. You might need new boots, ha ha!'

Madame Collart thought the voice was a friendly French one, but that could not be right. Through her pain and the gloom, she focused on the arm that had freed her from the alley. It was the smoking man from the canal! He was the eyes upon her and had followed her here.

Her body relaxed. She took hold of his arm, almost an embrace, seeing a rough hand, scarred and burned. Now, she felt safe and her hand automatically went to the little secret pocket of her dress. The pocket was empty.

'The papers. Oh no, the papers!'

'What papers? Yours?'

'Yes, well no. I have false papers. No, they are not false. They are real, but not mine. They belong to a friend here.'

'The fall?'

'Yes, it must have been. I put them back after the square.'

'We must get them back, or your friend will be in serious trouble. Wait here.'

He left to go back out into the light. There were sounds of timbers being moved, of aeroplanes above and soldiers running in the street. There were voices in the alley. German and French. It seemed to be a conversation, but the German was too fast to understand. Perhaps it was laughter? Perhaps not. Suddenly, the ground heaved and a storm of dust and hot air rushed into the little darkened room. Splinters of wood and chips of rubble splattered into the wall of the open door, followed by an eerie silence. The German voices faded away, the only sound being like raindrops, raindrops of rubble, falling into the space outside.

Madame Collart had to move, she had to go now. Staying without papers might mean death. She had no status in Cambrai, and declaring her papers lost was insufficient for the Kommandant here, with the French Mayor being little more than a puppet. She had to find Madame Lefebvre's papers and get back.

Outside, her eyes ached in the sun. In the alley, she saw a scene that made her pained body gasp, the outlines of three bodies, all together. Two Germans in clean uniforms, both dead. One struck on the head, the other killed by a piece of metal lodged in the small of his back. The third was her French rescuer, his face blackened, killed by flying stones or metal. In his hand, were the little identification papers, folded neatly.

Madame Collart took them, quickly placing them back in her little pocket. She crawled from the alley into the street. Her head still ached and the pain came in drumbeats, preventing her from thinking clearly. In the street, mercifully, French citizens were audible and she called to them for help.

They dragged the body of the French man from the scene, leaving the two Germans behind. They made sure his papers were in order and then tended to Madame Collart. One of the men asked her name. But Madame Collart never wanted to say the name out loud. To say it would be a lie. Papers can deceive better than any voice, so she passed over the identity papers instead.

'I know Madame Lefebvre! You are not her?'

'Oh, Lefebvre? Oh dear. Well, perhaps our papers were mixed up. The factory cloakroom is very small. I have done it often, by mistake.'

The French face was kindly, but unconvinced. Even so, he placed the papers back in Madame Collart's hand and no more was said on the matter. She was lifted to her feet and found she was able to hobble, unaided.

'Time to get home now, I will be quite well, thank you.'

'I will come with you Madame.'

'Oh no, it is no trouble. I will be able to walk home by myself.'

'Very well, Madame... Lefebvre.'

They shared a nervous smile and parted. The factory was just across the street. In the entrance, a friendly face spotted her and came over to assist.

'Madame Collart, were you in the explosion there?'

'Yes, Michel, I was.'

'We must get you home, you are overdue.'

At the pale green door, Madame Collart knocked once and entered alone. In the cool of the room, she sat upon the small stool by the fireplace. Before saying anything to anyone, she let the years of frightened anger surface, just for once. Thoughts of Amelie, Francois and Hugo in her painful, bruised head. The tears felt cleansing, washing away the dirty grime of the war, at least for today. A strong arm was placed on her shoulder, it squeezed her flesh a tiny, almost imperceptible amount.

'I must have the papers, Madame, I am sorry to ask.'

The door closed, Madame Collart was alone now with her thoughts. She slumped forwards onto the table, the tears dripping from her face and pooling on the unswept stone floor.

Tomorrow, she might have to do this all again.

.

CHAPTER THIRTY-NINE
CAMBRAI, APRIL 1916

After the busy movements in February, the German Army came and went in quite regular routines. Lorries, cars, motor bicycles, cycles and carts came and went in patterns. I began to understand the uniforms, the numbers and the language better. Kurt was attentive and appreciative of my company still. It was obvious that he thought himself in love with me. For my part, my feelings for Kurt were uncertain. Every time we were together, it was necessary for me to focus hard on everything that I said to him. My language shielded what I said, which meant being extra careful with my words. That seemed convincing enough. But I would not speak German to him, ever, and I reminded him of our pact at the water pump, that I would teach him French.

Kurt kept his side of the arrangement. Father worked on ambulances and carts, we were fed and housed. My behaviour was so convincing that almost every day, something would be thrown at me. I just hoped it was mud or horse droppings. Stones hurt, words did not, but human waste hurt most of all. Mother was struck by a bucket of vomit. The bucket cut her lip quite badly and the foul fluid burnt her eyes. But it only served to make us all the more resolved to our work in the shadows. Now it was all for the Collart family. I would step out with Kurt for the Lefebvre family and to provide cover for our work. Everything else that I did was for poor Amelie. Had circumstances been different, I am sure we could have been friends.

As the year turned, we noticed changes in the movements of the Germans. More troops began to arrive, more carts and horses, more droppings to be flung and less time spent with Kurt.

'Odile, you may have seen the army is moving again. Something is to happen soon, there are changes afoot. I must go south for some time. Not too long. You can all stay here, for I will be back soon enough.'

'What is to happen Kurt?'

'It seems the English are planning an attack.'

'The English?'

'Well, British, yes. They are in Albert and moving in more troops. I think perhaps that makes you happy?'

'There is nothing to do, except live my life here. Whatever happens, will happen. To you and to me.'

Kurt smiled a tight smile and was gone. For how long, it was impossible to guess.

The railway lines and the station were now being bombed by aeroplane almost every day. The morning stillness was broken with the sounds of engines, whistles and explosions. None of the bombs ever fell near where we were. Clearly, they knew of our presence and tried not to hit our homes. I wished that they would hit the factory, but they never did. Sometimes aeroplanes chased after one another in the sky, sometimes they were hit and fell to the ground. I was sure the men would be killed. But despite the bombing, we were not moved and we were told to carry on with our work, as if nothing was happening.

Occasionally Madame Collart would ask again for Mother's papers. Mother worried every minute that they were not in her possession. The Germans were meticulous and they had everything recorded, even rations and food allocations. Without her papers, Mother was more vulnerable and helpless.

Then came the day that Madame Collart asked me to go with her. I stepped into the cool little room behind the green door where there were familiar faces and faces that were new to me.

'Odile, today you must come with me. There is an important message for the British. You must help to assemble the words, as you can speak English. Will you come?'

I felt an unexpected rush of excitement. My English was simple, but writing in English reminded me of the note I had left for William and somehow made me feel closer to him again.

'Of course, Madame. Kurt is away and so there is no need for me to be here, if the factory can release me. But what Papa will say, does not bear thinking about.'

'Good. The factory will say you are ill and confined to bed. The supervisor and his deputy already know you are with me. They will tell the Germans that they have confirmed your absence. Because of your special relationship with the German boy, that will be the end of it. Your Mother will tell your Father something. But we will be here to look out for you. So, good. Here, you must see this.'

Madame Collart took out a dirty shirt. It was a man's shirt and it had been worn for what looked like a month. It smelled of stale sweat and lavender oil, which was odd. The arms were yellowing and almost rotten. Why on earth this shirt was being shown to me was a complete mystery.

Then, the wily Madame placed on the table a small bowl of clean water into which she put two grains of salt. Carefully, she dipped the corner of the shirt into the water and left it soaking.

'There, that should do nicely. Now Odile. I need you to translate this for me please. You must absolutely forget what you are writing here. Try very hard to train yourself to forget these words.'

Madame Collart took out a sheet of plain paper, no bigger than the palm of her hand. She smoothed it out over a small cloth.

'Here, Madame. I have the iodine water.' One of the new faces handed

Madame Collart a small bottle of pale yellow liquid. She poured it over the paper, blowing it dry as she did. Then, held near the warmth of a shaded candle, dark patches appeared, followed by words, in German and French. Tiny, perfect letters emerged, in neat little rows. This was painstaking work and it gave me the first notion of how important this job was going to be.

'Odile, read the lines in French and try to think of the best English words to use. Monsieur Joubert here will write them down and we can then take them to the British. Here, careful now, there is no copy and this information may as well have been written in our blood.'

Monsieur Joubert stepped into the light, but said nothing. He sat down and took a tiny piece of wood from his pocket. It had been sharpened to a point, to write on another tiny piece of paper. He stirred the little stylus in the water where the shirt was soaking. He wrote the date, invisibly on the new paper.

'Madame, the ink is invisible. This is incredible!'

'It has been soaked onto the shirt and it is now in the water. Come, Odile, let us be quick. Every second this note exists puts us in more danger.'

'There is no movement outside, Madame Collart. You should proceed.' The voice from the shadows moved away from the window, and all eyes were fixed upon the little sheet of brown paper that contained tiny words and a sheet of blank paper, being written on invisibly with a little wooden nib.

'The words should be, ah, the Somme defences, it should say, have two major weaknesses, which rebuilding has not sorted. Certainly the word is rebuilding, but I do not know how it should be spelled in English.'

'Joubert, do you have that?'

'Yes, quickly continue.'

I looked at the French and some German words.

'The lines are on a forward slope, white chalk – could it mean the soil of chalk?'

'Lines? Mademoiselle Lefebvre, could that be trenches?'

'Oh yes, yes of course, trenches. This next bit is easier. The defences are strong towards the – call it the front trench – with a regiment of two – is that battalions? Two battalions near the front-trench system and the reserve battalion divided between the... This is a German word. It is unfamiliar. Could you leave it in German? *Stutzpunktlinie,* is that something point?'

'Yes, leave it in German. The British will know it.'

It was extraordinarily tiring, reading the tiny letters and trying to turn them into English, my heart was racing and my palms were sweating, but it was essential to keep going.

'The second line, all within two thousand English yards. Is yards correct? It is a measurement most likely. Most troops are one thousand yards off the front line, in new, um. This word must be dugout, every hundred paces for thirty men.'

'Dugouts? That is bad for them. These things go underground.' Madame Collart shook her head.

My eyes ached, but the next lines were easier.

'You should write, the gathering of troops' trenches – on a forward slope, is good for artillery. Germans are afraid of shooting directed by watchers on marked white trench lines.'

Most of these terms meant little to me and it worried me that Monsieur Joubert was writing down nonsense. But after a time, my English started returning and became more fluent, giving me the confidence to keep going.

'The digging of a new third line beginning May, civilians moved from Flers/Courcelette and Le Transloy. Ammunition and grenades moved to Front. Large numbers stored in Bapaume and Cambrai and along AB road. AB road? That probably means Albert-Bapaume, could that be right, Monsieur Joubert?'

'Yes, I will write it in full, just in case. That was good Odile, very good.'

'But you know what this means?' Madame Collart leaned forward as she spoke softly.

'The Germans have deep trenches in which to hide if the English attack.'

'And not just the English, Madame, there are others, as well as the French.'

'More of them to die then, poor boys.'

When the note was finished, Madame cut it neatly into ten small strips. She took five and handed me another five. Then handed me two pairs of gloves.

'Put on the first pair and wrap the papers neatly around each finger. Then carefully put the second pair over the top. To anyone looking, it is just paper. You need the special iodine water to turn it into anything else.'

Monsieur Joubert picked up the French note and put it onto the fire, and we all watched it burn to ash.

'After all the effort to get this, the note burns in a second. Adieu Jean, Alain and Raymond, we thank you, and so will France.'

Madame Collart took my arm and checked my gloves were on correctly.

'It is a fine day today and no one else will be wearing gloves. You need to look sickly, or tired. Not too much, don't overact, just pretend to be tired.'

'That will be easy, Madame, I feel tired all of the time.'

'We must go, are you quite ready?'

I looked at the door, then down to the floor, thinking that if in any way, this note helped my darling William, then it would be worth the risk.

Madame's hand was gentle, but firm. 'Now, Odile. It is time.'

At the canal, the road forked and we took a little path. There had been some damage to the houses and the shops here, so they were all empty. At the bridge, we stopped and Madame looked around anxiously to see if anyone was around.

'They are not here, they are late. They are never late.'

Two figures in the distance stood smoking, as was customary. One of them put down his cigarette and stamped on it once. The second man did the same.

Madame Collart turned to me. 'Someone is coming, but only one is here. It might be a trap, or something might have happened.'

We moved again, and a single figure emerged from the bushes, walking past, with barely a nod towards us. Then we stopped as Madame Collart dropped a glove onto the ground.

'Let me get this for you.' It was French, but this person was not from France.

'Oh, thank you, so very kind.'

The man handed back the glove and we moved along. The man disappeared. Madame Collart leaned towards me, whispering quietly.

'Slip your gloves slowly from your hands. When I squeeze your arm, drop the glove with the notes to the floor. Ready?'

A second man appeared from a doorway. As he left, he turned and locked the door. In his hand was a tiny book, the pages almost the same size as our note had been. As he passed, he lifted his hand to touch his cap in the breeze, but in doing so, he knocked my arm roughly. I felt the squeeze from Madame Collart, and dropped my gloves on the ground.

'I am so sorry, Mademoiselle. Let me. Here. I think June will be busy for us all. Good day.'

He picked up my gloves and handed me a different pair. They did not fit, but it did not matter. No one could have noticed. Inside the glove was the little book.

We walked back in silence and the man's words came back to me. What could he have meant? *June will be busy for us all.*

191

CHRIS CHERRY

CHAPTER FORTY
CAMBRAI, MAY-JUNE 1916

Madame Collart was now more often seen moving about in daylight, by the French and Germans alike. It seemed almost impossible that the Germans had not noticed the irregularity with her identity papers. But they did not. Sometimes she carried little notes to the British. Other times, she visited Amelie's grave, which she had discovered in the little church close to where they had entered Cambrai. I am sure her visits to poor Amelie offered her some comfort, but more than that, perhaps she needed to remind herself of why she was defying the administration, risking discovery on an almost daily basis.

Often, she asked for my help translating passages. Despite my best efforts, it was difficult to forget what I had seen. The British and others, like Canadians, New Zealanders, French and Africans were in Albert. The Australians, Indians and Irish were all gathering for something big. We all knew that, and we could see that the Germans knew it all too well. Each little notes we sent on its own contained very little, but over time, a picture of the war in my homeland was emerging.

The Allies were forming up along the Ancre and Somme areas. There was going to be an attack here. June would indeed be busy. The Germans were building a series of defensive lines. One of them was near my village in Bazentin. It was unbelievable, my little village being turned into a defensive fortress. Longueval, Pozieres and Martinpuich were now out of bounds to anyone except the German Army. Even Father was never allowed to go further south than Bapaume. It was going to be a big fight. We were going to be in the front seats of this performance. I wondered sometimes whether William was here. I could not sense him, but assumed he had joined the army. He did not seem the kind of boy who would choose not to fight. Perhaps, because he was so good with engines, he had gone up in the aeroplanes. It made me shudder to think it, as so many kept falling out of the sky over Cambrai.

In late June, the factory was moved from its building to another one, further out of the town. As we walked to the new factory from our homes, the aeroplanes sometimes dropped bombs on the railway, and quite often on a daily basis. Madame Collart had been lucky with the bomb that hit the alley. She thought it must have fallen from the aeroplane, or had been dropped by mistake.

German soldiers were everywhere. Kurt had not returned, but sent word in little notes to the factory that he was in Bapaume, moving lorries to the front line along the Albert road. Walking to the factory reminded me of that road. It was always breezy in the early summer, the fields flat and farmed by families that my Father knew.

In his notes to me, Kurt began suggesting that it might be a good idea to sign up to become a nurse. For now, it was voluntary, but soon it might not be. After some consideration, it seemed to me that volunteering to become a nurse would go better for me than waiting until I was ordered to become a nurse. It might also mean gaining privileges that did not depend on Kurt, and we would be less likely to be moved.

It seemed the Germans were expecting a battle quite soon. More lorries with red crosses appeared. Father liked to work on the ambulances, these lorries and carts with crosses, because it meant that Germans had been wounded. He was able to visit us just about every day lately since he had been calm with the Germans and they valued his skills as an engineer. They still treated him as a prisoner, or an enemy, but no longer beat him. The soldiers here were from a farming area of Germany and they knew the type of man my Father was, and he understood them well in return. We were given rations every single day. Father still thought it was because he had earned them, although he did seem to be getting more suspicious. But the mud and the stones thrown by the French reminded me every day that it was alliance with the Germans that made our lives bearable.

Towards the end of June, the Germans opened the hospital in Cambrai. My instructions had been simple. *Wash and clean, offer food, if allowed. Do not touch any wounds, unless instructed. Learn the German words sometimes written above the beds.*

On the ward for the first time, I saw the damage war could inflict on a body. At that moment, I had expected to be inwardly glad to see so many Germans wounded because it might convince them to go home and leave us in peace. But that moment passed in an instant. On both sides were lines of dusty, scarred and bloodied men. They were being tended by German and French nurses, trained and caring. All I could do was offer a hand of comfort to the enemy. I had no ill feelings to them at all, at least not whilst they were so gravely ill. Never had I seen such a sight, a mass of bandages, beds, blood and steel instruments. As I walked the wards, offering food, apples and a word in French, I felt almost helpless.

'And the battle has not even started yet, you know, Mademoiselle.' His French was good, for a young German boy. 'The English are shooting big guns at us, day after day. They have not yet come and already we are being ground to dust in the trenches.'

Over and over again, I heard this from the soldiers. They had all been in trenches, day after day, being shot at and shelled by the Allies. For each one here in hospital, there was still a hundred still waiting for the attack. It was this that made me saddest.

Originally, my job now was to work in the factory in the morning and work in the hospital in the afternoon. But now, I was working at the hospital all day, taking food and offering kind words and comfort to those soldiers able to sit up and talk. Generally, I would give them apples and books. Most of them understood our situation, and many said they were sorry, but that the war was not their fault and even so, God was on their side. They were fighting for freedom. I could never understand them and so I always replied with the same question.

'Is it good to fight for freedom in another's country?'

Father was now working again in Cambrai. I would see him now, most days in the square taking apart a cart or lorry, or giving it a check before it went out to the battle lines. Each day, they would come back carrying the German wounded, hit by exploding shells and bombs. But still the Allies did not come, still they did not attack.

This changed at the end of June on a cold and wet afternoon. The lines of ambulances were stopped from leaving the station on the edge of town. Usually, it took them nearly a day to leave and return to the lines. But today, they were prevented from leaving. I called to Father, he could barely hear me over the noise from the square and the beating of the rain.

'Papa, what is happening today? Why is no one leaving?'

'The British are shelling the roads and the trenches. Ha! All the way from the Somme to the Ancre! God bless our Allies, Odile. God help these fat pigs, now.'

'Get on with your work Lefebvre, you miserable bastard.'

Father waved his oil rag at the officer and went back to his work. He had a smile on his face though, which was always good to see. Perhaps the leads in his hands would somehow melt in the heat of the engine.

I could sense something in the breeze. The air coming from the south somehow smelled of burning. It was a strange sensation. I lifted my head into the breeze, the rain falling lightly on my face, which I always loved, when it was warm in summer. Suddenly, I felt the ghost of a hand on my shoulder, a warm touch, curling around me in the breeze.

'William, my love. You have come to me! But this Odile does not know if she can ever touch your face again. You must go to your work, my love, whatever it is. You are close, and I feel you near to me. It may be true you are there, it may be that I am imagining this as a silly girl. Darling William, if you can hear me, come for me. Take me away from this and protect us all from the enemy.'

Even as I said the words it made me feel foolish. I had promised myself to let him go, and it hurt even to think of him. He was surely lost to me, forever, alive or dead. Deep down was the knowledge that I had to let him go and yet...

The breeze turned cold again, the rain dripped from my chin and my back was cold and wet. It was time to go inside. I waved again to Father at the steps of the hospital and he waved back. It was almost normal and yet it could not be.

When the wind blew from the west, I could hear quite distinctly the sounds of big guns. No one knew whether they were German or British guns. But something was going to happen, and it would be soon, there was no doubt. How it would all end was now less certain. Initially, everyone had expected the Germans to be sent home quickly in 1914. Then it seemed they would be here forever. But now it seemed the balance was tipping back. Was there the slightest chance that this might bring an end to their rule of France? I dared not ask, dared not dream. Mother told me that she sensed a change and also felt that something might happen soon, which would surely change our lives.

I looked at the lines of stationary ambulances. There were orders for them to stay until at least first light tomorrow. If these all returned full, then it could be as many as five-hundred wounded. This was only one of many stations for ambulances and one of many hospitals. I began to sense the scale of death that might be coming. And I also sensed the passing of something, the end of a rhythmic tapping of life. It was now becoming a drumbeat, matching itself to the tune of the guns in the distance. Their anger and insistence became louder and more intrusive.

Finally, it was time to turn back into the hospital to look into the terrified faces of the boys who had been trapped beneath that anger of their unseen enemy.

At least, unseen for now, but hopefully that would soon change.

CHAPTER FORTY-ONE
CAMBRAI, JUNE 1916

'Odile, my apologies for you must be tired. But you are needed urgently to translate a message that must get to the English tonight.'

'No need for apologies, Madame Collart. Tired or not, we must all do whatever is necessary to aid the effort.'

I took the proffered note, and read it quickly. 'There are also some numbers here…'

'Yes, we think this is soldiers and units, something to do with maps. See, look, this must mean Second Army. Quickly Odile, we do not have time. This must be with the English tonight.'

I began translating into English.

'Let me see. Yes. *Germans building at Poz. Ridge and valley to Long defended. Ammunition stores in Bap. Cam. LT and Windmill Road. Good Luck.* Does that mean what it appears to suggest?'

'Yes, it does. It looks like the attack is anytime now. Odile, there is no time for me to get your Mother's papers. You must go – you will be watched and safe.'

There was no time to dwell on what was in my hand. Whatever it was, however helpful it might be, it had to go tonight. It helped to think that it would make a difference, a silly girl's daydream that this might help William to live, if he was here.

As before, the note was written on the special paper, with the water ink made from the dirty shirt. Carefully, I tore the paper into neat strips and put on my gloves. The strips were so small that they caused me no worry at all. My only problem might be explaining why I was out when it was not allowed. Perhaps I might be lucky, and meet a silly young soldier. Then again, I might not, and would not see the sun rise again.

The night was damp, but clear. All lights were out, except for a few dim candles. Sound came from the guns in the distance, signalling the coming of an attack by the Allies. It vibrated around the walls, and the ground heaved and shook in a rhythm, as if a great animal were beneath the surface.

Unusually, the Germans were nowhere in sight. The sentries were out of sight, if they were there at all. My times scavenging secretly for food helped me to conceal myself, assisted by the dark shawl and black dress, borrowed from Madame Collart's secretive friend. Finding my way to the canal was easy in the darkness as the route was familiar to me now. Madame Collart had cleverly highlighted to me the alleys and hidden passages to move through if necessary. The meeting at the canal had been hastily arranged. It was not known who would be waiting for me, or how the note would be used. All I knew was that the drop had to be made before midnight.

At the canal, there was no sign of anyone, so I hid in the bush on the bank, where no one would ever see me. It was cool, but not cold and it should be simple to stay here unnoticed for a little time. I remembered the rules. *Wait one hour longer than the agreed time at night, if you can, no longer. If the note is not collected, throw it into the canal, do not think twice about it.*

It was hard to be certain, but it seemed that at least an hour had passed with no sign of anyone. There had been a faint rustle earlier, maybe a footstep above my head, but it had disappeared and I felt no presence over me watching out. The drums rolled in the distance, the guns were firing through the night. This was a big attack and a lot of effort had gone into the planning, that much was clear to me. The Germans, who had been attacking in the south east had paused to draw breath. I knew that their second army was here. Kurt had told me all about the units, and soon there would be the fight. My hospital would be full soon, and probably all of the others too.

My thoughts were interrupted by a rustle from boots scraping the ground. The sound stopped, a grinding of a heel on the road. Whoever it was had stopped and then turned to look around. There it was again. Shorter steps, faster, perhaps anxious? Was it a German boot? Listen Odile, work it out. Was it a German boot, or the shoe of a civilian? It stopped. The grinding again. Whoever it was seemed certain that something was here. It had to be my contact, it simply had to be. I had to take a look.

It was possible to lean out of the bush quite a bit before my head would be seen from above. The growth was too much in the summer to see through in the dark, so I had to risk it. My blouse caught on a small branch, snapping it with a sound that felt louder than the guns in the distance. I froze. Nothing. The boots or shoes were silent. But they had not gone away. Then there was a voice!

'Madame? Madame? It is I. It is quite safe, we are quite alone.'

He said *Madame*, but no name. Why no name? Could I trust this voice? He sounded French, with no hint of a German accent. But that did not always mean safety. Some French had sold themselves to the enemy. *Better to be seen as collaborators than cowards*, Madame Collart always said.

'Madame Collart, it is Robert!'

That was it. A confirmation of the contact. At least, there were no reasons to doubt it.

I got to my feet and moved out of the bush.

'Ah, Mademoiselle. It is Mademoiselle Lefebvre?'

'Yes, Monsieur Robert.'

'It is Robert, Mademoiselle. You have the urgent information?'

'Yes, there is a note for you. I have one question from the note. May I ask it?'

'It really isn't a good idea to ask—'

'Robert, I have risked my life tonight. Please?'

'Quickly then, ask if you must. But I might not answer.'

'Who are 12 Field Operations?'

Robert looked up.

'You must never mention that again. Ever. Do you hear me?' His tone was fierce and it frightened me. Then there were footsteps and a soft voice in French.

'Come on Odile, we must go.'

I handed over the little slips of paper to Robert. He looked up and his voice had softened.

'Mademoiselle, you must not have knowledge that can help our enemy. Thank you and good night.'

He turned and disappeared into the cover of two crumbling walls that had been bombed by the aeroplanes.

Whatever I had given him for 12 Field Operations had to be important and I hoped it would make a difference. Once again, I was alone. The voice behind me had also melted away. It was time to go home. Quickly, I scanned the streets and moved in the shadows. The sentries were still missing from their posts, but lights were on where the Germans were housed. I could hear humourless German voices shouting loudly at each other, and the sounds of many people moving about.

As I finally crept up to the corner of our street, it became clear that German soldiers were forming up. There must have been three hundred, about to move out. In front were carts and two cars, just moving off. The officers were occupied with papers and orders. No one looked at the little girl skulking in the shadows. I returned to the little pale green door, knocked once and then entered. All was dark and silent.

'Madame Collart? Madame? It is Odile.' No sounds or shadows were discernible in the darkness, and the room was cold. The fire had not been touched since my departure three hours earlier that night.

'Goodnight Madame. I will return in the morning. It is my sincere hope that the note was well received.'

Back outside, I felt a little uneasy that the house was empty. Madame did not have any papers, so she could not risk going outside. But where could she be?

It was impossible to sleep that night, surrounded by the alarm of soldiers moving out, and disturbed by the memory of Madame Collart's empty house.

CHAPTER FORTY-TWO
CAMBRAI, JUNE 1916

Madame Collart shut the door. The little note that Odile took with her contained something very special for the army coming to rescue them. Well, she liked to think they would come to rescue them.

'Good luck little Odile. God protect you better than He did my little angel.'

She moved across the room to the little candle and shielded it from the window, where a draught risked extinguishing the tiny flame. It was now dark, almost eleven, yet still the lorries at the railway rumbled on. At least the road to the canal would most likely be quiet, with the Germans' attention concentrated on moving troops to the Front. It was now quite clear that was what was happening. Suddenly, there was a knock at the door and it opened, in the agreed manner of the silent family in the shadows.

'Madame, it is me, with the information from the French you asked for. It is in plain language, but I have not read it. The French said to bring it directly to you. My apologies, but the movement of the soldiers has delayed me. They are expecting something big soon, it would seem.'

'Thank you. I will read it presently. When will they come?'

'The French think it will be in the morning. Last day of June, feels right. Knowing the English, they will come at nine, according to the clock, of course!'

'It cannot come soon enough. And do you think it will be relief for Verdun?'

'Only if it brings the whole army here, which it cannot. I must leave Madame. Goodnight to you!'

The figure left, closing the door firmly behind him. She watched the figure melt across the road into the shadows as the man disappeared. Then, she turned to the table and the little note that he had left behind. She split the little glue seal and opened the paper slowly, taking a deep breath before reading the words. Information had finally come in about Hugo in Verdun, her silly son who could barely dress himself.

Her eyes drifted to the few words on the note. When she had read them, she sank to her knees, the little sheet of paper dropping gently onto the table.

Madame's chair rustled a little and then tipped over into the silence of the room. The little candle burned down, flickered, and when it was nothing more than a little pool of grease, went out without another sound, sending the room into a darkness, drawing to an end the lives of the Collarts in the Great War.

CHAPTER FORTY-THREE
CAMBRAI, JUNE 1916

'Maman, we should go to Madame Collart. I have a very bad feeling, who knows why, but can we please go to her now?'

'Odile, it is still dark. The Germans will be suspicious, and they will investigate everything about us, Kurt or no Kurt. No. We must wait until morning light.'

'Please Maman, I beg you. The room. It was dark and cold. It is never cold, even if it is often dark. The door was open as usual, but no one was in the room. Please. It is making me sick with worry. Something is wrong.'

'Oh Odile, very well. Come, let us go. Perhaps you should bring some milk, or some other excuse for being about so early in the morning. It is still dark.'

I put on some clothes for the cool morning. Mother simply wrapped her shawls more tightly.

'We will pretend that someone is ill. Odile, this is a big risk. Are you quite sure?'

'Yes Maman. If Madame is well, then that will be good. Perhaps I should have looked through the house more carefully before leaving.'

At the little pale green door, Mother knocked twice and opened the door. The room was in darkness, but the tiniest light crept into the window as the day started to win against the night. On the table, the little candle had burnt down completely. This was truly worrying, and I had not noticed this in the dark of last night. Next to the candle was a small sheet of paper that had been unfolded. Quickly, I picked it up and held it against the window, where the tiniest amount of light allowed me to read the words by straining my eyes.

Regret to inform. Chasseur ap Hugo Collart. Killed by SF 0715/0720, 21 February16 in defence of the City Walls of Verdun. Identity confirmed by tag received by RC. Note: Unable to trace family.

'Mon Dieu! Maman. We must find Madame Collart!'

Mother raised her hand towards me.

'She is found. Madame is here Odile. Bless you Madame, she has found peace at last.'

'She is here? Oh no!'

I had not come as far as the second room last night, thinking the house empty. In the shadows, Madame Collart lay on the floor, remnants of her scarves wrapped tightly around her neck. The chair was tipped over, with the special shirt still draped over the back of it.

'She must have used the chair Odile, but the scarves, oh my goodness, the scarves did not hold her weight. I hope that she did not suffer too long. Oh Odile, hold me darling.'

Mother and I held each other for a short time, whilst we both took in the scene. We had to move fast and give Madame Collart some dignity. It would soon be fully light and she had no identification or status with the Germans. They would be suspicious and would ask questions we could not answer.

Madame Collart did not look like she was at peace. Her face was pained and her thoughts had clearly troubled her at the end. I tried to draw her eyes shut and calm her face, but it was difficult. Mother leaned over to her and looked into her face.

'Forgive us, Madame. Forgive us for not doing more for Amelie whilst she lived. Our frightened lives together were filled with pain. Rest now. We are sorry for what we must do now, to keep you safe from the enemy. I am sure you, of all in France, would understand why we must do this.'

Mother took my hand and squeezed it tightly. The dark force of her inner strength came to the surface once again.

'Odile, search the house from the very top to the cellar, if there is one. Burn everything that will burn in the fireplace. Quickly, do it now, including the note that you found.'

'But Maman?'

'Madame Collart is dead. That note tells of her son's death, does it not?'

I nodded, as tears formed in my eyes.

'Then there are no more Collarts. Whatever is left here gives her away – us as well. You understand? Come, let us get to work.'

Mother put a blanket over Madame Collart and left to find our friends. In upstairs rooms I found nothing of any interest to anyone. The few clothes there could be used without suspicion and there were no papers anywhere. All the floorboards were nailed and the drawers of the little cupboard were empty. There were no secret papers or anything else to help the Germans.

By this time of the morning, a lit fire would not arouse suspicion, so I lit a small fire and began to burn Hugo's death notice and the little sheets of paper. But I left the shirt, in case it might prove useful to those who knew what secret it held in its fibres. Before long, Mother returned with the factory supervisor and the smoking man who was with me last night.

The supervisor spoke. 'Oh Madame, God's rest to you. But you will not get any just yet.'

The two men picked up Madame and rolled her in the little carpet. At either end they folded a blanket.

'This is very dangerous. Are you sure this is the right thing to do?'

'Do we have a choice, eh? We cannot leave her here. At least in the church we can bury her secretly, no?'

'Right, let us go now, before it is properly light.'

We watched them go. It would be clear to anyone that the two men were moving a body wrapped in a carpet. Any soldier nearby, and they would be in big trouble. They disappeared around the corner and were gone.

'Odile, did you burn everything that might act as information for the Germans?'

'I did not find much, but everything I found I have burned.'

'It was Hugo?'

'Yes Maman. Killed on the first day of the German attack on Verdun.'

'You are quite sure the house was empty last night?'

'Well, it seemed empty. There was no light and no sound. I did not really look, but just assumed...'

'If there was no sound, Odile, Madame must already have been dead and there was nothing for you to do.'

'Thank you Maman. I hope that is true.'

'If there was no sound, then life had left her by then, Odile. Let us hope she gets the rest she has earned and the thanks of France she deserves.'

We waited until nearly six, but there was no sign of the others. I began to fear the worst had happened.

'We must go Odile. You are due at the hospital at seven.'

We both stepped outside and closed the door, able to move about more openly as the day had begun. Mother gambled on the Germans not noticing her dress was for the night and not the day.

I arrived at the hospital just before seven and was quickly sent to offer food to those men who were allowed to eat. There was some fruit and a sticky soup that was nutritious, if not delicious. In my ward were soldiers suffering from the effects of the bombs. Many had nervous jerks and there was a lot of uncontrolled shouting. Others had light wounds to their legs and arms, but were otherwise quite well on the outside. It was their minds that had been damaged.

Stop dawdling Odile and get on with your work! I snapped out of my thoughts and went to the first bed.

'Here is breakfast for you, soldier.'

The soldier on the bed did not look or reply, in French or German. He simply glared ahead towards the far wall. I picked up the spoon and offered a little of the sticky soup to his lips. They opened almost automatically and took in the liquid. Without another word, I did it again. After ten or so mouthfuls of soup, he simply would not open his mouth again. He did not look at me at all. This made me feel shy and inadequate, unable to communicate. He was an enemy, but it did not feel right somehow. Not here, with this man. He could have been my uncle. At the next bed, the soldier looked at me and spoke in French.

'Hello Mademoiselle. Thank you for caring for us. It is difficult and strange, ja? But we are just soldiers you see. Do you understand?'

I smiled, but said nothing, feeling overwhelmed by the time spent with Kurt, being beaten and humiliated by soldiers, watching my Father threatened and beaten, and my Mother being passed from soldier to soldier like a fabric doll. Every possible emotion came to the surface in the face of this uniform. It was confusing. How should I react? I wanted to care, and I wanted to hate in equal measure. I did not know what to feel at that very moment.

'If you like, I can feed myself. Some fruit please Mademoiselle?'

'Oh, yes, of course. Here you are.' I all but threw the apple at the soldier and ran out of the ward to hide in the nurses' room. Underneath the table, I breathed heavily and fought back the tears.

'I have tried to let you go William. I have tried to let my love fade in order to live in this war. I have tried to hate the Germans, for everything they have done to us. It is hard, my love, it is hard to understand what has happened to us. I beg you, come and get me now, William, for I cannot bear this anymore.'

Thoughts of Madame Collart being carried as baggage through the streets came to me. And little Amelie, bruised and defiled by the enemy, my Father beaten for sport. My mind was slipping from me, sending me down into an incomprehensible world, making me feel helpless and powerless.

Then footsteps echoed outside the room and I feared another beating. When the boots appeared, they were neatly polished, and the starched white uniform could mean only one thing – I was in trouble and would be punished. After all of this, I cared not for whatever would be said or done to me, as it could be as nothing compared to what I had already seen.

'Odile. Poor thing. Whatever is the matter with you?'

Almost shocked by the softness in the voice, I looked up at the senior nurse. Her face was kindness itself. Somehow, this woman had a little compassion left in her for me and it felt truly wonderful.

'Never mind. Look, come here and let me take a look at you.'

I emerged from under the table and stood in front of the senior nurse, my cheeks wet from tears and their salt stinging my sore lips. She placed a warm hand on my shoulder and drew me slightly to her. I wanted to bury my head in her uniform, to hide inside for safety. I had not felt safe since Father held me on that day when the car was finished.

'Such a young girl should not have to see such as this. But these soldiers are just young men, like your own brothers perhaps? Here, take the apples again and let us try to help those soldiers not able to feed themselves, hmm?

Come, let us try again and we will hear no more of this little incident. Of course, I should punish you Odile, for running away. Perhaps send you back to the factory again? Well, this is your punishment. You are to offer apples and pears to the soldiers on the ward every day in July. It is considered to be quite dull work, but it will suit you well. What do you say?'

'It will suit me very well, Madame, thank you. Very well.'

'Good. Do not think that I do not know what is going on Odile. I understand all too well. Now, get along and on with your work. The soldiers are hungry.'

'Yes, Madame.'

I looked at her, straight into her face. What did she know? Was she talking about Mother? Madame Collart and the secret team? Kurt? Where we had been? I dared not think. Everyone had secrets here, half-truths and deceptions. At its lowest, it was us all just trying to survive. But Madame was French and her accent was from the north. Perhaps she knew more than I thought and perhaps she might be trustworthy.

Cambrai was now full to bursting with German soldiers and the equipment of war. Carts, horses, lorries and gun carriers were everywhere. Armament officers shepherded the bullets and bombs and when these were moved in great numbers, the streets were cleared of French workers and civilian prisoners. It was clear that something big was happening again. We had not seen so many soldiers since early February, but this was different. Perhaps it was our turn to attack. I hoped so.

The evening of the thirtieth of June was more pleasant than anything had been for almost two weeks. The drizzle and gloom cleared and the evening was warm and fresh, the rain having washed the streets of dust and dirt. The noise was ceaseless and rough, the aeroplanes buzzed over the railways, sometimes dropping bombs, which exploded with anger and death. Our little part of town and the hospital were never bombed, and it made me think again of Madame Collart's notes. Perhaps some of these notes explained why we were not bombed.

I finished my duties as it began to get dark, at almost ten in the evening. This was exhausting, but still better than the factory and much better than any camp we had been in. Kurt was still away, perhaps at the Front, moving lorries and sending supplies to the soldiers. Each time he came into my thoughts, it made me reconsider my feelings, and it made me feel a traitor to France and to William. But then I looked around and thought of Mother and Father. The war had deprived them of their dignity, their purpose and the tools for their own survival. They were still young and healthy, with lives to live and dreams to fulfil. My head felt heavy and I looked to the floor.

I thought a little of Henri, my unseen and unknown brother. It was

Madame the nurse brought him to my mind, *like your own brothers perhaps*, she had said. What would he be like if he were alive now? Could he have helped Father to shield us from the Germans? Would he have made things better for his little family? Or would he have perished on the wire of Verdun, as Hugo had done? Hugo, who died on the first day of that battle it seems. At least he was saved the indignity of coughing his life away, or of looking at himself in the mirror to see only half his face looking back.

When I looked up again, carts were passing. There were whistles and calls to the horses, and the rumbling of wheels and the sounds of hooves were ceaseless. The horses seemed brave, moving towards the sounds of guns without concern, just as stupid as the Germans, riding or marching off into the unknown distance. It would seem that whatever was going to happen, was happening now. This day had been so different.

At eleven, I was inside. Still the carts moved forwards. Still the gun carts and drivers whistled through the town. We were not allowed onto the streets. Had there been a message to pass tonight, secret shirts and tiny strips of paper would not have got through the mass of heaving, pulsating grey uniforms facing the villages of the Somme Valley. At midnight, tiredness defeated me and I forced myself to bed. Sleep came and went fitfully that night, and kept me waking and turning. I was uncomfortable in the warmth of the short night at the end of June. It marked the coming of a new month, and the coming of a new uncertainty.

The morning came early, and the rumbling of guns was loud and constant, the movement of carts unceasing. It was a wonder that anyone could sleep through this. It was just light, and I rose and stepped to the window. The glass was cool, but the sun would shine today.

I was due at the hospital at seven. Until then I watched the carts go by, uneasy with a sickness inside that would not calm. There was a heavy weight inside that wanted to remind me constantly of the loss of this war. The loss of almost everything that I had known. There was nothing for it, I left early for the hospital. I might as well be useful, rather than sit about here worrying about something I could not understand.

Outside, the morning sun was warming, but not yet hot. The path to the hospital was blocked with soldiers, who grumbled and complained as they went. The infantry marched and swayed to a beat. The horses' hooves beat a hypnotic rhythm, often calm, sometimes urgent. It drew me towards it before I realised I was wandering into the road. Something was trying to fill my mind, as if I were trying to think, but my thoughts were behind the clouds. I stood, breathing heavily, a pain in my stomach.

'William? You are here. You have come to me. My loving friend. God protect you and keep you safe. You are here, I think.'

My thoughts of William were strong and moving around me in warm waves. I could see his face above the corn in the fields, his dirty shirt framing his shoulders as he waved to me. He was there, with Madame Villiers, in the chill of winter, pushing the motor bicycle. At that moment, I felt so safe, loved and warm. But the feeling passed quickly. The cool breeze, not yet warmed by the sun washed away the warmth. I looked up, and saw the hospital was in front of me.

But the air was filled with a dull roar and a rumble. Something had happened! A large, almost unimaginable explosion somewhere near the battlefield. I knew not what it meant, but it must be important for the attack. The soldiers in the street must also have heard it, and moved about their duties all the more earnestly.

I ran into the hospital. Although my ears felt strange, it seemed that the rumble of guns had stopped briefly before starting again. The senior nurse called to me.

'Ah, Lefebvre, we have orders to clear the wards. We have until noon to report the number of empty beds we can manage. This hospital has been designated officers only from now on, so all of the other men will be moved out to Rue Charlemagne. The more serious cases will be going there directly. Your job is to move their personal effects and documents. No mistakes now! Quick, to it.'

The urgency in her voice must have meant something more than usual. Her kindness from yesterday had matured to the quiet efficiency of the medical staff here. My mind was in turmoil as I gathered up the little boxes of effects. Still, the guns were audible, but the noises and notes were different. It made me uneasy, creating a worrying tug at my heart and in the pit of my stomach. The attack was happening, I could feel it. Everyone could feel it. We had known it was coming and it was here.

'I know you are there William. I cannot explain how, but you are here, somewhere out there in the fields. My love, my English boy. Have you found me?'

I moved across the street, back and forth and my hospital uniform meant that the soldiers let me cross. The little red cross had a deep and powerful meaning, for enemy and friend, soldier and civilian.

When I returned to the ward, I felt a little unwell, and thought perhaps carrying the large boxes had tired me. I had just made it to the little toilet and was sick. A wave of pain overcame me and then passed. Then the terrible smell made me sick a second time. The little bar of carbolic soap had a powerful scent that made me feel faint. I had not eaten, which was a relief. No one had seen me, so I quickly resumed my duty feeling hot and faint.

CHAPTER FORTY-FOUR
LA BOISSELLE SECTOR, SOUTH EAST LINE

The evening was clear and calm, and I was able to look at the sky from the trench. Just a little patch was visible amongst the bobbing helmets and bodies filling the front lines. On my left, the little village of La Boisselle – a village I had come to know very well. To my right, the next village of Becourt. It had been a small, farming village, innocent and hidden from the bustle of the larger towns. Now it lay in near ruins, shelled by all sides in the turmoil of the early war and once again it was in the centre of the war, on the front line.

It would soon be light, and time for me to move off. I had chosen to go with the second wave. Some said it was harder to go in the second wave, because it meant watching the first wave go into the unknown. It meant knowing that their fate, whatever it was, would certainly be my fate.

I read Cowling's little note to me one more time before putting a match to it, as ordered.

Major William Collins RE
(Attachment 12 Field Ops.) 26 June 16

This is our time. We are rolling up our sleeves and showing the enemy the strong arm of the British Army. Our Allies are with us, amongst us, leading and following. This is the moment, when we cast our hat to the enemy and he will know that we are here. If we succeed, then General Rawlinson gets what he wanted, open war again and the chance to roll up the enemy to the coast. If we fail, which I am certain we cannot, it might mean the end of us all. Remember your job. You are not an infantryman, a soldier of the line. You are to observe, to watch, to think. Learn from us, use your experience to help us. Your time is coming, Major Collins, your chance to recover the drive I saw in you. A need to succeed and what a place to be able to do it, eh? In your own home. Live, William, that others around you may be spared the trenches. Live so we can learn the mastery of our craft.

A little surprise! Your award of a bar to your Military Medal has come through. It is the first one that I have seen. It came for a Serjeant Collins. Do you remember him? No more though, William? I need you to live and to ensure success in our little operation. We will get to them, you will have your chance, but this is not the place to stand. Burn after reading, if you don't mind.

Arthur Cowling Col. OC 12 Field Ops

In your own home. Odile drifted into my thoughts often. I looked around at the soldiers filling the front lines and wondered if they shared the same thoughts as me. Of a girl, of a hope, however distant and unreachable. I stepped away from the wall to allow soldiers to pass, crouched down, and burned the little note under the shelter of my coat so the light would not be seen. As it caught light, I saw the words for the last time.

This is our time.

Once again, I looked again at the sky, which was clearing and promising to be fair for the coming morning.

'This is our time right enough, all of us.' I wandered along the trench in search of a little tea. The Grimsby lads were well known for sorting out a decent ration of tea.

CHAPTER FORTY-FIVE
CAMBRAI, JULY 1916

We had all been dreading this moment. It did not matter that the wounded were Germans. They were still people and citizens – just not of France. Whatever had happened to me up until now, just for a moment, moved from my mind, leaving only compassion, forgiveness.

It was almost dark when the first ambulances arrived. The officer ambulances were a little different from those for the enlisted men. Bullet and bomb, however, saw no distinction of rank. It was clear now that the attack had happened and that it was a major battle. There was a constant stream of wounded – dusty, silent men, uniforms in tatters, or missing. Most had a stare, and grim faces focused on one another for fear of falling. The line moved slowly to where medical orderlies and nurses met them at the steps, moving them into three lines. The lines coming up the steps were men with flesh wounds, but who could still walk and sometimes talk. They were given beds on the communal ward, fifteen to a room. They would be tended and dressed, given medicines and comfort and then sent on to a larger hospital to recover, and likely fight again. Mostly, they were junior ranks and many were able to speak to me in the awful French of the German soldier.

The second line was moved along the street to the side door, which had been the entrance to the mortuary before the war. Now it was the entrance for stretchers, which were brought in one at a time. Most contained unconscious and more seriously wounded men. I was not allowed to nurse these soldiers as I had not yet been trained. There was a third line, a mixture of walking wounded and stretchers. Their uniforms were different to the Germans. From a distance, I imagined them to be British or French. For the first time since the Germans had appeared over the horizon, I saw the uniform of a friend. A wounded, hurt friend, but somehow it made me feel better. That line was also long and I was expected to tend these soldiers in any way that I could.

For the next five days, the lines of wounded coming in to Cambrai continued, almost without a break. Many went straight to the railways, to get trains to Germany. These men might return, but not for some time. Many had lost limbs, were blinded or behaved in the strangest ways. Some were tied to the orderlies with what looked like pillowcases or sheets, so that they could keep moving. They had the oddest expressions, and their uniforms just sat upon their shoulders, rather than the men wearing them proudly. This was a tragedy to observe, for friend or foe.

Father was able to visit us in the evening of the fifth day. He had been working hard on ambulances, almost without a break. It was clear that he still felt anger towards the Germans, but he showed it less outwardly. The sights were wretched and deflating to see and feel. It was punishment enough that the enemy was suffering so. The pain was still visible. For every one of these injured, there would be at least one in a British hospital, from the other end of the gun, just as hurt. I tried not to imagine one of them being William. Each time I thought of him as a broken body, like those here, it made me feel sick. I wanted to help, and almost *needed* to help this wave of broken men, which helped me to hold back the anger of the invaded.

The French soldiers were kindly to the French nurses as they probably knew the world we had been living in. We were not allowed to speak openly, so any conversations had to be brief and strictly related to the medical care being given. But when the French soldiers and French nurses spoke quietly and quickly, the Germans could not follow us.

They told me that the French and English, or British as they had come to call them, had taken Fricourt and the east bank of the Somme River. Fricourt was a large village, near my home, and it was in French hands again. The English, from places called Manchester and Liverpool, had moved into Montauban and Mametz. They were getting closer, and it was painful to imagine the destruction to the villages now.

The wounded French did not know of Bazentin, of Longueval or Ginchy. Perhaps the battle had not reached there. I knew now that they were not coming for us and we were not likely to be moved from here. I knew from Kurt that the Germans were building lines of defence near my home and also some work was going on here, by the canals. It seemed that this was to be a stronghold for the Germans, and we would be in the middle of it.

'Quick little one, you must move on before you are scolded. Courage, we will get them!'

That was a phrase I had heard frequently from the French soldiers. They realised that they were now prisoners of war, out of the trenches and perhaps they were glad. It was not like that for us. We were still in the middle of it. I had begun to think them lucky.

On the tenth day of the battle, the lines of wounded had subsided slightly. But this was because new hospitals had been set up hastily in other parts of the region, and not because fewer soldiers were being wounded.

Four stretchers were brought into our ward. Four stretchers like any others that had been brought in day after day. I was told to assess one of them immediately. Me, with almost no training!

I just had to get on with it and pulled back a sheet to discover a body, which at first seemed lifeless. A French uniform filled with a corpse. The face was blue, the lips black as soot. Had it been painted? But, there was life. His breathing was shallow, so he was alive after all – if that was a blessing I could not see it. Blood smears in his nose and down his uniform, but no wound that I could see. The uniform was complete, no holes or punctures, so he had not been shot, or hit by a bomb. But he was blue and barely alive. Something terrible had happened to him. One of the German stretcher bearers looked over my shoulder.

'Gas Fräulein, er sterben wird.' *He is dying.* Of course, I had seen dead bodies before, the dead of the lorry in the open, the dead of the camp. But this was an insult, a lingering suffering that pulled my soul and turned my skin to ice. The German voice snapped me back.

'What are you doing staring, Lefebvre. Quickly now, let us get him inside and tend to him.'

'But what can we do?'

'We make sure that he can breathe, make him comfortable and wait. There are no medicines for this. His lungs are burned and only time will tell if he will recover. Come now, quick to your duties, he cannot tell you he is in pain, but he is.'

As we moved the stretcher indoors, each movement caused more pain, even though our efforts stemmed from compassion and comfort. Suddenly, my anger at the Germans surfaced, but only briefly, before I realised that this war had no favourites, only victims. The poor wretched body in front of me convulsed and a thick clot of blood filled the man's mouth.

'It is his lungs, Odile. Help me to empty his mouth so that he can breathe.'

We tilted his head towards us and the blood ran down his face, forming a pool. As his head rested back, he stopped breathing. I stared at the body. Once a fine boy, now a corpse with black lips, lying on the floor of a stinking hospital. The fight for survival had not diminished one bit, but the fight was becoming different. We were all just one step from death and had to stay aware, thinking every day, and there was so little opportunity to help our brothers in the fight.

I slept uneasily that night, having been restless since this battle started, and tonight was no different. The face of the gassed soldier filled my dreams. Jean-Baptiste Martin. He was seventeen – the same age as me. Somewhere, his Mother worried for him and hoped for his return. Hopefully, she would be told that he died quickly, doing his duty, and not suffering on the floor of a German hospital. At least the last voices he heard were French, the last touch he felt was compassion. Many others, perhaps millions, would have no such comfort. It made me feel a little better to think it so for his family. Tomorrow, I would have to do it again, the day after and the day after that as well. This was my life now. No dirty blouse, but a suffering heart.

In my dream, William and Kurt were walking together, talking as if they were brothers. They wore no uniform, bore no scars and smiled in friendship. They looked back to me and waved and it made me feel both frightened and elated. As my eyes opened at dawn, the black lips and the lines of ambulances came back into my mind. I remembered that dreams can lie.

There was no point in my working in the hospital if I was not able to clear my head and help. For two days, I was back to giving out apples and comfort. It was hard with the German wounded. They had gassed Jean-Baptiste, and it was as if each one was personally responsible. It was stupid and immature of me, but his face, his face!

The morning was spent with German wounded. I remember just tossing the apples at them, with barely a cursory look. My mind was really on the evening's plans. Father was allowed to take me to the motor station where the ambulances were being kept. Yes, the machines were fascinating and I missed the smell of oil and petrol. But it was more important to be with Papa.

My dearest Father was still here, thanks to Kurt. However, Kurt was either still away, or had chosen not to see me. Each time Kurt came to mind, I was confused. My heart belonged still to William, even though I had left my final thoughts for William in our secret place. But now there was Kurt. He was not William, but he was kind and strong, and he had given us so much when I had given him so little in return. He had given without expectation so far, although that might change. But whilst the opportunity was with us, it made sense to make the best of my life and I could not wait to see Father.

The clock ticked around to six, and the wards were busy, but quieter. The nurses and the doctors had worked out a system to bring in new patients and to move on the less wounded more quickly. A hundred new stretchers no longer created ripples of panic. No more did the sights of disfigured and broken bodies shock me to the bone. It was all in a day's work for this war and it seemed set to continue.

Father was in his usual white shirt and overalls. He saw me and smiled broadly, then embraced me deeply, kissing the top of my head. Always his little girl.

'Come, let me show you the ambulance gearing. See, it flows all the way to the axle bearings so there is no vibration. What do you think?'

'It is very inventive, Father. Is this your design?'

'Yes. We have spent a month on the lathe, making up wooden models. This is the first full-size lorry.'

We both pored over the ambulance. Father, I knew, just wanted to be normal again. He wanted his little girl back, a girl who was pleased with every moment her Father spent with her. I wanted to be that girl but we could not go back in time.

'Odile, I know what you have had to do to help us. Of course, I have known about that officer for some time. Did he bring us here, to enjoy more comfort and less suffering? It worries me, Odile. It worries me what the cost has been to us, to you. Should I be worried, little one?'

Father only called me little one to remind me of more innocent times. It angered me a little, but it quickly subsided.

'Papa, do not worry. We have all learned to live and survive in this war. I have grown up much, and seen much. I know what I am doing, what it is necessary to do for my family. Kurt is kind to me, to us. He cares and I must let him care, for we do not know where this war will take us.'

Father took the rag he was holding, polished the bearings that really did not need it and then tossed it to the ground.

'Take us? We must win the war, Odile. We must send these, these...' He gestured towards the nearest soldiers, 'these Germans home again.'

Papa turned to them again, 'I know that you can hear me. Of course I want you to go home again. This is our country and you are the invaders.'

The soldiers turned to face Father. They stared for a second, then looked at me and turned away again.

'Papa, you must not do this. We have been with the Germans long enough. It does us no good, only harm. We have advantages here—'

'Advantages? Like Madame Collart?'

My heart leaped into my mouth.

'PAPA!'

'I am sorry Odile. We are speaking too fast for these fools to hear us. I know all about Madame. Her poor daughter. She was such a pleasant young girl. What of her, eh? You think you will be any different? What happens when this boy tires of you?'

'He won't. I am certain of his love for me.'

'Love? A German boy and the poor beaten French girl. It does not seem like a meeting of souls.'

Never had I spoken with Father like this before. He was different. Even the day he hit me, he was not as harsh as this. He did not know of my secret work, but he was trying to tell me something. I wished he would simply say it. Our world was no longer innocent, but filled with danger and death.

'But Papa, it is for us to survive this war, however we can.'

'Be that as it may, Odile. Just remember you are the daughter of a proud French family. I have seen the stones and shit thrown at you. There are enough horses here for that to continue for a year. We can live without the favours of the enemy. We can survive. I can survive and protect you.'

I stepped towards Father, taking his hands in mine. He grasped my hands in return, gently rubbing my wrists.

'Darling daughter. Darling Odile. Your Mother and I suffered much for you even to live in this world. It would break my heart that I did not fight for you to stay in it.'

I leaned up and kissed Father.

'Yes, I know Papa, all too well. It will be fine. You will see.'

I sat and watched Father continue on the engines. He would look up and smile, seeming content now that he had said what he had needed to. Perhaps in his way, he had made a little peace with the Germans, at least for now.

CHAPTER FORTY-SIX
CAMBRAI, JULY 1916

I returned to the hospital in the late evening. More patients had been moved out and away to other hospitals and only the very seriously wounded remained. Men who might not last a day, or even this night. So there was little for me to do as I was not allowed to tend those German wounded who could not speak and sit up. The French had been moved away, or were the less seriously wounded cases. I was restless still, feeling a deep sense of dread in my body that pulsed to the tips of my fingers.

Mother was restless as well. When I finally arrived home, she was sitting at the tiny table, the dim light from the candle barely reaching past the table itself.

'Can you hear the guns, Odile?'

'Not really, Maman. What does that mean?'

'Something might have happened, or is happening. I do not like it.'

'Are our lives now lived to the rhythm of big guns, Maman? Is this to be our world?'

'For now Odile, yes. Look. There are messages to take. We must continue the work of Madame Collart. Will you come with me?'

'Messages? But the town is full of Germans. We will not be able to move anywhere without arousing suspicion.'

'You have your nurse's uniform. The hospital on the Rue Charlemagne is near to where we must deliver the message. You must go very soon. Will you go?'

'Of course, Maman. The uniform, yes. That might work.'

'It will have to work.'

So, as I had done previously, I set out into the night towards the canal. Mother had been given a message at the factory. Perhaps it had been sent by telephone, or in person. We did not know. Perhaps the message contained something vital. If it did, why give it to a frightened girl? If it did not, why risk my life? Perhaps it was better not to question, but just to act.

The night was cool and clear. Every step was filled with foreboding, walking through the busy night, carrying a secret message, dressed as a nurse. I was entitled to dress this way, but not on this business. It was a very great risk. I did not know if it could possibly be worth it.

I was at the canal quickly, having attracted some attention, although the waves and whistles of the soldiers seemed friendly enough. No soldier had asked for papers, nor held me up in any way, simply moving aside, tapping their caps and wishing me a good evening in German. It was dreadful being on my own, feeling alone, uncertain whether anyone was watching out for me – certainly, there was no sign of the cigarette smoker.

I stepped down and along the path to the bush. No one was in sight, or approaching from the distance. But it was early, so there was no need for concern. I waited past midnight. Anytime now, my contact should arrive.

Finally, there was a tap-tap on the path. It was an old man with a walking stick made from a tree branch. I looked to the path. A man was smoking a cigarette, when I looked to him, he threw it to the ground, stamping on it twice. He turned his back and walked away. The man with the walking stick approached me, looking directly into my eyes.

'Cool evening at this hour? Perhaps the summer is turning quickly?'

'Yes, it is cool. Hopefully the summer will continue though.' It was terrifying, I will admit. The smoker had indicated two men were here but there was only one and I did not know him

'I think perhaps there will be news tomorrow?'

'News?'

'Yes, there will be developments. A little surprise perhaps. One can never be sure, but I would listen for the signs. The birds sing a strange song at this time of year. What do you think?'

'Perhaps, yes. Look, I don't know if—'

He raised a hand towards my lips.

'The nights are short, especially tonight. Quickly, and then you must get back to safety.'

I passed the tiny papers to him. Then the old man looked up towards the bridge. He turned and moved away, down the path.

'Look to the dawn.' He was gone.

I stood there, suddenly alone again. The cigarette man was gone, the old man tapping back down the path now no more than a spot in the distance. Panic grew in my chest, my heart pounding too fast. What to do now? The rules were simple. Turn and go, without another glance.

The streets were dark and quiet. It was busy on the main routes through the town as the soldiers moved towards the Front. But away from the roads, it was less busy. There were quarters for officers and the administration of the occupation. Once or twice, voices or footsteps were heard, but I remained unnoticed. At the other end of our street, there was a small gathering of soldiers, smoking and drinking something hot, as steam rose from their cups. It was not possible to avoid them, it was late at night and I should not have been on the street. It was all I could do not to run away, but I needed to be ready for them, and so I thought of Maman and what she would do in this situation. How would she use the soldiers' weakness against them?

I approached them, keeping my head up, so as not to look at all suspicious. A nurse's uniform was a currency that could take me to safety if all went well.

One of the soldiers had spotted me. He tapped his friend on the arm and nodded in my direction. They muttered something in German, it was too fast and too quiet for me to understand it. One of them called to me, perhaps they had not realised I was French.

'Ah! Frenchie? Ja!'

This might not be an easy conversation. One of the other soldiers turned around and stared directly at me.

'Hello Mademoiselle! You look lovely this night! Are you going to the hospital now, eh?'

'Yes. I have been summoned to tend your wounded from the battlefield in the south. I must hurry quickly.'

'Not so fast eh? Less quickly! What is your name Nurse Lovely?' There was a roar of laughter. Three of them were staring at me, looking me up and down.

'My name is Mademoiselle Lefebvre and I am late now for the patients.'

The youngest soldier grabbed my arm. 'All in good time. Where is your Papa, eh? Fighting us in Verdun? Ha!'

'He is quite well and working for the administration somewhere in France.'

'Ah! I see. Good. Perhaps you and I could—'

'It is very late now and I must be allowed to pass.'

I looked straight at the first soldier and spoke very calmly and softly to him, making sure every word was clear.

'Sir, you would not like it if your daughter was held by the arm in a street, late at night, in your town, by a group of soldiers unknown to her now would you?'

The grip relaxed from my arm. The three soldiers looked blankly at each other. Perhaps a thought from home had wandered across their minds. And perhaps I had learned Mother's method of knowing how to cut to their souls quickly, especially the older ones with daughters like me.

'I am sorry, Mademoiselle. But if I may say, you are most beautiful.'

'Thank you sir, and good night.'

They all tipped their caps at me, and walked off.

'Until tomorrow night then. I will be here ha ha!'

I did not look back and it was an effort to stop myself from running. When I returned home, I collapsed, trembling, into Maman's waiting arms. The night had not been easy – for either of us. We had had easier nights and we had lived through much worse ones. For now, we sat quietly in the dim light, while I reported back to Maman, taking care to leave out the discussion with the soldiers.

'Odile, can we bear this much longer? Can we truly live through this, or are we just existing in this place?'

221

'Maman, think of Father. He is here with us and we are with him. Poor Madame Collart, little Amelie. Think of the families destroyed, at least we have survived.'

'It is to our wits we must turn again, Odile. You must make sure that German boy is in love with you. He may be the only true friend we have left in this awful war.'

True friend? I had never imagined Kurt to be a friend. Unusual company perhaps, a necessary tool in our survival box, but a friend? That sounded dangerous.

I was due at the hospital in the morning, for the feeding watch. It was, I suppose, a kind job. But the soldiers were still the same ones who had invaded my country, the same ones who had killed the Collarts, and the same ones who kept William from me, curse them.

It was still dark when the most terrible rumbling of guns came from the front line to the south. There was clearly a renewed attack by someone, somewhere near to Longueval. There were flashes of light, and bombs bursting, in the direction of Longueval, perhaps further south – it was hard to see and to judge the distance. But it made me feel sick inside, and I knew Mother felt it as well.

Almost as soon as it had started, it ceased and we returned to quiet. The little clock ticked around to three-thirty. Dull thuds and vibrations continued throughout the night and on into the morning. Mother had already gone to work when I rose at six, desperately tired, as I had been for all of July. When I set off, the weather was warm and still. I wondered what the attack was and what had happened the previous night. It gave me a bad feeling, but that seemed normal enough. The war was a slow grind for both sides. The trails of ambulances were not becoming any shorter, but nor were they getting any longer…

CHAPTER FORTY-SEVEN
MID-JULY, 1916

At the hospital, there was calm, but everyone's movements seemed more urgent and considered, with each nurse focused on her job. Something had happened last night that had the staff on edge. The senior nurse, who had once been kind to me, now spoke purposefully and harshly at everyone. She turned to us, her lips grimly together, a faint pink stain along the length of her apron. We were beckoned to follow her along the long corridor of the hospital.

'Quickly you two, come with me. We have much work to do. There will be no handover this morning, as all staff are to remain on duty. Casualties are expected from the Front at any moment. We are expecting three hundred today. They will be here by nine-thirty.'

I was expecting to be given a basket of fruit, as usual. A silly gesture amongst all of the wounded. Of course, kindness must give way to the suffering today.

'Odile, you will remain here, preparing beds in this new ward. Remember, two pillows, crisply plumped, an under sheet, top sheet and one blanket only per bed. Hurry you have fifty to do in one hour. Off you go.'

One bed a minute, which meant no time to waste. As I worked, I imagined who the occupant would be. Some poor man in a stinking uniform, covered in dirt and sweat, blood and goodness knew what, dropped on to these crisp white sheets that smelled of the hospital. Some poor man who had been dragged from the battlefield on a stretcher, bumping along in an ambulance tended by my Father. Some poor man who was lucky to have been found, according to the stories we had been told. This was not to be a good day, whichever army prevailed.

The first casualties arrived before nine. They had been in front-line trenches and in the artillery to the rear close to Martinpuich – almost at my own home. Their wounds were every kind of horror, and we had no time to stare and to stand in shock, we had to treat them quickly.

As usual, the French doctor and the senior nurse met the wounded at the large entrance. Many were sent to the old mortuary entrance for stretchers. Others walked in through the step entrance. One man had lost both of his arms and the stumps were tied up with rope made from his shirt. He was walking in! How could that be possible? But there he was and he was not alone.

Lines of grim faces, all German, stared back at me. This was no time for small talk in broken French and German. This was a purposeful day filled with wounds, operations, amputations and dressings. For each horrible wound I saw, the next was the same or worse. The lines seemed endless. I had been given little training for nursing and yet here I was, tending the most awful insults to the human body. I cursed the Germans, every single one of them, to my very soul. They had taken everything from us. I had not forgotten the beatings, the humiliations and the torments in the camps. I saw Amelie in my head, her broken body that had suffered unimaginable humiliations. I saw Madame Collart in the house with the pale green door, scarves tight around her neck, and the damaged bodies at the roadside, from the start of the war.

It was these men before me who had caused it. It was these blackened faces of pain, with bright red, weeping flesh under their uniforms. The burnt and shot, the deafened and blinded. I could easily have increased their suffering for all of the suffering they had caused my family, my friends and my fellow citizens. And also for any suffering they were meting out to my poor William. But of course, I could not, for these were no more than poor boys, poor soldiers who had been brave for their country and did not deserve what had happened to them.

I looked down at the hand of the soldier now in front of me. He had lost much of his face in a clean wound across his jaw and nose, perhaps a shell had burst near to him. His nails were dirty and bleeding, his palm cut and swollen. I held his large and filthy hand in mine. His fingers closed and gripped my hand a little tighter. His chest rose and fell, and I sensed a calm inside. Then his chest fell and did not rise again. I stood for what seemed like minutes holding his lifeless hand. He had passed. His last moment spent holding my hand, the hand of a friend.

'Don't just stand there Lefebvre, quickly now. Get the orderlies to move him out, we must use the bed again. It is not too soiled, so just change the under sheet, come now!'

In an instant the soldier was gone, his name never known to me. Immediately, a new man, with equally terrible wounds had replaced him. These were the less serious cases. The most badly wounded went in through the mortuary. I dared not imagine the state of those fellows. The lines outside the window were growing. These soldiers had been brought along the Albert Road and had arrived quickly from the battlefield. But there would be more, arriving later from the same battlefield, whose journey would have been filled with far more trauma. Evacuation from the field on a stretcher under fire, being tended to at an aid post by an overworked orderly, followed by an arduous journey over shell holes and temporary roads. Roads that I had seen being built when I had gone to Martinpuich.

The thought of Martinpuich, reminded me once more of the little note that I had left William. It really was foolish of me to have risked so much to go there. My tormented mind had craved some sort of normality, and somehow it had made me feel a little better, putting on paper my true feelings before the war took me. Now, it had taken me further away from my life and my love, and into a world of bandages, blood, suffering and the devil.

Perhaps I was losing touch with the world around me. Having tried so hard to keep thinking amongst this terrible suffering, thinking was now the one thing that I wanted to avoid. Not thinking would allow the numbness to overcome me, to deny the pain and suffering around me, to shield me from the wounded lined up here. But I could not stop thinking and so I took a deep breath and looked down at the new occupant of the bed. Already he seemed weaker and his breathing shallower.

'This soldier has been shot cleanly in the back by a bullet. There is a bullet hole to dress and clean to stop the bleeding. See, here is where the bullet came out. It is much bigger as the bullet probably broke apart, or it spun as it slowed down. It is not near to his spine, so that will be good. But the bleeding is bad, or was. He might need to be tied down to stop him moving and opening the wound again. Can you manage that Odile?'

'Yes Madame. I think I remember.'

'No apples today, Odile.' She put her hand on my shoulder, squeezed gently and moved on. The senior nurse still had time to understand.

All day this continued. The register showed three-hundred-and-thirty wounded from the battlefields of Martinpuich. One soldier said he had been in a trench in the Bois de Forcaux. That was the wood I had once walked in with William, just over the field from our house in Bazentin.

At eight in the evening we were allowed a break. Most of us just went outside, some to weep and some to simply take in some fresh air in the evening calm. But tonight was not calm. Outside, Germans were moving about with excitement. Something must be about to happen.

We learned that the civilians in the factory had been allowed out at seven-thirty, but had been told to remain in the square. Perhaps it was to be an identification check, or perhaps the puppet mayor was to make a speech about working hard and remaining calm. There was an air of anticipation, as if the carnival was coming to town.

Then I saw it.

CHAPTER FORTY-EIGHT
CAMBRAI, MID-JULY 1916

At first, it was not clear what I was looking at. On the right were lines of German soldiers with torn uniforms and wounded bodies. On the left was a group of German soldiers with clean uniforms, and armed with rifles and pistols. They were leading another group of soldiers, some with strange round helmets and some with bare heads. Most of this group had a bandage or two, but they all had their heads down and were almost asleep, propped up by the man next to them. Their uniforms were not known to me. Then, I heard shouts.

'Oh my God, these are English prisoners!'

The uniformed men I was looking at, with their round helmets, were British soldiers. They were prisoners and they were being paraded down the street in front of the whole town, a town still full of French. We had seen some French wounded, not that many, which upset us greatly. But this was a stream of prisoners, large numbers of men captured in the battle.

'My God, they look so tired and thin. Things are not too good on our side, are they?'

The waves of fear in the crowd were almost visible. If the prisoners had been strong and defiant, it might have been something. But these men were dirty and wounded, with torn uniforms and their heads down.

One or two of the crowd tried to speak with them in French, but the Germans pushed them back.

'No talking, fuck off French pig.'

But I could speak English well and pushed to the front. 'How are you?'

'Oh, not too bad miss, thank you!'

'Where did you come from?'

'A village called Bazentin something! Cheerio'

My heart nearly stopped. I moved along the lines, pushing people out of the way, I had to know more.

'Bazentin-Le-Petit? Is there anything left?'

'Sounds right. No miss, maybe the odd wall.'

This news made me want to scream at the Germans. My emotions were flowing in all directions. The line halted at the end of the road. The soldiers gathered themselves together again. It was clear that they had been marched all the way here, to make them tired and weary, so they would look beaten. The dusty roads had covered them with dirt, increasing the effect.

I turned back to the English soldier. 'The village. You say it is gone. Did you take it?'

The soldier looked directly at me. He looked weary and afraid, perhaps haunted by the battle. He smiled at me.

'Yes, we cleared the village this morning.'

'It is my home!'

The other soldiers looked up towards me. Perhaps their struggle had a purpose after all. Then there was a voice from the back.

'Better take a fucking broom with you luv!' The whole line started laughing and marched off, a song starting up somewhere near the back.

The French looked at each other and shrugged. Our English would have been too fast for them to understand any of the words. They looked to me as I started to push back to the hospital.

'What was that? What did they say? Why did they laugh? Did we win?'

A warm glow rose from my stomach, tingling into my arms and hands, eventually warming my face.

'They are coming, perhaps this is the end.'

I arrived at the hospital just as the last of the prisoners was paraded through the square. The effect created was most likely exactly as the Germans had intended. The French saw their captured friends, worn, weary, dirty and afraid.

But I had seen the German wounded. They were no victors. This war saw no winners, just young men ground slowly to wet dust. As I reached the steps, I smiled and said to myself, 'My darling William.'

I entered the cool of the wards, took a deep breath and walked to the first bed.

CHAPTER FORTY-NINE
CAMBRAI, MID-JULY 1916

The hospital was now full of wounded, including French and British. In fact, there were British, Canadians, and two Australians. I was allowed to visit them and to take them apples as a kindness. A lot of the food for the soldiers went missing, or was tampered with by the French. The Germans informed the civilians handling the food that they would eat from the same stocks, so if there was anything out of place, then they too would suffer. But once the British and the Allies started to arrive in the hospital, less food was taken or destroyed.

New hospitals had opened – wherever a roof was still in place, the floors could be made into wards for Germans. There were a lot of them as well. More and more German nurses arrived and they were not at all kind to the French ones. More than once, I saw a French girl slapped, or pushed around by these nurses. To the wounded, however, the German nurses showed kindness and care, irrespective of which uniform they wore.

Father was kept in solitary duty by the Germans because working ambulances were a high priority and he worked from dawn until nearly midnight each night. Then, he was kept under guard in his little room in the motor station.

On the fifteenth of July, we received news that more prisoners were to pass through on to trains bound for Belgium or Germany. Once again we were to expect a parade of captured men. Some of the French wanted to stay away, but were not allowed. Others wanted to shield their eyes, or turn their backs, but that was considered an insult to the soldiers.

This time, we also paraded. At the head of the procession was a German military band playing terrible tunes, much to the delight of the German soldiers. The French threw insults at them, including some horse dirt from the road. Some were beaten for it, usually ones innocent of the crime. From upper windows, showers of stinking yellow liquid were thrown, which sometimes drew a response from the guards. Mostly though, the German soldiers simply marched on, as if nothing were amiss, amid all our noise and shouting.

After the soldiers had passed through, then came the procession of the prisoners. Most wore their tin helmets and their uniforms were as tidy as they could manage. Tonight, the prisoners showed their strength in defiance of the enemy. They called out in English to the crowd and the crowd waved and shouted. But anyone getting too close was pushed back, or kicked, until they did not call out again. Some of the soldiers were wounded and one or two were diverted into our little hospital.

For the next two days, I saw a steady stream of German and British soldiers in the hospital. Side by side, they did not seem to be mortal enemies. Once denied the battlefield, they became men who could otherwise have been brothers – my brothers, little Henri as a man.

In the daytime, the lorries were parked in the square to be worked on in good daylight and I could often see Papa from the balcony of the wards. I did not enjoy visiting the German officers. They were rude and insulting, their feeling of superiority over the French clearly visible, even in an unfamiliar language. I wished Kurt was here, but I wished for William more.

The hospital was quieter. The long lines of wounded had been seen and assessed, moved to bigger hospitals, or to houses adapted as little hospitals for special care. These officers had been moved here overnight, arriving from the battlefield in motor ambulances, cars and carts. Mixed in amongst them were officers from the British wounded, apparently picked up by Germans from the battlefield, in acts of kindness that seemed rarer these days.

The new factory was away from the square so I could not look out and see Father at all, but I hoped that his work was not too heavy. He had looked so tired recently, he was still Papa, but it seemed that the fight had gone out of him a little recently. Daily lines of broken ambulances kept him busy and he did not mind this work so much. He was an engineer, not a mechanic, but he loved turning a spanner and maybe saw this as skilled work and not slavery.

The little house with the pale green door was now locked. No longer could I knock and enter, as I had done for some time. I did not know what had happened to the mysterious occupants, but they had probably fled, moved or perhaps even been discovered. All I knew was no one asked me to move any more messages to the British. Perhaps the messages were only for this battle and the job was completed. In any case, not knowing everything helped to keep me safe. Often, I had wondered how much Madame Collart really knew.

Back at the hospital on the eighteenth, I spent the day moving between the larger and smaller hospitals, fetching, carrying and taking food and fruit to the wounded. Some of the other citizens had volunteered to do this as well as those of us who were forced to be here, now that the hospital had French and British officers. It was quite an event, twice a day, visiting the prisoners on one side and the Germans on the other. It was interesting to see the French. The French nurses tended to throw the apples at the German patients, sometimes this got us into trouble. This strange parade was not enjoyable, and I tried to shield my face, not wanting a pleasant word, nor wanting to offer comfort to these lightly wounded German officers. Too many damaged bodies had taken my emotion away to leave any to waste on these arrogant fools.

At the end of the evening, I tossed the little basket in the corner, took out three apples from under my skirts, and hid them in my apron. The three of us had fresh fruit more often, thanks to the Germans. We decided not to share fresh fruit with the French around us for now, for we did not want to bring more trouble on our shoulders. But, large sugar and flour rations would appear in Maman's factory now and again, along with mysterious packages of meat and cheese. The hospital stocks always being adjusted accordingly so that the stores officer never realised, or never said. I did wonder sometimes. Even so, Mother and I would still occasionally feel the pain of a stick in a darkened alleyway, or the feel of cold horse manure down our backs. It was still difficult to work out who were real friends and who was the true enemy.

CHAPTER FIFTY
MID-JULY 1916

Three days of fighting had apparently taken place somewhere near our home in Bazentin. The names of Longueval and Delville Wood were mentioned many times, often followed by a wince or a frown. It seemed that the Germans did not to want to be upon the exposed ridges of my home. These ridges, once so peaceful and full of the sounds of the seasons, instead of the new sounds of big guns tearing up the ground and grinding men to dust.

Still, the wounded kept arriving, but the lines were mercifully shorter as more hospitals had been set up. More wounded British arrived, and these men looked particularly desolate and alone, surrounded by unfamiliar uniforms, the language unknown to them and in pain, anxious for their fates.

Kurt returned on the evening of the nineteenth of July. Immediately, he had spoken with his commanding officer, he came to find me. He appeared pleased that I was nursing Germans and that we had everything that we needed.

'Odile, my dear. Let us walk this evening. The last days have worn me down and I am in need of repair. Will you come?'

'If you order me to, of course.'

Kurt looked at me sharply, a look of hurt in his eye. The time apart had hardened me towards him again. I had to quickly gather myself or betray my feelings.

'Order you? But I thought…'

'Sorry Kurt. It is just that everyone has been ordering me around every day for ages – especially the German nurses, they are the worst.'

He laughed. 'Worst? Ah, oh yes, I see! They are the most terrible. They must be, or they would go insane.'

I looked down, feeling my harshness fade a little.

'Yes Kurt, let us walk tonight. But not here, for here there are too many dying men. This is a place of the dead, a city of the fallen.'

He did not reply, but gently took my arm. At least now, in my uniform, I would not attract unwelcome attention. This uniform shielded me from them all – French and German.

'Odile, it has been so hard for me the last days. We have been moving soldiers day and night without a stop for breath.'

It was hard not to tell him what was really on my mind, but I remembered the delicate games being played by those on all sides.

'I am sorry, Kurt. Truly I am. Still, you are here now, how long do you have?'

'Four days and then I must go to Koln to supervise the movement of men. That is all that I am allowed to say. For how long, it is not possible to say. But you can rely on me to make sure you are cared for and safe. You have a nurse's duty now and that makes it better, yes?'

'Yes. But it is not the same without you. The soldiers and the people are different when you are not here.'

He thought for a moment, stopped and then turned to me.

'Come with me, Odile. Come to Germany for the rest of the war. There must be a way to arrange it, somehow it must possible. Will you come with me?'

It was an impulsive outburst. Clearly he had not planned this, had not thought of what he was saying. Maybe a Fraulein in the fields in Germany would have jumped at the chance. But here, one step from death or life at the back of the tit lorry, I could not consider it. Being surrounded by my family and having the comfort of doing something for France helped me to keep my nerve. In Germany I would be helpless, trapped, alone, isolated and without any means to help France. Here, it was bearable, just. There, it would be unendurable.

'Oh, Kurt! What are you saying? How could that be possible? Perhaps you should find out and then ask me again when you are quite sure.'

Again, he looked at me carefully, as if reading my face and interpreting the tone in my voice. My thoughts were calm and clear now. I was the daughter of a French man and woman, driven from their homes by that uniform.

'Very well, I will do that! Come, let us finish our walk.'

As we walked, I wondered what would come next. It was clear to me that I was gambling my life. There were kindnesses and pleasantries, gifts of food and clothing, a little privilege from a German officer's rank. But the instant Kurt sensed any crack, an inconsistent remark or betrayal in my voice, he could turn against me and my family. He already had reason enough to despise Papa. In a second, we could be cast back to the camps, to live as beggars, uncertain of any future. We would never receive a little blue book, or the gift of milk. We would face certain death, death in sight of our own home.

In the morning, there was a little fog and dampness in the air and I hurried to the hospital. Kurt met me briefly on my way to the ward, and walked with me, holding my arm. It was an effort for me, but I tried to relax, so that he might not think he was holding a piece of wood. Perhaps it was my pliancy, or perhaps he had been thinking while he'd been away, but as we parted, he looked deeply into my eyes.

'Odile, I do believe that I am in love with you.'

This declaration stunned me. In the past, I had kissed Kurt, my mind on

William, and it was obvious to me that he had strong feelings for his little French girl. But this was a sincere, determined and deliberate confirmation of his love for me. He looked at me, clearly waiting for a reply in kind.

'For my part Kurt, I want nothing more than to be here with you.'

Before they were even out, the words soured in my mouth, my tongue thickening and betraying my soul. Kurt peered at me.

'What does that mean?'

'It means... it means that is all I can give for now. Until the war... well until the war is over. Don't you see Kurt?'

'Yes I see most clearly, Odile. You do not love me.'

'Give me time, my dearest. Just a little time to help me understand my feelings for you and for your country.'

Kurt nodded, and seemed content with my words for the time being. At least my choice of words had caused no harm, but they could hardly be construed as loving.

'Very well Odile, I will see you this evening, before it is time for me to go away again.'

I smiled, waved, and went inside quickly. I was late.

Some of the soldiers had been moved away to another hospital, with the British being moved to the building used to keep prisoners away from the wounded German soldiers. This building overlooked the motor lorries as they were dispatched to the battlefields. The parking place was no more than a minute from the British building, and occasionally I saw Father pretending not to look through the windows.

He was not often allowed to see Mother and me, being forced to work on the lorries all day and most evenings. The ambulances were in need of constant repair. The roads were hit all the time and ambulances would drop into holes, having their wheels torn away, their engines caked in mud, soaked in water or hit by British bombs. Still, it kept Father busy, it kept Mother happy that he was alive and it kept all of us away from the terrible camps. I felt certain that they still existed and imagined even now that we might yet be dragged down again into the horrors of the camps.

The evening came all too quickly, after a day spent changing dripping bandages, boiled in large copper pans. I was not allowed to speak to the soldiers, but was occasionally allowed to take them books to read, or to bring them water to drink. The soldiers had the same terrible injuries, day after day. Arms and legs, stomachs and faces, blinded and mute, deafened and paralysed. It was awful to see the way that a body could be damaged, destroyed in a moment by the war in my villages. Our peace shattered by this monster, out of all our control and no one and nothing seemed able to stop it.

In the early evening, I was allowed to move the less seriously wounded men onto the small balcony overlooking the street. When I was pushing one of the wheelchairs out, I saw Father down on the street, looking agitated and coming towards the hospital. He kept looking over his shoulder, left and right, as if expecting some silent creature to pounce. It made him appear suspicious and surely the soldiers must have also noted his odd behaviour.

Without making myself look suspicious, I made an excuse to find a blanket and disappeared back inside. Then, I walked calmly the length of the corridor to the stairs, and almost flung myself down them to the street to find my Father.

'Papa, please, what is it? I know something is not right? What is it?'

'Oh Odile, it is the most incredible news. Odile! Not here, we must go inside.'

Thinking quickly, I moved us both towards the little doors to the mortuary. For now, it was quiet. The ambulances had not yet arrived for the evening.

'Papa, please! Is it Maman? Are you well? You seem unhurt?'

Almost without thinking I was stroking his arms, looking for a wound.

'No, no Odile. It is the most incredible news.'

He took a deep breath and looked straight into my eyes. His eyes were tired and wet, but in them I could see the fire again.

'William is here. He is here in Cambrai!'

'What do you mean William? My William? Where? How?' My body coursed with wave after wave of nervous energy and everything started to spin around me.

'I am quite sure it was him, I spotted him in the building where the British are being kept. He is a little older and the war has done something to him. But it was him. He is a soldier, you were right.'

'Oh, Papa, is he badly wounded?' I hardly dared ask.

Father nodded. 'It appears so as he was using a stick, but he was at least walking. He looked right at me and he recognised me!'

'Oh, my poor William – a wounded prisoner.'

For now, I could say no more. Tears filled my eyes and Papa embraced me. The war flooded over me until I was under the waves. Held by Papa, I did not try to fight the tears. I wanted to be strong, but this was my beloved Father. With him, I could be weak and exposed and I cried until my chest hurt and my throat ached.

'Courage my love, at least William is here and no longer on the battle fields.'

I wiped my eyes, still not fully able to believe my own Father's words.

'Did you manage to speak with him?'

'No, but he is here in the war. Alive and well, and he remembers. Odile, what do you say?'

'Oh my darling William. You are here, here in this war. My boy from over the sea. Tell me you have come for me.'

'Odile, you can arrange to see him in the morning. Can you not be in the party that takes the rations to the British prisoners?'

It had not occurred to me that I could see William at all. Clearly shock had overtaken my thoughts. But the urge to look upon my love overtook me.

'But of course, the apples! The little treat for the prisoner soldiers. Oh Papa, you are wonderful!'

'Quickly, back to work Odile. We can speak more later. I will arrange to come tonight, if it is allowed.'

'Oh Papa!'

My Father embraced me once more before I left. He smelled deeply of oil and grease, and I was transported home again, for a brief moment. To the sound of the funny car and the swish of the harvest. The driving rain on the slopes and the fog in the mornings. There it was, lovely safe Bazentin. The little village that the war had taken as a prize.

So, William had to be in the new building, where I saw the British soldiers being taken. The prisoners were on the upper floors, because it was normal practice to keep them away from German movements.

'Madame. Will we still take apples to the other hospital, now that all the soldiers have been moved?'

'What? Why do you care, hmm? What is it to you? You are assigned to this hospital, my girl. The German nurses will not allow it.'

'Thank you Madame. But why can we not take some comfort to them? Would it be possible?'

Madame put down the sheet that she had nearly finished folding. She thought for a moment.

'An act of kindness, eh?'

'There are British prisoners, Madame, fighting for the liberty of France.' I thought these words would help, but it seemed to anger Madame and she stood upright and glared down at me.

'Go and get on with your duties, girl.'

With that, she swiftly gathered the sheets that she had been folding. Then she called over her shoulder without turning.

'Be quick and finish by seven, then come and see me immediately your duties are completed.'

I was both excited and anxious. William, my love, the force that held my world together was here. But Kurt was here too, for a little longer. This was almost too much. Joyous and elated inside, but outside I had to be calm and composed. Our lives depended on it.

Kurt came for me at six. I told him about being on duty until seven and then having to go and see Madame. He promised to come back. I sensed a change in him, or was the change in me? He looked disappointed, as if the shop had sold out.

At seven, I was finished. My duties done long ago, aching for the clock to come round. The evening was cooler, but clear.

'Madame.' I stood outside the door, and waited to be called in.

'Come in Lefebvre and close the door behind you.'

'Madame.' I bowed my head slightly, to the senior nurse.

'Report to the nursing supervisor at eight in the morning, at the steps of the Town Hall wing of the new hospital. I have, with the agreement of the Kommandant, arranged for a small group to visit the soldiers. It is for Germans only, so you must not speak. Your role is to assist the soldiers as they greet some visitors. There, what do you think?'

'Madame, it is most excellent. Thank you.'

I left. The little party was for the Germans, but I would be in the hospital where William was being cared for. It was close enough. Perhaps I would get to see him, if only fleetingly, but it would sustain me for the rest of the war.

Kurt came again after seven. He brought a small flower for my hair. I felt as though all eyes were upon me, just for wearing a flower. But I did it for him, for Mother and Father, and for the hope that I might get to see William. I stayed in my uniform, as it provided protection – perhaps I was moving under orders and not for my own sake. But the flower betrayed me.

'You seem quiet, Odile. Have you had a long and trying day?'

'Yes, the bodies of damaged and dying men are on my mind. It is hard to see the joy in the evening. I am sorry.'

'It is no matter. Time with you is quite enough.'

Kurt stopped. He looked at my eyes, not into them. I thought he was reading me, trying to see through me to the deception inside. Perhaps he was satisfied with what he saw.

'I am in love with you Odile and I will do everything possible to protect you and your family. Your Father is less of a concern to the army now, as he seems to believe that his work has earned a reward. But it is you Odile. It is your beauty and spirit that sustains me in this war. Do you know this?'

'Yes Kurt, I think so.'

'Do you? Do you realise that I wish you to come to Germany and to be with me. To be, in time, my wife? Do you now understand?'

'Of course. But remember what I said. This war will keep us apart. It would not be possible for me to be your wife until this war is done. This war between Germany and France. This war between you and your dreams, me and mine.'

This time, the second time I said this, the words had less effect.

'You have made your position clear. But the Germans will be victorious and you will be mine, Odile. I want you, and I will have you.'

Kurt took my face in his hands, firmly but gently, as he tilted my face to meet his lips. He was soft and welcoming and kissed me deeply. I tried to think only of William, of today's discovery, and what I was to look forward to in the morning. But my thoughts were washed away by Kurt's touch. My mind was drawn to his lips by his kiss and my body softened to him, drawn towards his power and energy. Was it the uniform or him? Country and home? I lifted my hands to his, placing them gently upon his fingers. My touch made him move forwards, kissing me more deeply. The world around melted away for a moment.

'Now I understand Odile, and I think you do as well.'

Afterwards, we watched the end of a show in the square. The Germans continued to entertain us with a show once a week. It was a thin coating of politics over the brutality of their occupation, and the citizens knew it. But they had to attend and participate, just as with the hospital and prisoner parades.

Despite this, Kurt was kind and warm, attentive and considerate. He was to leave that evening for the Koln railhead. He would be gone for some time. I knew he would send for me, once he was settled. This time, he would not be concerned with Mother and Father. This time, I would be alone and exposed. With William so close and yet so far away in this town, my mind was a wind storm of uncertainties, horrors and hopes.

Tonight, perhaps more than any other since leaving the camps, would determine our futures. Thoughts of Madame Collart, Amelie, Father and Mother, danced about my head. Kurt's arm was strong, protective and willing. But William, was now here in this place, a living being, not just the memory of a warm glow of happiness – a memory now softened by time. This was agony. Not a physical pain, from a beating or an insult, but one all the more awful for its ability to cut through me.

I looked to Kurt's face again. Not the face of a brute, but the face of a kind man, the saviour of my family, perhaps. Father was in better spirits, Mother was working and surviving. I could manage. I could survive. I could do this.

We walked to the hospital so I could collect a fresh uniform for the morning. If William did see me, he would see me looking well and cared for, so he would not worry for me. Father had said that William seemed to recognise him, so perhaps he did think of us still. Perhaps he even thought of me with fondness. I would know tomorrow.

Kurt left me at the hospital steps. He held my face in his hand and I felt myself leaning in towards his touch. My whole body was in turmoil, my stomach churning over and over. I hoped my face gave nothing away of the conflicts inside of me.

'I will see you soon Odile, but it may be many weeks. The Germans are moving some citizens and troops from Cambrai further north. It may be that you must be amongst them. I will bring you to Germany, if it is possible. You will be with me, Odile, once my arrangements are complete.'

'Very well, Kurt. Goodnight to you.' I looked to his face, his youthful eyes bright and clear. His face was near to mine, his breath on my face, his finger brushing my ear. With a jolt, I realised something for the first time. I really *wanted* him to kiss me.

CHAPTER FIFTY-ONE
MID-JULY 1916

I arrived at the hospital at seven, having hardly slept. My dreams were once again filled with William and Kurt playing their almost nightly game in the fields of Bazentin. First one, and then the other, would find his way to me. I was torn between the life I wanted and the one that most likely lay before me.

In my new uniform, I prayed no one would notice my old one hidden in the store pile to keep the uniform piles the same height. My old uniform was a little grey, but hidden in the pile, it would hopefully not be discovered for some time. It was a risk worth taking for the sake of saving William from worry.

There were two baskets of fruit to take to the hospital. Madame had left me a note, ordering me to be back strictly on the dot of nine. She had arranged some nice apples, taken from the top of the pile of provisions. Sometimes, I did wonder about Madame, how much more she knew, and whether nursing was her only occupation in Cambrai. Of course, I never said anything, but perhaps the clues were here for me to find.

When I hurried over to the officers' convalescent building, my heart was pounding almost out of my chest. I could barely hold the baskets, my limbs felt so weak.

In the entrance were five younger girls, perhaps fifteen or sixteen years of age. They were carrying neat parcels of books from the library in the town. They were here to give the soldiers something to read. Whatever they had in their hands was in French or German. I wondered what the British soldiers might have to read. Doubtless the Germans cared little for the substance of the visit. It was the meaning of it that mattered, and it was clear what was going on.

Before going in, I pulled up my shawl over my ears, hiding my face from the onlookers. If William was here, this private moment was not going to be a public spectacle.

We were escorted up the stairs to the officers' convalescent ward. The French signs had been replaced with German ones. The French administrator was there and tapped each girl on the head as she passed. The German soldiers looked on with a mix of boredom and indifference.

In the ward, there were two British uniforms hanging on the wall, and I nearly shouted out. But I dared not, for this was a moment of danger as well as joy if William was indeed here. I was directed to the first bed – a young German boy, no more than nineteen. A young officer, like Kurt. He spoke to me in German.

'Thank you for your visit. It means so much to us.'

Somehow, his voice calmed me. This boy would have been kind, had he worn the uniform of a different colour. I did not want to throw an apple at him, but I dug to the bottom of the basket and picked out a small one. I felt compelled to speak to him in the perfunctory German sentences that I now repeated so often.

'It is a duty I am pleased to perform, sir. I hope you enjoy your apple.'

The words were cursory, the meeting brief. No doubt the watching administrators would make much of this. How had this been done so quickly? Who was at the heart of this public exhibition? But there was not time to think as a firm hand pushed me on.

To the other Germans, who simply stared at me, I had no kindness to offer and just tossed them the fruit. It was a small act of resistance, but it made me feel better. The eyes of the British soldiers were on me, and if William was here, he would be in that group. The thought made me so nervous that I could hardly stand.

I passed the first bed.

MSMITH – ENGLISCH.

I picked a larger apple from my basket, stepped around the bed and gave him the apple. Without daring to look up, I simply passed it and nodded when he thanked me in English. My body was coursing electricity, I could feel the spark of each nerve.

The next bed.

WCOLLINS – ENGLISCH

It was William.

I could barely keep my legs from folding. It was dangerous and exciting. This was my darling, my beloved, my missed and wounded darling. He was here. I took a shallow breath and looked up.

It was the face I loved. Here was the face that sustained me, gave me life, spirit and energy. Here was my boy from over the sea, here was my William. Just a little older, black around the eyes. But beautiful as ever. His eyes melted my soul. As he looked at me, it was clear that he recognised me, his eyes widening a little, almost unnoticed. His breath quickened and his body stiffened slightly.

As I reached out to place an apple into his hand, I brushed the back of his hand with my finger as I used to do, wanting to feel normal. It sent sparks through my body. It was forbidden to speak to the prisoner soldiers, but it was hard to keep my words to myself. I wanted to throw myself at William and bury myself into his chest, his arms around me, protecting me, a blanket of safety to take away this war. I lived a lifetime in those seconds. Lingering for just a second longer, looking deeply into his eyes, I dared not stay longer. The firm hand again turned me away and on to the next soldier, a German boy. But after that, everything was a blur, and only William filled my head.

On my return to the hospital, the senior nurse looked me up and down carefully – she must have noticed my new uniform.

'Odile, you do not look well. You seem pale and drawn, perhaps a little feverish. We cannot risk fever in the hospital, when the men are already so weak. You must go home until it passes.'

For the morning I wandered the street, safe in my uniform, protected by the Germans, who saw nurses as allies and saviours. The French would not dare touch me, as the Germans protected their nurses, whether German, French, or English.

I wanted more of William, wanted him in my soul again but all I could do was aimlessly wander the streets. It felt good to go unnoticed, but this time with no secret purpose.

Eventually, I reached an alley with a view of the windows where William was kept, hoping to glimpse him. I wanted to feel connected to my love, my darling English boy. So I stood in the breeze of the alley, not caring to eat or to move.

In the late afternoon, those soldiers able to walk were allowed onto the balcony, possibly to enjoy the sun away from the gaze of the general population. And there was William, standing strong and alone! He waved to me, but it seemed a very polite wave. Was he trying to tell me something? Perhaps not. Perhaps we were both having to act a part for the German audience, a play to the enemy for us both to live.

So, I just looked at him, with no hint of recognition, of love or joy. It would endanger us both and prevent any further contact. The risk of discovery was now too great to allow me to remain. It was time to leave, being seen by the Germans could mean disaster.

Despite the risk, I was drawn back to William in the evening and watched the balcony. A glimpse of him across a window would suffice. My white uniform would be visible in the dark and he would know it was me. If he would only leap from the balcony to see me, or run across the street, take me in his arms and away over the low hills of the ridge to the safety of the south. But this was a hopeless dream, a silly girl wasting time.

It was not late, but it seemed to darken quickly tonight. Suddenly, two lorries arrived at the building. They were not ambulances and seemed empty. These lorries had previously taken us to the north and it almost made me sick to see them again, bringing back memories of poor broken Amelie and the little blue books. I wanted to see what was going on.

Two guards flanked the rear of the lorry. This meant only one thing. A movement of prisoners. The guards were armed, so no Germans would be going with them. But who was to be transported?

My God! It was William. He was escorted out of the building, his hands tied in front of him. He was pushed into the lorry and onto the floor in the middle. He was leaving! A desperate urge to run to him overtook me. He was going again from my life. This time, might be the last time. The lorry quickly lurched forward.

There was no time and I rushed down the little low hill to the road. He saw me! I ran to reach the side of the lorry, but it had increased in speed. I reached the road as the lorry moved away, with William looking right at me.

'William, my darling, take me with you. Please! Take me! Come back, my love. Come back to me. Come back to our life.'

But it was no good, only futile words that he could not hear. But I kept running, wanting every possible second of seeing his face. The guards were jeering and laughing at me, but I kept looking straight ahead towards William. Somehow, my skirt got trapped, throwing me forwards, my hands outstretched in front of me. Now covered in dust and dirt on the ground, I looked up as William disappeared. Still on the ground, my insides felt torn, and my body bitter at the parting. Two soldiers came over and lifted me to my feet. Their German voices were harsh and unfriendly.

'What the fuck are you doing, you silly girl! Why are you running behind a prisoner lorry? Get the fuck away, or else.'

I stood in front of them, dirty and in pain. Memories of the camps flooded over me. My time with Kurt counted for nothing here, for they surely did not know him.

'I am sorry, one of the guards is my, is my... friend!'

'Ha!' The soldier looked me up and down a little. 'I suppose he is a lucky man, eh? What do you think Josef?'

'Yes, a lucky man, this little French slut running after him. Now fuck off, or I will find something of my own to detain you, eh?'

The voices of the camp came over me. There were no fences here. Quickly, I turned and fled.

'She has a nice little arse, Josef. Maybe we should bring her back, ha!'

Their horrible laughter followed me, convincing me that at any second a clammy hand would pull me back. I ran home without stopping or looking back.

'Maman, William is here! I have seen him in the convalescent building. But now he is gone. Taken away from me.'

'My God Odile! William? Are you sure? How? Do you think Kurt had him removed? Could he know?'

'No, Maman. Kurt has no sense of my having any affections other than for him.'

'Good, good. Have you seen your Father? You should tell him as well. How did you come to see him?'

'It was the nurse supervisor. She arranged for me to go to the building after Father had seen William on the balcony.'

'So your Father saw him first? Good. That will raise his spirits.'

The day's excitement had drained and worried me, and it was an effort to say any more. My mind, already a whirl of emotion, needed rest, to settle and calm.

'Your uniform is a mess, Odile, whatever did you do?'

'A small tumble coming home, it is no matter. It will clean very well.'

Sleep came easily that evening. But at nearly midnight there was an unexpected knock at the door. Mother woke me quickly.

'Are you expecting a visitor, Odile? Quickly, think girl. Are you expecting a caller?'

'No, Maman!' Could it be William, coming to get me? No, silly girl, that cannot be possible.

'Dress quickly Odile, we need to be ready.'

Mother went to the door, brushed down her dress and touched her hair. We had to look calm and remain in control.

When Maman opened the door, it was to the nursing supervisor.

'Oh! Madame, please do come in. What brings you to this house so late?'

The supervisor entered and I closed the door. Our visitor pushed back her scarf and chose her words carefully, her eyes scanning us both.

'It is business relating to Madame Collart.'

This made me petrified. How could she know Madame? What did she know?

'Do you understand what I am saying? In the past, you have passed information to the British. Well, that information came through me.'

Mother softened just a little, but still looked wary. In this place, it was impossible to be sure who was a real friend.

'The Germans suspect a resistance in Cambrai. They know that something is going on, and they may soon discover the truth. So we are closing down the operation, tonight. You will not mention our operations to anyone. We will maintain a watch over our friends, but we can no longer operate. Do you both understand?'

'Yes Madame.' Mother and I replied almost automatically. Satisfied with our responses, she nodded and turned to leave.

'Just one more thing, Odile. How was he today?'

'Madame, how could you—'

Madame raised her hand. 'I will see you at seven, sharp!'

CHRIS CHERRY

CHAPTER FIFTY-TWO
JULY-AUGUST 1916

With Kurt away, the hospital routine ground on. Each morning in bed, my first thought was of William and of home in Bazentin. And each morning at the foot of the steps to the hospital, a new line of wounded greeted the staff. The battles ground on, but the threat of evacuation faded each day as the advance of the British slowed. As each day passed, the silent optimism of the French was replaced by a sunken resignation. Daily proclamations from the administration office of imminent defeat added to our misery.

In August, the weather turned a little. The rain came down for a week and this slowed the movement of troop transports and halted the occasional bombing of the railway. The wounded still came in daily, but on wagons now, since the ambulances kept breaking down in the wet conditions.

Our hospital was full and it was not possible to accommodate any more wards or beds. Soldiers were being treated in the corridor and on the steps, even in the rain. Some factory workers had been moved to work at the hospital in the daytime, Mother amongst them. She was set to work tending wounds and replacing bandages and dressings, and it gave me comfort to know she was near.

Kurt was still in Koln and there was no word from him. William was lost to me once more as it was impossible to find out where he had been taken. Then, at the end of the month, we received word that the hospital and all of the staff were to be moved north, outside of Cambrai, to a large tented hospital. The daily bombing of the railway was getting more intense and closer.

The staff spent a week packing essentials into large boxes, which were taken by wagon to the new site, north of the canals. Father was put to work loading wagons and ensuring that they were all in good condition to transport the equipment, the beds, and finally, the wounded.

At the end of the week, the wards were quite empty. The nurses were to be kept together, in separate accommodation, until it was time to move. In the new hospital, the nurses would sleep in tents, alongside the wounded. Mother would mostly likely be separated from me once again since married French women were kept apart from the unmarried girls. It was unbearable now that Mother was near me again, and after my family had come through so much, that we would once again be separated. Not at the point of a bayonet this time, but at the tip of a lancet.

In September our plans changed completely. In the middle of the month, the war intensified and we were told that the British, along with soldiers from New Zealand, Canada, Africa and Australia, had launched a massive attack, just south of Bapaume. The tent hospital in the field was now also full and so the original hospital in the town had to be hastily re-opened.

By now, German casualties were littering the streets and once again my morning and afternoon duties were to stand at the steps whilst the three lines of wounded men were directed. But this time, it was different. Now it was me deciding who could be helped and who might die within a day. Each time my arm lifted to the left, a soldier went down the steps to the large entrance, to the 'dead door' as it was beginning to be known. Me, with no qualification, having the lives of soldiers at my mercy. How things had changed from the camps, where the power was with the uniform. The uniform now depended utterly on me for their very life. It gave me no comfort.

The evening of September fifteenth was the worst. Casualties arrived all through the night. The sound of angry guns filled every gap in the air day and night. Whatever was happening to the south was immense and the struggle could be felt in the sweaty wetness of the air. By now, uniforms became more mixed. British, Canadians, New Zealanders and Germans came in almost together as one body of dying men.

The Bois de Forcaux had apparently been taken, High Wood falling at last to the New Zealand soldiers. Flers had been captured and I remembered the little lanes from my childhood. Flower-lined tracks between the fields, open land with a warm breeze. But not today. Today, it was a battlefield, with bones and blood driven to the chalk beneath, a terrible fate for my beautiful country.

None of us slept that night. The casualties kept coming, line after line, with blackened and bloodied faces, and wretched uniforms. The sounds of the guns beating out a rhythm shattered the air, almost turning the ground to water beneath my boots.

I felt sick for most of that night. The smell of the dying mixed with the heady scents of operations wore me to a ghost, just pacing the floors and wandering from ward to faceless ward. No more apple duty, no more kind words for the suffering. Here, it was dealing with blood-soaked wounds. Me, with no medical training at all, being asked to hold responsibility for a man's life. Perhaps one of the very soldiers who had pushed my Mother from man to man, or one who had beaten Father.

William was constantly in my thoughts. My grazed knee ached when I remembered the lorry, seeing him go, watching his lovely face disappear. It did not matter, because William is seared on my soul and I can remember every line on his young face.

The rest of September passed in a flood of wounded. The German medical machine had finally began to sort out the wounded men and had separated most of the enemy soldiers. This meant the British were fewer in number now, and the German cases coming to us had already been sorted. The 'dead doors' were no longer used, and the worst cases were taken directly to the large operating hospital.

Mother had already been sent back to the factory, along with the others who had been sent to help out. Now, it was time for me to decide whether to stay and train properly as a nurse, or to return to the factory. The factory would allow access to Madame Collart's circle of deception. But the hospital would allow me to live freely amongst the Germans. Kurt would be back soon and he would either want me for himself, or to cast me out to find my own way. Whatever fate was to bring now, it would be soon.

CHAPTER FIFTY-THREE
LATE 1916

The hospital routine moved each day to a rhythm of quiet resolve to heal the wounded and to care for those who had been courageous enough to stand in the line – the German line. Now, I was only one of four French women working in the hospital. The others were nursing supervisors, with authority over the German nurses. As for my supervisor, it was still difficult to be sure of what she knew, or how she had come by her information.

On some evenings, I would follow my senior nurse in the shadows – this skill never forgotten. But there was nothing to see at all, no meetings, no furtive movements. My curiosity was unbearable, but my curiosity could bring danger to us both, so that had to be the end of it. The war seemed no nearer conclusion. The lines seemed to have moved little and our lives were balanced between perils as much as they had ever been.

One day, Mother came to the hospital, running up the steps and straight past the line of wounded in the corridor. She must be looking for me and it could not be good news since her face was ashen and she was wiping tears from her eyes, straining to see me in the gloom.

'Odile, you must come now. Please hurry. They are taking away your Father. He is going right this very minute. Quickly.'

There was no time to think, or to understand what Mother was saying. I left immediately behind Mother, carrying my skirt ahead of me. The nursing supervisor was in her little office, but she did not look up.

'Why Maman?'

'I do not know Odile. This is terrible. We shall all be cast to the camp again.'

We ran down the steps, attracting calls from the lines of wounded. It was forbidden to run in uniform, as it caused unnecessary alarm. But Papa was being taken from me! Perhaps we had been lucky to have him with us, but that fortune had now changed for some unknown reason.

'Maman, be calm, it will be well. Kurt will surely help—'

'Kurt has done this, most certainly! What did you say to him, Odile?'

'Nothing, Maman! I have not seen him in many days.'

'Well your Father is being taken away and there is nothing we can do about it. Hurry now.'

We ran to the station yard and through the wooden fence that was there to keep civilians away from the military transports. A couple of soldiers looked over, but when they saw my uniform, they went back to their duties. Father was red faced and terrified, with a large soldier either side, gently holding his shoulders. As if he were under arrest by two of his big brothers.

He was being addressed by a small officer in thick glasses.

'Sorry Lefebvre, it is not permissible, there is no time. You have been lucky enough up to now to have your wife and the girl with you. Well, your time is up, now get a move on.'

'Please, Herr Major, at least allow me to tell them that I am leaving?'

'No, absolutely not. The lorries are already loaded. Get on the train now, or you will be tied on if necessary.'

Father looked up from the floor and looked straight at Mother. He looked devastated. For the first time, worry was clearly visible on his face. This man who had lived and carried us through the camps was to be taken from us, where and for what reason we did not know.

Father spoke to the officer. 'Yes...' There was a momentary hesitation and Papa's shoulders rounded just a little, his fire was already out. 'Yes, Herr Major.'

Father turned to where his family stood by the wooden barrier before being moved onto the train, without being able to say goodbye to us. He looked so very weary and worn as the train moved away. But then, he glanced quickly left and right, and dared to wave at us.

'Goodbye, Papa. I will take care of Maman for you!'

'All love, Pierre. Bon chance!'

Father began to gesture that he would write. But as his hands completed the imaginary note, a soldier pulled him by the shoulder and my Father was gone from our lives. It felt to me as if a door had been left open on a cold night. The wind swept through me, the door unlocked, my house open for anyone to pass through.

'God help us Odile, because if He doesn't, no one else will.'

Maman tugged my arm and tried to lead me home. It was tempting to go with her, especially because she needed me. Certainly returning to the hospital to tend the men who had done this to us was not my preference. But I did not dare to stay away any longer, and had to leave poor Maman to her misery.

The rain began to pour and did not stop for over a week. The casualty lines grew a little shorter and the winds were a little colder. Winter was coming to northern France, which would mean a renewed struggle for survival, irrespective of whatever friendships had been forged in the warmth of summer.

Father had gone, in little more than the blink of my eye. We had been given no opportunity to come to terms with his departure, nor to find any way of keeping our family together. It was as if he was gone forever, but the torture was only increased by hope as we looked for his return each day, knowing that he could not.

It was now clear that the efforts in the Somme had not been successful in breaking the spirit, or the lines of the enemy. The war was to be continued into 1917, with the turning of the year offering no opportunity for celebration and joyous remembrance of times past. Instead, we had the cold winds and biting rain to greet the new year and the first snows kept the streets clear and the hospital quiet.

The ground froze in January, which allowed some transports to move and the Germans made the most of the opportunity to move machines and men around the lines. Cambrai remained busy and it was from one of the daily trains from Germany that Kurt emerged early one morning.

Since the hospital was so quiet, I was at home tending to Mother as she was ill. It was exhaustion, but it might have been something worse had I not spotted her fever developing. She would be well, given plenty of rest.

The knock at the door startled me, and its confident rap roused me from my tired daze. It could only be Kurt, and my mixed feelings surfaced again. I had reached a quiet reconciliation of William being alive and in my heart. Kurt was a confusing memory of fondness, perhaps based on his ability to care for us. But my world had changed since that day in July.

'Odile, my love. I have missed you.'

Kurt pulled me to him and kissed me deeply. I wanted to resist, wanted to pull back and tell him, but I dared not betray my family. Far better to betray my feelings instead.

'Kurt, I am so glad to see you here safe and well. Have you been far?'

'I was posted for a time back to Germany, to the railhead in Koln. Moving lorries and equipment, making up camps for soldiers and machinery. But I am back to Cambrai. But only for one thing, Odile.'

His words made me shudder, knowing what he would say next.

'I am here for you.'

'For me? Whatever does that mean?'

'I have come to take you with me.'

Father was gone, and I wondered what would become of Mother as Kurt would have no intention of including her in his plans. I needed time to think, and time to plan. This was always coming, I had known this for some time, but it was too soon after Father's departure. Kurt could see it in my eyes. The fear, the worry and perhaps even the thinking.

'You do not need to decide tonight. Do not feel that you are being ordered to Germany. Far better if you want to come with me. That our love for each other is enough to make you decide to come. Perhaps you will accompany me to the café this evening? I am meeting some good friends and would like you to meet them.'

'Yes I will, Kurt. Just for you.'

So, I was to be taken to Germany. Just until the end of the war perhaps and then... Well it was difficult to imagine a time without the war. My world had seemed full of this tragedy and nothing else. I wanted to speak to

Mother, but she was weak and needed her rest. The last thing she needed to hear was news of my departure, so soon after Papa was taken away.

Before agreeing to go to Germany, I had to find out whether Maman could be cared for. The factory manager would be the best person to ask for help. I put on all of my clothes to keep me warm against the night air. The wind was bitter and the air still brought the smells of war into my nose. The whole town simply smelled of burning and it still made my stomach turn over.

The factory was quiet. Some bombs had hit one corner, but had not damaged the roof too badly. The wind caught the edge of the iron sheeting, causing it to rattle through the whole building. The manager's apartment was above the offices. He was lucky, for coal and wood were made available to him and his life was comfortable. If only the Germans knew the truth. Perhaps they did.

'Mademoiselle, please come in, come in.'

'Thank you. I have come about my Mother.'

'You have? Is her condition worse?'

'No, no. She will make a full recovery, fortunately.'

'That is good, very good. Here, have something warming. A toast to Madame Collart?'

Hearing her name made me jump back to thoughts of Amelie, of holding her broken body in my arms. We were only children then, but it was not so long ago.

'Yes, Monsieur. Please, Kurt is taking me to Germany. There is no longer any choice.'

The manager's face became stern.

'You always have a choice Odile. Did you choose this life for yourself?'

'My Father is now most likely in Germany, or on the borders. He will be working as a slave no doubt, for those who do not care for him. Mother is ill, but if I stay, we will lose the protection of the Germans, and her health will be badly affected. You know where my heart truly lies and it is not with them. But if I refuse, we will be cast back to the camps.'

'There are no camps like that here anymore Odile. True, there are punishment camps and camps for the homeless, but the early days are past and the Germans have procedures in place for citizens. Administrators and all of that. We may not like their occupation, but it is more settled now. More civilized.'

These sounded like the words of a coward, a betrayer of our country. Perhaps our last ally was gone, perhaps the manager's comfortable life with no hardship had forced this conciliation with the enemy. This man would not help Mother.

'Thank you monsieur, I must get home now before the cold of the night sets in.'

'But you have just got here. What is it that you came for? Perhaps you wanted to ask if I would care for your Mother if you were to leave?'

'It was not that monsieur. It was to ask if there were any extra hours available for me. For some extra coins.'

He looked at me suspiciously, but said no more. He opened the door to the street, the cold air curled around me and he shepherded me onto the street. The door slammed hard behind me, telling me everything I needed to know. My only ally was Kurt. The little resistance movement had perhaps crumbled after the failure to break the line in the summer. Madame Collart was gone. Mother was sick, but she would be strong again, provided Kurt did not withdraw his support. She needed me here, but leaving her was my only way to protect her.

Kurt was my only hope for survival now in this war of the lost. He must never find out that I depended utterly upon him, but not in the way he must truly want. My true love for William must forever remain secret from Kurt, to survive, to protect my family, and to find my darling English boy again.

In the early morning, Kurt met me on the hospital steps, greeting me with a small flower. It was the first snowdrop of the turning year. A little beauty in this grey harshness, but its purity brought me no comfort.

'So will you come, darling Odile? Will you choose to live your life with a soldier of your mortal enemy? Could it be that history remembers us not as enemies, but as friends?'

'Am I to come as your amusement Kurt? Am I to be a trophy from the conquered lands?'

Kurt looked pained at my remark.

'Odile, my love for you is quite sincere.'

His expression was open, and part of me felt badly for him. 'I am sorry, Kurt.'

'I would have you as my wife, if the war would allow. But it is not that simple. Perhaps one day, but for now, this is all that I can offer. I am, at least, an officer with standing in Germany. Such things are permissible if things are managed politely.'

Politely? In this war of brutality. Lying not more than fifty paces behind me are the broken bodies of men fighting this war in my home villages. On my own garden perhaps there lie one hundred bodies of men – men who would not think this a war of politeness. Resentment filled me. I tried to control my emotions, but the thin veneer coating my deceit would not hold back my anger.

'You think such delicacies are important, when we are all ankle deep in blood, Kurt? When the bones of our brothers lie scattered across the fields of France. Take me, I cannot stop you. There is no weapon in my hand no one at my shoulder.'

Kurt dropped the flower and ground it under his heel, and narrowed his eyes at me. But even in the face of such a warning, the words continued to flow from my stupid mouth.

'To even think that your own sensitivities are important when the dead lie amongst us. See, even now, look, there is a body of a German in the street. Did he care for such things?'

Kurt turned on me, his face red, but his voice controlled.

'Odile, I have kept your family together and away from harm. Even while your Father did all in his power, to destroy you all.'

Briefly, I opened my mouth to protest, but Kurt was not going to be interrupted.

'I am no brute and would not take you against your will. I have cared for you to the point of ridicule by my own people. Yet you cast this care aside with such ease.'

'Of course I know that. But I am frightened to my bones at what will happen to us, can you not see that?'

'Of course. That is why I give you a way to escape this war. It is willingly offered.'

Kurt stretched his arms wide apart, in an almost biblical resignation to my decision.

'If I refuse, what then?'

'I will leave your lives forever and promise never to disturb you again. Any other action would be too painful to me and perhaps also to you?'

The choice had been offered. Any further attempt at refusal would risk my parents' safety. Finally, here was the moment where I had to choose between my family's safety and my love for William. Perhaps William was back in the trenches and already dead. Perhaps I was no better for having seen him. I must choose Germany over France. My poor country bleeding on her knees, with the enemy standing over her with a bloody knife. How could I abandon her now? But what difference could one girl make?

Acceptance would commit me to life as a German wife, a life of being the enemy, held in contempt by every French soul for the rest of my life. The enemy growing from within. But it also offered one tiny golden light. I would survive, and have choices if I was brave enough to find them. It would protect my dear family. That counted above all in the balance.

But he wanted an answer now. Across my mind came all of the memories I held in my life. Maman, Papa, the funny little motor car, the day I met William in Albert at the little café in the square. Then the terrible lorry with Amelie, the strange journeys, the deaths, the beatings. Then Kurt covering us with his care. My mind was a whirl of emotion, but I was drawn to the conclusion, forced to reply.

'I will come Kurt.'

But I did not stay to see his face, instead running up into the hospital. Finally, I had committed to a future away from everything familiar and trustworthy. It was an uncertain future, but one that would be free from this terrible war.

Inside, I locked myself in the lower sluice, a place full of the war where dirty bandages were boiled, washed and stretched out to be used again. Soaking buckets were everywhere to remove the blood and dirt from sheets, clothes and blankets, to remove the mud from our fields forever mixed with the blood of the dying.

There was a knock at the door. This was the sluice after all and in constant use. But this knock was gentle, as if intruding on a private meeting. I opened it, expecting to be in trouble. In the doorway was the nursing supervisor, looking kindly. She placed her fingers to her lips and entered in silence.

'So you are going then, Odile. The walls may be thick, but the sound still comes straight through them.'

'How could you possibly know?'

She placed her hand on my face and stroked it gently.

'Odile, there is much that is known in secret, you of all people will know that. Madame Collart and Amelie were not strong enough to survive, but you are, even if it does not feel like that now. Think about your future. You can survive this war, Odile. There is much for you to live for. Here take this and go.'

She pressed a small scrap of paper into my hand.

'Read it, learn it and destroy it immediately.'

'Thank you Madame.'

She stood up and held me gently for a second or two. The clinical smell of her uniform was comforting in that moment, the comfort felt by a thousand wounded souls.

'As soon as you have finished, right, back to work, Mademoiselle, you are already late onto the wards.'

She left me and I read the strange words, a name perhaps, again and again, repeating them in my head, trying to turn them into a picture to help me remember. Finally, I looked around the sluice and decided to soak the paper in the foul water and then put the paper into the drain.

CHAPTER FIFTY-FOUR
LEAVING CAMBRAI 1917

The station was full of soldiers and equipment. Kurt had told me to wear my nurse's uniform, which would ensure courtesy without the need for explanation. I would accompany a group of wounded men and help where possible despite my limited training. The time had come to be strong, to do this and survive. It was so much less than the camps, barely a hardship at all.

Mother was unable to come to the station. Her fever had subsided, but her muscles were weak and she was still worried about Father, since there had been no word about him. Before my departure, I had visited her briefly. She was in her bed, surrounded by pillows, looking pale and older than her years. It was unbearable having to leave her. But Kurt had promised me that he would leave good orders for her care. Orders that would be honoured, whatever unit was in the town.

Maman squeezed my hand and leaned forwards to kiss me.

'Darling child. Be careful and take our love with you. Trust no one and take nothing as granted. Be watchful and think of your parents with love. We will be here for you when you return, for you will return to your beloved France.'

She leaned back and I stroked her head and kissed her on both cheeks.

'Goodbye Maman. I will love you always.'

I was to travel from Cambrai to Koln railhead and then finally to Dusseldorf, which was at least three days away, since the trains moved slowly for the wounded. As I stepped onto the train I was shocked at its coarseness and quality. The carriages were cattle trucks, the straw flints still visible in the corners. The men were packed in thirty to a truck, on the floor on stretchers. Wounds and dressings were already soaked through and there would be no orderlies or medical help available until Koln itself. Men would certainly die on this journey, and the train would no doubt have to stop and remove them.

The carriage for the hospital teams was already converted for troop use. There were six orderlies and four nurses travelling with me, but there was no equipment, fresh bandages or any water or food provision. This was the enemy, but more than that, it was humanity. Suffering was appalling, whoever it affected. I had seen suffering often, but never as awful as this. Amputations were barely healed. Many wounds seeped yellow and red fluids. Stomach wounds bled black and red. These men seemed to be the condemned, not the rescued. The battlefield would not be their final resting place, but for some, it would surely be a railway siding in the middle of nowhere. This was no way for anyone to die.

As we moved off, it was possible to hear the cries of the wounded with every bump and jolt. Each time the carriages ground together, there would be a hideous chorus from those in pain. Kurt had arranged my passage in the more comfortable hospital carriage, but it was really only a storage area with a few extra seats and fewer occupants. The staff were German and looked at me suspiciously. They never spoke to me directly, but they were certainly talking about me in their language.

The journey was terrible. The rain was cold and the wind came through the sides of the carriage. It had been lined with linen and canvas to help with the equipment, but the sheets just flapped and got wet, making the whole carriage cold and damp. It was miserable enough for those of us without wounds, God only knew what it was like for the wounded men.

There were no blankets, or covers against the weather and the train did not stop that often, but travelled desperately slowly.

I looked up to see the nurses' faces, stern and unforgiving. They might be wearing the same uniform as me, but they were the enemy also, perhaps appearing even more sinister for being hidden in friendly costume.

At night the train rumbled on and sleeping was almost impossible. The cries of the wounded pierced the constant rhythm of the wheels on the tracks. The train only stopped to allow the dead and mortally ill to be taken off to spare neighbouring comrades any unnecessary terror. Though God alone knew what eased the terror of the mortally ill being left alone. Although my future was considerably less bleak, I was also alone, with no one looking out for me, headed towards a strange country – the enemy's country. My only protection on arrival was a note in my pocket containing instructions in German, for the staff at the station and directions to my new accommodation in the nurses' quarters.

I had surely made a terrible mistake. Kurt would not be with me for some time. Was this purely a journey to serve a master? Father was lost to me, away from his family and alone in some place. Mother was also alone, but those citizens who knew her secrets would care for her, and she would now be safe. This journey was for Maman, to preserve her safety, and also for my hopes of finding William. This gave me some comfort at least.

Whenever I tried to sleep, at the moment where my control dissolved, I feared attack, or being thrown bodily from the train without ceremony. It was impossible to trust anyone. We stopped frequently, lurching to a halt, which jarred everyone on the train, causing the wounded to suffer even more. Once it was because we were being shot at by an aeroplane and once because the railway lines had been damaged by a bomb.

Gradually, the fields began to look less damaged and less part of this war. All of the signs were in German, of which I understood little, and it was confusing, never knowing whether I was already in Germany. As each day passed, the nurses and orderlies in the carriage seemed ever more frightening and intimidating. They wanted nothing from me, nothing of me and nothing to do with me. At least they had not beaten me, or thrown rotting food or shit at me, and they had not tried to kill me – a blessing of sorts, and an improvement on where I had been.

On the fifth day, there was a stop that lasted half a day. The others got off without looking at me and left me in the carriage. I never once considered trying to escape because of the risk to my parents if I did not arrive when Kurt expected. He knew where to find my Mother and Father and that was enough to keep me on this terrible journey.

When I finally felt able to leave the train, the sun was weak and the air was cold, but it was glorious to have the sun on my face. Out of the wind, it almost felt warm. No one tried to stop me and no one asked for my papers, so I moved about the little station without anyone asking me anything.

On the ground, a small group of heavily bandaged soldiers crouched around a comrade. His leg was covered in a black and red stain, which looked bad. It was weeping, with the look of broth. He was crying out and there was nothing anyone could give him. One of the soldiers saw me, I tried to hurry by, but he came to me. He spoke quickly in German and it was clear what he was asking, even though I did not know the words.

I had to confront this terrible wound, on an enemy, far from home. The sweet and sickly smell from the dressing was almost unbearable and made me feel sick. But at least we were outside and the wind took away the worst of it. The bandage was almost solid with a crust of tissue and pus. The wound was black, with a brown and green sheen sliding up the man's leg. All I could do was ask for water to wash the worst of it away. Fresh water was brought in a dirty bucket, but it was all there was since nothing had been shown to me on the hospital carriage.

Once I had washed the wound, it was obvious that the wound was badly infected, with black and green tracks going along the tissue. If these tracks went too far, the blood would be poisoned and the patient would die. Tissue needed to be cut away if this man had any chance of survival. He needed the surgeon, but there was no surgeon on the train and this man might die. There was a small box of sheets on the train. These were not sterile, but better than leaving a wound uncovered. I ran back and picked up the box. The sheets were yellow, but clean enough.

Soon, I had the wound bound again, having washed it as much as possible. But without surgery, this soldier would die and his comrades would know this. Being soldiers, they would have seen this before. All I could do was to stay with him, which was no hardship since no one else wanted to be with me. The poor man could not speak, so no language was necessary, for him, but his comrades wished to make sure they were leaving him in good hands.

'You are French nurse?'

'Yes, er ja.'

'You can be helping my friend?'

I decided that French was my best option.

'A little. But it may not help.'

'Ha, in the arms of a beautiful woman. We are not lucky, like him!'

They all went off together, content that their friend was being cared for. I had been no help at all. The poor man smelled terribly, and the damp sweat that had soaked into his clothes had dried to a white and yellow crust. His uniform was still dirty from the battlefield and it was covered in blood. His wound had initially been dressed by a skilled hand, but where and when I did not know. This man had not been in a hospital, perhaps just a clearing station and then onto the train. The number of wounded outside Cambrai was large and not everyone was fortunate to find a hospital in time.

For an hour I stayed with him, holding his hand and cradling his head in my arms. There was nothing else to be done. One of the men returned with a warm drink for me. It tasted of beef fat, it was warm and welcome.

'He would say thank you, nurse, if he could. He will die content in the hands of a woman, eh?'

I smiled thinly, wishing this man in the hospital in Cambrai. If he had made it there, the diseased tissue could be removed and the wound might have healed. Left like this, he would be dead in a few hours. But almost immediately, his breathing became heavier and shallower, and he was struggling for every breath. With each rise of his chest, he rasped, as if breathing in nails.

The other men returned with a blanket and placed it around my shoulders, making me realise how cold I was now. Then, the man's breathing stopped. I did not move for some time. There were no words to tell his friends, but I did not want to leave his lifeless body cold on the floor alone. So I stayed there, until it began to get dark.

The train driver appeared and the orderlies from my carriage came past, at first not noticing me. Then one of the nurses saw me there, clinging to a dead body. She looked at me for a few seconds, taking in the scene. In German she called to the others, who quickly came over and picked me up, pulling the blanket tighter around me. I was shepherded to the train again and sat now on a stool, not in the corner, but at the front. The dead soldier was picked up and placed on a stretcher and taken away. I never knew his name.

Once on the train again, it was a little warmer. The nurse who had helped me up took off the wet blanket and found a smaller, dry one to help me. She spoke no French, but her attitude to me changed in that moment. She rode with her arm around me, keeping me warm. The bottom of my uniform was still marked with black and yellow slime, which she cut off with scissors and then threw it out of the carriage. If only that could have happened to the poor soldier, he may have lived a little longer and in less pain.

By the time we finally arrived in Dusseldorf, I had received smiles and nods from the others on the train. Had we shared a language, it might have been different; I still felt alone, but less lonely. When I left the station, the guard at the barrier waved me through without asking to see papers! It was not possible to move about France without a check, but in the heart of the enemy country, I was free to move. Given the choice, I could have walked the streets all day and night. But it was cold and windy, and I was very tired. The orderly at the front door of the nurses' accommodation was expecting me and welcomed me in as a colleague. He spoke to me in German, but I did not understand him.

'I am sorry, but I do not speak German.'

He looked puzzled, but showed me to my room.

It was a small warm room and the bed was immaculate and soft. It was impossible to comprehend the ebb and flow of this war. When I first met Kurt, I was sitting by a water pump, terrified of Thomas and the tit lorry. Now, in the centre of the enemy machine, I was unsupervised and free to move. But I decided that sleep was most important. Anyway, I was hungry and sleep would help me to deal with that. I washed in the water put in the room for me and helped myself to some scent from a little bottle, which was most unexpected and welcome. Then I locked the door and fell asleep, almost without a second to think about my fortune, or fate.

During the night, I awoke in the dark, suddenly afraid of where I was and thinking myself still alone rattling on the train in a moment of unguarded sleep. But the room was still, the door was locked, the bed was soft and the room was warm. I had not known this blissful feeling for years. My body was still dirty, but I did not care in the face of salvation that overwhelmed me.

I rose and washed my body in the water. The darkness was oddly reassuring, making me feel less exposed and anxious in the little room that was now my world. Faint noises came from the station, and the movements of trains continued, but these sounds were of life, not of death. There were no guns here, and no trembling of the earth beneath the convulsions of war. Here was enemy ground, but Kurt had given me a shield of safety. It was now up to me to make use of it and save my family during this awful time.

After washing, I dressed again in my uniform. It was not clean, but it was all there was until I could exchange it in the morning. I sat on a little stool, remembering times when life seemed simpler. It was occasionally harsh perhaps, but filled with as much love as it was with cold and boring housework. Father's voice echoed around me in the room, chastising me for dropping a bolt in an engine, Mother telling me off for dropping the clean linens on the garden path, or Madame Villiers outraged at my daring to pinch apples from her garden, or a turnip from her field.

It made me smile remembering this life now gone forever before its time. Replaced by iron gates and grey uniforms, shouts and bombs, guns and the screams of the dying. I was only seventeen and had witnessed so much that would change me from the girl I should have been. Perhaps a girl married to a gentleman farmer, like my Father, working in my home, enjoying the air, the rain and the woods around my home.

The Bois de Forcaux on the hill was bleak and yet warm under the summer sun. The wood in Longueval was peaceful, and created places to hide between the farming tracks. The walk down the hill to Bazentin-Le-Grand revealed the little farmhouses puffing smoke from their chimneys. These must all be gone now, exploded to dust in this war. A war that has not touched Germany but that has taken everything from me.

Now I imagined William walking through the fields above the village, or past the old windmill to Longueval. It made me sad and tears ran down my cheek. At least this time they did not leave tracks in the grime on my face.

'William please hold on for me for I will return to you. We may be old and tired, we may not even survive, but please be comforted in my love for you, wherever you are.'

Somehow, despite the hardness of the stool, I had fallen asleep. When I awoke, it was full daylight and my back was stiff from a draughty window. Outside, people moved about freely in tree-lined streets. It looked cold and their clothes were drab and uncomfortable, but there were no soldiers asking for papers, or taking away prisoners.

A sudden knock at the door startled me.

'Mademoiselle, I have some clothing for you, orders of the Kommandant.'

The girl at the door had excellent French. I opened the door slowly and a red-faced girl pushed a bundle towards me. It was another nurse's uniform. It was different to the one I was wearing and it was far too big. But it smelled clean and fresh and it was good to remove the one I had been wearing for over a week.

'When you are changed, I must take you to the nursing school. You will be there until you are trained. I am Eline. You are Odile?'

'Yes I am. Thank you, Eline.'

I quickly put on the new uniform and stepped in to the hallway. All my instincts for trust and suspicion had now been thrown through the window. It was difficult to know who or what to trust. I was already a casualty of this war and just hoped it would not hurt too much when the end finally came.

We walked in the weak sunshine to the hospital. Inside, the wards were large and spacious. This had been a grand house in years past, but now, it was turned over to the military. To my dismay, it was still quite close to the front line.

'Now, there are three French nurses here, and you will be the fourth. You are not trained yet, but we will make sure that you get your training here. Have you ever worked with cases of *Kriegsneurose* before?'

She spoke to me as if expecting me to know all about medical conditions. All I had seen up to now were blasted and broken bodies, and men with faraway stares.

'Sorry, but I have not heard that term before.'

'The English are calling it shell shock. Combat hysteria? You have never heard or seen it? It is quite distressing the first time that you see it, but you get used to it you know.'

'Shell shock? Combat hysteria?' The words did not mean anything to me.

'None of the men speak at all, ever. Anything they say seems, well, unintelligible. Are you sure you have never seen this?'

'Ah, now that you say it like that, it sounds familiar to me. May I ask, why the French nurses are here?'

'The French nurses are here because the German nurses find it very distressing.'

'Oh, of course. And why can we move about so freely?'

At this, she put her hand on my shoulder and smiled. 'Because you chose Germany over France my dear.'

The blood drained from my face. It was not like that at all. I had not forsaken France, and was only here for the sake of my family. I was no traitor to my beloved France.

'Of course, we are all really here for our families. But sacrifices have to be made. You will get used to it after a time.'

Was this a terrible mistake, choosing a comfortable life when so many were sacrificed daily on the battlefield? It made me ashamed and sickened, and my clothes felt dirtier here than ever before.

'Right, I must show you around. By the way, Sister was most impressed with you on the train. She said you seemed a sullen, miserable girl for days, until Duren, when you helped a dying man pass in comfort. That has earned you a little respect here already. You will fit in quite well, perhaps.'

Eline took me around the wards, which were large and airy. There were no blood soaked bandages here, and no serious wounds, or at least none that were visible. The smell of decay was not present here, but young men wandered around, waving and saluting, throwing clothing and effects. This was distressing, but at least these men were alive. That was surely a good thing?

'These men here, we have categorised as the least affected. They can walk unaided and are not in danger of harming themselves or others. We need to make sure that they eat and drink enough. Some of them can even wash and dress and otherwise care for themselves, if you see what I mean. Sometimes these men are allowed visitors, but only when we think that they are calm enough to be seen by family as the families get very distressed.'

In the next ward, the beds were separated by little wicker fences and curtained rails. These men were perhaps not so fortunate, but we had moved on before I could ask any questions. We reached the next ward and Eline hesitated, just for a second

'In this ward especially, you should take a deep breath before entering. The smell can be interesting, but these men are the more serious cases and you may find this a little distressing. The doctors think that these men will never recover from their experiences. But do not feel sad or let them see you upset because it makes things worse for them. You have a great responsibility to these men. When you read where some have been, you may understand more. Though you have come from a town on the battlefields, so perhaps you are better prepared than I was.'

I had an idea what was behind the large oak door of this almost secret ward. The end of June last year brought men to the hospital who were badly affected by the constant shelling all around them. Strong, wilful men were reduced to cowering in corners, with faraway eyes, minds not living in the world we inhabited. Of all the injuries that I saw, it was these which had created the most lasting impression. As instructed, I took a very deep breath.

The door opened. At first it appeared to be like any other recovery ward, if a little unkempt. There were men in beds who were dressed in uniform or night clothes. But on closer inspection, all was not as it should be with these men.

The first beds on the left were empty, but all around were the possessions of soldiers. It seemed that the men were to found underneath the beds, complete with blanket and pillow barricades. A hand emerged from one of them, trembling and clenching to the rhythm of a tortured voice. The man next to him reacted to every noise with the same anguished cry. Already my legs had turned to lead, but I had to go on.

The last four beds contained soldiers in uniform, lying on top. One lay with his hands over his chest as if praying. He was talking to himself in a low voice, in very rapid German and I could not understand what he was saying. Every few seconds his arm flung itself violently upwards onto the metal pillar of his bed. Fortunately, a pillow had been tied to the post to soften these repeated blows.

The last two men were rocking forwards and backwards, amidst constant trembling. The awkward, painful movements looked distressing. They had been doing this for some time because their skin was red raw with the repeated twisting of their uniform against bare skin. Dressings had been attempted and removed. Food had been offered and rejected. These men were sick but it seemed nothing could help them.

On the far side were five beds separated by sturdy curtains so that each man was kept in a private space. The first man was invisible to us on entering the ward, but from this end his movements were all too visible. He repeated the same movement whenever there was a sound above a whisper. He would sit on his bed, with a book, open but clearly not being read. The sound would make him leap off his bed and underneath it, scattering his sheets in his haste to take cover. He would remain motionless for a few seconds, then take a wide view all around from the end of his bed, to see if all was well. Then he would return to the book again, drawing the sheets around him.

'He will do that fifty times an hour, if we let him. We offer something to calm him down, but it is quite useless to try. He was in the line at Delville Wood, it is somewhere in northern France.'

'It is a short walk from my home in Bazentin!'

'Oh really? I am sorry. It looks to have been bad there. I did not know.' She placed her hand on my arm and moved me along.

The last four were mostly standing, as if on parade. Their legs wobbled and buckled, but they kept trying to stand upright. The grunts of pain and frustration cut me deeply. They were trying to be normal inside, but their bodies would not obey.

'It would be comical if it was not so desperate. These poor fellows, I try to talk with them every day. Of all of the men here, these four are the ones that upset me the most. I can feel their agony and torture as their minds try to take some control of their bodies again. But it is no use. Their fixings and fittings are mixed up, forever fused by the shells and bombs. Make sure you come and give them a kind word each day, will you? It does not matter if it is in French, it is the kindness in your voice that works.'

'Yes of course, Eline. I promise.'

We stood and watched the men for a few moments. Not for any other reason than me wanting to understand what they were trying inside to accomplish. Stand upright, hold it a second and then the legs buckled, falling forwards and backwards, to both sides. Again and again, sometimes the flourish of a salute, snapping heels together. But this just made them less balanced and they would tumble again.

'But please, do not try to help them stand. Just move things out of the way and be kind. If they are on their feet, then do try and help them steady their balance. It will be hopeless, but perhaps they are better each day, it is so very hard to tell sometimes.'

My whole life felt like it had been turned upside down. It barely mattered that I was here in Germany, tending Germans with a German boy at my side. It no longer felt like I was here under sufferance, or as an obligation to my family. I felt almost destined to help these men, to try to ease their suffering. Perhaps these four men, above all others.

These men were no enemy of my country. These men were as much victims as Madame Collart, or Amelie. They were broken by war, as easily as if they were eggs being smashed on the ground, and the damage to them was too great to put them back in order. These men were not dead; to these men, the dead were the lucky ones. For the very first time, most unexpectedly and to my shame, I felt angry at the French and the British, and even at my poor William, for not ending this war and for firing the shells that had damaged these men.

All four had photographs of women at home, who were probably like me and anxious for news. I felt confused. Perhaps it was the separation from home, perhaps it was already inside me. It felt corrosive and I would have to be careful.

CHAPTER FIFTY-FIVE
DUSSELDORF SUMMER 1917

Kurt took up his transport posting in the July of 1917. By this time I had spent almost five months in training in Germany. I had learned some German, but did not want to use much of it. They made me come, they can work around me. But I still had to survive, to eat and to understand what was happening around me, so I learned the words. The nurses were all German or Austrian, apart from the four of us from France. A Scottish nurse had been here for a short time, but she was moved away. It struck me as strange that she would be here, but it seems she was in Belgium when the Germans attacked and she became trapped.

During my training Eline was friendly to me. It was good to hear her French voice since she was the only reminder of home in this sterile town. Over the months, she became more curious of my arrival in this town and my journey from the Western Front.

'Out of interest Odile, why were you not moved to Switzerland? Your village was evacuated and in the trenches, so what happened?'

'We were moved north and some others were given passes, but my Mother and I – along with another family – were brought back. It was supposed to be for our safety, but I am not so sure these days.'

'Oh. Well I was living in Lille and escaped north, through Armentieres and on into Belgium. I ran out of food and money and was captured – the stupid soldier thought me a spy. But I managed to convince him that I meant no harm.'

'How did you do that?'

'How old are you Lefebvre?'

'Nearly nineteen.'

'You have never had to, well, deal with a soldier in that way? You have a soldier friend. Surely you must have?'

'I see. No. Kurt does not seem to think that way.'

'He is a man, Odile. Believe me, he wants the charms you hold beneath your skirts. Has he never even tried to…?'

'…Well a little. But I say no and he lets it go. But that may not last.'

'Has he not proposed already?'

'I will not marry whilst the war continues. He knew that from the first discussion on the matter.'

'You have been lucky so far then, especially given your looks.'

'I try and keep alert, Eline. It is my only weapon.'

Eline sat back. Perhaps she was thinking of her own journey here and how it could have been different. There was sadness behind her confident demeanour. A sadness of a virtue lost perhaps, just like poor Amelie.

Each afternoon, Kurt collected me and took me to the nursing quarters. I was not allowed to visit him at his parents' address as the military did not permit him to visit his home. In any case, his family would most likely not welcome me anyway. He tried to find ways to help me adjust to life in Germany and appeared satisfied that I was out of the war and dependent on him. Maybe he just wanted me to lift my skirts, but maybe he was more sincere in his desire for me. It was hard to be certain, but inside me was the strong feeling that something most likely had to change.

Kurt sometimes brought me news from France. He neither spoke of German victories, nor of advances by our armies. He talked more of the towns and villages and occasionally brought news of my Mother. He had sent word to care for her in the German hospital at St Quentin, but the Germans had moved back from there to somewhere called the Hindenburg Line. Mother was apparently well but unable to work. She was looked after by German nurses under the orders of Kurt's officer friends. It was just as well since the French in the towns would be unlikely to care for her. If only they knew the truth of Maman's war.

So, with news of my Mother came the realisation that I was trapped. Trapped in a chaperoned world of hospitals, guided utterly and completely by Kurt Langer and his whim, though he was always kind, caring and attentive. There was no malice in his words or actions, and his behaviour was most gentlemanly, especially when compared to other Germans. Here, I completely forgot the French struggle, but I never forgot William. He was a constant at my side every day and I could never let him go, even if I had slipped from his life. Kurt had to remain under control and my feelings for him must always be set against those for my parents. I heard little from Kurt about Papa, but I did know that he was under Kurt's command. This meant I still had to be careful, never forgetting my real job here.

The evenings in the summer were pleasant. I was not treated with suspicion in the town, although I was rarely allowed out as freely as my first night here. The people of Dusseldorf were wary of the French girl in a nurse's uniform. But when they heard where I was working, they softened completely, understanding what happened in the hospital.

Kurt would be gone for many days at a time. When he was here, it was always briefly, supervising train transports at Koln, so his time in Dusseldorf was brief. I think he tried to arrange meetings with his parents, but it never seemed possible. Something, somewhere held him back. Perhaps I was just a fancy, after all.

The hospital days were tiring and wearing on my soul as the poor soldiers – victims all – never recovered. Whereas a wound was deep and bloody, it could be stitched and the body would repair it, at least to the point of tolerance. But a wound to the mind was hidden. A world inside torn apart, as if the bomb had passed through and rattled around the skull, consuming the man from inside, never letting him back. For some of these men, it would have been kinder to have shot them in the trenches.

The morning rounds were the hardest. The nights always brought more terror and shouts. The shouting was mostly incomprehensible but sometimes it was possible to comprehend orders being issued in faraway dugouts. At least I could hide behind the barrier of language, but it wore the German nurses and orderlies down – it was plain to see on their faces. The German staff tolerated me but they envied my ability to escape the shouts and usually sent me in first, as if that could make any difference.

When I entered the ward through the large oak door, there would sometimes be a man clinging to it on the other side, thinking it a trench support. He would claw at the beam, trying to reach imagined safety. My poor men stood to attention from sunrise to sunset. Their faces were constantly wet with the sweat of exertion and with saliva from their tortured mouths cursing themselves for each failure to obey their brain's command. I would steady them first, calming them with a song in French. It did not matter what I said or did, it was always the voice that was important.

Men who had served at Verdun, Messines and the Somme were here. Each battlefield told its own story. Our armies had set off mines in Belgium and some of these soldiers had been above them, their minds blasted from their bodies and perhaps still lying out there on the hills.

In particular, I looked out for the soldiers who had been on the Somme. There was the soldier from Delville Wood, but there had been two others. One had been at La Boisselle, perhaps near my uncle's house. The other had been at Mametz Wood, holding a bayonet to his own neck in a hole in the ground with two dead British soldiers. According to his notes, he had been there for at least five days.

As the year went on, I wondered if this war could ever end. The brutality and hardship suffered by millions of men seemed to have no effect on those deciding the outcome of the war. The grind continued and undoubtedly the lines of wounded would continue in Cambrai, along with many other places. But at the end of the line came the forgotten ones. No one knew quite what to do with them and no one wanted to claim these most terrible victims of this terrible war.

The visitors' room was mostly empty. On those days when a visitor did come, the heartbreak seemed to be worse than a bereavement for the visiting relative. Seeing their sons, husbands and brothers living tortured life tortured by the shells of a cursed war. Part of me wanted to tell them it served them right for invading my home, but I could not condemn them further. The Western Front had condemned them well enough and whatever debt I felt they owed France, they had paid over and again.

At the end of the year the first snows came to the town and I was moved to a larger hospital in the north of the town at Kaiserswerth. It was an enormous space, with every kind of medical treatment available. What energy and strength the town still had left was sent here. This was an academic hospital and not one created by the war so my nationality meant little or nothing here – I was just another overseas nurse studying.

Just before Christmas in 1917, Kurt came to see me. His face was earnest and bright and the outside world seemed to mean little as he stared into my eyes and then kissed me.

'Odile my love, I have such wonderful news. As you have been accepted at the Kaiserswerth, my Father has agreed to a visit. He understands that it would be right for any girl to want to know her German family and he now accepts my choice.'

These kind words delivered softly by Kurt, felt like a sentence of condemnation. Now, I was entangled to a point where it would be impossible to get free. But I tried to think only of my parents and their safety, and not of myself.

'That is good, Kurt. When are we to see your parents?'

'Tomorrow, at six. I have to be back to the station at nine, so it will be a good time to meet them. Then you can return with me. Isn't it wonderful?'

'Yes Kurt. Tell me, where are you to go again?'

'I am not supposed to say but we are hoping to move more troops for the new year. We are hoping to win the war at last. It fills me with hope as we can then marry. Remember your promise!'

'Promise? I have not offered a promise Kurt.'

'You said you could not consider marriage until the war was over. That is what you told me, Odile.'

'Yes, but it was not in acceptance of a proposal!'

'Well, I have plans for that… but that is not for now. For now it is good that that my parents accept you to be my betrothed.'

'It is all moving very fast Kurt—'

'Too fast? You have been here many months now. Surely you know why you are here? It is because I love you deeply Odile Lefebvre. I have loved you from the first time I saw you at the water pump. And I have proved my love repeatedly through helping you and your Mother – and of course your troubled Father. You remember he was shot with a gun?'

'Of course I do! You do not need to tell me—'

'Do not think me a fool Odile. I know your affections are linked to my ability to care for your family.'

'But Kurt, it is more than that.'

'It must be so, Odile, for I have used up many favours to offer you the very best to demonstrate my love. At every turn, I wanted only to show you my care. To take you from those fucking camps of shame, God knows we hated them, bastard country boys taking advantage of the girls—'

'Please, Kurt, there is no need—'

'There is every need Odile, for have I not shown you a way out of your trenches? Have I not allowed you the peace of life with your parents at your side? Do you know how hard that was to achieve?'

'Oh Kurt! I do not care for you simply to gain favours for my parents. I care for you because *you* are caring and strong.'

'It makes me glad to hear you say that.'

Kurt reached out to touch me, but there was more to say.

'But please see things clearly. You invaded my country, taking whatever you wanted, whenever you wanted. That cannot be the basis for love, it is a false foundation. Can you see that? To me, your uniform means starvation and beatings, the stealing of our virtue.'

My anger surfaced and tears filled my eyes. Kurt's eyes glistened, but it had to be said, or my body and soul would not forgive me.

'I know Odile. But I did none of those things and only joined the army for the life it offered me. Could I disobey? Has the French Army never invaded other countries? Can you ever see me as anything other than a device for comfort? Can you ever love me deeply?'

He was backing away from me, his outline set against the grey street below. Some people had stopped to watch. Kurt was sincere and he had helped us. Could that not be enough? Perhaps for most girls it was but I loved another man. One with a kind soul and sincerity, and one who honoured his country and his girl, seeking not pleasure but love.

In my mind, Kurt and William appeared again in the field in Bazentin walking between the crops and speaking coarsely to one another, soldier to soldier, brother to brother. It was almost unbearable and I wanted to get back to my poor saluting patients, for at least I could treat them honestly.

'Perhaps Kurt. Let us have this meeting tomorrow and we shall see. Give me time. For I am the beaten enemy, am I not?'

It was not intended as an insult, but his face darkened. He took off his cap, smacked it against his arm and placed it on the ground.

'Here. It is me, poor Kurt Langer, naked in front of you. Not a soldier, not a vicious enemy, not the Hun, but just a German boy. An unlucky boy in love with a French girl, who gives him nothing but scorn and disdain. You hide some secret underneath, and you keep a visible contempt for the Germans on the surface. Here I am, just you and me Odile. This is all that I can do. Is that enough?'

I looked at Kurt standing with outstretched arms, his cap in the dust. Indeed he was just a boy, with a beautiful kind face. But it was not enough, he could not win my heart as I belong to another. But I bent to retrieve his cap and when I rose his chest was heaving deeply and his face was wet with tears. I dusted his cap, wiped his tears with my thumb and drew him close.

'I have never lied to you Kurt. But for love to blossom, there must be no threat of punishment for failure. Love cannot be a hostage. Love cannot be used as a currency. Love cannot be used as a weapon. It is a lesson we must all learn.'

I drew him gently to me and kissed his lips.

'Until tomorrow, Kurt Langer.'

CHAPTER FIFTY-SIX
KRIEGSNEUROSE WARDS 1917

The afternoon at the hospital offered no time to reflect on what had happened that morning. I had become more accustomed to this life and accepted it as payment for safety. These men expected nothing from me and I had the power to choose whether or not to care for them. But this power offered no comfort to me, for these men needed care above all else. I would not wield power over these broken men, for they deserved my best. Perhaps my love was better invested here, if I could hold my world together.

As darkness came early that winter afternoon, the men wanted only comfort from terror. Their eyes were focused on some faraway danger coming for them in an unseen world, and they did not notice me come to them with warming drinks. The bed legs offered more comfort than my actions so I spent that evening under the bed helping a new patient settle in. He continually asked for more bullets for his empty gun and he kept repeating that the French were coming over the hill. He seemed to see their ghostly silhouettes armed with rifles held high. Sentry duty on the Mort Homme.

The new man sat mostly in silence, frightened by the calm. The guns had silenced his mind forever, leaving behind the echo of a shell that filled his ears with fear. He dived down, caring not that his head kept smashing against the floor. Blood flowed from his head, a wound that would never heal as he repeatedly struck his head against the stones.

No one came for him. No one rescued him from this shell crater. He was struck on every side by fire and screamed his rage at the French for killing him. He was convinced he was dead, in Hell. I could only listen, with one hand on his shoulder, trying to stop him from dashing his own head against the hard floor. But it was no use.

By the end of the evening my uniform was spattered with bright fresh blood and the doctor had to sedate him. His wound was stitched and dressed while he was calm. But when the medicine wore off, he tore at the dressing and his wound until it bled again. I wished fervently that a French soldier had taken his life.

'Lefebvre, let him be for now. There is nothing more we can do tonight. Here, help this man to bed. He is going home tomorrow.'

'Home? To a house with a garden, or a window with a view?'

'Yes, but it will give him no comfort. He is being sent home as there is nothing else we can do for him. He may live fifty more years with the guns still in his ears.'

This poor man was only twenty-five and he had been shelled for a month near to Bixschoote in Belgium. His notes told of his rescue from a dugout that had been buried four times and each time the men had dug themselves out using their bare hands and playing cards. He spent hours leaping from his bed at the least possible sound, diving for the door and survival.

'His Mother has said she will take him. I do hope she knows what to do.'

'Should he be allowed home at all?'

'Probably not but he does not try to injure himself and he is no danger to others. What can we do? He won't die of Kriegsneurose, at least not directly.'

The next day was a rest day for me. Kurt would not arrive until the early afternoon. Eline was on duty at our old hospital and the other two French nurses were much older and sought one another for company.

I decided to risk an unchaperoned walk, which was allowed but not encouraged. Even when not working I was still required to wear my uniform. This was helpful since the uniform offered some status in the town and helped to get around any language problems. Around the Kaiserswerth, people were used to seeing foreigners. Some had a fascination for the French, but it soon became clear that they only wanted to know how it was to have been defeated and occupied. I cared not for that type of conversation.

The day was short and cold and there was not much to see in this town in wartime. There were soldiers around, although they looked young and poorly fed. They tipped their caps to me, which was almost amusing. One even helped me to cross the road, which I almost objected to until I remembered my training. A nurse was treated with respect and the nurse should treat nursing with respect. So I smiled and offered my arm, as was the custom.

When I arrived at the hospital, it was chilly and my face was red. Kurt was waiting for me at the little hill under the steps. He looked worried.

'Are you quite well, Kurt?'

'Odile, hello. Yes. Come on, we do not want to be late.'

We walked in silence for a while with Kurt walking fast and me walking slowly. As a result, he was a step in front of me, showing his anxiety about this meeting. It occurred to me that my own Father should be present at such a meeting for the sake of propriety. But since this was impossible, I kept the thought to myself so as not to increase the tension. I decided not to speak until Kurt chose to break the silence.

'My Father has secured you an occupation once the war is over and nursing is no longer required. You can work as a nanny for a family in the town since looking after children is acceptable for a woman in Germany.

The children's Father was killed in France in 1916 and the Mother and uncle need help. It will be a good position for you. What do you say?'

'But Kurt. Did I not say yesterday?'

'But you simply can't say no after all that I have done. I have cared for you and your family, rescued you from the camps and brought you here. Remember the dirty, stinking, shithouse you lived in? Not any more. Now you can have baths and scents you could never have imagined.'

I could see his intent more clearly now. He had grown bolder as we neared his family, where he could leave the safety of politeness and reveal a deeper purpose for me.

'Odile, I have been patient long enough. I will marry you, and you will remain here with me. All I ask is your hand, willingly given. Why should you deny that to the man who saved you from… rape?'

The word made me stop and shudder. My God! He wanted me to exchange my safety for my life. He wants me here, at his pleasure. I did not know what to say or do next so I said nothing. Kurt did not speak again until we reached his parents' home.

'We are here. I wish you to meet my sister first. She is seventeen and silly. You might find her amusing.'

The girl emerged from the door. She may have been seventeen, but she was a child to my eyes. At seventeen I had seen people blown to pieces by bombs, girls with grunting men's hands in their underclothes, and men beating others for a morsel of food. This girl had most likely never been out of her little lace-covered bedroom.

'Liesel, this is Odile. Odile, this is my sister, Liesel.'

'Hello Odile, I very pleasing to meeting you.'

Her attempt at French made me smile. I wondered what she thought of the war and doubted she had formed a hatred of the French. Perhaps she would just find me interesting or different.

'Good afternoon Liesel. I am pleased to meet you as well. Liesel, will you show me around your garden?'

This seemed such a contrived meeting, I hoped to move us along, or this would be an awful evening.

But Liesel knew no other French, which meant falling back on my sparse German. It made me sorry to use this language at all.

'Oh Odile, it is so cold at this time of year. But look, there is the lawn. Father has some ideas for planting vegetables for the war but they will not grow as the soil is too dry. We have planted turnips in every spare bit of garden. Father sends them to the army cooks to make soup for the soldiers. I help him sometimes.'

I detected no bad feeling in her, only a sincere desire to make polite conversation. Perhaps Liesel might turn out to be an unexpected and unsuspecting ally. This would be good perhaps.

'Odile, come, we must not stand outside all day. Father and Mother wish to speak with you. By the way, it is not customary to embrace or shake hands with them."

Finally, the moment had come that I had been dreading since first realising Kurt would be more than just another soldier. We waited until his parents came to the door

'Mademoiselle Lefebvre, this is my Father, Herr General Langer and my Mother, Frau Langer.'

Kurt's Father did not speak directly to me, and addressed his questions to Kurt.

'My boy, this girl is cold. Let us go inside, off the street, hmm?'

'Yes Father.'

'Tell me, Mademoiselle, are your Mother and Father alive?'

This was a surprising first question from Kurt's Mother, since our countries were at war with each other. Hopefully my German would get me through the afternoon's questioning.

'Yes, Frau Langer. They are both well. Your son has helped them much.'

'Ah, that is our Kurt!'

Frau Langer gripped my arm and led me into the small sitting room, where some drinks had been prepared. For most of the time, Kurt and his Father talked of war. I wondered whether his Father had any real idea of what the Germans had done to France since war had changed so much since he was his son's age.

Kurt's Mother tried hard to be kind but every few words were mixed with glances towards her husband as if checking whether her toleration of the French was too much. It was already too much for me and it was impossible to like this family when my own was torn apart by the war. How dare they live so safe and secure, without knowing what was really going on? I wanted to tell them of the poor soldiers in the hospital and watched carefully for my opportunity.

'Tell me Odile, I hear that you work in the institute?'

'Excuse me, Frau Langer?'

'Oh, the Kaiserswerth?'

'Ah yes. I work with soldiers suffering from Kriegsneurose.'

'Oh? What is that?' Kurt's Mother looked genuinely interested.

'It is a disease of the mind. Something new perhaps. It is from living in trenches for such a long time, being bombed or shot at. It damages the soldiers in unimaginable ways—'

'Hmm Kurt, sounds like men avoiding the front lines to me. It was never like that in my days in the army.'

It was very strange being interrupted by someone who was clearly listening to me, but then addressing himself to his son. Frau Langer was squeezing my arm and Kurt looked increasingly uncomfortable, but I avoided catching Kurt's eye and continued.

'Sorry sir, but no. The men are not avoiding. They have been blasted by real bombs. The war has taken their sense and lost it forever.'

'What? How?'

'Men are alive, but they are really dead. They continue to breathe but their eyes do not focus, their limbs do not obey and their families do not recognise them. They live, but life has left them. They have fought for their country, but their country cannot do anything for them.'

Frau Langer's hand gripped my arm more tightly so that it began to hurt.

'And you tend these men, Odile? A French girl, tending Germans?'

'Yes Frau Langer. I do.'

Frau Langer glanced at her husband. His face softened almost imperceptibly. Perhaps he realised that Kurt had not brought the enemy in from the cold, but just a girl from another country. Frau Langer certainly seemed to take this softening as approval of some sort.

'Odile. When Kurt is in Dusseldorf, you must visit us and we might get to know each other better. For now, I think Kurt and his Father want to talk of the war. Perhaps Liesel can show you her room?'

Although Liesel was only fifteen months younger than me, she had seen nothing and I felt like the nanny to a child. It was not her fault that we had nothing in common but I wanted her to know more so she would be a stronger woman, when the time came. I talked to her of nursing.

'Yes, I had thought of nursing. Next year, in June of 1918, I will be allowed to apply to the institute. It seems very exciting. Will you tell me more of your experience?'

'Liesel, there is too much to know and you do not want to hear of all this war has done. But I will say this. Be kind first, be honest and make up your own mind in this world. There will be plenty of people to tell you their opinions, but try to find your own.'

Liesel looked puzzled but did not question further. I looked at her dresser full of clothes – none of them rotten, or stinking of sweat or shit. None of these delicate garments would be worn with bare breasts and a helpful breeze. But I did not wish these things on her since innocence was a precious gift to be treasured for as long as possible.

Strangely, that room gave me comfort, perhaps reminding me of my own home as it might have been now. I felt no resentment to the girl but to the unfairness of fate. Liesel was open and joyful and the war had not taken this from her yet. And with her brother's work keeping him from the Front, perhaps the war would not touch her at all. I envied her, but despite everything about us being so very different, I liked her immediately.

The time came for Kurt to leave for Koln. His Mother embraced me warmly, and his Father nodded courteously. Kurt told me that it was a sign that they had given the first stage of acceptance. How would they react when I made my way out of Germany? Kurt walked me to the hospital and his mood was lighter but still determined.

'Odile I do wish us to be married, that is no secret. Perhaps this can be soon and you will grow to love me and my family. My Father is seeking a legal clarification. Perhaps we can marry in Germany even before we win the war.'

'Do you ask this of me, or do you tell me to marry you?'

Kurt's mood hardened again.

'Can I not order you to go from this place to the next? Can I not move you at my own whim? Yes I can. Odile, I will be married to you. I have waited over a year for you to love me. My friends suggest throwing you over a barrel and having done with it. But I do not want to know you in that way.'

'And I should be grateful for such mercies! Is that what you mean?'

'I love you Odile, but that love must be repaid. You are safe and comfortable. Your Mother is alive and being cared for. Your Father is working and not stuck in some punishment camp. Would you betray them by rejecting me?'

There was nothing for me to say and I dropped my eyes to the ground. He was clearly angry.

'I thought not. Go to the hospital. I will come for you upon my return in three weeks.'

'Kurt, please I only... I do not want this life, if we are not to be happy.'

His eyes darkened. 'Go now and not another word.'

He quickly turned away, snapping his heels as he went.

How little my life had truly moved on. I was still a defenceless girl, my only true power was when I was alongside Madame Collart, working in secret for the defence of France. What was I doing here, little more than the fancy of a German officer? One who had appeared to love me. I had been mistaken to think that coming here offered safety for my family. Their lives were now thrown to me as barbs, by this new Kurt.

The new Kurt had real menace in his voice now that he was safely at home with his poor French girl, the conquered trophy. I despised him for it and there was certainly no hope of love, or even respect. Perhaps I might have been able to accommodate him once, but no more. There was never really a choice, it was just my instinct to survive. From that day, I promised to improve my German, if only to help me escape.

Kurt was gone until December, which was good for me as I felt comfortable in the hospital. Although I was training to be a nurse in Germany, I now had no intention of staying here. Every day brought new opportunities to speak in German and learn how to hold a conversation with ease. However I could engineer an escape, I would, but it would require great caution because Kurt was part of a machine that consumed the ground behind it and in front.

The routine in the hospital was unaltered. The patients' faces changed little and their conditions continued to be complicated and delicate. More and more work had been done to understand what had happened to these men. Research was being carried out on Verdun, the Somme and the battles in Ypres to gain an understanding. What had been previously termed battle fatigue or cowardice was finally recognised as a terrible insult to the human mind. I saw this insult every day, these dancing men trotting down the corridors with no mirth in their eyes. Truly, we could do little to aid them.

But in November, the hospital administrator received a paper written by an English doctor. The suffering undergone by these German soldiers had happened to men from all nations in the war. But the paper described ways to treat the victims. As a result, we were asked to try massage and music, and the doctors tried hypnosis. For the first time men emerged from the fog of terror – not all, but some – and I began to love my work. Perhaps I could even stay, just for these men, just for a short while.

Whenever possible, I volunteered for the exercise therapy sessions in the new gymnasium. If I could be strong and fit, I might manage the leap for freedom if it ever became possible. The sessions were tiring with repeated movements for the men to learn. But it did me good to see them and to feel the difference inside me as well. Exercise and German, repeat the movements and repeat the phrases. Work hard Odile.

I was taught how to use my body to push away men who came at me. It was all good training and raised no suspicions. Each day, a frightened soldier would lunge towards me, thinking me an enemy soldier in a trench. Each day, I would move them away, hands down, returning them to their beds. This was good.

CHAPTER FIFTY-SEVEN
DUSSELDORF DECEMBER 1917

The winter came early, bringing with it the promise of snow on the ground by the new year of 1918. Kurt returned briefly at the beginning of December, his head full of transports and movements. He said nothing of our previous conversation but his mood was mechanical, running but not spontaneously.

'I will not be here for Christmas. However, we will visit my parents before I leave as I will be gone until March. You will see why soon enough. You will remain at the hospital and you will live at the nursing quarters. Do you understand?'

'Does this make you happy? Is this how we will be with each other?'

'No, Odile, but it is what you want.'

It was clear that all was not well and I feared that at any moment he might be upon me, taking whatever he felt himself entitled to. There was no tenderness in his voice now, only harshness. Perhaps his comrades had hardened him by suggesting that he use me as he wished. He had resisted their suggestions so far, but perhaps the hope of winning my love had curbed his will.

'You have not written to me, Kurt. Has all been well?'

'I will write when I wish, but you may not like what I have to say.'

Kurt left again just before Christmas. Dusseldorf was grim and I was lonely, unable to reach out to my parents. Often, I sat on the street benches near to the little hospital where I had first worked. I was deeply conflicted and felt that I would lose this gamble of love. Kurt was gone to me, and it was only a matter of time before he realised it. What would he do? Perhaps I should offer myself to him as a barter for affection, a new start for our love.

Something inside stopped me thinking further of it, hoping it would not be necessary. I did not love Kurt, that much was clear to me. Whatever happened with him was never to be love and so I would need to be strong. It was essential to get away, but going anywhere now could mean death – not just for me, but also for my parents. If only William was here to save me, to save us all.

'My darling William, what have I done to deserve this? Is it foolish convincing myself that I am in control when this war has consumed me as it has consumed you? Can we still find our love? If not, then I cannot live this life without you. My only comfort here is thinking of you.'

I felt William by my side, his touch comforting me. I rose from the bench, realising it was just starting to rain on us – on me – William was only a figment of my imagination.

'Kurt, you were only ever a means of survival and you are angry because all you wanted was my love. I have failed to be what you wanted. Punish me if you must, but do not accuse my parents of the crime of emotional deception. They are innocents.'

I spent Christmas Day on the wards. There was a little meat thanks to one of the farmers bringing us some chickens and rabbits, which went into a stew.

Some of the men were showing wonderful progress. The four wobbling men at attention could stand still, although we never managed to stop them from trying to salute. The exercise classes had worked for some of the less damaged minds and had also helped my own fitness. I could now lift a considerable weight and easily deflect the grasping arms of a wounded man convinced that I was his enemy.

The hospital administrator wanted the staff to be healthy, so it was now policy to move nurses around because some wards were distressing. It was well known that time on the Kriegsneurose ward was wearing and caused suffering to the nurses. As a result, I was moved to a simple convalescence ward in February of 1918.

In time, I began to feel more accepted, no longer a French tramp profiting from some fortune of fate, but a nurse making life better for wounded men. It did not matter that these men were German for I had emerged from the pain of France to the pain of everyone caught up in this tragedy.

But I no longer wanted this uniform around my shoulders. The fire of my anger had faded to bitter embers. All I wanted was peace and to return to William. I wondered whether he would love this woman who was now so different from the one I might have been, a woman now torn to matchwood by this war. It was possible to look forward a little to a future that was now shrouded in a veil, and not one lined with fire.

CHAPTER FIFTY-EIGHT
RECOVERY IN ENGLAND

The winds from the Solent rushed up and over the house overlooking the little inlet that was probably used by smugglers centuries ago. The corridor was the coldest place but I needed to walk this corridor to regain strength in my legs and my back. Although I had to be helped at every step, the doctors had said that in time, my legs would recover enough to walk for myself. The thought of recovery kept me strong even though my back and sides ached constantly.

Most likely these injuries would bring an end to me one day. It might not be for many years, but they would stalk me to my end. But I carried on walking like a sick old man, even though I was only twenty-one. Besides, walking made me tired enough to sleep. Without walking, my sleep would be filled with shouts from the Grimsby Chums as they went after the Germans and the mine. Horace Watkins would dive once more to the ground, his body convulsing at the explosion.

Odile was an ever-present companion in my mind. On those days where desperation and loneliness overtook me, she was there with her perfect arms enveloping me with a love that the war had not yet taken from me. Mostly, I remembered our meeting in the French hospital, the sight of her face and the touch of her hand, such a small thing kept me alive and in love.

'Colonel Collins?'

'Yes nurse? Ah Margaret. Hello to the tender hand of the General's daughter. How are you today?'

'Well, that was to be my question to you, Mr Collins! I see you are in a better mood today?'

'My mind is filled with this bloody war, Margaret. But it is probably over for me. I won't be recovered before the summer and by then *my* General will have forgotten me.'

'Are you still going to try and find Odile? You won't give up on her will you?'

'Oh no, she has protected me from this war, well not actually in body, but my goodness, on those dark days, she was there for me.'

'And she still is, I am certain of it.'

'How can you know?'

'Call it a woman's way. You told me that she was in the hospital in Cambrai in July of sixteen. So that means she survived the invasion for two years. She lives for you still.'

'But her letter? I can remember it, but...'

'Your French is terrible, you have probably got it all backwards. Look, I spent a year in France in fifteen and saw a lot of men and women together. The war does something doesn't it? It is hard to bear, but above all else is the human need to survive.'

'This was difficult for me to hear, Margaret, but you are right.'

'And of course it would be no different for Odile. Perhaps she has had no choice but to use that German boy to protect her. And she still came to you in hospital, didn't she?'

'Yes she did! Perhaps having so much time to think makes me imagine anything and everything.'

'Quite. May I ask something personal, now that we are speaking in familiar terms, Colonel Collins?'

'Of course. A man in pyjamas and slippers cannot defend himself from a starched white uniform for long!'

'Ha! No, I was wondering. Please don't think that I intend offence. In fact, quite the opposite.'

'Come on, you want to ask why no one comes to visit?'

'Yes, you are able to receive visitors and your mind is where it should be, mostly.' She paused and smiled. 'Yet no soldier or civilian has come to you. Why are you left alone?'

'I do not want to see my family until I am recovered and am more certain of myself. It may sound strange, but that is how it is. And as for the military...'

'Go on...'

'The General seems to feel that seeing men in uniform and discussing the war may tempt me back to duty.'

'You want to go back?'

'If there is anything left of me that could possibly be of any use, then I would like to do my bit.'

'Well, according to your records you have done quite a bit sir, more than your bit.'

'Margaret, on the first of July I was in the trenches, east of La Boisselle, under the big mine that went off. The blast was unbelievable, the explosion of that massive mine bursting into the air and tearing the ground to dust with dirt, blood and debris falling around us. Do you know of it?'

'No one could forget that day.'

'Well I had been speaking to a young private from Lincolnshire and his only fear was letting his mates down.'

I sat back, still ashamed that I had not done more on that day. Margaret's warm hand rested on my arm and squeezed a little, urging me to continue.

'He was waiting with his chums. Then GO! Away went the men, along with the young private. He lifted his pack up the ladder, went over, took one step forwards and then his body was lifted into the air and onto the wire. He was still alive, but motionless.'

'Oh my goodness. What was the poor boy's fate?'

'He died on the wire, mercifully killed by a bullet in the chest.'

'That is truly dreadful William.'

'That boy he gave everything he had to give, Margaret. While I still have arms and legs and a mind to think, it is for me to carry his pack into the trenches. I must do his bit for him, and I choose it willingly. Do you see?'

'Yes, but you cannot win the war yourself, can you? It is not possible.'

'No but whilst there is breath in me, I must carry on for those lads we left behind.'

Margaret's hand patted my shoulder. I knew she understood.

'Rest a little more, sir. I will bring you another blanket so you can stay out a little longer.'

She pointed to the Solent and the line of steamers pushing out for the continent.

'You can watch the war from here and I will fetch you at tea time.'

I closed my eyes on the steamers and thought instead of the fields of Bazentin. All that came to mind was Odile, trying to find me, lost in the destruction of the village we both called home.

CHAPTER FIFTY-NINE
DUSSELDORF, MARCH 1918

The sun shone brightly on the first day of March 1918. Kurt arrived on the morning transport train. His mood was more pleasant towards me and it seemed that his anger had eased a little. But something told me to remain wary.

'It is lovely to see your beautiful face again, my love. How I have missed that smile and your uniform. Quite the nurse now, eh? How is your German? Shall we try a little?'

'If you wish, it has improved as you can tell. It is good to see you Kurt. How has it been for you? Do you have any news of my Mother and Father?'

'Ha! Well, I am happy because plans are in place to push over the trenches at last. At last, the Empire can finish the job! We can win at last. We can... sorry Odile for not thinking. I do not mean for more war, I mean for it to end.'

'With Germans on the winning side, and guns on French soil?'

'Perhaps, but an end to the war is in sight! Can you not see that?'

'All I see are the faces of men struggling to hold on to their minds. You would not know that because you are not—' I broke off, knowing I had said too much.

'Not what? A Sturmann? Would you love a trench rat? Does that make me less of a soldier – less of a man – to you?'

'No, Kurt. But a nurse only sees the soldier after the fighting is done. There are no victors, only victims.'

Kurt calmed, perhaps embarrassed by jumping to the wrong conclusion. But it told me something about how he thought about himself and it gave me something to consider. *Oh, Maman, you would also have seen this. You taught me well.*

'Odile, I will go to the Alderman today to discuss my desire to marry a French girl. He is a friend of my Father who has just taken up office. The Alderman will be amenable to an old friend, eh?'

'Kurt please, not here or now. Let us walk a little and enjoy the fresh air.'

'No, Odile. I will see the Alderman and we will marry very soon, before I am due in St Quentin next week. I have only two days of leave here.'

'Very well Kurt.'

I had to sit down. Kurt went to the Alderman and left me alone in a small café, whose owner knew Kurt's family well. Clearly, he did not trust me to remain unguarded.

Outside the café, I watched what was left of German society go by. Over the months their clothes had become greyer and more worn looking. The wearers themselves had grown thinner. Perhaps these were the first cracks in the effort to wage this war. Or perhaps they were only visible to the eyes of a French girl from the camps.

Almost unnoticed the Germans changed. But I saw everything, since I knew how long fabric would last, and could see the tell-tale repairs to rotten seams. I saw the gaunt complexions, the stooping gaits, the tired worn souls trying to be normal. There may not have been guns or beatings on these streets, but this was a population imprisoned by the war, just the same.

But these were not my people. I had nothing to share with them and could not find the energy to try. And certainly I could not marry a man whose brothers were in my country, taking whatever they wanted, whenever they wanted it.

I thought of my parents. *Papa, I have done enough, more than any loyal daughter could do for you. Maman, perhaps you are no longer in bed, but strong and recovered.* Perhaps Mother was once again taking on the secret work of Madame Collart. How could I betray their struggle in exchange for my life in Germany? But Father must find his own way. I would find mine, and it would not be here with Kurt. On that I was now resolved.

Perhaps Kurt's veneer of civility would vanish with my words. He might kill me, violate me, or even take what he had maybe always wanted to take. But that was nothing compared to an utter betrayal of my kin. I was living a comfortable lie in Germany. In France, the French spat at me for allying with the enemy. In Germany, the Germans did not spit at me, but I was no more accepted.

My only salvation here was the hospital where my soul was spared, and where I gained strength to know what was right. Kurt would not like this, but he would live with it. It would be my final act of kindness to him. There was no longer any confusion over where my heart lay. Today, Odile Lefebvre would become a woman.

Kurt was gone for over two hours and I moved inside as the day grew colder. I was given a little pastry, which was hard and salty since butter and sugar were more expensive than perfume in this country. The population was feeling the war inside and out. When Kurt finally returned, he seemed upset and angry.

'The Alderman says that whilst our union is legally permitted, now is an unwise time to marry. He thinks we should wait until a time when people might be more accepting of a marriage like ours.'

'Then it is settled, for now.'

'We will marry Odile, you will take me and I will take you. *Then* it will be settled.'

Although this place was public, with people at nearby tables, whilst the subject was on our lips, it was best to cast my words to fate.

'I will not marry you Kurt. Whoever wins this war, I cannot be your wife. I say it again in French and German, I cannot be your wife. *Ich will nicht deine Frau zu sein.*'

Kurt looked at me, his face reddened and eyes glistening. He shook his head, as if once he found my words in his head, he did not believe them.

'How dare you. How fucking dare you defy me like this? After I have cared for you. After the lorry, the beatings, your Father— I saved you from the hands of the devil and wished you here, safe.'

He sat in silence, drumming the table with his fist. But then he stood up abruptly, the chair falling backwards and knocking into the next table. The occupants of that table said nothing but quickly stood to leave. Kurt tried to pull the table away to get at me, but it was heavy and just scraped across the floor with an ear-splitting squeal, as if reflecting my own fear. The café owner lunged at Kurt.

'Kurt, your Father is—'

'Fuck off, Herr Gruber. Just fucking leave me alone.'

'But I have customers!'

'Fuck them as well! How could you Odile? How dare you? You are not permitted to do this. You will be my wife now, you will accept me as your husband and I will have you.

'Kurt please!' I gathered my clothes around me, they were my only protection. The table was still in the way, but Kurt had both hands on it pulling it backwards. Finally, it crashed over and the cutlery and crockery smashed to the floor. Then he was upon me. I expected a beating on the spot and prepared for the hammer blow to my face.

'Odile, I love you, truly, but you take all this from me and cannot give me your love. Why?'

'Kurt, I cannot marry you, I will not be your wife. I cannot say it more plainly. I care for you and truly wanted to love you, but I cannot.'

He pushed me towards the door. My skirts caught the corner of the table and I fell to the floor. He grabbed my legs and dragged me backwards, humiliating for both of us, but he was determined to have me outside. I got to my feet and stood in front of him. He grabbed my arm roughly, pinching my skin, so any movement sent sharp pains to my neck.

'You will walk calmly. I live in this town and have standing and reputation. You will not humiliate me further, you stupid ungrateful little *schlange.*'

He pushed me towards his parents' home and I feared he was going to rape or kill me. No doubt his Father would cover up my death, perhaps scolding his son for his behaviour, whilst he dug my grave. No one would come looking for me. Kurt could tell the hospital anything and they would never question my disappearance. My papers were issued by Germany and could be revoked if I escaped. All along, I had known this might happen, but when it became reality, it terrified me. He had called me *schlange* and his former tenderness had gone.

My arm hurt and my pain was clearly written on my face as people passing us simply looked away. I was desolate and without a hope for survival. At the gate to Kurt's house, I left my soul for only God to find. Whatever happened from this moment on, I was ready and could blame no one but myself for playing Kurt this way.

'Get inside. How could you? I love you! Loved you. I gave you everything. You owe me everything, you would have been dead had I not been there for you.'

I stumbled up the steps, falling on my hands and sending pain shooting up both arms. My hands went numb and it would be impossible to fight back while this pain echoed through my body.

Once inside, Kurt spun me around. Again, I expected a searing pain, or a beating. But he looked into my eyes. His face was an angry red and his eyes were narrowed and hawk-like, ready to strike. It was little wonder that the people on the street had looked away without a word.

'You fucking ungrateful bitch. I gave you everything. I risked my reputation to bring you safely here. Do you know how hard that was? I protected you. You and your family of fools. Do you know how hard it was, how many favours it took?'

'But it was not all favours, my Father is a good engineer—'

'Ha! Your Father is good with engines, but he is a fool to insult Germans. Would you like to know what fate was intended for your Mother and you? You were destined for the camps in Lithuania. I got you out, pretending you were to go to Switzerland. Did you never wonder why you went so far away, only to come back? Your Father was the worst. He was to be shot! But who do you think fought for leniency, eh? It was me, Odile, me! I rescued you all. I wanted your love, I deserve your love. You led me to believe you loved me and I brought you into the heart of my own family.'

'Kurt, I do owe you much, but I am not a prize. Marriage is not a barter or a transaction. I am not a commodity.'

'You were to be *killed* Odile! Those camps in Lithuania – no one survives that cold with nothing to wear but the dirt and blood on their bodies.'

He was screaming at me now in German, his whole body convulsed. But still he did not lunge at me.

'Kurt, please. I have tried, but to say that I love you would be a lie. Then we would both have to live that lie. Should either of us have to do that?'

'Does anyone truly love? Are not all marriages a compromise between love and duty? So this is your final word Odile, you are resolved to hate me?'

'I do not hate you – you have been so kind to me and my family. But I am quite certain and must be strong for both of us. I do not love you. *Ich will nicht deine Frau zu sein.*'

'We shall see about that. You will come with me.'

Kurt pulled me upstairs to part of the house I had not seen before. His words were harsh and his movements tense but perhaps he would not now kill me. Why take me upstairs alive only to drag me downstairs, dead? This was the end of any kindness from Kurt. My own stupidity had cost me dearly and my body was to be the final price.

'In here. Move!'

He pushed me into a sparsely furnished bedroom and I looked around for something to defend myself. Kurt came straight in behind me and I now expected to be raped. I made peace with myself and thought of Father, Mother and William. At least they would never know of this moment.

Kurt came to me, held my face roughly in his hands, and then pushed me roughly to the bed. My neck hurt as my head jolted backwards. Even in my fear, I could feel his torment and realised that he was not fighting with me, but with his own emotions. His rough hand grabbed my blouse, moved down to my waist and then stopped.

'Odile, you will stay here until you are calm. You will reconsider your thoughts. You will remain here until you agree to marry me. It may be a loveless marriage for you, but it will do for me. You will be mine. I want you and I will have you.'

I sat up and pulled my blouse together. The top two buttons were open, the threads of the third were pulled but they held, but my underclothes were ripped. I closed my eyes against the unbidden memory of the tit lorry. Here in Kurt's house, open buttons would invite more pain, not earn a reward, so I grasped them tighter, feeling that it was the only power I had.

Kurt leaned down to me, his face over mine, looking at me, at my neck and shoulders, my stomach and my breasts. Then he moved back and pulled me up by my arms. With nothing to hold it shut any longer, my blouse came open. He looked down at my bared breasts and stood motionless for a few seconds. Then he blinked and looked away, shaking.

He kicked a small stool against the wall, muttering curses in German, holding his hands to his head. I was terrified and dared not move. How naïve I had been! All my exercises in the gym were useless against a fit man – especially one so determined and driven by his rage. Escape was clearly a foolish and impossible dream.

Finally, Kurt turned and left, slamming the door behind him and I heard the dreaded sound of a big door being locked from the outside. Then I heard him slump down on the other side, and the sounds of a man crying vibrated through the door. He whispered to himself and it was only possible to make out a little of what he said. *Odile, what have I done? What am I to do now?* What he was to do, I dared not think. But he had not raped me when he had the chance and he had not killed me. Perhaps I would live for William after all.

I sat on my side of the bedroom door with one hand on the lower panel with Kurt on the other side. There was just the thickness of a door between us but we were a world apart and always would be. I looked down at the remains of my underclothes. My breasts showed red marks from when he had pushed me down. Perhaps seeing that he had marked me took away his anger. Perhaps he realised himself less of a man for treating a woman this way.

Kurt finally left, his boots tapping loudly as he descended the stairs, calling angrily to Liesel. Her soft voice came from the garden and I wondered how he would react if his sister were ever treated the way he had just treated me. Perhaps he was just a man after all, with the war taking its revenge upon him now.

For the remainder of the day I was locked in the room without food or water. How had Kurt explained this situation to his parents? I was late for the hospital and would be missed, but any enquiries were unlikely to go any further than the nurses' home.

Kurt did not return that evening. I was hungry and thirsty, but these were not new experiences for me. I could catch the rain, I could survive. Survival was now the driving force of my soul and a new energy rose in me. The camp cat in me emerged once more and I began thinking as a prisoner again. It felt more comfortable somehow, perhaps the way it should be. It felt better being a prisoner of the enemy. As Kurt's intended I had felt more trapped than I did now behind this locked door.

I had spent the night on top of the bed, fully clothed. In the morning, I heard slow footsteps and something heavy being heaved into position outside the door. But then the footsteps went away again. Much later, Kurt came to open the door. I was unsure of his intentions but no longer feared death and calmly awaited his entrance. The lock jammed, perhaps it had not been used for decades, and he swore and cursed on the other side. It upset me because it made him angrier than he might otherwise have been. As the lock released, the door opened with a jolt and the key skittered across the room, and under the dresser. Kurt did not seem to notice it had gone or to care where it had gone, but I knew exactly where that key was.

'*Scheisse, Gottverdammt.*'

Kurt entered and stood in front of me. He appeared calmer, despite the frustration of the lock.

'Good morning Odile. You might like to hear that Germany has won the war. A massed army of our guns is ranged against your friends and your country. So you will come around in time, that is certain. Until then, you will not leave this house without my permission. But perhaps you have reconsidered your position already, eh?'

My mind raced. What did he mean by winning the war? Could it be true? Or was it a lie to manipulate me? But I was resolute.

'My position has not changed Kurt. I can never love you. I will never marry you.'

These words seemed to have little effect on him and he continued as calmly as if I had not spoken.

'Odile, you do know that I can yet bring shame and humiliation on your parents? Papa is building new ambulances in Marburg. He seems happy there and he knows you are well. But there are always drains to clean and shit to clear for troublemakers...'

He looked at me with a hopeful expression and when I did not reply, he simply carried on.

'You might like to know that Maman is recovered and working as a doctor's assistant in Lille. She enjoys it there and she is happy that you are safe. Such a handsome woman your Mother. It would be the work of a second to find her work in the brothels.'

I was utterly shocked at the calmness in his voice, the words laced with poison. My mind tried to remain calm and steady but my legs trembled and a pain rose to my chest.

'Yes I understand Kurt, I understand all too well. What of you?'

'I am to be here and there. My Father does not know of this bargain that you have made with me. He has given his permission for you to be housed here after your formal release from the hospital. It is so sad that the strain of caring for the soldiers with Kriegsneurose has affected you so badly, that you have had to take an indefinite leave of absence. The hospital administrator wishes you well and understands your condition. He is pleased that our own family doctor is up to the job of looking after you. Breakfast is served.'

Marriage to someone they did not love had been the fate of many women for centuries. If Kurt truly loved me, he would not behave this way towards me. But this war has taken the soul from us all.

'I have no clothes here, Kurt, I have nothing. All my possessions—'

'Have just been delivered from the hospital. The porter has left the trunk here, outside your door. You will be quite comfortable, whilst you make up your mind Odile. Make up your mind, I insist.'

So that was it. Every loose end had been tied. Again, I was in the custody of the Germans but in a situation all the more frightening for its outward appearance of normality.

'Odile? Odile? You are here! Oh, I am so glad! Come quickly, we have pastry for breakfast. A treat, fit for an emperor!'

Liesel's earnest face appeared at the top of the stairs. There was no malice in this member of the Langer family. She took my hand and tried to lead me down the stairs.

'Liesel, I must first wash and change. Give me five minutes, will you?'

'Yes, but not a minute longer! I absolutely insist.'

Insist. How different the word sounds in her kind voice.

It surprised me that there were still two clean uniforms in my trunk – clearly the porter had not thought to remove them. There was also the nice dress that Kurt had given me for our evening walks and a plainer dress for days when I was not in the hospital. A very meagre collection, but that was it. Perhaps these clothes would be of use in the future.

I went to the large bathroom to wash, removed all of my clothes and noticed the little line of bruises down my body. My arm was very red, with four distinct finger marks visible. The red marks on my breasts were swollen and had darkened. One would be visible under my neck, whatever my outfit as I had no powder to dust it, nor scarf to conceal it. On my face were three red bumps, but these blemishes were merely tokens of my age. Looking at my reflection was not enjoyable.

I wondered what it would be like downstairs as I washed and dressed. Once ready, I descended slowly, carefully surveying the rooms and occupants. There was no sign of Kurt, and his Father looked to be out for the day, doing something political possibly. In the parlour Liesel was already seated with a place set next to her for me. Frau Langer came striding down the passage to meet me.

'Ah Odile, it is good that you are awake and that you will be joining us. How do you feel today? We are sorry that your work at the hospital has affected you so badly. Come and eat with us.'

'Thank you Frau Langer.'

The pastry was hard and salty just like the pastry in the café and it looked to have come from the same place. Perhaps Kurt or his Father had made peace with the owner, although it was hard to see quite how they would have managed that. I tried to eat delicately but I was very hungry.

'So, Odile. What are we to do? It is best to be occupied so perhaps you and Liesel can make some new clothes for yourselves? You must know your way around a sewing box, no?'

'Yes, thank you. That would be very nice.'

'It will be good to try to be normal.'

Frau Langer bustled about, trying to make the best of what was an odd situation. I did not know what she knew and did not dare to ask. But when she leaned across the table to take the milk she glanced at me, and her eyes flashed to my chest. Her face reddened and she knocked the milk jug against the candle, knocking it over.

'Oh dear me. Liesel dear, please pick up the candle and then take Odile to our day room.'

As we passed the doorway, Kurt's Mother passed me a thin scarf.

'We don't want you catching anything, this will keep you warm Odile.' Clearly flustered, she avoided looking at me directly again as she went about her business.

Liesel and I spent the morning together, with me trying to discover what she had been told.

'Liesel, what do you normally do in the daytime?'

'Oh, normally it is school for me but it has been turned over to the authorities for the army. Boys as young as fourteen are trying to join the army! Your German is very good, Odile. Do you understand all that I say?'

'If you speak slowly, yes. I am keen to learn more of course, so let us always speak in German.'

'Oh yes! Well, the girls have been told to help the war by making uniforms, or to pack parcels for the men in the lines. It is fun and not too boring. Better than school!'

Liesel sewed as if it were the only thing she had ever done. The needles that I was used to were made from sharpened bones that tore at the fabric as I sewed by the fading light of a stinking candle.

When Frau Langer left the room, Liesel quickly showed me a newspaper headline. Earlier in March, the German Army had broken through and had tried to march on Paris. It made me feel sick. Kurt's words had not just been idle boasting after all. This was the worst news I had heard since coming to Germany and it was time to make a move. Trying hard not to lose my composure, I handed the article back to Liesel in silence.

'Odile, it is good that you came here. Are you glad that my brother rescued you and kept you safe?'

The needle in my hand slipped to the floor, the thread swirling behind it. *Rescued!* Kurt, you are no longer the boy I thought you might have been.

'Yes Liesel, very glad and happy. I am grateful and thankful for your kind brother, as are my Mother and Father, of course.'

Liesel smiled and went back to her sewing.

'You almost sound German sometimes if you speak slowly. And you will soon get even better. I can make a dress in a week so shall we make one for you first and then one for me? We could make it from the same material. Won't that be funny, for us to be dressed the same? Like the sisters we are to be?'

'Yes let us do that!'

Strangely, I began to think that Liesel could be my key out of this country – along with the key I had retrieved from under the dresser. I needed Kurt to be able to imagine his sister in my place and me in hers. It might soften him towards me, which might give me the one chance that I needed.

As the days passed in captivity in Dusseldorf, spring turned to early summer and my routine became more comfortable through familiarity. First, I would teach Liesel some French, encouraged by Frau Langer, and then Liesel taught me German. The clothes that we made were in the German style, being wide in the shoulder and narrow at the waist. These were so different to my French clothes that it would be possible to hide in plain sight of the soldiers. The more clothes we made, the better and stronger I began to feel.

'Father tells me that you are to remain indoors, as you are absolutely not well enough to go out. But shall we go into the garden? It is a little cold but the winds are getting a little warmer. Shall we go? Please say yes!'

'Of course Liesel. Let us take a little walk around. You can tell me all about Dusseldorf. Mainly, I am to stay indoors in case any emotions from my hospital work overwhelm me. The garden will be fine.'

Liesel was now a willing but innocent player in my strategy to leave Germany. My plan was unformed but whatever it turned out to be, Liesel had to be the key to it.

June came and my confinement drew questions from Liesel but visitors were not informed of my stay. If anyone asked, I was described as a prisoner nurse, kindly allowed by Herr General Langer to stay here and recover from my experiences. What a kind man the General had been and how fortunate it was that Kurt had found me.

In late June Kurt was called away, brusquely informing me that he would be training near to St Quentin. His words were thrown at me and it did not convince me that he was telling the whole truth. There was no tenderness in his voice and his body was tense, harsh and unwelcoming. But I no longer cared, in fact it suited me all the better. Herr Langer chose not to be near me at all, but Frau Langer was kind and I often wondered what she had made of my bruise. Perhaps she had completed the puzzle for herself as her kindness held no obligation and she seemed to genuinely care for my health.

But I had a real friend in Liesel and she appeared a total innocent, and her youth, her gender and her position offered me hope of salvation.

'Liesel, show me again how you pin your hair in the mornings. I should like to try it for fun.'

'Oh yes please! Come on, I will show you, it can be such fun.'

We went into her room, which was small, intimate and personal to a growing girl. Here, the war had no importance and it felt strangely uncomfortable to have no reminders of the conflict. The furniture was new and it was puzzling how Kurt's family were so wealthy during a time of uncommon hardship. But then this was not the front line, where furniture had been burnt for warmth. The war was here, but it was possible to avoid the worst with a little effort and a willingness to pay above the normal rate.

'See Odile, like this. One pin in here, careful not to prick your head and then take a handful of hair like this, up and then over, never the other way around. Now you try.'

After a few tries, our hair was pinned in exactly the same way. Now our dresses and our hair matched. I looked at Liesel and then at myself and we laughed at ourselves. A casual observer could easily take us for sisters, but could they also think we were the same person? Liesel's photograph would be seated, so the difference in height would not matter, and a casual observer would not have us both together for comparison. Liesel *wanted* to dress like me, I *needed* to dress like her. I had to be her and not just look exactly like her. My impression needed to be exact. My plan was forming and it was exciting and dangerous in equal measure.

CHAPTER SIXTY
DUSSELDORF, JULY 1918

With Kurt away I felt bolder and wanted to leave the house, eventually intending to escape. But Kurt's Father was absolute in his strict instructions. For my own good, I was not to leave the house or garden. What did he truly know? Irrespective of what he knew, I was never let out, not even with Frau Langer or with Liesel.

As June turned to July and I was on the verge of turning twenty, I began to feel the creepers from the vines moving around me, hemming me in. I had to go soon or I would find myself forever trapped here.

Liesel was always kind. I did not wish the war to reach into her life and tear the soul from her little pale frame. I could not imagine this young girl surviving the torment I had suffered. The war was also in this house of course, but much of it was in the form of maps and words – the real war was happening somewhere else. To the innocent Liesel, Kurt was a towering god whose iron will would protect him and see him through. That I was in some way connected to Kurt, gave me some power over her. If I was careful, this power could serve me, but I could never hurt her or leave her forever changed as I had been.

As the summer wore on, the news from the war became progressively depressing for me in my little Dusseldorf cage. Now that I was so obviously well, Kurt's Mother had presumed I might return to the hospital. Clearly my extended presence was now causing some embarrassment from whispers in the streets. However, my return was forbidden and a letter from the hospital confirmed as much, informing me that my training had been terminated for *conduct leading to dereliction.*

Kurt's Mother must know more than she showed on her face, but I wanted to ask her if she knew me a prisoner here. Would she protect her son or regard another woman with sympathy? She was impossible to read and I presumed her lost from me.

Although Kurt did not write to me once, I did see his letter to his Mother, upside down on the parlour table. The only word I understood around my name was *embarrassed by her behaviour,* which was enough for me. No one in this house truly cared and would not miss me. My only real fear was Kurt and what he might yet do to my Mother and Father. It would take but a simple word, if his position were to be believed.

Each morning Liesel and I took a short walk in the garden. We now had three similar dresses and my hair was now the same length as hers. It was not quite the same colour, but it did not need to be. I had to survive one convincing glance, as a second might prove fatal.

'Liesel, are you allowed to visit the train station? Perhaps if you are, you might bring me the news sheet? The papers are difficult for me to understand as the language is too hard for me to read. I know it is printed each day, would you bring one to me?'

'Of course, Odile. That will be easy. I don't know why you cannot come with me as you seem quite well now.'

'I am well on the outside, Liesel, but inside I am still in a great deal of pain.'

'Oh, sorry!' She leaned over and kissed my cheek. 'There, is that better?' I warmed to her touch.

'Much better, thank you.'

She smiled at me, content that she had made me feel better. I watched her manner, her gait and her hands. All of this would be important come the day to leave. She was little more than fifteen months younger than me and yet I felt like a Mother to a young girl, such was her innocence.

'Mother thinks it might be a good idea for me to volunteer at the hospital two mornings a week. What do you think?'

My heart raced. It would put her in a uniform that I also possessed, offering me a perfect cover for my escape. The hospital was so close to the railway station this could be very good indeed. Bless you Frau Langer, for considering the possibility. I had to be calm and not betray my excitement.

'It would be the perfect way to get you out of the house and into the real world. You don't think the sight of sick men would upset you?'

'Hmm, no. But they are young men and I am a young girl, one of them might—'

'Do nothing of the sort! It isn't allowed and no good can come of that thinking. You would be caring for them, not looking for a husband.'

'Oh Odile, a husband! But I am nearly of that age.'

Where I had been, the very last thing on my mind was looking upon the damaged souls as husbands. She could not have known of the truth of the Kriegsneurose wards and I had no intention of telling her any of that. But if she had a regular routine that took her to the hospital and station it would provide me with a perfect opportunity. She had to do it.

Liesel brought home the papers she needed to apply to the hospital. She had to write a letter to ask permission to join and give reasons why she should be chosen. I told her what was important and the girl devoured every word, writing furiously as I dictated in my improving German.

'You know, Odile, you are my sister in every way. You can write my language as well as all of us. Especially the medical words. Well, I suppose you were a nurse. You even sound like me now, what fun!'

Liesel visited my first hospital for an interview. I was careful that she should not look to the institute or any hospital out of town. When she returned from her interview, she was smiling broadly as the hospital had accepted her unconditionally, impressed by her passion to heal the wounded.

Her training would begin on the first day of September, 1918. I could wait until then. Kurt was not due to return as the war had moved him to a new posting further south, but I did not know where. Even his parents did not know, or would not tell Liesel. I did know that Kurt had applied for a commission in the infantry, but had been turned down. His Mother was pleased, but Kurt and his Father would be bitterly disappointed. I rejoiced, it served him right and I never wanted to see him again.

In August, something new happened. The triumphant newspapers in the train station suddenly stopped and Liesel came home empty-handed each day.

'Something very bad must have happened. The soldiers rush around angrily and walk into people in ignorant groups. They must have lost a battle. Well, we have lost a battle but I cannot find where.'

I felt the wind change. It was almost imperceptible but it gave me hope that the war might be reaching its last days or months. Soon, it would be time to go. Liesel's first day could not come quickly enough.

Because something had changed, there were sudden changes in the local hospitals and Liesel's plans were altered. The hospital she was due to go to had been quickly turned into a battlefield hospital, which had no time to train new nurses, and she was now needed urgently in the middle of August.

On her first day at the hospital, Liesel looked every bit the young nurse. She was already much thinner than when we had made her uniform. The tightened rations and increasing shortages quickly affected her face, which was now much more hollow and made her eyes appear darker.

'Now remember Liesel, you will not be able to dress wounds and give medicines at first. You will scrub, clean and wash dirty bandages. You might have to run the sluice, do you know what that is?'

'I was shown that bit. The nurses call it the—'

'Not here! Besides, I know what they call it! Off you go, you do not want to be late on your first day.'

'But I am an hour early?'

'An hour early in matron's book, is just on time. You will see.'

'Until this evening Odile. How I wish you were with me!'

She disappeared round the corner. Her Father was nowhere around but her Mother was behind me, waving her off. Today was not the day, I still had much to prepare since staying alive once I left would be the hardest part.

I had considered trying to walk to Switzerland, which meant going south perhaps. But Germany was not known to me and I was uncertain whether I could use the transports. There were so many restrictions. A nurse would be allowed almost any transport she wanted, perhaps even not paying a fare, but still needed the right papers. Trains seemed to be the best option. But first, I had to get out of Dusseldorf.

It was necessary to develop a new routine, which was easier now Liesel was at the hospital. If I was regularly to be found in the day rooms, I would be quickly missed. But if I remained in my room, I could be alone almost all day and not missed until after mealtimes. If I was clever and kept Liesel leaving an hour early each day, that should give me five hours to make my escape. The train station was twenty minutes away, the trains to Koln were twice daily. This was the most dangerous part with many opportunities for discovery.

Hopefully, the chaos of war would provide enough cover to secure passage onto a train bound for Koln. When I had first arrived, the checks were thorough, but papers were only glanced at. It was the questions that made the difference. With Liesel's papers and my knowledge of nursing, it should be possible and my heart raced with excitement. I tried to study maps secretly, but those in the Langer's books were not detailed and already out of date.

CHAPTER SIXTY-ONE
DUSSELDORF, SEPTEMBER 1918

September was cold and food was increasingly scarce. The war was rapidly deteriorating for the Germans. That heady optimism back in March had faded fast. The army had advanced but had not broken through. In fact, it seemed that the very movement forward had left them short of supplies. The last exertion had put out the fire in the belly of the army and of the people. It seemed they were now in full retreat, pursued by the armies of France and her Allies from over the sea.

By the first of October, the city was almost out of food altogether. I began to see the same animal behaviour that I had lived with in France for two years. In the street, prices would be agreed and then changed immediately, especially for sugar and butter. Milk was bought as soon as it arrived, with farmers now coming into the streets, sometimes being robbed and beaten for the precious liquid.

I was a strange observer behind the glass, watching the city collapse into chaotic scenes of rivalry and bloodshed. The authorities issued law after law but they were always a page behind the men and women in the street. Wages were increased as an emergency measure, but it only pushed up prices and caused more resentment. Workers were on strike. Even in the factories making weapons of war, there seemed little incentive to work since the loaf of bread that was barely affordable in the morning would be five times the price by evening. Of course, it would be a stale black army loaf stolen from the stores a week ago. At first, it amused me, seeing my family's fate revisited on the Germans and biting them just as hard. But that amusement soon disappeared as time passed and nothing improved.

Word came that Kurt was being transferred to the front line at Verdun, having finally been accepted into the infantry. I imagined that it was because the army was so short of soldiers that it would be the fate of all men in Germany. Even though Kurt was a specialist in moving men and equipment, even he now found himself with a rifle in a trench, fighting for his life.

Part of me almost wanted to imagine him trying to stand by a bed and offer a salute, his mind taken away forever. I cursed the very breath he took for what he had done to me. It shamed me wishing him to suffer so, but he was no friend of mine now and I would never be his wife, whatever he did to me. This imprisonment only drove me to resist him all the more. He did not truly know or understand me at all.

I wanted news of William, to know that he was living and where he was for I refused to imagine him dead or as a casualty. I had seen him wounded, but perhaps not too badly and did not want to think of him like that again. In my mind he was fresh and free, smiling and light. If we ever met again, we would perhaps wonder whether life could be the same, hoping that we could find each other again.

News reached Dusseldorf that the British had again attacked with force using tanks in France. This had driven the Germans back almost every day to the fortified lines, and beyond. Even the most political of papers now talked of peace. Perhaps Germany would simply stop fighting. The people here had seen and lived through enough. The sons and brothers who were still alive had done enough. It felt like time to stop.

Kurt's Father still maintained the rules of the house, forbidding me to leave, even more so now that France was rising again. Liesel frequently questioned her Father, in her own innocent fashion.

'Father, certainly Odile is quite well now. Perhaps she could accompany me sometimes to collect the papers?'

'Do not ask this again, daughter. She is French and cannot be seen on the street. It is humiliating having her but we are stuck with the wretch. When your brother returns, he must marry her. That is my final word and there will be no further discussion on the matter.'

Liesel and I were truly as close as sisters. She was my only link to the world with her whispers of sympathy, her dreams still alive and burning bright in the darkness. But there was a new hurt in her eyes now that she had seen the wounded in the hospital. Certainly no husband there, of course.

Kurt's Mother was quieter and more distant. As time passed, the shield of the story wore away, exposing the cruelty beneath. Frau Langer surely knew what her son had done, but I doubted she understood it all. She probably supposed me without virtue or dignity, a cheapened woman fallen from society and now protected or imprisoned by her upstanding son.

We all had much time to reflect on it and every reason was explained by the facts of our lives. It was a horrible, embarrassing and humiliating existence and felt like I was being tossed just enough food to ward off starvation, without causing further embarrassment to the family name.

The frosts came early. Now, I was confined to my room more and more, with the family hardening towards me. I was a prisoner still and Kurt was the only one who could free me. He had decided on this action but how little he considered my feelings for him now.

This was no way for any of us to live our lives. But the world was changing fast around my little room. People were on the streets almost every day and the authorities were arresting men and women daily. Why, I did not know for I was locked in my room until mid-morning. Frau Langer said it was for safety at night. Something odd was happening, but I did not know what.

One morning there were open fires in the street. The shop opposite had been closed for some weeks, but it was open today, handing out small cakes. People were smiling and rejoicing. Elsewhere, above the tops of the buildings, there was smoke from other fires. Carts and motor cars were absent from the street. It worried me, perhaps something, somewhere had gone badly wrong and I was to be in the middle of it.

I had not eaten for two days and just after first light, there was a crash under my window – someone was breaking in to the house. Herr Langer stepped into the street and shouted at two men. One of them hit him over the head with a lump of wood and he slumped to the floor, holding his head. I thought for a minute it was perhaps because of me, but no one came inside. Herr Langer was dragged away, his hands tied with rope. There were no other sounds downstairs, but I dared not move all day.

At nightfall, Frau Langer appeared at the door, a handkerchief to her lips. She kept her face hidden and hurried away and out of sight, locking the door behind her. I wondered where Liesel was today, hoping that she was safe at the hospital. I was so hungry and thirsty, I used the lost key that no one knew I had. On my hands and knees, I crawled to the bathroom and drew the little jug to my lips. The cool water was not fresh, but tasted sweet to my lips. After drinking the whole jug, I crawled back to my room, locking the door behind me. Then I sat at the window and waited to see what happened.

In the early hours, I awoke from a light sleep, still slumped at the window. Frau Langer was returning, trying to be quiet. Her light feet made quick work of the stairs and she came to my room, knocking lightly, something she had never done before.

'Odile, Odile, please wake up. Herr Langer has been arrested. No one will say why.'

'Frau Langer. It is nothing that I have done, how could I do anything, locked up here?'

'No it is not you. I must go to another part of town, but you will remain here with Liesel. There is no word from Kurt about what to do with you. I bear you no ill will, Odile, but you must not be seen out in the streets. Things have changed and you absolutely must remain here.'

'But Frau Langer—'

'Please! Not another word.'

The door slammed shut and I was locked in again.

A new routine fell into place now. Liesel would open my door and we would eat in silence, a terrible, miserable existence. The food was meagre, sour or stale. Vegetables, when Liesel could get them, smelled terrible, a smell I remembered well, but never at a German's table. Liesel looked sick. She was now a nurse in the infirmary looking after underfed civilians to keep them apart from the lines of wounded, pouring into the city from the battlefields.

Dusseldorf had never been a large hospital for the wounded, it was only ever for those at the end of their convalescence. But now casualties arrived direct from the battlefields. Although I could help, I was not permitted to do anything other than exist in this half-life of the shadows.

There was shouting constantly outside and the sounds of breaking glass every day. One of the windows in the Langer house was broken, repaired and then broken again. The costs for repairs was huge, so many windows were simply left unrepaired.

One Sunday evening was particularly cold but people were on the streets shouting and singing. From every corner, the people in the street came, singing songs and drinking a spirit that was made in bathtubs and mixing bowls at home.

Without warning, word came that Kurt would return home briefly in October. He was still in the infantry, but had been granted extended leave for a week. It transpired he had been buried for a time by a shell and was recovering from weakness. His Mother came back to the house the day before to pretend everything was normal again. She opened up the house at a great risk to the family, but her Kurt was coming home.

'Odile, Kurt will be here in the morning. I do not know what his plans are for you, but he expects your consent to marry. It is not so wise, but it is his decision. The Alderman has already agreed since the war will soon be over. Marriage will be accepted, if there is a Germany left to live in.'

'Am I to be given a choice Frau Langer?'

She hesitated, perhaps as Mother to a daughter, this bit her hard. She looked up at me slowly, brushing her apron in front of her.

'No Odile, you have no choice. Perhaps you must be grateful for Kurt's love for you, and for his taking you from the war. You are alive today only thanks to my son.'

So that was it. In plain words. I was a slave and nothing more.

The morning train bringing Kurt was early. I was ordered to be up and dressed to greet him as if nothing in the world had happened. Liesel went off to the hospital as usual even though she was tired and thin. She looked like me almost two years ago.

Kurt came home and greeted his Mother warmly. For a time I heard voices downstairs but remained in my room, too frightened to leave. He came for me just after ten and I did not know what to expect. The door was not locked, but he clearly expected it to be as he turned the key and then had to turn it again.

'Odile! I have not seen your face in many weeks. You are thin and weak again, I remember that look on you. You remember me? The man who rescued you from the rapists and the murderers? Have I yet earned my reward? What do you say?'

'You are expecting a reward Kurt? What reward could this be?'

'You are my reward Odile. Your soul and your love.' He hesitated and looked at me slightly sideways. 'And your body.'

'So that is it, you do just want me over a barrel then?'

'No, Odile. I insist first on your hand. I care not now for the niceties of love and respect. I have delivered you from death and you owe me for that kindness. It is not too much to ask that you love me. You should see the girls in the fields Odile. Tired, sick, dirty, diseased and unloved. Passed from man to man, as much the property of the army as the guns and the bullets. Here you are, safe in my home. So I ask, what say you?'

'Kurt had the Germans won this war, I might have had to give up. But you have not won and I will not give up. Germany is in retreat and peace may come before you are wiped from the floor of France.'

Kurt's face tightened. He picked up a vanity brush and threw it at the wall, where it dug a deep groove in the old plaster, near to where the little stool had left its mark on that terrible day.

'How dare you say that? It is nothing like that. Be thankful that France still stands. If we had our way, it would yet be on its knees, begging for our forgiveness.'

'But France is not on its knees, is it Kurt? France stands and I am a daughter of France. I insist on being allowed back to my home country.'

'Never. You will remain here, you *will* remain until we marry. It is all arranged. The Alderman, the papers, my Father. He has been released now that he has renounced the Kaiser. All is set. If you will not marry me, I will drag you to the altar and then I will drag you to our marriage bed, by your hair if needed. You will be my wife Odile.'

He smiled without humour at the last words, which he repeated slowly.

'You *will* be my wife Odile.'

He moved towards me, stretching out a hand. His touch was cold on my face, as he slowly ran his thumb over my lips. His hands were rough and smelled of oil and tobacco. I expected him to touch me, to take off my clothes. It would not be possible to push him off as I was tired, weak and frightened. His hand wrapped itself around my waist, drawing me towards him. His touch softened a little, his voice gentler close up. But his words carried barbs like the wire buried in the bodies of the men in Cambrai.

'Odile, you cannot imagine where I have been. I am no longer the kind Kurt from the camp. I will not be fucked around by anyone anymore. I could have you now, here, on this bed. But I will not cheapen my family's worth by taking you now. So I ask you one more time, as Kurt Langer, the man who worked every hour to keep your family together and safe. All those days in the camp, girls buying food with sex, but never you? What was her name? Collart. She was free with her favours, but where is she now? It may not have felt like it, but you were truly safe from the war, eyes looked out for you. All I ask is for you to marry me.'

Hearing Amelie spoken of in such a way made me shudder. My lower lip gave way and Kurt had seen it.

'The answer is still no, Kurt Langer. It is still no even with the hand on my back that could snap my spine like a twig. Whilst the lust in your eyes fires a need to violate me, it is still no. I cannot marry a man who imprisons his love in a room, forcing her to submit. You should have killed me when you had the chance. This is not love Kurt. The war has taken from you the man you were, I understand that. Let me go unhindered to *my* people, the people I truly love.'

He let me go with a jolt, I almost wanted him to become angry. Instead, he backed out of the room, looking directly into my eyes as he did so.

'So be it. Now you will never leave this room. My love for you will fade, but my need of you....'

The shadow of the door darkened his face and he was gone. Kurt closed the door quietly, the lock clicked and he went downstairs. He spoke a few words to his Mother and left through the front door. At the gate he put on his cap, drew himself to his full height and strode off into the crowd.

For the next two days, meals were brought to me by Liesel, now strictly forbidden to speak to me, but her face was still kind. The door was always then locked by Frau Langer. Liesel was no fool, but she loved her Mother and her brother. Clearly the foolish girl thought we had quarrelled and that this would calm and pass.

I could hear loud concerns being expressed in conversations downstairs. Kurt and his Mother would speak plainly of my continued presence with Kurt insisting he was making preparations for marriage, with my consent. For the sake of propriety perhaps, Frau Langer did not ask me, and Liesel acted as though all was well, if a little unusual.

'Well I suppose you cannot marry, not whilst there is war, unrest in the street and no food on the table. It would not seem proper. Perhaps Kurt is waiting until an opportune moment? Let us talk of the hospital, there is so much to tell you.'

Kurt visited me very rarely during his leave. When he did, finding me unmoved and unchanged, he always became angry and left quickly. I truly believed that he would soon kill me, instead of marrying me. It worried me whether he had caused harm to my parents. Had he had an opportunity? If they were in Germany at a reprisal camp, then he may yet still be able to harm them.

These thoughts were deeply unpleasant, I was unhappy beyond measure and considered simply jumping from the window. There was no opportunity to escape. Any means were denied to me. I had a plan, but it depended so much on access to Liesel, and whatever access I did have was fleeting. I needed more from her. I would again seek her companionship as a sister. If nothing else it would take my mind away from dreams of Kurt hanging from a wire in the street as a reward for his behaviour.

When Kurt left, it was to an army training camp that would help him to recover. A new Germany was coming and it would need courageous men to lead it. His departure without any word of farewell mercifully signalled time that Liesel and I be together openly. Hopefully it would deliver a way out of this degrading nightmare.

In Dusseldorf men and women demonstrated on the streets with signs, throwing bottles and bricks at public buildings, especially at the old recruiting yard across the road from my room. Very few men or boys signed up to fight now. The shortages affected most people but by no means everyone, and resentment was clearly visible on people's faces. All of this was good for me and my chances felt improved. I grew in confidence and lived now in anticipation of the opportune moment.

Early one bleak October morning, I awoke with energy and a feeling of peace and joy that I had not felt for months. It inspired me to think of the future with optimism. The plan, its time was now.

CHAPTER SIXTY-TWO
OCTOBER 1918, A PLAN FOR HOME

Let me see. Up early enough to get my hair done just so, exactly the same as the photograph. Yes. Leave at eight, make sure I am not seen in case she goes the same way. At the hospital registrar at eight-thirty, latest. Need to be in a clean uniform, make sure it is still exactly the same, as hers. The officer on the door in the mornings is a fool, he will not even ask for the time of day. I just hope the list has not changed.

Identification, yes, that will be crucial. It has to be just right. I will have to go in and make a request first, and then forget all about it. But what are the clues? Parade, cover for unusual movements, less attention to detail, less time to check the facts. Yes, parade it will be. I hope that it provides just enough cover to get away. Nothing left to chance. Nothing.

Oh yes, permits! The system has not changed in all the time of the hospital, so it might be possible. Need to make sure the right people are on the desk. How can I do that? That does not matter, just ask for the right kind, without too much detail. Well, that will have to be left to chance, it cannot be helped. Thirty minutes to deal with the confusion. Good, this is good.

Perhaps young Eisner, no, it will have to be his Father of course. Yes, Herr Professor Eisner. The station will be crowded, no one will care. The times work to Koln, after that, well, nothing can be done for that. If you go straight to the station, you won't get on a train, impossible. The permit is the trick to this adventure. Yes, please think about a permit. Badge, permit, train. Perhaps an excuse to travel. Nothing left to chance. Nothing except...

CHAPTER SIXTY-THREE
OCTOBER 1918, A PLAN FOR HOME

'...Odile, will you please come into my room right now, I insist. You must help with my hair? It will not stay in place today. I must not be late as there is a civic parade later.'

'I am here, Liesel, what do you need?'

'Can you pin it for me? There are some stronger spare pins on the top that Mother gave me yesterday.'

Liesel handed me a few of the special ones that I was never allowed to use myself.

'Maybe you should wear it straighter today, here let me pin it up on top, see? You look very professional and efficient.'

'Efficient? I like that Odile. Yes, that is perfect, thank you. Take a good look, what do you think?'

I quickly placed the spare pins in my pocket with a well-practised hand and noted which uniform Liesel took with her. Before she left, I saw her apron hanging behind her door with her essential hospital identification sticking out prominently. Unlike my old one, this was a full pass, a proper German citizen nurse card. I had a split second to decide. I stopped at the door and turned around.

'Liesel, you look every bit the trainee sister. What time is your parade?'

'Noon, why?'

'Who is he then?'

'Who do you mean?'

'Who is the man you wear the rouge for?'

'I am not wearing any rouge?'

'Aren't you? What is that in your pocket?'

'Well, maybe a little for later, so as not to look so pale. He is the new trainee doctor I told you about, if you must know. You know! Herr Doctor Eisner's son.'

'Of course I know, Doctor Eisner himself is the administrator of the admissions and assessment wards. Now don't forget your rouge.'

'Oh Odile! Truly, you have the eyes of a *hawk*. Good. All is well.'

If only she truly knew how I have learned to spot the tiniest details and lock them away for later, just like the special hair pins. As I turned out of the room, I dropped my hand into my pocket, releasing the little card onto the pile of pins. Liesel's hospital identification was safely in my possession and the clock was now ticking.

The picture on the card was of her in uniform, but she was not wearing anything on her head, as was the rule. Her hair was tied up above her head, making her neck appear long and her ears small. This was good for me, because my neck was long. If I did not smile, I could look quite like Liesel. If there was to be a parade, then she would need the whitest, crispest uniform possible. I still had mine and had kept it clean and pressed in case it was ever needed again.

Liesel's Mother no longer waved her off now that her routine was so settled. Through my window, I watched her turn off the street and had to move right away, there was now no time to lose in case Liesel realised she did not have her identification. If I was lucky, she would not be asked at the door and may not notice until the end of the day.

It took no time to change into the crisp white uniform that the porter kindly left in my trunk all those months ago. From memory, I recreated Liesel's hairstyle on myself. It was good enough. My hair was finer, but it would certainly look the same to a busy and distracted man, and that was all that was needed today.

I picked up a spare scarf and two dresses, one of which was exactly like the one Liesel was wearing in the photograph of the family together. I bundled everything into a small bag. It was different to a nurse's bag, but would a railway guard notice? Quickly, I added a few items that might be of use. Then I opened the door to my room, with the little key that had rolled into my possession all that time ago.

When I left the room, I locked it behind me and went down the stairs, praying that no stair would creak and give away my exit. Liesel's Mother would assume that I was in my room and no one would go there for a little time. The front door was too risky, but if I went through the garden, the prim hedge would be no obstacle. Frau Langer peered closely out of the big window at the front, so I was quickly through the passage and away into the garden. The light was poor but the weather was clear, at least.

My heart pounding, I hurried along the same road Liesel would have taken towards the hospital, still avoiding Frau Langer's view from the front window. As I finally neared the hospital entrance, I decided to wait a moment, long enough for there to be no chance of us meeting.

Then I used the little path to the side and rounded the corner, into the main entrance for stretchers, beds and wheelchairs. The entrance was wide and busy, with less chance of a guard asking for any papers. The door was open and three soldiers in uniforms turned to me, tapped their caps and clicked their heels. They wished me a good morning and I gave them a shy smile, as was the correct response.

I was inside and had to move fast, but without arousing suspicion. I knew the building well, and could move about as a nurse unhindered. But if recognised, I would be in trouble and that would be the end of my escape. This was the most dangerous part of my journey and my stomach ached, making me feel sick.

At the administrator's desk, I looked for an unfamiliar face, one that could not know me as Odile. I would not use my identification, in case they knew Liesel. If they did, then the familiarity would be too great for my disguise. I took a short breath and purposefully approached the desk, making sure it was a man.

'Good morning. I have been sent to collect a travel permit for this morning, travelling to Koln railhead. I am sorry, but it was forgotten yesterday and so I need it quite urgently.'

'We have many permits here, what was the name?'

'Langer.'

'Langer?'

My heartbeat shot up and I nearly panicked and ran out. The man seemed to recognise the name. My legs made the smallest movement towards flight. My brain kept me there a little longer.

'Yes, Liesel Langer.'

'Nothing here.' He did not know Liesel, or I would already be in trouble. He did know the name though, but that was good. It added some life to my story. I calmed a fraction.

'Who ordered it?'

'I think it was Professor Bauer.'

'No, it would not be him. He is on sick leave.'

My nerve failed a little again, I tried to remember which other nurses or administrators would have the right to request travel permits. I could not think of one. But fortune was with me, just a little.

'Most likely it would be Dr Eisner, did you come from the apothecary today?'

Suddenly the name leapt out. Of course! Only this morning Liesel had mentioned Eisner again.

'Sorry I did, yes. It was Herr Doctor Eisner, it is an admissions and assessment journey.'

'Well, I have nothing in the day book. It happens. Wait a moment.'

'Berndt. Got any of those train passes handy? I just need to write one out for this lovely young lady.'

'Where to again Fraulein?'

'Koln railhead.'

'Why there? We haven't any new cases coming in do we?'

'I have been instructed to collect three men, walking convalescents for admission.'

'Very unusual that Dr Eisner has not been down himself. Why has he sent you?'

'Busy man, I expect.'

The man looked down.

'We all are Fraulein, we all are.'

I heard the card open and the little stamp was pressed on to the paper. That was it. I had a train permit to Koln. The first step to France.

'Here you are. You are very lucky. Frau Meier would have sent you back with a ticking off for not bringing the right paperwork, or the doctor himself.'

I knew Frau Meier well. 'Does she still have that moustache?'

Both men laughed loudly, my cover story now firmly secured.

'Ah, keep your voice down! You had better watch your words Fraulein Langer, she can hear through walls and around corners.'

As I picked up the card, I had to concentrate to make sure my legs would work. I took the first step. One done, all the rest yet to come. I stepped out of the hospital, patting the card in my hands as I went. This would look like official business and if I was purposeful enough, I was free.

I did not look back, but walked as fast as I could straight towards the train station. The daily news sheet carried the train times. I had not read one for a month and prayed the times would be the same. At the station, the crowds were small, which made things more difficult, but the sign above the entrance raised my spirits.

ALL MILITARY PERMIT HOLDERS TO THE LEFT. PRIORITY PASSES PLEASE ADVANCE TO THE FRONT OF THE PLATFORM. ALL CIVILIAN, NON-MILITARY SUPPORT AND OFFICIAL WAR PERMITS PLEASE WAIT IN THE COMMON ROOMS PROVIDED.

Hospital passes were always priority, they never issued the ordinary kind. I simply walked through the two guards, smiling weakly, a shy look working its magic as always. On the platform, I immediately approached two young officers who were smoking, to help pass the forty minutes to the train departure. A confident conversation with them would ensure my passage went unhindered. The best German I could manage, it had to be.

'Can I help you Fraulein? Are you lost?'

'Just in need of a cigarette. Do you have one?'

'Oh certainly, for a beautiful nurse in a hurry. Here, take one and keep one for later. Smoking eh? That is uncommon behaviour?'

'I'm a nurse you know? There is not much to concern us, we have seen it all and treated it all. It is nice to see a healthy soldier for once.'

'Ha, I can see that. Tell me, young nurse, what is your name?'

'Liesel Langer.'

'Langer?'

My heart dropped. He knew Liesel or Kurt.

'Yes, Langer. Why?'

'Nothing, I am sorry to cause offence. I used to know a Langer. He ran the transports from Koln to the Front.'

He did know Kurt. I needed to be careful. 'I am his little sister.'

'Lucky that I did not tell you what I think of him! Have you studied in France by any chance? You sound a bit French, if you don't mind me saying?'

'Oh, I worked in a hospital south of Lille for two years, at the front line. I had French nurses all around me. It catches. I think they are a little German as well now, ha!'

That seemed to work. I could place myself right in Cambrai if I needed to with names, dates and units.

'I was in Cambrai, July of sixteen, when I first started nursing. The day after the British attacked. The Third Guards had it badly. I nursed over a hundred men from the Switch Line.'

'They were almost wiped out. The worst day was later, where was it Rudi?'

'Some piece of shit village near Longueval.'

The sound of my home being uttered in that guttural voice drained the colour from my cheeks. Had they seen my face? They had.

'Something wrong, Fraulein? You seem suddenly a little ill?'

'Oh it is that name! Many of the soldiers that I treated came from the battle there. A place called Dell's Wood?'

'Delville Wood. Truly a Hell on earth. You were there? No wonder the name makes you look so ill.'

'I was there, Rudi is it? The line held at a cost. I treated some bad cases from Flers a little later. You know it?'

'I do. We were in the same part of the world, Fraulein Langer. We are lucky to come back, I think.'

The train came early. I was careful to check that Kurt was not on it. Of course he would not be, but I was always watching.

'Fraulein, my friend and I would be honoured if you would join us? Your permit is a priority I see, so you can come in the officers' carriage with us? Will you do that?'

'Yes I certainly will, thank you.'

'No, the honour is ours, thank you.'

So that was settled. On a train to Koln with an armed army escort to offer me every assistance. Madame Collart would be cheered by this sight.

The train pulled out of Dusseldorf, bound now, without stopping at all, for Koln. Like a cork from a bottle, it slid up and away, in a small explosion of relief. Dusseldorf was perhaps not a bad city, but it had dark memories of terror and evil and a man changed from kindness to hatred. I moved to open the little window a fraction.

I took out the key to my room. I wished that I could thank it for saving me, but in my hand, its cold shape reminded me only of my torment. I flung it from the window back towards the city. Then I turned away, promising never to return.

'Where are you from Fraulein Langer?'

'I am from Dusseldorf. The Old Town. Do you know it?'

'No, we are both from Munich, just here for training. Sounds charming.'

'Oh it is, the castle and the institute. I was tending sufferers of the Kriegsneurose.'

Both soldiers stiffened.

'My God. I saw it in Kemmel. Horrible way to die.'

'But you don't die, that makes it all the worse. But it is still a death, a death where you are breathing and warm, but the life has been taken away, replaced by a waking torment that does not subside.'

This caused both men to quieten and reflect on their own experiences. It was some time before they wished to speak again. I chose to try and sleep, not knowing when sleep would be mine again.

The journey to Koln took almost the rest of the day. It was slow and the railhead was choked with troop transports for the war, the wounded and the dying. Beaten, but not yet gone, Germany was on the brink and perhaps this would give me cover.

At Koln, I needed to be particularly careful. Transport into France was now much more restricted and there were signs everywhere. I would not be on a direct train to France. If I wanted to get back, it had to be by other means.

'Will you join us for a drink, Fraulein? Just to say farewell for now?'

'I am really busy, you see I must—'

'Please, we insist, just for boring you with our nonsense.'

The guard at the gate was checking passes and permits. Mine was genuine, but I worried all the same. It was expressly stamped as a transport permit, not a city visitor permit.

'Come, I know a nice little café just outside the station.'

'Evening Sir. May I please see your identifications?'

'There, soldier. The same bloody card I give you almost every week, you stupid peasant.'

'Very good sir. And yours sir? Thank you. Fraulein?' A deep breath and a confident thrust of the card.

'Sorry Fraulein, this is a station only permit. You are not permitted to leave the station. It is a condition of the issue, you see.'

'We have invited her for a drink, you woodentop. Can't you see that? We will have her back by nine Mother!'

The guard looked anything but amused.

'Very well sir. Thank you.' He tapped his cap as I passed. Out of the station, but still in the heart of Germany.

The drink was pleasant. I was offered food and gladly accepted. Every bit of energy would serve a purpose somewhere I felt.

'Fraulein, we must be on our way. Let us settle this bill and leave you in peace, before General Woodentop comes looking for you.'

'Thank you and good day. It was a pleasant journey shared with you.'

Both soldiers clicked their heels together and left me alone in the café. Being alone was unusual for a woman, but perhaps not a nurse. The rules seemed different for nurses. The waiter left me alone, seeing as I had been with an officer. This earned me some thinking time.

From here, I could get a train to Stuttgart and get in to Switzerland with little problem, if I was clever and careful. Trains went across the border in towards Basel, but I did not know for what purpose. It would be easy, once I was on, to be asleep, or to be nice to the guard. I could get a light train to Aix-La-Chapelle, which the Germans called Aachen. A seat of Charlemagne! Yes, I would try to go here. I could beg a trip to Liege as a nurse who had lost her orders. Once in Belgium, I could find a way to disappear for no Belgian would think badly of a French girl.

Either way, I decided to go back into the station and try to find another train. I tried to see any train times or departures listed, but none were visible. Perhaps it had been unwise to leave.

But here, outside, I was free. Koln railhead was huge. Every destination was possible if I could only find a way onto a train. But outside, no one even noticed me. I was not watched or followed and nothing was thrown at me. I must not let this chance slip. Everywhere were uniforms.

There were no trains to Aachen today, or tomorrow. The next train would be a special train for war families to visit the battlefields in the very north of Belgium, which was perfect in every way. But, for these trips you needed a specially issued pass, since the war was not yet ended. I did not have one, only Liesel's identification as a German nurse. But I had come this far and to give up now would be madness. To be on that train, I needed to be in the station today. Entering the day after tomorrow would be a problem as my pass would have expired.

I returned to the same gate, and was pleased to see the same Herr Woodentop on duty. He simply tapped his cap and let me pass without a word. I was back inside again. Back where the trains could snake me to freedom. A tantalising prospect, as yet beyond my grasp.

There were two little rooms to rest in. I could pass the remains of the day there. I knew that the station did not really close, but I had to find somewhere to stay, if not sleep. My uniform must not get dirty or creased, I had to look at all times, like I was at work. I was unaccompanied now, but as a nurse, there were rules to the game I was playing and I must not be found out.

The station was always smoky and dusty, as the trains steamed in and out, smoke billowing from the smoke stacks. I needed to be behind a wall to protect me from the dust so I found a small store room. It was big enough to sit in and small enough to stay hidden. Inside were three packing crates, empty and clean inside. Why they were here I did not know. The door was unlocked, but there was a lock on the door. If I was inside and the door was locked, I would be trapped and might starve or die of thirst.

Great caution was necessary. I stepped inside at the last possible moment that I could be on the station. Then I tore a little strip of wood from the crate and jammed it into the lock. Now it could not lock, but the unlocked door could be opened at any moment. Inside I would still be instantly visible but I had to chance it, there was no other option.

I tore the side from one crate and climbed into the next one, tipping it on its side. I was now lying in three crates. It was cold but I would not get dirty and could wash in the morning. My hair would need to be tied again, but I would face that when I stepped out in the morning. It was the smallest of details, but it could make all of the difference.

I woke as the station came to life. It was daylight, but it could still be early. Fortunately, I had been undisturbed. This little store would be good tonight as well. I stepped out, and slipped quickly to the small washroom reserved for employees to clean off the soot when working with passengers. I washed everything I could reach and then went to the day waiting area. It had only two stools and was really to help elderly passengers recover from the bustle when the station was busy. As a nurse, I was not allowed to enter the lounge at the end of the station. I would only have water to drink, but that was sufficient for my needs.

The day passed very slowly. Sometimes a soldier or a young man out of uniform would pass a word or two, fascinated, but not suspicious of my French accent, but I needed to take care all the same. I wondered about changing out of my uniform and travelling on as a civilian, perhaps a war widow. I knew enough names of the dead and I could remember dates and places for a number of them, which would be enough. But I needed that pass. No, Liesel would have to do for a few more days.

I went to the small counter to find more information about my journey, hoping to gain every advantage I could get.

'Excuse me, sir. I need to check a journey for my Mother. My uncle was killed in northern Belgium in fourteen, near the forts in Liege. He is buried there. When is the train leaving?'

'Tomorrow Fraulein, at eleven in the morning. You know it is already full and you can only travel with a ticket.'

'Yes, she has one. What else will she need?'

'It was attached to the ticket. There is a special bill of travel, to allow German citizens into Belgium again. It will be checked at the border. Once in Belgium, she will be issued a receipt to return. It is stamped for three days only, so do not miss the transport on return.'

'If she has not got the bill to travel, can you issue a new one?'

The man laughed. 'The only other way in is to try the Schleiffen Plan again. But she will need a few more friends to help. Next person please!'

So, I needed a ticket and a bill of travel. Being Liesel Langer would not help me get either of those and I would have to find another way onto the train.

I was hungry and this made me tired. Food was scarce everywhere and nothing was wasted. The turnip winter was long past, but Koln was not normal. A French girl was still one step from trouble and I needed to get out.

The evening was colder. The store room was lonely and cool and the boxes were undisturbed. No one had been near here all day. I felt safer and fell asleep quickly, knowing that I could not miss the train the next day, even though I did not have a plan to get on.

It did not really get dark in the station. The door let in light from the lamps, its yellow glow was warming and comforting. My sleep was filled with dreams of the war, my imprisonment and Kurt. What had happened to the kind enemy? It was the war of course, with no possibility of finding the past again.

But then, I was woken by a bright light streaming into my dream. The door had opened. A small man had entered, he squinted in the dark and then unbuttoned his breeches. Had he seen me? He might have done. Was he going to come for me? Possibly.

Then to my shock and relief, a stream of warm urine flowed from his breeches, over me and onto the wall opposite. It splashed over me, my face, body and my uniform. The bag of clean clothes was in full view, away from the boxes, but he seemed not to have seen it. He finished and with a grunt and a sigh, then stepped backwards.

A shout came from the station and the sound of footsteps running. There was more shouting and some scuffling of feet. The man was taken away. A face peered in to the store, grunted and left, slamming the door behind him. I almost dared not risk staying here in case someone returned to clean up.

The smell of rapidly souring urine sickened me. I sat upright, wet and terrified, back in the camp again. But I was wiser now and all that mattered was my sight and my hearing. Nothing, no more noise and the lamps on the far side of the station were dimmed for the night. I had to stay awake and dared not risk sleeping again but I would change clothes in the morning, just in case.

I rose early, when the first passengers arrived for the transports. The small clock in the station told me it was five fifteen. The first train would depart at six. Once on the platform, splashes of a greying yellow colour were visible all over my uniform. Quickly, I found the little washroom and cleaned my face and hands, splashing my hair so that it could be neatly styled again. I would still have to look like Liesel, so I repinned my hair like the photograph. My second uniform was creased and looked like it had been in a bag for a week, but I had no choice.

I wandered the platform openly, reasoning it was the safest option. At eight, an elderly couple arrived, with a servant helping with a large trunk and a perfectly polished valise. The man was unsteady on his feet and walked with two canes. The woman walked with one ivory ball-topped cane, which told me everything I needed to know about this couple.

As a nurse, I had a social standing that could be made to fit in anywhere. I could be the daughter of Prussian aristocracy, if I could act the part perfectly. So, I walked up to them and spoke directly in my clearest German.

'Good morning sir. I can't help noticing. Can I be of assistance? I am a nurse and waiting for a train, so I am happy to help.'

'Oh hallo, Fraulein. Thank you, yes. My wife cannot walk too far or too quickly, ha! I can manage, but the arm of a pretty nurse offered willingly is too good to refuse, no?'

'My name is Liesel Langer, I am happy to make your acquaintance.'

'Oh, ladies first now is it? I am Herr Manfred von Ehrlich and this is my wife. Langer? From Dusseldorf?'

Not again, it cannot be so! Was I to be so unlucky with this old man?

'Yes, sir, from the Old Town.'

'Ah, so not Maximilian Langer?'

'No sir. Not he.'

'Good, because the man is a scoundrel and still owes me money.'

For the first time in a very long time, I laughed. 'If I may ask sir, which train are you taking?'

'Eleven, to Liege. We are going to see the place where our sons were killed. They both died in nineteen fourteen, near to Mons at the start of the war. They were cavalry officers and both died on the same day at the end of August. We have tickets and these damnable bills.'

'Let me stay with you, if I can be of help. I am on the same train.'

'Ah, excellent. It is a comfort to know we can get about, if you would be so kind. Brother? Uncle?' He looked over his glasses and lowered his voice a little. 'Sweetheart?'

'I'm sorry? Oh, I see. Er Brother. Killed near the fort in Liege.'

'Ah, it was bad there. They say it was the Belgians or British, startled into fighting. Bad days they were. You would have been quite young then, what? Twelve?'

'Thirteen sir, a very good guess.'

'Never had a bad eye for the ladies, so I am told.'

'Manfred, leave the poor girl alone and come and sit.'

'We have a ticket for the station lounge. Will you join us?'

'I am not in possession of that type of ticket.'

'You aren't one of those Langers then are you?'

'No sir.'

'Stay with me, they know me here. I will sign you in.'

The lounge smelled of leather and sweet flowers. The difference between the outside and the inside could not have been more stark. As soon as we went through the door, my stench became much more apparent to me. The fresh flowers made a difference and I sat away from the Ehrlich couple.

'Will you have something to eat for your trouble?'

'No, sir, I am quite settled, thank you'

'Nonsense, you are a thin as a plank. You, young man. Fetch something to eat for our nurse will you?'

'We only have mutton broth, sir, but it is fresh.'

Herr Ehrlich looked at me and raised his eyebrows.

'Broth will be perfect, thank you.'

Herr Ehrlich nodded approvingly. 'Good, good. Bring bread. Not that stuff, the good bread.'

I did not even know that there was a good bread. Things could be had for the right price. Prices were certainly high enough already.

The broth was delicious, especially to a hungry body. I tried to be delicate, but I think I did eat too fast. Herr Ehrlich noticed, but his only response was to order another portion.

'My dear, no one will take it away. It is like you are in a prisoner of war camp, ha!'

I tried not to choke at the words. 'The very thought, sir.'

'I suppose the food in the hospital is not so good.'

'Terrible sir, more sawdust than vegetables.'

That seemed to satisfy him. The food and water were good. I was back to my best. My uniform was worn, but I looked travel weary, not dirty. I had found a solution to my problem and that brightened my outlook enormously.

'Sir, if I may, shall I go and check your tickets for you?'

'No, no my dear. I will need to do that. We are on a special arrangement. But you can come with me.'

It took an age to walk around to the ticket table. It was a temporary arrangement. The young man at the desk did not know the wind that was about to hit him in the face.

'We are to board the eleven o'clock train to Liege. My name is von Ehrlich and there is a ticket in my name and one for my wife. You will also have a booking in the name of Langer. Kindly see to it that this arrangement is made the same as my own.'

'Yes sir. Sorry, we do not have a ticket for a Langer? Is it Herr or Frau?'

'She is standing here, you fool. This is Fraulein Langer. Check again.'

'I am sorry sir, no Langer. We have a Wagner, a Frau Maria Wagner.'

'Then that is the one, boy. Sort it out quickly, my legs are old and weak.'

'Of course sir, I need them to be countersigned before issue. Just a moment.' I watched him go. If he returned with a stamped ticket, I was as good as in Belgium and home.

But the boy returned, empty handed.

'Sorry sir, the officer is not at his desk. I will have them signed when he returns. Can you collect them in an hour? You are quite early.'

'Well of all the...'

I brushed Herr Ehrlich's arm lightly, not wanting a scene and the chance of freedom denied at the last moment. Liesel's identification was surely known to be lost, the French girl absent, the administrator in the hospital with a record of issuing a permit to Koln. A telegram could already be on its way. I did not know how much they cared. Would Kurt come after me? Most certainly.

'I will take Herr Ehrlich back and return in one hour. Be sure they are signed, will you?'

'Yes of course, Fraulein, I will make sure your reservation is amended and signed as well.

For an hour I paced up and down, telling the Ehrlichs that I wanted air. The document that could take me home was only a short distance away. The chance of a life would come again. Maria Wagner. If she arrived now, it would be hopeless again. I prayed that there was a mistake somewhere that I could benefit from. I prayed as hard as a beggar girl could.

The hour could not have passed more slowly. The train was brought in to the station and was being coaled and watered, ready for the fires to be lit. This was my train to freedom. It looked beautiful to my eyes.

I returned to the desk after fifty minutes. The smile at the desk told me everything. I relaxed, the fire inside me burning brightly again.

'Ah, Fraulein Langer. Here, your tickets and bills. All in order, right into Liege. The train will stop at Aachen overnight. I do not have any details of accommodations for the night, it is arranged separately. But all should be in order.'

'Thank you, Herr Ehrlich can be awkward and he does not like to be upset.'

'He is not the only one! I am sorry that this is a journey with such sorrow.'

'Thank you, yes sorrow.'

Yes, sorrow. But not for Odile Lefebvre travelling as a Maria Wagner, carrying identification for Liesel Langer.

I returned and helped the elderly couple onto the train. The carriage at the rear was reserved for special travellers. It was longer and the fittings were more luxurious. A name card was placed on our seats. One had been laid out for me in the name of Frau Maria Wagner.

'Stupid fools, getting the name so wrong.'

'Yes, they are.' I smiled and looked down, as my foot left the ground.

CHAPTER SIXTY-FOUR
DEPARTURE FROM KOLN AT LAST

The train did not want to leave and it seemed an age before it left. As the carriage lurched forwards, I looked again at the little ticket table. There were two men sitting there, unaware that they had just saved a life today. During the first part of the train journey, which was more painful than joyful, I tended the Ehrlichs gladly. These people had shown me much kindness and also a blind eye perhaps. I thought of Maria Wagner, unknown to me. She was clearly to travel to visit a dead relative, but her absence was my salvation. She could not know how glad I was that she was unknown to me still.

At Aachen, the army boarded the train and no one was allowed to disembark. They demanded papers gruffly and without favour to anyone. Herr Ehrlich showed his tickets in perfect order. I took out my identification and tickets, with my heart racing with the knowledge my ticket was actually in the name of Maria Wagner. Of course, my only identification was in Liesel's name and I handed her papers to the soldier with my heart in my mouth.

'Your identification papers are for a Liesel Langer. Your ticket has been changed, it seems, from the original Frau Maria Wagner to Fraulein Liesel Langer. Can you explain this?'

My throat was dry, my armpits prickled and a drop of perspiration ran down my spine as I tried to make a response that would not condemn me.

Herr Ehrlich intervened on my behalf. 'Soldier, I demanded that the ticket be corrected! Please, this is most extraordinary! Leave our poor nurse alone.'

The soldier raised a hand to silence him.

'Enough old man. Perhaps this can be sorted. For now, keep silent.' Herr Ehrlich deflated and sat back in his comfortable seat. The soldier would not need to unshoulder his rifle to obtain the elderly man's obedience.

The soldier turned to me, as I held out my papers again to explain.

'Not here. Off the train Fraulein.'

'But she is our nurse!'

'Not according to this register, sir. You are listed as travelling as a couple.'

On the platform, still on German soil, I could see army uniforms everywhere. The soldiers held my arms lightly, but I was certainly not free to leave. Having been free in Germany, I was now prisoner again near the Belgian border. There was no way to make an escape from here.

'So Fraulien, who is the real nurse in front of me, if indeed you are a nurse?'

'My name is Liesel Langer.'

'Your identification states Liesel Langer. You look exactly like the photograph, but you occupy a seat intended for Frau Maria Wagner, a booking that was altered only today. Is that not a little odd?'

'Yes, I suppose. I am a nurse at the military hospital in Dusseldorf, number six. Herr Doctor Eisner sent me to care for Herr Ehrlich.'

'Where did you travel from today?'

'Dusseldorf to Koln. I took this train at Koln, as instructed, a nurse for Herr Ehrlich.'

'So who is Frau Maria Wagner?'

'I do not know her, perhaps it was a mistake at the hospital. She may be a nurse.'

'But you have her ticket and got it changed?'

'Herr Ehrlich made them change it, as he believed there had been a mistake by the hospital. As I said, Maria Wagner may have been another nurse in the hospitals. There are many different ones. I do not know Maria Wagner.'

'Good nurse are you? Attentive?'

'Yes, I am attentive. Why do you ask?'

'Sounds suspicious. You understand what I am saying?'

'Yes.'

In tears now, I was taken roughly into the holding area. I was in custody in Germany with my identity in doubt, and now it was all too much for me. One call to the hospital and I was as good as dead. It had seemed a neat trick to occupy Maria Wagner's seat, but now it had been found out. I was too tired to think about a way out. I could only hope my wits would preserve my life in this awful place.

Two hours later, the door opened and a glass of water was placed on a shelf. A little card was stuck to the bottom, but nothing was written on it. The door was then opened and a drunken soldier stumbled in. The glass of water slipped from the shelf and smashed on to the floor. Little shards of glass scattered across the wood and stone floor.

'What a nice bit of arse! I see you have plenty upstairs as well, eh?'

He lunged at me.

CHAPTER SIXTY-FIVE
DUSSELDORF, OCTOBER 1918

'Let me be absolutely clear, Langer, for the very last time. You did not request a permit in Herr Doctor Eisner's name?'

'Herr Professor, I knew nothing of it until I passed Herr Doctor Eisner and Nurse Guttmann in the corridor and Nurse Guttmann wished me well for my trip to Koln. I had no idea what she was talking about—'

'But that was *yesterday*, you stupid girl! You have no knowledge of a trip? No memory loss, or forgetful misadventure? You should have reported the anomaly. Are you playing a trick?'

'No Herr Professor, I have no knowledge of any trip, and my identification has either been lost or stolen.'

'Stolen! Why would you think that?'

Liesel shifted uneasily from one foot to the next. She hated lying, and she was neither expert at it nor good at concealing it.

'I do not know sir, it was only a suggestion.'

'Nonsense girl, you must have placed it mistakenly in the laundry. The travel permit is a mystery, it is almost certainly a trick being played. Either way, this must never happen again. Do you understand girl?'

'Yes sir.'

'Good, out with you.'

Liesel left in tears. She knew perfectly well what had happened but was unable to tell anyone, least of all the hospital staff.

'What do you think Sister?'

'I think as you do, sir. A childish trick designed to embarrass the poor young men on the desk. I think she is sweet on one of them.'

'Then that is the end of the matter. We were all young once.'

'And the identification card?'

'No doubt she will find it in the laundry, stuck to the inside of her pocket. Issue her with a replacement and charge her for it. That will prevent it happening again. Stolen indeed, the very thought. No more need be said on either matter. We have too much work to do. No harm has been done.'

The professor stood up to leave and smiled towards the sister.

'These young nurses and their high spirits. It seems a long time ago now, but I remember those days! My son will be in trouble if nurses behave like this, ha! Who knows what goes in their little minds.'

They shared a smile and he left.

Liesel had heard the shouts, the thumps on the ceiling and the angry and unjust locking of the door. She had known what was really happening. Her brother was now so different and he had changed so much in this awful war. She was now very frightened of her brother, she still loved him, but the brother he had been, not the man he had become.

The girl smiled to herself, pleased that she had read Odile's intentions so well. Liesel was vigilant and noticed everything but knew she gave the appearance of trusting innocence. She revelled in her clever ruse to get her Mother's special hair pins to Odile so that her hair would perfectly match the photograph on her identification.

Although Liesel had been reprimanded, there was a spring in her step and she almost ran home. The house was empty and Odile was gone. She picked up one of the little hair pins that had been left behind, turning it over in her hand.

'Bon chance Odile. Viel Glück. Perhaps one day, you will honour me with a visit to your home and permit me to meet the man you truly love, for I know that it is not my brother.'

CHAPTER SIXTY-SIX
AACHEN, OCTOBER 1918

The drunken man's arm rose to grab my throat. But I had seen this at the hospital many times before and was ready for a man whose reactions had been slowed by cheap schnapps. I simply lowered my head and he fell over me and onto the floor with a thump, cutting his hands on the broken glass as he landed.

'Bitch!'

He was drunkenly trying to get up from the floor and cursing loudly. His noise risked alerting others so I had to act quickly. Surprise was my only weapon. I raised my heavily booted foot and stamped as hard as I could on his arm. The snap told me it had broken. The man's scream was blood curdling so I needed to leave.

As I raced for the door, he hooked his good hand onto my foot and I fell forwards. Then he was upon me and had me face down on the floor with his body weight on top of me. He was trying to lift my skirts, but my nurse's outfit helped to prevent such an intrusion as he could not find the hem to raise it.

When he raised himself a little to aid his fumbling, I waited till his arm was bent and caught in my skirts, then I pushed upwards, rolling him over. His broken arm was crushed and he shouted in pain again. I aimed my elbow in his face, but missed, crashing my arm against the stone. It hurt, but it was only bruised. As I rose to my feet I kicked him as hard as I could in the head. He was no longer moving.

I stood up panting, unsure of what to do next. The sign on the door was written in chalk. It seemed I was to be detained and questioned on suspicion of spying. My uniform was smeared with blood and it was obvious that I had been in a fight. I ran outside into the bitterly cold air.

There was no time to waste. Liesel's identification was stolen and perhaps the alarm had been raised when the soldiers had tried to verify my story. But I was deeply confused, alone and afraid of every person around me.

The train was empty and the doors were unlocked, so I crept inside. But I could not stay here as the man who attacked me would soon be discovered, along with my empty room. They would search for me and it would be easy to find me here. All I could do was run, there would be no chance to sleep as I must be wary of everything around me.

Darkness came without the alarm I was expecting. The empty room must as yet be undiscovered. With any luck the drunken soldier had recovered and decided to sneak away rather than explaining how he'd been overcome by a small French girl.

The railway carriage still had a little warmth in it. I moved forwards towards the engine where the boilers were hot and would stay warm all night. The little hot pipe running towards the first carriage brought enough heat to keep my hands and feet warm and dry and that was enough.

Here I was at the border, aiming for Belgium, just a short distance away. On the run again, but without anyone to help me. So close to Belgium and the friendly faces there, if I only knew where to look. I tried to recall the words on the little scrap of paper that Madame at the hospital had made me commit to memory.

As dawn came, there was still a comforting silence. No alarm, no soldiers running to find me. Either I was not important enough to search for, or they had not discovered my disappearance. Either suited me as long as the train left shortly. The ticket and bill in my pocket were still valid, but I would need to get off the train before the soldiers came aboard to check everything. Then, I would need to reboard as a passenger.

'Where is the girl, name of Wagner or Langer?'

'Door is locked, has she been taken for questioning? He likes to start early.'

'Is that what it's called now, *questioning*?'

'She was pretty handsome, you must admit.'

'Lucky bastard officers get all the advantages. What do we get? Stewed cabbage for breakfast. My mouth tastes like an iron bar.'

'Well, let's leave it for an hour, he might have finished by then.'

'What does her paperwork say?'

'Needs to be put back on the return train to Koln, as soon as possible, escorted all the way. No further action. Just had the wrong paperwork, Koln's fault it seems.'

'That's odd. What was she up to?'

'Nothing apparently. Tried to forge a ticket to save paying the fare officially. But the truth is her dirty old Uncle Ehrlich tried to smuggle his little tramp into Belgium – lucky old bastard. For a joke, I put espionage on her door, ha! Spying on Uncle Ehrlich!'

'So that is what *you* call questioning then eh?'

'Absolutely. Come on, I'm cold out here.'

Cautiously, I slipped from the train and moved around the front of the big engine as the passengers began to emerge from their simple accommodation rooms. There was no sign of Herr Ehrlich or his wife. Perhaps they had been given something grander than a temporary hut by the railway.

I watched to see if there was a ticket check, but there was none. Soldiers courteously helped the passengers back on to the train, up the steps and inside. I had to chance it or they would surely find me here when the train left so I merged into a little line of passengers. The soldiers were unfamiliar to me.

'Good morning Fraulein. I did not see you travelling yesterday.'

'Someone put me on the wrong carriage, by mistake. I have it right this time.'

'Ah, you look cold. Here, we have blankets in the storage box.'

The carriage was already warming up. We were all given warm drinks and the train prepared to depart. The next stop would be Liege and maybe our identification would be checked again. Hopefully, word had not spread of the mysterious Langer or Wagner girl.

I settled in the carriage, intending to sleep. The journey to Liege would take me out of Germany and into Belgium. A country administered by Germany, but full of Belgian citizens. One of them might be prepared to help, especially with the words in my head, remembered from Madame's little scrap of paper.

As the train departed, a soldier entered our carriage, looking around and clearly searching. He saw me and approached. Although I did not recognise him from yesterday, my heart began to race. So near to the point of salvation, only to be struck down.

'May I join you, Fraulein?'

'Oh! Please, yes.'

'It is good to pass a journey with a nurse. My Mother is a nurse in Cambrai. Have you been to the Front at all?'

'No, I only ever worked in Dusseldorf.'

Too late, I missed the opportunity to explain away my French accent. Hopefully the sound of the train would make me hard to hear. I would say as little as possible and try to sleep.

'Ah, the Front is a terrible place. But now we are all done in this war.'

'Oh?'

'We are lost. We have played our last cards and it will all be over very soon.' He sat back and closed his eyes.

'Will there be peace?'

'Of a kind. One without bullets, perhaps, but not one without conflict.'

I sat back watching him carefully. He was an educated man, wanting to sleep. Perhaps he was to be the last German soldier that I was to see. And this one did not want to jump on me or hurt me.

We reached the border at about noon. There was no ceremony or firing of guns to mark the occasion, just one of the soldiers remarking that this was roughly where the border used to be. So, I was in Belgium! I was closer, but not yet safe. I was the wrong side of the lines still. Perhaps Switzerland might have been the more sensible choice.

The train rumbled in to Liege, the border town that was attacked by the Germans in the very first days of the war. The battle that drew my Father to the army, knowing that there would be a war. His skills as an engineer drew him into this conflict, condemning his family to the camps. Perhaps I should have blamed him, but I was his daughter and his fire burned in me as well.

With a jolt we came to a standstill. Nurse Langer was finally in Liege. Now I had to come up with a real reason to be here. I had no onward travel arrangements, and could see no chance of making any.

I saw Herr Ehrlich disembark, a step in front of his wife. Both of them slowly moved towards a waiting car. It was a large grey army car, the only one near the station. Money had its advantages but it would not pay to chance my luck a second time. Perhaps they would be suspicious and inform the authorities.

At Liege, there were carts waiting for one or two of the passengers, but most walked. There would be another train south, but it would not go as far as France since the war was too close. I approached the smiling attendant at the gate.

'May I take you name, please Fraulein?'

'Langer, Liesel Langer. I am visiting a deceased relative.'

'But you are wearing your nurse's uniform and this is not a medical transport. How is this, may I ask?'

'It is all I have to wear. I donated my other clothes to the families of dead soldiers in Dusseldorf.'

'Of course.' His tone softened immediately. 'And the name of the deceased, please?'

'It is…' I did not know of any German soldiers who had died so far north in the early days. My mind raced, trying to come up with a name.

'…oh, it is too painful even to say his name. I am sorry.'

My tears were real enough, just not for a dead German, and they bought me a little time to think.

'Oh, I see. Here, have a seat, am I right, is it *Fraulein* Langer.'

'It is. Herr Wagner and I were due to be married.'

'So sorry, Fraulien. I will check my list. Ah, here we are. Herr Wagner. Pieter Wagner, a professional soldier – so sorry – cavalry officer, was killed at Amel-Ambleve, August fourteen.'

He looked again at me and then at the soldier standing behind him, then back to me. Something was wrong, but I did not know what it was.

'The transport to Amel-Ambleve leaves very early in the morning. The arrangements have been made for all visitors to rest this evening in Chateau Arnoulx, over the road here. It is very comfortable and we have hot water available, if you need some.'

I stepped over the road with my little bag of dresses. The uniform in the bag was smelling quite sour and I was worried that it would transfer to my civilian dress. The uniform I was wearing had a blood on it that meant I always had to cover it, which might look odd. The hot water meant that I could at least wash everything.

The room was already warm and dry. No locks on the doors and no guards watching me. Out here in Liege, Liesel Langer could have wandered freely, beyond the risk of discovery. No call would be made here for a missing identification, not for a single French escapee. I *was* Liesel Langer and had the dress and the photographs to prove it. But I had to take on Maria Wagner's deceased husband or maybe even her Father. Perhaps she was coming to see her Father. That would certainly explain the look the attendant exchanged with the soldier.

Hot water was brought in to me and I filled a tin bowl to the brim with the delightful steaming liquid. A little soap had been provided and I undressed, wary that someone would come in. As I washed, the worry faded for I was safe in the guise of a protected German citizen.

My body bore deep red marks from the soldier in the cell, my arm was bruised and stiff, and I smelled badly of my own body. I lapped the water over me with a sense of joy, over and over, washing the dirt and grease from my skin, my hair, cleansing in an almost religious rite of passage to freedom. I was not free yet, but I could now taste it on my lips – along with the soapy water.

Never had washing been so nourishing for my soul. Away went the memories and the bruises would soon fade. The wash was refreshing and I felt reborn, as if I had finally washed Germany from my body, leaving only a dirty scum across the surface of the water. So, it was done! Liesel Langer had done it.

'Bless you, dear Liesel. Of all the people in my life you have done more to help me than anyone else – all without your ever knowing a thing. Someday, I will find you and thank you properly.'

But the time was not now. There were things yet to do.

The short journey to Amel-Ambleve was easy, but it was taking me away from the main railway lines. I had to find a way south to cross into France. At Amel-Ambleve I had to visit the cemetery where Herr Wagner was buried to complete the deception and cancel any doubt.

I now saw why the faces in Liege were amused. Herr Wagner was a forty-year-old cavalry colonel. Thank you Herr Wagner. I hope that Maria will visit soon and that I have not hurt her by taking this place.

But I could not linger to unburden guilt. I had to move before the return journey tomorrow. So I walked to the corner of the cemetery then ran as fast as I could until my lungs ached. I ran leaving Maria Wagner behind in the cemetery at Amel-Ambleve.

The village nearby was quiet but not deserted. After a while, I found an empty house. Although it was empty, it might not have been abandoned and so great caution was still necessary. Once inside, I tried to find food and water. There were dried ingredients but nothing to eat immediately.

Since there was nothing worth staying for, it made sense to keep going as I was neither French nor German here. Briefly, I considered changing out of my uniform, but if there were still Germans around, then my uniform would be best. I needed to find the civilian administrators and hope that they were not in the pockets of the German officers.

After walking south all day, I took shelter for the night in a little shed. Inside was cold but dry and there was a pile of old sacks for warmth. I would sleep up against the door. That way, if anyone tried to enter, it would wake me and I would have time to react and not be taken by surprise. Tomorrow, I would bring Liesel back to life. Sleep came easily. I was tired to my bones and had no choice but to close my eyes.

Early in the morning, I was awoken by voices nearby. They were speaking a language I could not understand exactly. Perhaps it was Belgian farmers with a local dialect that was hard to distinguish. I looked through a tiny crack in the door and saw a man and a woman who were probably married to one another.

There was not a German in sight and it was a good opportunity to try their kindness. If any Germans did arrive, then Liesel Langer would simply be a lost nurse. It was better than the alternative. I opened the door and the couple both turned and looked at me. The woman put up her hand to her mouth but the man remained motionless. I spoke in German.

'Excuse me, but I think I am lost.'

'You are?'

'I am yes. I have come from Germany to Liege in a train bound for the cemeteries.'

'Then why are you here?'

'I am not going back. I am escaping a life of misery and pain, can you understand that?'

'Oh, I see. Why should we trust you?'

'Look at me. Do I have the look of a spy, or a German officer?'

They looked at one another, shrugged in the traditional country manner and moved towards me, opening their arms.

'Quick Muriel, we must get her out of sight. This way my dear.'

I followed without questioning, hopeful that these people were not in pay to the Germans, not this far north. They took me into their parlour and asked me how I had found myself in Liege. I told them as much of my story as I dared for them to believe me. My heart poured into their parlour, overflowing with emotion.

'My poor child. The war seems over perhaps, you know the Germans barely make a sound here. We know someone you can talk to who may be able to help', she looked down and in barely a whisper continued, 'in a very particular way. He is the administrator, but he is a true Belgian, if you really understand what I am saying. He is my brother and no friend of the awful Boche.'

'Thank you, Muriel.'

That afternoon, I met Muriel's brother.

'Liesel Langer, eh? German?'

I took a deep breath and silently prayed that my memory of Madame's note would not let me down.

'Sir, this may sound strange, but do you know of *Léopold Philippe Charles Albert Meinrad Hubertus Marie Miguel*, at all?'

'I see, I see. Be truthful now, what is your real name? Your French name, my girl.'

I took a deep breath, trust had to be taken for granted, I gambled everything on this one moment in Belgium.

'Odile Lefebvre, daughter of France and, sorry if this is a bit wrong, *and I place my trust in the Prince.*'

He stood upright, clearly he recognised these words.

'You know what you have said?'

'Yes sir.'

The administrator offered to shelter me and to find a way to pass me back to the French, avoiding the front lines. I stayed with his family for nearly a week.

Then the most wonderful news was received. There had been an agreement signed to end the war. The people in the village gathered, with me amongst them, to celebrate the end of the war.

It came so abruptly in the end, but I was safe. Saved from unimaginable horrors to return home, whatever home held for me now. It was impossible to imagine the destruction and I did not want to. All I wanted was to turn the corner from Contalmaison and see Father and Mother waving me home, with William in the garden, cleaning the motor bicycle. But I knew it could never be.

The administrator arranged a cart to take me to Charleroi, now that I could travel openly. It was slow, but eventually we reached the main road at Verlaine. Belgian soldiers were moving miserable-looking German prisoners and I was offered a place on the lorry, as Odile Lefebvre. At the roadside I looked at the picture of Liesel before tucking her away.

The ride was still slow, but much faster than the cart. The soldiers were kind and wanted to know my story. When they heard of Kurt, one of them turned around and spat on the prisoner soldiers.

'Fucking animal Boche. I hate them.'

'Please don't, the war is over and that is all that really matters.'
He turned to face the Germans.
'You hear that, fat pigs? After all this, she still feels for you. You can't understand me, can you, you thick ignorant country pigs.'
So the journey went on. At Charleroi there was a small British and Belgian hospital. I would go there to see if I could to arrange transport as a nurse. Perhaps they might see me as a colleague in need of a favour. Inside was chaos, with nurses everywhere. A voice shouted at me in English.
'You are either late, or early. Whichever does not matter. Come with me, Nurse Cole. There are patients waiting.'
'Sir, I am not Nurse Cole. I am a nurse, but my name is Odile Lefebvre. I am sorry, but not assigned to this hospital.'
'You are a nurse though?'
'Yes.'
'Where did you do your training?'
'Kaiserswerth Institute in Dusseldorf. In the Kriegsneurose wards.'
'Really? You certainly have a story to tell. Well, you are now on my team and we have fifty in today.'
'Fifty? The war is over.'
'Tell that to the patients with influenza. We have lost three today.'
'Influenza?'
'Yes, there has been a terrible outbreak.'
So it was. The hospital was full of patients with influenza. Soldiers, beggars, homeless people, and also nurses and doctors. Four of the weakest patients were German, no one talked to them, leaving them to sweat alone in pain and discomfort.

I was torn in two. There were so many ill people here but I wanted to go home to France without delay. But to what would I return? Desolation – a flattened, shelled misery. I had seen photographs of the Front. I decided to stay a little while and try to find out about my parents and my beloved William.

My stay extended to three long weeks, as I could not have lived with myself if I did not help. Besides, I was now amongst French and Belgian people. There were also doctors from Canada, America and England. I asked the English doctor whether he could help with some information, but he was not in the army. So I had to wait for news, continually asking until it was possible to get news from the old front lines.

The influenza knew no boundaries of class, age or mercy. Doctors were struck down and died, sometimes within days. Nurses were affected, children, the old, wounded, underfed and weak souls all died of the terrible sickness.

At Christmas in 1918, the wards were full of the sick and dying, but there was also a certain calm in helping the sick and I was fully absorbed in my work. Matron came to me one day to tell me that trains to France would soon resume on the old Brugge to Paris route. She would see to it that I was on a train, as a thank you for my work.

I did want to return home, but it was not possible for me to leave behind these sick people – people who had survived the war only to be struck down at the very brink of salvation. No, it was not possible to leave them yet. There was work to do.

In early February news came that the transports were again to cease until the influenza outbreak had been managed. The disease had spread all over Europe, with soldiers and grieving families carrying it around. Travel, unless on urgent business, was stopped. The long lines of sick came in each day and night. Many did not leave again, and died unmourned. I put off all thoughts of home for the time being and stayed to be the best nurse I could.

In April 1919, I volunteered to move to the army convalescent ward, to look after the men who were preparing to transfer to hospitals near their homes. They also suffered influenza and I wanted to save as many of these men as possible. After surviving the trenches, these men did not deserve to die of influenza.

The senior nurse was a wonderful English lady, who provided a strange and comforting connection both to William and to Madame in Cambrai. It was perhaps the way she spoke and the movements of her body. Deliberate, practiced and confident.

'Ah, the new French nurse, but from Germany. I see. What a splendid surprise. But you *are* French? You have had a fair old war haven't you? Odile isn't it?'

'Yes. And you are Clare?'

'That's it. Clare Witham, from darkest Lincolnshire. Here, give me a hand with these towels. Got to keep everyone cool, you know the drill, eh? Germany. That must have been awful. You weren't er, on *their* side?'

'No Madame, I was not on their side.'

'Madame, gosh that is funny. Call me sister on the wards and Clare when we are not! If anything it's Mademoiselle, but that would be soppy.'

As we made our rounds, Clare and I exchanged our stories and we became friends. Clare helped me to write to the British to find out what might have happened to William. We wrote countless letters but heard nothing back.

April turned to May. Influenza was finally coming under control with the aid of new medicines to help the symptoms, along with more plentiful food and milder weather. It began to feel that we had climbed over the summit, at last.

In June I found Clare stood in the doorway to the little nurse's dormitory. The rows of empty beds had been testament to the scale of need at the height of the influenza outbreak and to the toll of lives it took amongst the nurses.

'Clare, now that things are quieting down, I am going to make a real effort to find William.'

'Why don't we go to the army office in Bruxelles? There are plenty of British there organising the clean-up. What do you think?'

'Thank you Clare! Anything to find my darling William again. Mother and Father as well. I just want some news from home.'

'Then let us get you some Odile!'

So off we went, with genuine passes issued in our own names. A stocky officer in the army service corps met us and promised to find out whatever he could. Clare lied that William was her brother in the hope that he would try a little harder to find him. Still, we had to wait for two whole days before returning for an answer. It felt like an age before we could return to Bruxelles.

'Right ladies! William Collins. There are eighty four fellows with the name of William Collins registered in the services.'

'Eighty-four!' It would take forever to find William.

'Don't take on so, there are only two in France. One is the quartermaster of the Durham Lights. The other is with some queer Field Operations mob with the Engineers on the Somme. Any idea which Collins it might be?'

I knew immediately. 'The Somme. It is him. Is there word?'

'Right then, that will be a Colonel Collins. Young chap for a senior officer. But that's what happens in war.' He paused a second, perhaps in deeper thought.

'Anyway, he was wounded to England, with a Blighty one, but came back to work with the Royal Engineers on battlefield clearance and recovery. Seems he is still there.'

'Clare, that is him, I know it!'

My heart leapt. My darling William was alive! The man I had tried so very hard to live for was alive and in France. My beautiful William had survived the war and I would come home to him.

'Captain, do you know exactly where my brother is and when transport might be available to the Somme region?'

'It says his unit is based in Albert. Anyway, why on earth would you want to go to that bloody place? It is a barren dead land. Who would willingly go there?'

'Me, sir. I am a daughter of the village of Bazentin-Le-Petit.'

'My goodness! Bazentin? You know it's... High Wood? You lived there?'

'I live there still, sir.'

'But that's not possible, it's rubble. I saw the mess at Montauban and Serre. Nothing there miss, I promise you.'

'All the same Cap, is there a way to return?' Clare pressed for an answer to her question.

'Well now, if you can get a hospital permit to make the journey, I can get you from here to Ghent and on to the train to Paris as a nurse. Won't be until July though, as they're still rebuilding that bit of the route.'

The hospital issued my pass in the name of Odile Lefebvre. I gave my name with a flourish and read the little card over and over, staring at my name. They most likely thought me a fool, but they did not know the story of my war. To stand and give my name, well, it was almost magical. July was only twenty days away. I had waited fifty months for William. I could stand one more until my darling was mine again.

CHAPTER SIXTY-SEVEN
À PARIS, JULY 1919

The train stopped often, but the journey was faster than I was used to. Most travellers were no longer faceless uniforms and angry soldiers, but real people, individuals who had suffered loss, become homeless or bereaved. The unheard-from victims of this cruel war. Crossing the border into France was such a relief. But amongst tired, distraught and ill people, I did not feel able to shout loudly that I was home. But I was joyous inside, with my heart above the clouds over France.

The journey to Paris took me through Amiens, near to the battlefields of my home. I looked out to the ground. Torn, scarred, broken. But we would rise again. We would love again. We would live again.

Paris was crowded with returning soldiers and prisoners, many of them barely adults. But I was not here to see the capital. I was here for a train home. The guard on the platform was old and grumpy at the passengers who were bumping along and not listening to his instructions. I smiled at him.

'Excuse me, monsieur. How do I secure a train to Amiens?'

'Ah Mademoiselle! Do you have a ticket? Do you have money?'

'No sir, neither. But I am returning home to Bazentin after the Germans sent me away.'

'Been gone a while then? Who are you with? Most are home now. Are you well, Mademoiselle?'

'Quite well, sir. But please, how do I—'

'Amiens, the troop reinforcement train leaves in just under four hours. There is only one platform marked for troops, you won't miss it. Tell the guard captain that Alain said to put you in the guards van, and that he still owes me for the whisky. That will secure your passage!'

'Thank you Monsieur, you have got me home at last.'

He gave me a wink and moved off.

Although part of me would have loved to see Paris, I could not risk the train leaving without me and I stayed close to the platform, hardly able to contain myself for four hours. To make matters worse, the train to Amiens was twice delayed, making the agony all the greater.

When I finally arrived at Amiens, I begged a lift from a kindly farmer who took me to the Albert Road in the back of his motor lorry. Although I was once again in the back of a lorry with that familiar smell, this was so very different. I was free.

In Albert, the farmer dropped me by the Basilica.

'Are you sure you want to be here, Mademoiselle?'

'Quite sure indeed!'

'Very well, good luck!'

But Albert *was* a shock. Buildings flattened to the ground, rubble and dust, wood everywhere. Even after these months of peace, France was not yet peaceful. Another farmer took me north on the Bapaume Road. The devastation on either side was brutal and shocking. La Boisselle was a deserted landscape of another world, torn and broken. There were crosses by the roadside, in great rows, tended by a few soldiers and planted with a little colour. That made my stomach drop to me feet.

'The Germans have destroyed us, Mademoiselle. Your village, is probably gone as well. Look here at La Boisselle. Do you see it?'

'See what?'

'Exactly. There is nothing left. Same for Pozieres, just along here it is worse. I can take you to Contalmaison, but I cannot take the cart any further. You will have to walk, I am afraid.'

'Very well, besides the walk will give me time to calm down.'

'Something wrong mademoiselle?'

'No – quite the opposite, thank you!'

At Contalmaison, the village was rubble, if it was there at all. It seemed to take forever to walk to across the bumps, holes and trenches from the war. I imagined the men there at night, frightened and suffering. I could not bear the thoughts, my imagination running in spirals. But I had already seen the destroyed men, with their disfigured bodies and twisted minds.

But we would heal and today could be the first day of my own healing. I needed William more than ever right now and hoped beyond all measure to see him today, to feel his presence next to mine. I hoped, prayed and pleaded for him to be here to love me.

Eventually, I reached the bottom of the road to Bazentin, leaving just the shallow hill to the village. My heart was wild and racing as I crossed a temporary bridge over a trench. There were lumps and holes everywhere, a British helmet and a piece of shell still visible in the hole. Ploughing was going on, but it wasn't all levelled yet. No crops this year.

The village cemetery at the bottom of the hill had been badly damaged and rotten wooden caskets were stacked up. But there I saw a face I knew! Monsieur Robain! He had survived the war, a man my Father knew and trusted! I called to him and he looked up, but did not recognise me.

'Monsieur Robain, it is Odile Lefebvre.'

His face opened up and he collapsed into tears.

'Mon Dieu, Odile, it is you! My goodness you are a woman now.'

'Yes, Monsieur. It is so very good to see you.'

He pulled me to him, kissing my forehead as if I were still twelve.

'You have come to see your William then? You know he is near your place. Of course, there is not much of it left! Not much for any of us.'

'Monsieur, you are quite sure William is *here?*'

'Yes, Odile. He is working to clear the battlefield.'

'Oh Monsieur! Forgive me, I must go to him.'

'Go quick. He was there earlier. It is good to see you. What about your Mother and Father?'

I called back as I ran. 'I don't know Monsieur, but hopefully I will know soon.'

My God. He is here, in my village. I was shaking, too excited by my whirl of love and hope. My eyes blurred. The sadness of the war fell from my shoulders a little with each step. Closer, closer to my love. No more could I be hurt by the war, my love is here. I would never, ever let him go.

I ran up the hill, not wanting to miss him another minute, and not caring if I arrived red in the face, out of breath and covered in dust. For soon I would see William. The love that sustained me from the first day until now. The love that gave me the strength to defy the enemy, to tell Kurt I could not marry him. The love that laced my dress for the trip with Madame Collart. The love that allowed me to stand with the women at the tit lorry. The love that saved my sanity in the institute. William was here. I could wait no longer. I wanted to see him, to breathe him deeply. To know I was in love again.

I turned at the top of the hill to the right. The church was gone, it all was gone. It was as if we were somewhere else entirely. But it was home. At the corner of the road, there he was! I saw him, with nothing between me and my love, my most darling William!

He was asleep and more beautiful than ever, almost a dream. I did not want to startle him so I gently brushed my finger on the back of his hand. He would know that touch, it could only have been me. He would remember.

'Darling William,' I whispered, 'my beautiful boy from over the sea. It is your Odile, your loving girl, who lived the war for you. Wake and kiss me, please. William, darling William. William?'

His eyes opened. I was trembling and my mind was racing all over France. This was really, truly him. He took a deep breath, blinking in the light. His beautiful face lit up at the sight of me, sleep still in his eyes. He placed his hand on my shoulder and drew me to him, kissing me deeply.

This time, I did not hold back my love. I kissed him, falling into his arms, wanting him to devour me in his love. His strong arms held me safe, keeping me warm and close. I felt the sun on my face, and the afternoon melted away as the war was finally at its end.

CHAPTER SIXTY-EIGHT
BAZENTIN-LE-PETIT SEPTEMBER 1919

My Father arrived home again in the middle of the night in September of 1919. He was devastated by the sight of the village. When he saw me, he fell to his knees, weeping openly and without restraint. The beatings and the sickness and the worry and the daily fight for survival poured from his soul. He gripped me tightly, holding me close. I had never heard my Father cry before. The deep breaths and tears ripped from what was left of him poured out and over us both.

'Odile, my little girl. I am so sorry I did this to us, brought the war upon us. We could have been safe, but I cursed us to live the life of slaves and wretches. Forgive your Father, forgive me please. I will never let you out of my sight again, my darling daughter. Let me breathe you in. God bless you Odile. My God, William. Is that you? Let me look at you. God bless you William.'

Mother was here now as well. Recovered from her illness, she continued to work in the hospital but never saw or heard from Kurt again. Each month, a little parcel arrived containing a few little luxuries. France was grateful to her, the parcels were all it had to give.

One day, William was standing talking to my Father for a while. They appeared deep in conversation for some time and neither of them looked at me. Finally, they stopped talking and William ran over and pulled me close to him.

'Darling Odile, my beautiful girl from over the sea. Will you complete my life and agree to marry me here in this village?'

There was only one reply that I could make.

'Oui, William, certainement.'

In secret, Maman and Madame Villiers helped to make a dress, aided by the ladies of the village. The custom of William's country was for a white gown. No one asked or showed any worry or concern for my virtue but I *knew*, and that was all that mattered. I was pure for my William, my husband, my love. I was all for him and only for him.

The fabric for my dress came from Albert. It had been rescued from a fire and it was impossible to get it clean, but it did not matter. We embroidered some little flowers, in the café style of the time, to remind us of the beauty of our village.

William had shown me where he had been in the war, it had made me very sad, but gave me strength that we would survive and heal together. What took us apart would bind us again, this time forever.

As each day passed, bringing me one day closer to my wedding I grew ever more excited. I wanted it all. The day, the ceremony, the gathering of the village and my husband to myself. I had imagined this day over and over, and how that day might end. I would be a woman, willing this time, to accept the touch of a man. My man, my beautiful boy from over the sea.

The morning of my September wedding was grim with autumn gloom but it did not matter at all. Today I would become a woman and my life as a loving wife would begin. William had been hurt by the war and I would be there for him. Our love was strong enough to survive everything.

Two young British Army officers appeared on horseback to greet me. I was startled for a moment and then realised their intention. A little behind them was a pretty gold and white cart drawn by two more horses.

'Good morning Mademoiselle Lefebvre. You don't know us, but we have a great desire to be your escort since your husband-to-be, is our very own Colonel Collins.'

'Of course, gentlemen. Your horses are quite beautiful. It will be a lovely touch.'

It seemed to delight them more than anything, to have their horses admired by a bride on her wedding day.

'The horses drawing your carriage are Magic and Bertie, by the way. They both survived the battle of Albert last year. Good horses, they will get you there.'

'Ha! Good morning Magic and Bertie.'

With a swish of tails, we were off. The gun carriage being drawn in front was pristine and it was clear that many people thought a great deal of my beloved husband-to-be. The gloom had cleared a little, enough to see reflections in the polished brass and iron from the carriage.

For a moment, I recalled my captivity, my life in the hospital, and scraping for food in the camps. But here I was, in love and about to be married! I wished that Liesel and Clare could have been here, and Madame and Amelie Collart, and of course, Madame from the hospital. I let them stay in my mind as we climbed the hill.

'Mademoiselle – may I be the last man to address you as mademoiselle? At the top of the hill we must move along, since we must be in Albert this afternoon. Congratulations to you both and may I say what a lucky man the Colonel is, to be marrying France's most beautiful flower. Good luck and adieu!'

The other solider called over towards the church. 'Good morning sir and good luck!'

Then I saw William looking wonderful in his smart uniform. He was a little thinner than I remembered, but every bit the handsome officer he had become. I hoped that he would like me in my dress. A lot of ladies had worked hard in dirty candlelight to finish this with me.

After the ceremony, when I was no longer Mademoiselle Odile Lefebvre but Mrs Odile Collins, a handsome man in a pristine uniform approached us, smiling broadly.

William squeezed my hand. 'Mrs Collins, prepare yourself to meet General Cowling!'

So this was General Cowling, my new husband was clearly deeply moved by his presence. William had spoken of him often with a love that I did not know could exist between two men that were not brothers.

'Congratulations, Colonel Collins, Mrs Collins, enchante.'

He shook William's hand, embraced him warmly and then he kissed my hand. Were I not now a married woman, I might have blushed.

The day passed in a joyful blur. As the evening turned to the night, William and I stood inside our new home and I looked into the face that had sustained me for so many years. The memories of those years flowed over me until the one image that remained was William's face, so dear to my heart.

'My darling Odile?'

'Yes, mon cheri?'

'The guns have stopped.'

The air was cold and damp and I shivered. William's arms circled my body and a flood of his warmth came over me. I leaned back into him, safe and protected from the hurt we had survived. He turned me to face him with no roughness in his movements. Gently, he reached down and buttoned up the top two buttons of my wedding dress that had somehow opened. An unexpected shock rose from deep within me at this touch. William's gentle hands on me, securing my top button. Oh how my life had changed.

I placed my hand on his chest to feel the warmth of his heart, beating with mine. As one we were united. As one we would live our lives together.

'I think it is time we went to bed.'

He took my hand and I moved him gently into our little bedroom. I closed the door, breathing deeply and stepped up to him again.

'My darling William. For four years I have wanted you near me. The war has taken nearly everything from me that I am, but it has brought you back to me. I love you and want you in every way. My love, I am your wife. I have protected my soul for you and it is here for you now my husband.'

I looked down at the three buttons on my dress and again undid the top two. But I hesitated at the third.

'William, will you open the last button for me?'

He looked down in the light of the single flickering candle and undid the third button softly, his hands trembling just a little.

EPILOGUE

The postal boy ran up the path, gripping an envelope tightly, panting for breath. At the front door he pulled the large chain to summon the householder.

'Good morning, Herr Doctor Eisner. I must give this to Frau Eisner personally.'

'It is quite all right young man, you can give the envelope to me and I will give it to Frau Eisner.'

'Excuse me, sir. My instructions are quite clear. It must be delivered straight from my hand into Frau Eisner's hands, otherwise I shall be in a lot of trouble.'

Eisner raised his eyebrows slightly but smiled as he turned to call his wife.

'Darling, this young postal boy insists you receive a letter directly from him. He was polite, but quite insistent.'

Frau Eisner appeared at the door and collected the letter from the boy. She turned to go inside while her husband dropped a coin into the boy's hand.

'This envelope looks like it has passed through the hand of every postal boy in Germany. It is covered in stamps! Whatever is it, anyway? Most unusual.'

Herr Doctor Eisner looked down at the grubby envelope.

'Look, it was posted to my Father's old hospital. Come along my darling, open it. The suspense is driving me insane. Who do you think sent it?'

'I do not know. My goodness, look at my name as well!'

She opened the envelope warily. Out came a photograph of a handsome man, dressed in an immaculate British Army uniform, leaning on a stepping cane. In front of him were two adorable little children, with smiling round faces, dressed in matching sailor suits. Twins! It made her laugh to see them. The woman in the picture was so familiar looking. In her arms was a little baby, perhaps only a few weeks old. She turned the picture over to see if there was anything on the back. There were just a few words carefully printed in perfect German.

> To my little sister, forever in my heart
> William, Odile, Arthur, Armandine and baby Henri

Liesel looked again in the envelope. She tipped it gently and a little hospital identity card fell out, torn and creased. It had been wet many times and the photograph was scratched.

'So you did make it home, Odile. You read my plans, my clever sister. Now my heart can truly rest at last.'

ABOUT THE AUTHOR

As well as time spent as a military historian, Chris Cherry leads an education consultancy, which inspects schools and colleges to help improve outcomes for young people in the UK. He has also spent much of the last twenty-five years researching the effects of the Great War on the lives of ordinary people, innocent of the blame for its cause.

Chris is also an active member of the Manchester 500 Advanced Motorcyclists Group, which offers support as an observer for the Institute of Advanced Motorists/Motorcyclists.

In his spare time, he is a volunteer with Blood Bikes Manchester. This charity transports blood and blood products, donated human breast milk samples and urgent controlled medications for local hospitals and hospices.

Chris loves nothing more than getting on his motorbike and riding off to the battlefields of Europe, seeking authenticity for his stories and adding human interest to the calamity that was the Great War.

He is also a full member of the Royal British Legion, the Royal British Legion Riders' Branch and The Western Front Association.

35508513R00201

Made in the USA
Charleston, SC
12 November 2014